ROCKHOLE

Dee Ann; Thanks for the great care and enjoy the book. [illegible]

Jesse Skiles

First Edition

PAGE PUBLISHING, INC.
New York, NY

First originally published by Page Publishing, Inc. 2019

ISBN 978-1-64544-950-8 (Paperback)
ISBN 978-1-64544-951-5 (Digital)

Printed in the United States of America

ACKNOWLEDGMENTS

Cover design by Garrick "Rick" Guth: *For an outstanding job of depicting a place from my memory and from a short, one paragraph description of an old man's fifty-five year old remembrance extracted from the dusty shadows of a dark recess in my mind. Excellent work Rick. To his wife Melissa Guth who, without her supreme knowledge of computer systems and her patience in teaching me how to use my new computer to my best advantage, saved me months of hard, unnecessary work.*

To my mom and dad: *My parents, Victor and Mary Skiles, bought me the Brother word processor which I used to write this book twenty-two years ago. At the not so gentle nudging of my wife and daughter, I recently retrieved the manuscript from an old-really old-floppy disk, cleaned it up and submitted it to Page Publishing. Again, my thanks to my parents, though posthumously, who gave me my start. I wish they could have lived long enough to see the product of that love.*

To certain family members: *These are the individuals who endured the agonizing and time consuming endeavor of reading this novel in its rawest form. They include my wife, Debbie, who has been my constant companion and strongest advocate for forty-three years, my daughter Tami who won my heart at the age of three months, my daughter Jessica who has been and continues to be a wonderful cheerleader for this book and my efforts in general and finally my sister-in-law Kathy who, if memory serves, was the first person to read this and offer encouragement. Kudos to each of you for helping bring this to light.*

To Page Publishing: *They saw the potential in my raw, unedited manuscript and was willing to publish it. Especially to Diana, who remembered me from three years earlier, when I first considered submit-*

ting it, and was more than willing to accept it. To Andy, my coordinator, who did a marvelous job of bringing this all together and for putting up with neurotic authors like me. To all those at Page whose names I don't know, who performed behind the scenes, editing, page design and cover design to make this book a success. Thank you all.

To my God and His Son, Jesus Christ: *They gave me the knowledge, discipline and especially the courage to follow this dream. I placed all my faith in them, and it has blessed me for many years. To the Father, the Son and the Holy Spirit. Amen!*

Prologue

The young woman stood perched on the edge of the cliff that jutted out slightly beyond the wall of rock below. She stared into the darkness horrified, frozen by fear and unable to move. "I must be dreaming," she whispered. "Of course! Any minute I'll wake up and everything will be fine. It was just a nightmare."

But it wasn't fine! She was awake. This was real?

The woman began to tremble as fear swept over her anew—her lips quivered, and her hands shook. She wrapped her arms around herself and tried to calm down, but she could still feel the quaking in her body. She closed her eyes, squeezing them real tight, but she could still see the shocking image in her mind.

Her head began to spin. She felt nauseated, like she was about to throw up. She was dizzy. She was losing her balance. She teetered precariously, about to fall into the darkness below.

Panic set in and she backed slowly away from the edge. Suddenly, she spun around to run up the slope behind her, but her feet seemed glued to the rock. She lost her balance and, falling backward, clawed at the air. She just knew that at any second, she would pitch over the edge and into the madness below. At a moment that could not have been timelier, her feet loosened their grip on the rock, and she found herself lying facedown on the ground. Beginning to lose her hold on reality, she inched her way up the short incline, scratching and scraping, while crawling on her stomach.

Halfway up, she jumped up to run, but a low-hanging branch slapped her across the face. Stunned and reeling from the pain, she screamed. Still clutching her flashlight in her right hand, she continued to struggle up the slope. She had just about reached the top when her feet slipped on some loose gravel. Once again, she found herself lying flat on the ground. Slightly dazed, she glanced behind her, fear creeping in again and numbing the pain.

"No! Nooo!"

She finally reached the top and started running along the dirt road that skirted the creek below and led to the main road.

She had to get out of there before it came after her too!

Her eyes darted from side to side, but her quick, furtive glances revealed nothing in the darkness. *Doesn't matter*, she thought. *You can't see it unless it wants you to.*

The young lady had been down this road a hundred times. She knew it like the back of her hand, but suddenly she felt totally lost, as though she'd never been there before. She swiped at a tangle of dirty, matted hair that hung aimlessly in front of her eyes. She tripped over something in the road and went sprawling forward, landing on her left knee first, then catching herself before doing any more damage. A sharp pain shot through her knee and up her thigh as the pointed edge of a jagged rock pierced her tender skin. Stifled only by her fear, she permitted a little scream to escape her lips before bouncing up and resuming her panicked escape.

She took a quick look around, certain the creature was right behind her, or maybe in the black dense tree line. She was terrified that the horrible thing was close.

She felt it. Somehow, she felt it!

She couldn't see it, but she could feel its strong presence. It... beckoned to her. Covered by the dark of night and guarded by the density of the trees, it was almost...yes, yes...pleading with her to come to it!

Gripped by unfathomable fear, she ran.

She clung to the flashlight, as though it were a lifeline, swinging it as she ran, the light dancing all around her. The one thing she feared the most, being alone in the dark, was happening to her now.

The creature was near. She was certain of it.

A barbed-wire fence separated the road from a field of rye to her right. If it were daylight, the girl would be able to see the waist-high weeds swaying in the breeze that drifted lazily through the valley surrounded by ranges of hills on both sides. But in the darkness, the weeds were thousands of invisible fingers reaching for her. She didn't know which was worse, the dark, dense tree line or the open, treacherous field.

A loud screech split the night like a huge machete. It elicited another scream from the girl just as she tripped over a broken tree limb lying across the road. She staggered a few steps before falling and skinning the other knee. As before, the pain gave way to her immense fear. She looked around for a minute, before leaping up and bolting away.

When she reached the end of the dirt road, a barbed-wire gate loomed ahead. Rather than take the time to climb between the rungs of wire, she scrambled over the top. The needlelike barbs pierced her hands, arms, and legs. The top rung grabbed her foot, and she landed in a heap on the other side. The razor-sharp barbs had torn at her tender flesh until she was a bloody mess.

She lay there for a moment before sitting up and taking in her surroundings. Suddenly, she stood up and at a dead run headed for the farmhouse where lights pierced the night. It stood like a lone sentinel cutting through the blackness, just a quarter of a mile away.

She stopped.

The light—her beacon in the night—had turned red. Bloodred! Everywhere she looked—there was blood. Then she remembered. The cool, dark water had turned a sickly red hue as the life-giving fluid spread out in an ever-widening circle over the surface of the water at Rockhole. And then it came back to her—Brian!

She screamed and screamed!

The earlier events had been blocked from her mind by fear and the horror of what she saw, but now she saw clearly—the horrifying images, the awful sight of just moments before.

Her screams bounced off the hills and echoed through the valley.

She stiffened. Someone, or something, was coming. It has come for me. "Oh god, I don't want to die," she whispered to the night. Then she fell to her knees, drops of her blood mixing with the dirt on the road.

Crying almost silently now, she uttered one last scream—as something grabbed her arm.

Carson Glen Baker

Lila (Baker) Clark

Franklin R. Baker

Curtis Baker

Carlotta Clark

Derek Clark

Curtis Baker
Sharon (Long) Baker
married Oct. 1998

Franklin R. Baker
Carlotta Christine (Clark) Baker
married March 1896

Derek 'Slim' Clark
Betty (Long) Clark
married 1904

Harry N. Baker

Deborah (Clark) Baker

Homer J. Baker

Imogene Lucille Baker

Jeffrey Baker

Seth Baker

Deborah Clark

James Edwin Clark

Robert Eugene Clark

Harry N. Baker
Deborah (Clark) Baker
married Jan. 1936

Seth Baker
Sarah Anne (Clark) Baker
married 1930

Robert Eugene Clark
Rachel (Baker) Clark
married Aug. 1930

Elizabeth Baker

Daniel Caine Clark

Daniel Caine Clark
Elizabeth (Baker) Clark
married May 1952

Brian James Clark

Christopher Stoney Clark

Christopher Stoney Clark
Susan 'Susie' Marie (Connors) Clark
married 1987

Daniel Caine Clark
Sadie (Cleary) (Connors) Clark
married June 1953

Brian James (Connors) Clark
Mary Jane (Connors) Clark
married 1970

Rachel Clark

Renee Clark

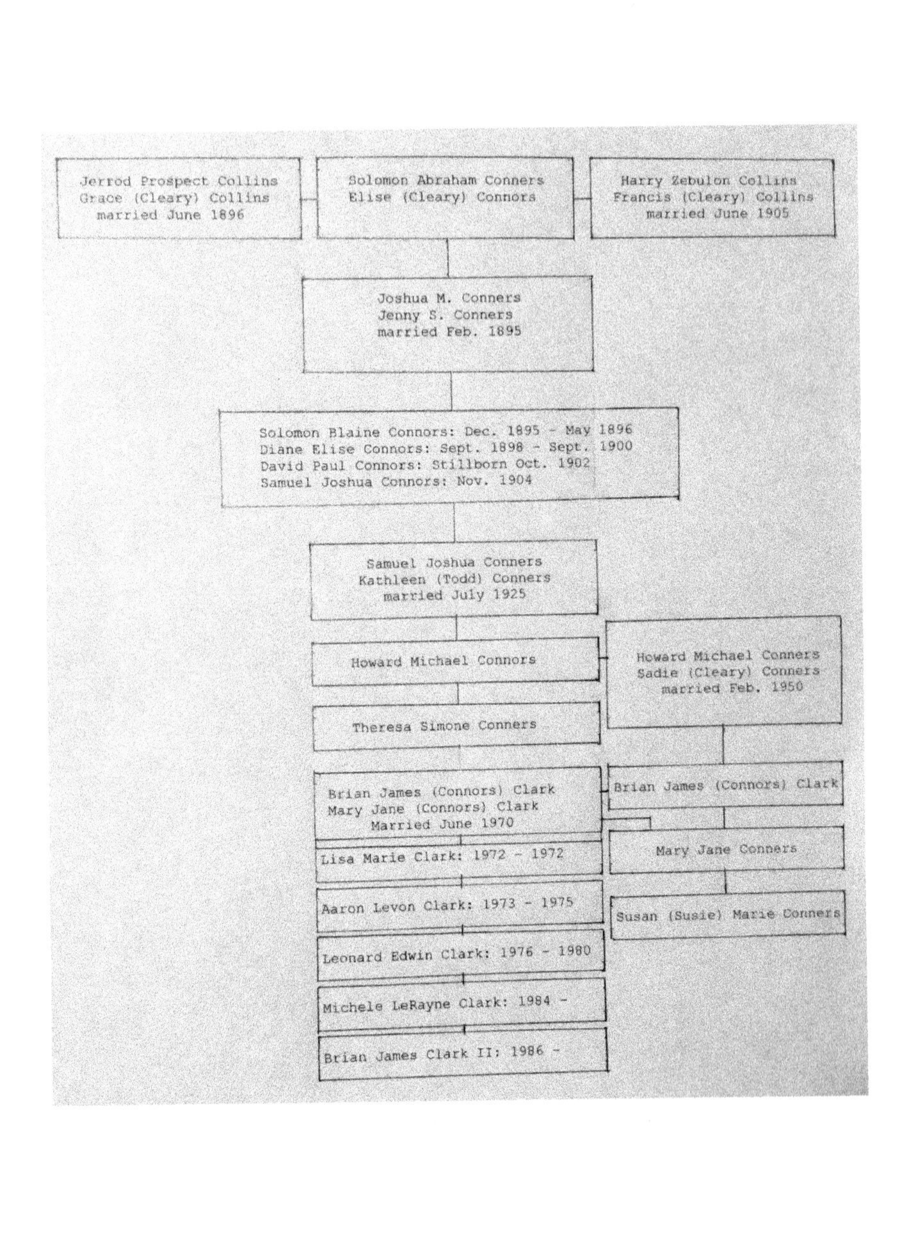
Jerrod Prospect Collins
Grace (Cleary) Collins
married June 1896
Solomon Abraham Conners
Elise (Cleary) Connors
Harry Zebulon Collins
Francis (Cleary) Collins
married June 1905
Joshua M. Conners
Jenny S. Conners
married Feb. 1895
Solomon Blaine Connors: Dec. 1895 - May 1896
Diane Elise Connors: Sept. 1898 - Sept. 1900
David Paul Connors: Stillborn Oct. 1902
Samuel Joshua Connors: Nov. 1904
Samuel Joshua Conners
Kathleen (Todd) Conners
married July 1925
Howard Michael Connors
Howard Michael Conners
Sadie (Cleary) Conners
married Feb. 1950
Theresa Simone Conners
Brian James (Connors) Clark
Mary Jane (Connors) Clark
Married June 1970
Brian James (Connors) Clark
Mary Jane Conners
Susan (Susie) Marie Conners
Lisa Marie Clark: 1972 - 1972
Aaron Levon Clark: 1973 - 1975
Leonard Edwin Clark: 1976 - 1980
Michele LeRayne Clark: 1984 -
Brian James Clark II: 1986 -

Chapter One

He could feel the sharp, clawlike fingernails digging into his back. He didn't know how long the scratches were, but they felt like they covered his entire back. At first, they felt like razor slices, like paper-cuts, but as the sweat began to seep into the fresh wounds, they burned with electrifying intensity. But the pain was partially masked by the strange goings on around him, drawing him in until he became a part of the odd happenings. It seemed unending; time was irrelevant, as though it would last forever. But surely it couldn't. His emotions and conscience imprisoned for all eternity. His adversary danced around him, filling him with a passionate and heightened sensitivity. Thrashing wildly, as though possessed by a demon, the relentless torture probed at his spirit while pain continued to nip at his consciousness. The razorlike fingernails finally released their grip, clenching into tiny fists that pummeled his body. Subconsciously, while keeping a wary eye on his foe, he tried to remember the last time he had been so badly beaten. But his mind was unable to search his memories, choosing instead to remain vigilant and responsive in the present. Suddenly her tongue searched out and found his mouth. It slithered in and out, probing the depths of that dark, sensual opening. The girl moaned loudly as her passion exploded and her senses came alive. As their sweat mixed, the salty brine lingered on her lips and on the tip of her tongue. Their fingers intertwined and squeezed tightly as their bodies shuddered in unison from the spasms of ecstasy. Then it was over.

Stoney Clark and Susie Connors lay side by side on the bed, breathing heavily, exhausted but content, while still holding hands.

Susie was a spirited young lady, full of zest, not promiscuous, though her family believed she was. Maybe if her parents could see her side, they would realize that Stoney was the only man she'd ever been with and ever would. Nevertheless, she remained a disappointment to her parents. When she went to work for Brian and Stoney in their hardware store, she thought for sure they would change their opinion of her. But unfortunately, some things never change.

As far as she could remember, it started when she entered high school, the day she decided to test the waters of parental control. She had been a brunette all her life. Her mother often bragged on her pretty locks and fussed over them when she was a little girl. Susie was never fond of the color. She had wanted to be a blond since those early days of childhood. In school, especially high school, the good-looking boys all liked blonds—and they did seem to have more fun, just her opinion—no matter what her mother said.

Sadie, Susie's mother, was totally against the color change and, in so many words, let her youngest daughter know it. She launched into a rampage letting words like *slut*, *wench*, *hussy*, and *tramp* trip off the end of her tongue. Susie had heard enough and finally moved out when her mother referred to her as a slatternly whore. That was the beginning of a strained relationship between mother and daughter that still existed. It was unfortunate, too, because everyone else liked her new hair—particularly Stoney. He once told her the blonder and the longer, the better. So except for an occasional trim, the only other thing she did to her hair was a blond rinse. Her goal was to have it long enough that it could tickle her behind—and it was almost there.

"Susie."

"Shh! You'll wake Michele."

Susie's lover and fiancé was also the brother of her sister's husband. And since her and Mary J.'s mother had married Brian and Stoney's father, after their own father had died, it technically made them related, but the whole thing was so complicated that folks stopped trying to figure it out a long time ago. The way Stoney and Susie saw it, since there was no blood relation between them, they weren't doing anything wrong.

Stoney had grown up in his brother's shadow but never resented it. To tell the truth, he admired and respected his brother and had been in many fights to prove it. Brian always said there was nothing to prove, but still the fights came. Of the two brothers, Brian was the brain and Stoney was the brawn. Stoney had defended his older brother many times when they were young. As adults, Brian had decided to return the favor by partnering with his brother in their hardware business.

Brian swung a deal with the local bank to finance their hardware store in a joint venture. Their partnership had worked well for three years now. When they added Susie to the payroll, it soon became a family business.

Mary J., on the other hand, was content to be a housewife, happy to let those three run the business while she stayed at home. Of course, stayed at home is a rather loose term. What she did most of the time was go next door and visit with Dala, her best friend, while Dala worked on her customer's hairdos.

In sharp contrast to Susie, Stoney had no problem with his looks. His hair was dark and wavy and hung to his solid square shoulders. It never looked messy, and he always kept it clean. Stoney was an even six feet tall and had the kind of lean yet muscular build most women adored. He had sinewy, smooth skin that effectively showcased his muscular frame. Most of the family saw him as a lazy sort that would never amount to anything. Regardless of what others thought, Brian had always been exceptionally close to his brother—and always, always sided with Stoney.

"Sorry," he apologized, still breathing heavily. Susie started to cover his mouth with her hand but instead popped him in the nose. Then she covered her mouth and burst into a light giggle, as he pulled away and touched his nose gingerly.

"Am I bleeding?" he asked softly.

"No, silly! I didn't hit you that hard. I'm sorry." she said, reaching out to touch it.

They were in Brian and Mary J.'s bedroom, which was down the hall and around the corner from Michele's nursery. They probably would not have wakened Brian and Mary J.'s six-month-old baby girl anyway. But Susie wasn't taking any chances.

"Where do you think they went?" he asked, still rubbing his nose. Both were relaxed now, leaning against pillows propped against the headboard.

"Rockhole," she chided. "Where else would they go to get away from everyone?"

"Maybe we should do that some night and make mad, passionate love under the stars after a refreshing swim," Stoney whispered seductively in her ear.

Susie thumped him on the arm with her fist. "You are so romantic sometimes. Why haven't you said anything before now?" she asked, jumping out of bed. Without waiting for an answer, she tiptoed down the hall and stopped in front of Michele's room. Clasping her hand tightly around the doorknob, she carefully turned it, not making a sound. Still walking on tiptoes, she crossed the room to the crib, leaned gently over the side rail until her face was close to Michele's checking to be sure her niece was breathing.

Susie stood beside the crib and gazed at the sleeping child with a love that only an aunt could feel. Down deep she wanted kids but just wasn't ready for them, and she didn't believe Stoney was ready for a family either. She was perfectly content with her relationship with Stoney just like it was. But there would come a day...

Her heart suddenly pounded as she briefly thought of the three children Brian and Mary J. had lost. Each death had torn a fresh wound in her own soul. Susie felt the losses of those three as much as her own sister had. So as she looked down on her niece's tiny face, it was with special affection.

Michele was sleeping so peaceful, lying there in her soft flannel sleeper that was decorated with circus animals. Mary J. wouldn't have bought this style, so Susie had done so. Aunt Susie had convinced her sister to keep using them at least until Michele outgrew them. She reached down and brushed a stray lock of hair from the baby's face. It was so soft, Michele's sandy-blond hair, that Susie let her fingers linger for a moment. She finally removed her hand and pulled the blanket over the child, leaving only her head exposed. Susie backed out of the room noiselessly and closed the door.

At the door of her sister's bedroom, she broke into a run, and three feet from the bed turned herself into a human torpedo. Stoney was lying on the bed with his eyes closed and was taken completely by surprise, when Susie landed on top of him. There was a loud whoosh as the air in his lungs erupted violently. She rolled off and sat next to him with her legs folded under her, shocked by his reaction. She wasn't sure what to do. So she did nothing but sit and stare in disbelief. "Should I call 911?" she cried. He made a couple of wheezing noises as he tried to breathe in some air. A minute later, he was sucking in great gulps of it as his lungs began to inflate.

"Nice…shot," was all he could manage to say.

"Sorry," Susie said, almost tearfully, disheartened. "I didn't think that would happen. My foot slipped just as I jumped. You okay?" she asked, nervous concern evident in her tone.

Stoney laid his head in her lap, and she gently stroked his hair. "I'm fine," he said, breathing easier now.

She twisted around until she was reclining against the pillows, cuddling and caressing him until the incident passed. She glanced at the clock on the nightstand. It was 1:00 a.m. *Time for more fun*, she thought playfully to herself. She ran her finger down his cheek and let it wander aimlessly over his hairy chest.

"Want to go again?" she cooed.

Just then the phone rang.

Delmer Matthews and his wife, Dora, were awakened by screams that pierced the night from somewhere across the ryegrass field that he planted every year. It shattered the nighttime silence, jarring them from a deep sleep.

"My god!" uttered the aging farmer, throwing the covers back and jumping out of bed. He raised the window shade and scanned the semidark field.

"What is, Del?" his wife asked, a scared tone in her voice. "Del?"

"I don't know. I can't make out a thing in this darkness." Dora had put her robe on and joined him at the window.

"Was that an animal?" Dora asked.

"I don't know. It's just too damned dark to see—No! Wait a minute. There," he said, pointing at something in the dark. "Someone is on the road." As if on cue, the moon peeked from behind a cloud and illuminated the road. "I think it's a girl," he said, a bit surprised.

"Well, go open the door! See what's wrong. Hurry up now, she may need help. I'll put on some coffee. Should I call the sheriff?" she asked quickly.

"Best to wait till I see what it is. Might not need the sheriff." He slipped on his house shoes and robe and quickly made his way out the front door of the old farmhouse. He walked at a fast pace down the road toward the girl, mindful of the loose gravel.

She had fallen to her knees by the time he got to her. Del leaned over and laid his hand on her shoulder. "Miss, are you all right? What's wrong?" She looked him straight in the eyes and screamed.

Delmer recoiled at the raucous noise and looked for signs of injury but couldn't see much because of the darkness. "Young lady, what is it?" he asked, gently squeezing her shoulder, which caused her even more panic.

Suddenly she grabbed his arm and yanked his hand from her shoulder. "No! Nooo!" she screamed. Del regained his hold on her, afraid she might run. It was obvious she shouldn't be alone. He tried to make some sense of her confused babbling but couldn't understand her. "Leave me alone! Get away from me!" she cried, trying to free herself. But the farmer had a steel grip and refused to let go. The girl continued yelling and screaming incoherently. "*No!* You won't get me too. Get away! Get away!" She started backing away from the farmer, her eyes wild and frightened. Del finally relented, letting go of her.

"Who's after you?" he asked, shouting to be heard over her screams. "Miss, I just want to help you. Can you tell me your name? You may need a doctor." The more he spoke, the more she shrank away, unable to hear or understand.

Suddenly, she collapsed falling into a heap on the road. Delmer pried her hand loose from his arm and then picked her up and carried her back to the house. Dora had the door opened, waiting for him.

Del struggled up the porch steps.

"Put her on the bed in the spare room," she told her husband.

"Call the doctor and the sheriff," he gasped, out of breath. After he laid the poor girl down, Del went into the kitchen for some water and rags to clean the girl's wounds. By the time he returned to the unconscious girl, his wife was off the phone.

"What happened to her?" she asked softly.

"Don't know," he told her. "One minute she was yelling and screaming and the next she just passed out. From the looks of her, I'd say she got into that barbed-wire fence, but I don't see anything really life-threatening."

"Well, I called the sheriff, and the doc like you said. They're both on their way."

"Good! Good," Del replied, beginning to wipe some blood from the girl's arms and legs. "How's that coffee coming, Ma?"

"Should be about ready." She nodded. "I'll go check on it." He took a blanket from the closet and covered the girl up. She moaned and rolled her head but then quickly settled into a restless sleep.

Thirty minutes passed, and Del had cleaned her about as good as he could. "Hello," a voice called from the front door.

"Hey, Doc. Come on in," Del responded cordially, opening the screen door. "Right in here. She's in the spare bedroom."

Dr. William Edwards had once had dreams of practicing medicine in a big city hospital when he was still in residency. He had always thought of starting a specialized practice, in gynecology. But for some reason, he ended up back in his hometown of Crater Ridge with a general practice that didn't pay much, had long unforgiving days, but was very much needed.

The five-foot, ten-inch silver-haired potbellied physician walked into the bedroom and immediately began to observe the girl's situation.

He pulled the cover down to her waist and began to examine her, poking and prodding the obvious areas affected. Finding nothing serious, he lifted the stethoscope from around his neck and listened to her chest area. Over her right lung, he detected a gurgling sound. "We'd better get her to the hospital, Del. Dora, is that coffee I smell?"

"Certainly is, Bill. You want a cup?"

"If you can make it to go," he said, giving her a quick smile.

"I think I've still got some of those paper cups left over from the fourth of July picnic," she replied. "I'll get it for you."

Daniel and Sadie Clark had an ongoing argument that started a couple of years after they were married. For nearly twenty-five years they had been having this same argument. It involved their inability to come to any discussion about what they'd found. Sadie had wanted to confront the family about it, but Daniel convinced her they should remain silent. Purely by accident, they had discovered a dark family secret kept hidden for two generations.

"We should tell the kids," Sadie said firmly.

"No!" Daniel shouted. "No one is to ever know." He looked at his wife, his stare never wavering. "Do I make myself clear?"

"Yes, Daniel, of course you do," she snapped. "But I still say they have a right to know. It's our fault for letting them get married to begin with. We should have told them before we ever let it go that far."

Daniel ran his hands through his hair. He suddenly felt very old as he rubbed his burning eyes with very tired fingers. "It's not something I want out in the open," he said weakly. "If we do, before you know it, the whole damned town will know. Hell, I wish I didn't know," he admitted.

"Daniel! I'll say it again. They're our children. They have a right to know."

He looked at Sadie, regret already building inside him. "We keep our mouths shut! The subject is closed."

Sadie gave him a disapproving look. No matter how long they'd been married, she was still a Connors—first and foremost. She and Howard Connors had two daughters, Susie and Mary J., from their marriage. When Howard died, she was left with two little girls to raise—alone. So out of desperation, she had married Daniel Clark. There wasn't love in the beginning. For her, it was more a marriage of convenience. She just didn't want to be alone.

What no one knew, except certain family members, most of whom were dead by now, was that she and Howard were second cousins but far removed. Surely there wasn't anything wrong with that, or so she had convinced herself many times. Sadie caught her breath suddenly! Did Daniel know about that? She'd never told a soul, especially not him. Maybe someone else did. She gave him a furtive glance. Nothing. He was completely stone-faced. Oh, God! What a nightmare!

Daniel's mind worked feverishly as he tried to sort through the horrible knowledge of his ancestor's incestuous relationship. He had thought his was awful until this. But what he and Elizabeth did was nothing compared to his grandparents. Franklin and Carlotta were brother and sister. That had to be about the absolute worst he could imagine. Daniel tried to remain expressionless as he sorted through it. He finally decided it was time for him to be honest with Sadie. At least he wouldn't have to live in fear of her finding out some other way.

"There's something I need to tell you," he blurted out. Say it before you change your mind. "It won't be easy for you to hear."

Sadie's eyes were as large as saucers. Oh my god! He did know. Or maybe it was something else. Maybe he was having an affair or worse. But what could be worse than that? "Yes?" she asked in a barely recognizable voice.

Daniel took a deep breath. "Elizabeth and I were second cousins," he told her.

Sadie stared at him. Was she holding her breath?

"Did you hear me? I said that Elizabeth was my second cousin. We were related before we were married."

Sadie was relieved and a little surprised. Truthfully, she had expected something much worse. She quickly shook it off but continued staring at him. "My god, Daniel, what have we done?"

"What Sadie?" Daniel didn't expect this from her. "Are you okay?" Not sure what to do, Daniel waited for her to say something. Sadie was usually the stronger of them. "Can I get you something?" he finally asked.

"I'll be fine, baby. I just need a moment." Sadie fanned herself with an unopened letter lying on the end table next to her. "Daniel, I have something to tell you too," she replied as she lowered her head until her chin rested on her chest. "Howard and I were also related before our marriage."

He squinted his eyes. "You don't say?"

"We were second cousins too." She spoke quickly before he could say anything else. She needed to get it all out while she still had the courage. "My father and his mother were first cousins," she admitted, her voice beginning to quiver a little. "Mary J.'s poor babies never stood a chance," she cried as tears welled up in her eyes. "And it's our fault. It's our fault they died. Oh, dear God! What have we done?"

"No, I don't believe that! I can't believe that!" Daniel leaned over and held her tightly.

"Oh, yes! It's our fault our grandchildren died," she sobbed. Daniel continued to console and comfort her, but it wouldn't be enough.

"Sadie, could we just not think about that right now, huh?"

She nearly lost her mind when the first baby died. Lisa Marie, their first grandchild, lived only nine months. Crib death, they called it. Purely an accident. Nothing you could have done. But Sadie knew better. That baby's death was the direct result of their family's dark past. And they had decided to keep it all a secret from their kids. Let them go on thinking it was just an unfortunate accident and not live with that dark cloud hanging over their heads—but now it was too late! Let them have a new start—but they would never have that, would they?

Next was Aaron Levon, who died at eighteen months. And then, Leonard Edwin, who they thought would outlive the family curse. He lived to the age of four before he died. In fact, he had just celebrated his fourth birthday. All that was left to them out of four grandchildren was little Michele LeRayne. She was six months old, and everyone held their breath every day that she would make it.

"Isn't three enough?" she cried out, looking toward the ceiling. "Isn't three enough?" She collapsed into Daniel's arms, a broken woman.

The sound of a ringing phone broke the ensuing silence.

Mary Jane Clark lay in the hospital bed, her blood-soaked, knotted hair cleaned, her several cuts and scrapes tended to with loving care and a few stitches. None of her many abrasions were severe or life-threatening, but she would need much rest but should recover soon. The pain and horror of the night's events, however, would linger for some time.

Susie and Stoney were the first to arrive at the hospital. They ran up to the nurses' station out of breath and frantic. "Mary J. Clark—where is she?" Susie asked, excited and breathing heavily.

"Are you family?" the nurse asked without emotion.

"Yes, I'm her sister. Where is she? How is she?" Susie was angered with the nurse's cool, detached attitude.

"I'm Dr. Edwards," said an elderly man with silver hair and a mustache that matched, approaching them from behind. He wore a white doctor's coat, and his smooth, soft voice had a calming effect, appeasing Susie's anger. He steered them to some chairs in a small waiting area.

Susie never took her eyes off the doctor, as though he might vanish if she did.

"Your sister was found out on County Road 135 tonight. She was in a state of shock, panicked and scared to death. She was covered with various cuts and abrasions. She has a punctured lung. She'll be fine, physically, with rest and care. I gave her a sedative and she's sleeping." Dr. Edwards averted his eyes for a moment. "I don't know what happened out there, but she's been through something traumatic. When she wakes up, she'll be disoriented, and she may not remember what happened. On the other hand, she may recall the whole thing, and her fear and panic could return. That's about all I can tell you." He finished with his hands spread apart to indicate he had no more answers.

"How did she get here, Doc?" Stoney asked quizzically. "Who brought her in?"

"Well, actually I did," he answered slowly. "But I'm not the one who found her. Delmer Matthews lives out there, at that first curve, he found her and called me."

Stoney and Susan looked at each other in dismay. It was Stoney who asked first. "Where's Brian?"

"I'm sorry. Who is Brian?" the doctor asked, confused. Stoney glanced at Susie, but she still stared at the doctor. After a few seconds, she forced her eyes away. Slowly and deliberately, she focused on Stoney.

"Brian is her husband," Susie informed him in a barely audible voice. "They were together."

"I'm sorry," Dr. Edwards said again. "I don't know. She was found alone. Neither Delmer nor Dora said anything about another person."

"Paging Dr. Edwards. Dr. Edwards, dial 449 please. Dr. Edwards, please dial 449."

"I'm sorry," he said for the third time. "I have to go. Your sister is in room 122. You can go see her now. I'll look in on her later." He smiled and walked off.

Dan Rogers had been sheriff of Miller County for twenty-two years, and he still hated getting called out in the middle of the night. This call came shortly after midnight. He had been asleep for only an hour. Usually when calls like this came in, it meant trouble.

He climbed the steps to the Matthews porch and knocked vigorously on the screen door. "Hello, anybody home?" he called out.

"Yeah, Dan. Come on in!" Del shouted back from the kitchen and walked into the living room to greet the sheriff.

"I was pretty sure you were," the sheriff commented. "Looked like every light in the house was on." He grinned as he accepted Delmer's extended hand and shook it with a strength that belied his small frame. Besides being short and light on his feet, Dan had jet-black hair and a boyish face. Most folks agreed, he looked more like a schoolboy than the county sheriff.

"Come on in and have a cup of coffee."

"I thought I smelled some of Dora's coffee when I walked up on the porch." He smiled cordially at her. "But I also thought I smelled biscuits too."

"Sheriff, you've got a nose like a bloodhound," she chided, giving him a hug. "Set yourself down there at the table." She busied herself with pouring coffee and serving biscuits and some of her homemade jam.

"Okay, Del. Why in the hell did you call me out in the middle of the night?" he asked while sipping his coffee.

"It's the strangest thing I've ever seen, Dan," he said with brutal honesty. He recalled the sequence of events just as they happened. Every few minutes, Dora would nod in agreement with Delmer's assessment about the strange girl and her odd behavior. The sheriff took a bite of his biscuits and washed it down with a swallow of coffee.

"There wasn't anyone else around?" Dan asked, puzzled.

"Didn't see anyone," Del said thoughtfully. "Strangest thing though, her being out there all alone. But she said something that didn't make sense, considering she was alone."

"You won't get me too.'" Dan recalled from Del's account before. He stroked his chin and stared at the wall.

"I thought she meant me at first," Del replied, "but now—I don't know. She had a wild-eyed look that reminded me of pure fear. It was scary…you know?"

Dan stuffed the last bite of biscuit in his mouth and washed it down with what remained of his coffee. "I'll go look around in them trees and down by that swimming hole. Don't reckon I'll find anything in the dark. You'll let me know if you remember anything else?"

"Of course, Dan. Of course."

"Thank you for the biscuits and coffee, Dora," he said over his shoulder as he stepped out onto the porch. "Good night, folks. Thanks for all your help."

"Night, Sheriff," they said in unison.

Susie and Stoney sat, one on each side of Mary J.'s bed. For an hour they had sat quietly watching the sleeping girl. She hadn't moved a muscle—not even a twitch to Susie's dismay. The only reason she knew her sister was alive was her shallow breathing and the annoying beeping of the monitor connected to Mary J.

"Mary J., I wish you'd wake up."

"Susie, Stoney?" Sadie murmured in a low voice. Susie flinched, startled by her mother's sudden presence. Sadie stared down at the motionless form of her oldest daughter. Daniel had gone to the other side and stood beside Stoney. He rested his hand on the boy's shoulder.

"What happened, son?" he asked. Stoney looked at his father. For some reason he was surprised his father spoke.

"Don't know," Stoney answered in a whispered reply. "The doctor told us they found her out on County Road 135." He quickly recounted what Doc Edwards had told them.

"What in the hell was she doing out there?" Daniel asked. "Was she alone?"

"They went for a swim. Brian was with her," Susie responded, her voice trembling slightly. "They went for an evening out. We were watching Michele for them when the call came that Mary J. was here," she stammered, her eyes filling with tears. Susie moved to the foot of the bed where Stoney joined her. He held her for a minute, something her own mother wouldn't do. Sadie hadn't so much as touched Susie.

Stoney leaned over and gave her a quick peck on the cheek and whispered in her ear.

Drying her eyes, she blurted out, "We have to go. We left the baby with Dala." Sadie nodded but kept her eyes on Mary J. "We'll be by later." Daniel nodded silently. Sadie ignored her. Daniel might be her stepfather, but Susie had quickly fallen into the habit of calling him Daddy shortly after her mother married him. She didn't disrespect her own father. She never knew him. He died when she was still a baby.

As they exited the hospital, Susie noted it was a beautiful summer night. The stars were shining in all their splendid brilliance, and the moon was full. Susie hooked her arm in Stoney's, and they walked in silence to the car. As she climbed in on the passenger's side, she asked, "So where are we really going?"

Stoney stared out the window on her side, focused on something only he could see. "To find Brian," he said evenly.

Sheriff Rogers was not superstitious. He got spooked from time to time—not the same thing. But something the girl had said to Del bothered him. What did she mean by "You won't get me too"? Dan shook it off. Some mighty freaky things had been known to happen around this area.

He turned his car around and eased it down the road in the direction the girl had come from looking for the spot where Del said he ran across the girl. Once he found it, he stopped his cruiser where the headlights would shine on it, got out and walked in a wide circle around the area. The gravel was obviously disturbed, scattered around where Del had struggled with her. Other than that, there wasn't much to see, except for a few drops of blood.

Suddenly he heard footsteps approaching from behind. He was still bent over, inspecting the ground. When he was sure the steps were close, Dan drew his service revolver and spun around in one smooth, swift motion.

"Wait, don't shoot," shouted Del, backing up a step. "It's me, Delmer." He pounded his chest over his heart.

"Good God A'mighty, man," Dan blurted out, "you scared the living daylights out of me. I must be a little squeamish tonight." He released the hammer on his pistol and returned it to its holster.

"Must be," Del laughed nervously. Something else came to mind a while ago, and I thought you might want to know about it."

"What is it, Del?" Rogers asked, sighing with relief. He wasn't sure why he was so skittish about this. It certainly wasn't his style.

Delmer was staring into the darkness that shrouded his rye field. "The first scream, the one that woke us, didn't come from here, on the road." He pointed through the darkness to somewhere across the field. "It came from over there, by the creek."

Mary J. felt like she was floating, or maybe soaring? It was difficult to tell. She was high above the earth, certainly. She relaxed and joyfully accepted the wind on her face. It flowed through her hair, but her hair didn't tangle or get in her eyes—it was perfect.

Strange, she thought silently.

Not a sound. She was unable to speak aloud. Mary J. moved her mouth, but nothing came out. Oh well, maybe she didn't need a voice. It would only destroy this perfect moment. Besides, the silence was golden, right?

Silently!

Suddenly, far below her, she saw Brian. She was about to call out to him, then remembered—silence. She contented herself to just watch him. Something she'd always enjoyed. He was a handsome man with finely chiseled features. Mary J. often showed jealousy not only of his perfectly smooth and unblemished skin compared to hers, but that other women appreciated his enormous good looks as well. Besides, she had to work hard to keep hers that way. Brian's came naturally.

Brian wasn't alone. She strained to see through the darkness. But could only make out the form of a woman. They were laughing and trading intimate moments.

Brian was stepping out on her?

She strained even harder to focus on the woman and then, embarrassingly, realized that the woman was her. They were at Rockhole for an evening of swimming and making love. God, how she loved Brian!

The interlude was a short one as Brian's demeanor seemed to change.

Suddenly, she remembered. The creature! She had to warn him. She could stop what was about to happen.

"*No!* Brian!" she screamed. "Don't go, Brian! Don't go! Please don't leave me. Her screams echoed through the hospital corridors. "Leave him alone!" she continued yelling. "Don't touch him! Stop! *Nooo! Nooo!*"

As quickly as the nightmare had come, it was gone. Mary J. sat up in bed, screaming at the top of her lungs and saying things that Daniel and Sadie didn't understand. Her panic-stricken screams stabbed at their hearts. Terror seized them. They could only stare in horror as the doctor and nurses worked on their daughter. They saw the lines on the monitor jumping up and down, fluctuating wildly like a polygraph needle. Then the sedative took effect, and Mary J. instantly calmed down. Her vital signs returned to normal, but her skin was pasty—as though her body was drained of blood.

"She'll sleep now," the doctor reported.

Daniel and Sadie remained motionless for a bit after the medical staff left the room. But something was terribly wrong. Their eyes met as a look of dread passed between them.

"You sure you want to go with me? There's no telling what we'll find out there," Sheriff Rogers warned the aging farmer.

"Yeah, I'll go. You just might need my help. Besides, this night is already ruined," Del said ruefully.

The sheriff shook his head. "It isn't any wonder you farmers have such a hard life." He grinned at Del. "You don't get near enough sleep. All right, we'll follow the path she most likely took. On this side of the creek, there's a dirt road that follows the creek for a bit." When they came to the barbed-wire fence where Mary J. had gotten hung up, they found bits of cloth clinging to the sharp barbs. Shining his light along the wire, they made another discovery. "My god!" Rogers exclaimed, reaching out and touching one of the barbs that was covered with some red substance. He brought his hand away and rubbed his thumb and forefinger together under the light. "Some of her flesh, I'd say."

They crossed through the barbed-wire gate and started following the road. The sheriff shined his flashlight from side to side, looking for signs of the young girl's trail. "We'll go as far as Rockhole tonight," he told Delmer. But they hadn't gone a hundred feet before they discovered more of Mary J.'s blood. "Look. She fell here," Dan whispered softly, pointing at the blood on a tree limb lying across the road. He held the light on the limb long enough for Del to see. They walked a little further along the road and found another blood spot on a rock protruding from the ground. They straightened up and slowly made their way along the road to the rock cliff overlooking Rockhole.

The sheriff was in the lead as they eased their way down the incline to the smooth rock surface below. He shined his flashlight around the area looking for signs of a struggle but didn't have to look far. It only took a few seconds of scanning to realize something tragic had happened here. Everywhere their light shined there was blood, a lot of it!

"My god! What happened here?" Delmer asked.

Among the other debris was a picnic basket, its contents strewn about the place and a blanket with towels and a few personal items lying on it.

Dan shuffled over to the edge of the cliff, followed closely by Delmer Matthews, and shined his light into the darkness below. "Oh my god!" he exclaimed.

Delmer gasped and began to reel at what they saw in the water below. He stumbled back away from the edge and vomited. "Oh, sweet Jesus!" he cried. After a minute or so, he returned and looked again into the water.

"Sweet Jesus!"

Chapter Two

February 28, 1895

Dear Mama,

I thought I would try one last time to explain to you and Daddy how Joshua and I feel about each other and how beautiful our love is. Please believe me when I say we never meant for this to happen. We don't know why it happened; it just did.

I love you, Mama. Please know that. I wouldn't purposely hurt you, but I love Joshua too. And I won't hurt him either. On the contrary, I would die for him. I think I loved him even before he was my brother. When we were yet in the womb, we were meant to be together. Surely, God must have wanted it so. For how could we have known about right or wrong then?

I know that twins share a bond closer than most brothers and sisters, but I think ours was unusually so. I can't ever remember a time when we were apart.

Well, I just wanted you to know that before I told you the real reason, I wrote you this letter.

Joshua and I are getting married. I knew that neither of you would ever consider coming, or we would have told you long before now. By the time you get this, we will already be husband and wife. Mama, please be happy for us. That's all we ask. And please believe me when I tell you it was a difficult decision, leaving you and Daddy. But again, we knew you wouldn't approve.

Joshua says hello. If you should decide to write back, just post your letter to general delivery. It will get to us.

I pray that you will find it in your heart to be happy for us. It was the only way. And perhaps find it in your heart to forgive us and maybe we could be a family again.

Your loving kids,
Joshua and Jenny

"This could quite possibly be the coldest day we've ever had," Solomon told his wife, shivering from the subzero temperatures that had held them captive for nearly two weeks. He had been out feeding the livestock, and the strong north winds seemed to cut right through his heavy parka. "I sure could go for a cup of that hot coffee you got brewing over there." He finished pulling off his boots and was standing next to the old potbellied heating stove in the middle of the room.

Solomon suddenly realized that Elise had been unusually quiet since he came in, nor had she moved from her chair at the kitchen table.

"Sugar, what's the matter with you?" Solomon stood with his back to the stove now, preferring to stick close to the heat. He stared intently at the woman who had been his wife for fifty-four years. Her skin was more wrinkled than a wadded-up newspaper and the color of an Indian in summer, but to Solomon Conners, she was the most beautiful creature on earth.

"Ellie, honey, what is it? What's that paper you're holding?" She was never this quiet. She usually prattled on about one thing or another all day long, even if she was alone. It wasn't like her to act this way. He crossed the space between them quickly. Elise was staring straight ahead, deep in thought.

"Well?"

"Joshua and Jenny are getting married," she blurted out in a rush of words. Solomon frowned and turned away. He had always assumed the kids would be close by and never considered they might choose a lifestyle other than the one they had been raised in. Especially Joshua. They left only two months ago, and the shock of how and why they left was just beginning to wear off.

Solomon could hear his wife crying. He cupped his hand under her chin and very gently tilted her head upward. "Ellie, honey, they're not worth the tears or frustration."

"How can you say that?" she practically spat the words at him. "They're still our children."

"No, they're not," Solomon retorted. "They stopped being our children when they made that blasted decision to run off and abandon us. Besides, there's laws about that sort of thing, aren't there?" He looked at her quizzically.

She almost snickered at his last remark. "I-I should write them," she said, her eyes moistening again. "What will I say? How do I talk about this?"

Solomon was half lying sprawled on the couch, where he had collapsed, a crumpled, broken man. Their hopes for their children, their grandchildren—everything they had worked for the past forty years, to build a family, to work the land together, three generations destroyed—so quickly, so easily.

May 12, 1895

Dear Mama,

I'm so happy you answered my letter. I was so afraid you wouldn't or that Daddy might not allow it. At any rate, it boosted my spirits just to see the envelope with your name on it. Besides, I'm convinced that most of what you said was Daddy talking. Your letter was austere and hurtful, something that's not in you. Though that was the response I expected, it was not the one I hoped for.

I plead with you to please tell me that was Daddy saying those mean things and not you. I couldn't stand it if I lost you completely, as I have Daddy. I know it was a shock and you have every right to be put out, but please think about it carefully and understand how strongly Joshua and I feel for each other.

Well, on to happier things.

Joshua and I have some wonderful news to share with you. I have just this morning come from the doctor's office, and he confirmed that I am with child. Isn't that simply marvelous news, Mama? You're going to be a grandmother despite everything. Please tell me you're happy for us.

We have been making all sorts of plans for when the baby arrives. Oh! By the way, if it's a boy, we're going to name him Solomon. And if it's a girl, her name will be Elise. Would you like to have a namesake? Daddy probably wouldn't approve. Anyway, Joshua and I agree on the names. I hope it pleases you.

The baby is due in December. We're not going to buy much of anything until we know if it's a boy or girl. Joshua is due to be promoted from teller to bank assistant in a couple of months. So we'll be able to better afford the baby's needs then.

I'm sending these letters through cousin Grace. I hope it's all right. I thought it better daddy didn't know where we are for now.

Well, I better stop and get this posted.

All our love,

Joshua and Jenny

"Another letter came for Elise today," Francis said thoughtfully. "I wonder why she's sending them here."

"I suppose you could ask her when she picks it up," Grace replied logically. She continued her knitting as she talked without ever dropping a stitch. "You know, it has to have something to do with Solomon and those kids. If she's sending them here, she must not want Solomon knowing about it."

Francis mulled that over a minute. "That makes sense to me," she agreed. "I thought I noticed a change in him these past few months. He just doesn't seem like his old humorous self."

"Well, if Elise wants her mail to keep coming here, she should tell us what's going on," Grace pointed out. Suddenly, she stopped knitting and let her hands fall to her lap. An involuntary gasp escaped her lips, and she covered her mouth with one hand. "It must have something to do with Joshua and Jenny. There's more to this than meets the eye. Mark my words."

"Yes, I think you're right," Francis agreed, nodding. "And I think you're right that she should tell us about it too. After all," she insisted, her mood perking up, "we might be able to help with whatever it is that's wrong."

"I seriously doubt that you could help in this case," Elise said from the front door.

"Oh! Dear me!" Grace cried out, pounding her chest repeatedly. "You gave me quite a fright."

"How long have you been standing there?" Francis asked, fanning herself rapidly with an old, worn-out magazine.

Elise fought back the need to cry again but swallowed her emotions while trying to decide whether to be truthful with the two sisters or try to deceive them with lies she and Solomon had been living since finding out about Joshua and Jenny. Truthfulness finally won out. "I was just about to knock when I heard my name mentioned. Normally, it wouldn't bother me to eavesdrop, because I'm sure that we're the subject of a lot of conversations. But then I heard my children mentioned and in a moment of weakness decided to be silent and listen. I apologize for doing such a terrible thing."

Having regained her composure, Grace was still resolute in her ambition to know the truth and help, if possible. "That's quite all right, Elise. It's probably better you heard anyway. But I don't understand, why you think we couldn't help?"

"We are family," Francis added wistfully.

"I suppose it's time someone knew," Elise cried mournfully. She sat in a winged-back chair across from the sisters and sobbed silently for a few minutes. They let her cry for a bit, unsure what to say, or do. Then quite suddenly, she blurted out the whole sordid affair. When she finally finished, she sighed. "So now you know. And it would be in everyone's best interest if you kept it to yourselves, especially around Solomon. He has completely disowned the children. I thought about doing the same thing, but…I still love them," she whimpered. "I just couldn't bring myself to turn against them." She buried her face in her hands and once again erupted into tears.

"Oh my god," was all Grace managed while Francis stared in disbelief.

There didn't seem to be much else to say. As the jagged edges of their individual thoughts doggedly ripped a hole in the fabric of their silence, Grace desperately tried to find something important to say, but alas, nothing came to mind. Suddenly she remembered the letter that came for Elise and sighed with unmistakable relief. "Here's a letter that came for you today," she said with a soft smile, extending it toward Elise. "It's from your children." She hoped it might help dispel some of the tension that had permeated the room.

Elise raised her head and only halfheartedly wiped at her eyes. She took the letter and held it pressed to her bosom for a minute, as though that might relieve some of the aches that tore at her heart. Without saying another word, she got up and walked out of the house.

"Well, of all the gall!" Francis snipped.

"Colene, help me! It's Jenny! Something's wrong! She's bleeding," Joshua shouted as he crashed through the door of the little clinic. Nurse Colene Whitaker was the only one around. The little clinic rarely needed any more than one person to attend it. The more-difficult cases always went to the hospital emergency room.

"Put her on the examination table in there, and let's have a look Joshua," the nurse directed him.

"I don't know what happened. We were sitting at the table eating supper and all, she doubled over, moaned, and turned as white as a ghost and then passed out. You've got to do something Colene. You've got to help her," he pleaded urgently.

"Calm down, Joshua. You're no help like this. Has she shown any other symptoms?" the nurse questioned him. "Complained about unusual pains, a high temperature, headaches, or anything like that lately?"

Joshua was looking at Jenny and shook his head. "She, uh… no, nothing," he stammered. "I didn't notice anything, and she never mentioned anything."

"You stay right there and watch her. Don't let her roll off." She grabbed a blanket from a cabinet across the room and covered Jenny to keep her warm. "I'm going to call Doc Harris." She left the room. Just then Jenny grabbed her stomach and yelled in pain. Joshua just stood there silently and watched Jenny with his hand on her arm. "Joshua! Joshua! Joshua!" the nurse shouted for the third time. She was trying to lift the unconscious girl to put a pillow under her head and straighten her up on the bed. "Either help me or get out of the way," she snapped at him.

That seemed to snap him out of it. "What's wrong?" Joshua asked. "Don't let her die. You can't let her die," he shouted, grabbing the nurse by the arm.

Dr. Harris hurried into the treatment room. "What do we have, Colene?"

"Her respirations are shallow. Her pulse is rapid, and she's clammy. She grabbed her stomach in intense pain before passing out," the nurse informed him.

Dr. Harris clipped his stethoscope to his ears and listened to her chest first and then to her abdomen. "The baby's heartbeat is strong," he said, straightening up and removing the stethoscope. "Joshua, has she shown any signs of anxiety lately?" he asked the boy.

Joshua didn't answer right away. He kind of fidgeted around for a bit, staring at Jenny.

"Now, Joshua. You can take all the time you want to answer my questions. But your wife doesn't have a lot of time. So it's up to you, but you might want to consider that the quicker you make your mind up, the quicker I can help her."

"Uh, yeah, Doc. We got a letter from our mother today," he replied hesitantly. "She hasn't been the same since. She kind of moped around all day, and then at supper, she just started crying."

"All right, Joshua. Why don't you go have a seat in the waiting room," he suggested. "I'll be out in a few minutes to talk to you." Joshua believed no one had caught his innuendo, but now he wasn't so sure. Doc Harris seemed suspicious. Joshua had slipped and said, "Our mother." Joshua started to protest, but he was gently shoved out the door by Nurse Whitaker.

"Colene, prepare her for surgery. We'll have to deliver this baby by cesarean," he instructed the nurse. "I'll see if I can ease Joshua's mind a little."

He walked out of the room and stopped in his office briefly before going to the waiting room. He poured a cup of black coffee and then joined Joshua. "Here. Sip on this for a while," he said, sitting next to the nervous boy. He tried to put Joshua at ease by explaining what was happening with Jenny. "She's going to be all right, son."

"I know, Doc. I have faith in you. But I can't help worrying. She's all I have in the world and I love her so much. Do you understand?"

"I think I do, son. I was young and in love once," he said, smiling at the young man. "Joshua, I think what's happening is that the sac that surrounds the baby and protects it has ruptured and is bleeding. If I'm right, it can't be fixed. And that baby can't live in there. It must come out, but it's not ready to come out on its own yet, so I'll have to take it out surgically. It'll take a while to do this. Just make yourself comfortable. There's more coffee if you need it. Just help yourself." He walked off and disappeared through the door to the treatment room, leaving Joshua alone.

Joshua propped his elbows on his knees and let his head fall forward until his face was pressed into his hands. He and Jenny weren't very religious people. They were made to go to church when they were kids at home. It's not that they didn't believe in God; they just didn't think He believed in them very much right now. But in this desperate hour and at a time when Jenny needed all the help she could get, he was willing to give it a try if God would listen to him. He hoped so, for Jenny's sake. Where else could he turn? Their parents wanted nothing to do with them. We're on our own, he thought miserably.

"God, I-I know You have every right to be mad at us a-and not listen, but this isn't for me. It's for my Jenny. And she never stopped believing in You, so do You think You could take a few minutes and hear me out? I'd appreciate it." He glanced around to see if anyone was listening in and then continued.

"God, she sure could use a little help. I know that Doc Harris knows what he's doing and all, but there might be something terribly wrong, and he'll need Your help to make it right, you know? So if you would just kind of watch over what he's doing and make sure everything goes okay, that'd be great. I can't make any promises as to our part in this, but we'll try to be better folks."

He thought it over and decided he'd said about all that needed saying. "Well, that's it, I guess. Thanks for listening. Uh…Amen." Joshua waited. It seemed like hours had passed. He sat there for a while after his talk with God and wondered if He had heard him. Joshua decided that He probably did. He paced around the small waiting room, finally deciding this was a waste of energy, he approached the door to the treatment room where Jenny was. Standing still in front of the door, he heard voices coming from the other side. He grabbed the doorknob and turned it. Nothing happened. The door should have swung open, but it didn't.

Joshua released the doorknob and returned to the waiting room. This was taking too long. Why hadn't someone come out and told him what was happening. Time passed slowly. He was becoming more and more worried by the moment.

"Joshua."

He sprang from the chair. "What is it, Doc? Is she all right? Can I see her?" He finally noticed the frown on Dr. Harris's face. "What's wrong?"

"Joshua, sit down."

"Oh my god!" Images of Jenny lying on the table dead flashed through his mind. He continued standing until the doctor forced him into it, then pulled another chair over and sat right in front of Joshua. He put his hand on the young man's knee and then began.

"Jenny's all right, now. She's resting comfortably. It was touch and go for a while. She lost a lot of blood. But she and the baby are doing fine."

"Then I don't understand, Doc. Why the long face? Is there something you're not telling me?"

"Joshua, there's something about the baby. I'm not quite sure what it is yet. I just can't put my finger on it. It's more of a feeling, really."

"I don't get it, Doc. What are you saying? Is there, or isn't there something wrong?"

Sensing Joshua's concern, he tried to explain further. "Have you ever had the feeling you were being watched, but there was no one around?" Joshua nodded. "That's what this was like. I…I don't really know," he said, shaking his head. "Look, just forget I said anything, Joshua. Okay? Everything's fine," he added, patting Joshua's knee. "Congratulations, you have a new baby boy. He's a little small because he was premature, but he's just fine. We'll watch him closely for a few days. There's nothing to worry about."

"Can I see them, Doc?"

"Sure can, son. Come with me." They walked in as the nurse just finished cleaning up from the surgery. "Colene, Joshua would like to visit with his wife and son for a bit. Not too long now, she needs a lot of rest. Later, she and the baby will be moved to the hospital where they can get proper and constant care."

January 4, 1896

Dear Mama,

Christmas finally arrived and with it our wonderful baby boy. That's right. Solomon Blaine Conners was born three weeks ago on Tuesday at 10:35 p.m. He weighed four pounds, eight ounces because he was premature. I had a problem with the pregnancy, and they had to take him early. But we're both fine now, so don't worry. He was fourteen inches long. His hair is kind of a silvery white and very, very thin. For a while, we were afraid something was wrong. And indeed it was. The sac around the baby was torn, and I was bleeding out. But Joshua reacted quickly, and he saved both me and our unborn child.

Little Solomon is fine, and so am I. Joshua thinks he looks like Daddy. I tend to agree with him. It really shows around the eyes and nose. I wish you could see him for yourself. Maybe someday, I hope. He is absolutely beautiful, Mama. I know it seems like I'm bragging on him and maybe I am. After all, we made something wondrous and are eternally happy about it.

Baby Solomon and I had to stay in the hospital a little longer than is normal. I had some complications, and the baby was too small to risk leaving here. Anyhow, we're both home and all is well.

I hear my little one crying, probably hungry, so I'll say goodbye for now.

All our love,

Joshua, Jenny, and Baby Solomon

"Mildred, I've been thinking," Ruby said, breaking their protracted silence.

"Well, I'd be shocked if you ever stopped." Mildred snorted. Most folks around here didn't put much stock in what Mildred and Ruby said or thought. They were known to be the town gossips, spinsters who usually stuck their noses in many places they didn't belong. They had never really done anyone any harm, outside the harm normal gossipers could inflict. But still, they had a way of getting under your skin. Kind of irritating, like chiggers, or ticks.

"Oh, posh and nonsense!" Ruby exclaimed.

"What about, dear?" Mildred asked, ignoring her comment.

"Joshua and Jenny," she said smartly. She had given it a great deal of thought and determined she was on to something. "Well, actually about the baby," she corrected herself.

"What about him?" Mildred asked curious now. She had been thinking about it too but hadn't dare broach the subject yet, afraid it might get back to those sweet kids. She didn't mind talking about them because that's what she did with everyone, but she liked them and didn't want to cause undue harm.

"I don't quite know how to put it," Ruby began. Then she smiled as an idea formed in her mind. "When we visited Jenny, and I looked at the baby, it's almost as if he were looking back at me."

"Of course, he is," Mildred snorted. "Who did you think he was looking at?"

I knew she'd make fun of it, Ruby thought to herself. "That's not what I meant. I mean like another adult would look at you. Like he knows who I am…and like he's forming thoughts about me." She paused while letting Mildred think about it. "What do you think?"

"I think you've finally lost it," Mildred snapped.

"What a terrible thing to say." Ruby shot back, drawing her lips into a thin line as they clamped together. She sat perfectly still, except for the age-old custom of twiddling her thumbs to keep her mind occupied and her tongue silent.

"I'm sorry," Mildred apologized. "I didn't mean that the way it sounded. Forgive me, dear."

"I know you didn't," Ruby countered, "but it still cut to the quick. Of course, I forgive you, silly. What should we do?"

"What can we do? It's not like we can prove what you're saying," Mildred replied.

"Maybe we should tell someone," Ruby continued pressing.

"Who? Who would we tell?" Mildred asked, miffed.

Ruby thought for a moment, then her eyes lit up. "How about the preacher? Wouldn't this fall under his umbrella?" She beamed, proud of her answer.

"I don't know," Mildred replied. "You know how the reverend is. Should we really do that to those sweet kids? This could really get out of hand."

"Nevertheless, I think that's what we should do," Ruby stated with certainty.

"God help us," Mildred prayed silently.

Joshua loved his weekends at home. After a long week of dealing with customers problems, disgruntled coworkers, and the ever-vigilant bank president, he was more than happy to take his frustration's out on the chopping block on Saturdays. Chopping wood had become his normal Saturday morning activity. That's what he was doing when Reverend Jeremiah Weeks dropped by on this Saturday morning.

The reverend was cut from the same cloth as most preachers from the late nineteenth century. He was tall and thin and possessed an unearthly ability to appear either super righteous or terrifyingly evil, depending on those present at the time.

Joshua was undaunted by the reverend, where most folks were greatly intimidated by him. This morning, Joshua waited to see which side of the minister would show up. "Morning, Reverend. What brings you out this way?"

"We have business to discuss," he replied shortly.

Straight and to the point, Joshua thought grimly. *The evil side*, he said to himself. Though he disliked these confrontations, he never backed down from them. He supposed that's what made him so good at his job at the bank. The trouble with this kind of person? They just had a way of twisting things to suit their own purpose. They could quote the Bible in support of any statement they might make—right or wrong. And in Joshua's opinion, this preacher was mostly wrong.

"Doesn't sound like a social call," Joshua mused. He couldn't imagine what business the preacher had with him, but from the set of the man's jaw and his open stance, it suggested he was preparing for a fight—and the preacher's piercing eyes looked like they could split the wood for him. "What's on your mind, Reverend?"

"There is some local concern about you and your wife's relationship," he began guardedly.

Joshua continued picking up the wood he had been splitting and stacking it in a pile. He never looked the preacher in the eye but asked, "What exactly is this concern?"

Reverend Weeks hurled a glare at Joshua with his dark, penetrating eyes that had been known to freeze the very depths of a man's soul. "This is a quiet, God-fearing community, son. These people don't need the condemnation that an unrighteous act is sure to bring on the town." He spoke with his preaching voice while pointing a bony, crooked finger at Joshua. "So think carefully before you answer my next question."

"Don't call me son!"

The reverend kept his arm extended, his finger aimed at Joshua as he asked the question, "What was the relationship between you and your wife before you were married?"

Joshua's anger had begun to well up within him even before the preacher had finished his question. "Watch how you talk about my wife, Weeks. We're not some of your parishioners you can browbeat into submission with your religious hocus-pocus.

"*Blasphemer! Blasphemer!*" Weeks shouted, continuing to point his meatless finger at Joshua. "You will both stand in judgment before God for your filthy, evil deeds of immorality. He has decided your fate and He will tell me what to do. The thorn in the side of this good town will be removed."

Joshua remained cool during the preacher's sudden outburst. He somehow managed a calm reply to the preacher's chilling address. "Preacher, you're through here. Get off my property and don't ever come back again." After brief consideration, Joshua shrugged and said softly, "Why not?" And then with as much venom as he could muster, "*Now get out of here!*"

Reverend Weeks eyed the ax Joshua held and, while unafraid, nevertheless spun on his heel and started back toward town. He walked everywhere he went. He didn't own a horse or a buggy and had never married, claiming it would have greatly interfered with the work God had for him. At the end of the short lane which connected Joshua and Jenny's property with the road, the preacher turned and faced Joshua one last time. "This is not over, Conners! You haven't heard the last of me!" he shouted, shaking his fist in the air. "*This is not finished!*"

"I feel just awful," Ruby told her friend.

It was odd to see Ruby acting this way. Mildred could usually depend on her strong will and a firm hand. But this time, she appeared unable to cope.

"About what dear? What has gotten you so upset? Is there anything I can do?" Mildred asked hopefully.

"No. But I heard that Reverend Weeks had taken steps to have Joshua and Jenny run out of town," she whimpered. "It's my fault. I should never have said anything."

"Can they do that?" Mildred asked, shocked. Then Ruby's last statement sunk in. "What do you mean you shouldn't have said anything? You mean to tell me you went to the preacher after all? You told him what we talked about?" She was astonished that Ruby would do such a thing.

"I thought he would just talk to them, you know," she proclaimed miserably. "But not this."

"Are you sure you heard correctly?" Mildred asked, her concern evident.

"I'm afraid it's all true," Ruby said, dismayed. "The bank president, Mister Chalmers, said it would be better if Joshua moved on. He released him with a letter of recommendation and severance pay and agreed to sell their property and forward the proceeds to their new home. They..." She broke down crying, her words lost.

"Ruby?"

"They...they have one week to clear out," she said, dabbing at her eyes with a handkerchief. "It's my fault, Mildred. It's all my fault."

"Now, you can't blame yourself for this. It's unfortunate, certainly, but you couldn't have known Reverend Weeks would go this far," Mildred said while comforting her. "They probably would have found out eventually."

"I thought that Reverend Weeks would just pray for them or something," she continued her tirade while ignoring Mildred's words of comfort. "I feel just terrible," she repeated.

"Joshua, where will we go? How will we get by?" Jenny asked, still in shock at the sudden turn of events. "I can't believe they're doing this to us."

"Jenny, you don't worry about a thing," he told her. "I'll always take care of you and little Solomon. You remember what we said when we were fifteen years old?" he asked with a rueful grin. "We said we would never let anyone, or anything, come between us. Remember how we used to hide just to be together like boyfriend and girlfriend? We were in love and we were determined. We always knew we'd be together. And we knew we might be found out someday."

"But where will we go?" she asked again.

He thought about it for a moment. There was a place he had heard about. It was in some hilly country with lots of trees and creeks and wild game. They could build them a cabin, hunt game, grow a garden, and never be bothered again. It would be their Eden, their paradise.

"I know a place," he said smiling. "You'll love it. It'll be perfect."

April 12, 1896

Dear Mama,

Just a short note to let you know we are leaving here. There have been some developments that make it necessary for us to leave our home. I can't really tell you where we're going, as I'm not sure myself. Joshua has spoken of it some but is very secretive of the exact location. All he has really said so far is that it is beautiful, especially this time of year.

Little Solomon is doing just fine. He is growing like a weed. I hope this move doesn't upset him too much. But I don't think it will. He is high-spirited and one of the happiest babies I've ever seen. We think also that this move will take a lot of pressure off Joshua. The banking job was becoming very stressful. Daddy will be happy to know that he's going to try his hand at farming.

Mama, I really wish you could see little Solomon. He is such pretty baby. I still marvel at the very idea that he's ours. Sometimes, I lay in bed at night and just listen to him sleep. It's all I can do to resist picking him up and holding him close the whole night.

Joshua thinks I'm overprotective and a worry wart. However, I can't help but feel there is something different about our little baby. It's probably just my imagination. You always said mine was overactive.

Well, anyway, I better get this posted. There's a lot to do before we can leave. I'll write to you when we get settled.

Our love forever,

Joshua, Jenny, and Baby Solomon

CHAPTER THREE

Susie and Stoney drove along State Road 38 in silence. She stared out the window at the near solid blackness of the night and watched as images flitted in and out of the car's headlights. Neither had spoken a word since leaving the hospital. This gloom filled silence was incredibly frightening and made her extremely uneasy. It didn't help that Stoney was so pensive and withdrawn. She didn't like it but understood that his immediate concern was for Brian.

Suddenly, a desperate thought exploded in her mind! Could Brian have done this to Mary J.? Could they have had a fight and... and it came to this? Could the pressure of losing three children have finally erupted into such horrible violence? But they never fought—about anything. Brian could never—would never hurt Mary J. under any circumstances. Of that she was certain. Susie had known them both their whole lives and had never seen two people more in love than Brian and Mary J.

Someone had attacked them at Rockhole. Mary J. had a special night planned, just the two of them, so they wouldn't have even suspected such a thing happening. They didn't have any enemies. There would have been nothing to gain by robbing them. Was it possible a gang had done this in order to rape Mary J.? If so... Suddenly her thoughts turned again to Brian. He might be lying out there hurt and in need of help. He might be... She had a terrifying thought.

"Stoney, we have to hurry," she cried suddenly. "Can't you go any faster?" she pleaded. Susie was beating on the dash with the palms of her hands.

"Susie, what the hell's gotten into you," he asked, grabbing at her arm. But she continued assaulting the dash.

"Come on. Let's go."

Stoney reached for her arm again but missed and jerked the steering wheel sending the car into a spin. When they finally stopped spinning, the car was racing toward the deep ditch. Years of rain and zero maintenance had caused the ditches to turn into small ravines. In the space of a split second, the headlights caught the reflection of a shiny culvert, placed there by a local farmer so he could cross the ditch into his field.

The front wheels made it just fine, but the right rear wheel just missed, vaulting the back end of the car into the air.

The last thing Stoney remembered before he lost consciousness was his head smashing into the roof of the car. He also recalled an intense pain in his legs as they were jerked from under the steering wheel.

Susie shot straight into the air also and mused about not wearing her seat belt. Strange to think about that while you're being twisted and tossed around. Nevertheless, it did—briefly as she was hurled into the back seat.

Sometime later, when Stoney had regained consciousness, he looked at Susie and said, "You could have gotten us both killed.

"Me? You were driving, bub."

"I was trying to stop you from beating up my car," Stoney complained.

"I'm sorry." She pouted. "Are you all right?"

"My legs are sore, and I've got a headache, but other than that, I'm fine," he retorted. "You coming to the front seat?" He asked, reaching back to help her.

She slid easily into the front. "Stoney, I'm really sorry," she said again.

"Why were you doing that? Beating on the dash." He pointed at the glove box. "Reach in there and get me the flashlight, please. We need to check the car and see if we can drive out of here."

She did as he asked and then opened the door on her side and climbed out. After a quick survey of the passenger side, she proclaimed, "All good over here. How about your side? No, wait a minute. Flat tire in the back and I think the fender might have a little wrinkle. Bring that light over here."

"This side look's okay," he said happily. "Just some weeds and dirt caught in the bumper and underneath." He shined the light on the right rear tire and confirmed Susie's evaluation. "Don't look like the wheel is bent. The tire is shot, though. Looks like it was cut on the end of the culvert. Fender is easily fixed." He heard her breathe a sigh of relief and gathered her in his arms. Only then did she cry.

"Susie, it's all right, as long as you're not hurt. We'll change the tire and be on our way. No harm done," he assured her. "At least the bounce landed the car on level ground. By the way, what were you so worked up about?"

Susie explained what she'd been thinking just before the accident. "Sorry," she apologized again.

"No need to apologize," he assured her. "Besides, I think you may be right. Help me with this. Grab the lug wrench and jack." He hoisted the spare from the trunk.

"Delmer, you going to be okay?" the sheriff asked. Delmer Matthews had seen a lot in his day. A farmer was killed when his tractor rolled over on him, a chainsaw got loose and severed a man's limb, an ax slipped and lodged in a man's leg, but this—this was unholy.

No, Delmer wasn't the kind of weak stomached person who threw up at any little thing, but this mess…He shuddered. "Don't worry, Sheriff. I'm with ya," he mumbled while wiping his mouth on the sleeve of his shirt. "You reckon that's that woman's fella?"

"That's what I'm thinking," Sheriff Rogers agreed. "We won't know for sure until we get the body out of the water and have it identified." He looked at Delmer. "Would you mind staying here while I go back to my car and radio this in? We're going to need some help out here."

Delmer wasn't afraid to stay by himself, but something made him uneasy about this. At least first light was just peeking over the treetops. "Yeah. Go ahead, Dan." He nodded. "I'll be fine here."

"I won't be long," Rogers assured him.

Delmer shivered. Was it the early morning chill, or was it the dark outline of a man floating in the water below, mangled by… what? He shivered again!

Watching Mary J. lying in a hospital bed, with wires attached and tubes in her, was more than Sadie could take. Mary J.'s hysterics had not only frightened her but had caused her daughter to lapse into a coma. The doctor had no time table for her to wake up. "It's totally up to her now," he had said. She's the only one with the key to unlock that door."

"The hell you say!" Sadie snapped.

They waited around all night, just in case. But when daylight came, they decided to take the doctor's advice and go home. It was probably best anyway. All these machines made Sadie nervous. An IV in her arm and wires that ran from monitors to Mary J., constantly beeping. It was just precautionary they said. To keep track of her while she was in a coma.

Shortly after they left, the nurse had entered the room to check on Mary J. and noticed some unusual readings on the monitor. She watched them for a moment but didn't think it was cause for alarm. She thought it best to notify the doctor anyway.

Five minutes later, the doctor was staring at the machine intently, while occasionally glancing at Mary J., searching for medical signs that trouble was imminent. Her heart rate had increased, her blood pressure was elevated, and she was sweating.

"I'd say she's having a nightmare," he mumbled. "Let's keep a close eye on her for now.

To Mary J. it didn't seem like a dream. Everything that was happening felt real. It all looked so normal. Still, she had the uncanny feeling of déjà vu.

"Where are we going?" Brian asked for the second time leaving the house.

"I told you, silly, it's a surprise. Now quit asking." Mary J. laughed cheerfully. She had been in a quirky mood all day and he hadn't figured out why.

"Okay, fine," he said with resignation. "Then just tell me what the special occasion is. It's not my birthday or our anniversary. What else is there?"

Mary J. shook her head vigorously. "One word," she replied candidly. "Surprise!" they both said in unison. "Just sit back and enjoy the ride."

"It'll be dark soon."

"Even better," she said with a sexy grin. "That suits me perfectly."

Brian took note of his surroundings. *The only reason we ever come out this way is to go to Mom and Dad's, or to...* Suddenly it dawned on him. "You're taking us to Rockhole."

Mary J., her mood supremely playful and flirtatious, blew him a kiss.

A boyish grin her reward, as his finger traced a line down her bare arm. He didn't always like these games she played with him. But he had to admit, he loved that goddesslike charm she possessed. It pleased him. "So are you going to fill in the blanks for me?"

"I don't think so," she teased. "Besides, we're here." She giggled, turning off the highway onto a gravel road. Mary J. found a place to park the car where it couldn't be easily spotted from the road. She preferred that no one know they were there. She climbed out of the car and opened the trunk. Brian could see a picnic basket and a blanket. She lifted the basket out and handed it to Brian, then picked up the blanket. "So are you coming," she quipped, her short pleated skirt flipping up as she spun around, exposing the back of her slender, well-tanned legs.

Brian slammed the trunk lid shut and caught up to her easily. He took the blanket from her and draped it over his shoulder. "Let's go." He climbed between the barbed-wire strands of the gate across the dirt road and then put his foot on the lower strand while lifting on the middle strand, parting the two strands for Mary J. to climb through safely. As soon as she had done so, she slipped an arm through his, and they strolled along the dirt road in the direction of Rockhole, a popular swimming hole for people around the area and a favorite haunt for beer busts.

Mary J. hadn't seen any cars when they drove up, so she was confident they had the spot to themselves. Besides, she had alerted the regulars about her plans. Everyone agreed to let them have their privacy.

They hurried down the well-worn path that descended to the rock bluff below. Mary J. was too busy looking at the creek to notice the vine lying across the path. She hooked the toe of her right shoe under it and suddenly skittered down the slope, unable to stop, and barreled toward the edge of the cliff. Brian reached out and grabbed her arm as she shot past him and just before she would have tumbled over the edge.

"Bri—" she started to scream. It died on her lips, however, as Brian jerked her to a halt.

"That was close," she whispered. "Thank you, baby!"

"Come on, Mary J. What's the worst that could have happened? You would have gotten wet," he teased, patting her on the cheek.

"I love you," he whispered in her ear while holding her close. "Will you marry me…again?"

Mary J. hesitated, then replied, "You mean you want to make an honest woman of me?"

"The only reason I'd have to do that was if you were pregnant out of wedlock," he said jokingly. "And if that were the case, yes, I would. I would definitely marry you again because I love you that much."

"Really? That's so sweet, Brian. But I'm already married. And I'm also—"

"You're pregnant?" he asked, interrupting her.

"Yes!" she said excitedly. Brian lifted her up and twirled her around, which emitted an excited shriek from Mary J. "I love you," he told her again.

"I love you too," she replied then suggested they spread the blanket, have a little picnic, and then get down to some real celebrating.

"That's how you got that way to begin with." He grinned at her. "How long have you known?"

"Not long," she assured him. She spread the blanket over a bare spot on the ground. "Straighten the blanket on your side, please."

She sat on the blanket cross-legged and began to unpack the picnic basket.

Mary J.'s legs were in full view as the skirt hiked up. Brian took careful notice of her well-tanned, slender, voluptuous legs. After seven years of marriage and four babies, she still had a beautiful figure and an enchanting beauty. However, his love for her went much deeper than casual sex.

Brian's senses dulled, as his mind drifted to another place and time. He felt detached from the world. He couldn't touch anything. He couldn't speak out loud. He couldn't hear any of the sounds around him, the usual animal noises, or the buzzing insects, birds calling from above. And the meal Mary J. had obviously taken great pains to prepare, not one whiff of its taste-tingling aroma tickled his nostrils. Was she affecting him like this? What was so different—

"Brian! Brian!" she shouted, tossing a small rock at him. "What's the matter with you?"

Brian snapped out of it, his focus returning to Mary J. He felt like he'd been gone for a while, several minutes at least, but it was only seconds. "All right, gorgeous. What are we waiting for?"

"For you to come back from wherever you went," she laughed.

"Let's eat before I starve to death." He scowled but not at her. Now why did he do that? What was wrong with him. He felt like something gripped him, like he was suspended in time. Suddenly, that feeling let go. He was himself again.

"Brian, honey, what's wrong?" Mary J. had moved across the blanket and was sitting next to him.

When had she moved? he wondered. "I don't know," he told her, darkness crossing his face. "It's like I lost time. Mary J., I don't feel right. Maybe we should pack up and go home."

"I don't understand," she said, cupping his face in her hands.

"What do you mean you lost time? You didn't go anywhere. You were right here with me the whole time. You're not making any sense," she said stubbornly. "Let's eat and then I bet...I can change your mind." She kissed him and returned to her original place. "You'll see," she said. "It'll be all right." He forced a smile. Something was definitely wrong. He suddenly lost interest in Mary J.'s little tryst.

Mary J. continued to unload the picnic basket. The first thing she pulled out was a camping lantern. "Here, light this while I get the food ready," she instructed him. Brian took the lantern and a pack of matches from her.

He fumbled with the lantern for a few minutes, and after nearly dropping it once, he finally got it lit. The lantern sent out a strong white glow that lighted the whole area around them. He loved the oily stench that filled the air.

By the time he finished, Mary J. had laid out a meal that would feed six people—fried chicken, corn dogs, fried okra, potato salad, pickles, cheese sticks, potato cakes, mincemeat pie, and a bottle of champagne.

"Jesus, Mary J.," Brian blurted out. "Who else is coming?"

She laughed that his sense of humor had returned, but at the same time, she harbored a feeling of trepidation at what had just occurred. She knew there was more to it than Brian had let on. The look in his eyes. That distant stare. But it wasn't like he was daydreaming. It was more lethargic, like he had no emotions, or his mind was blank. Mary J. tried not to think about it, but for some reason, the thought lingered.

Something was terribly wrong. Of that she was sure.

They ate and laughed and talked like two young teens in love for the first time. Brian was sitting with one leg bent, his arm resting on the upraised knee. He was extremely interested in the pretty young woman reclined on the blanket in front of him.

Finished with her meal, Mary J. had lain on her back and was looking up at the stars. She had one leg pulled up toward her, and her skirt had neatly fallen to her waist revealing, once again, a well-proportioned thigh.

Brian couldn't take his eyes off her exquisite bare legs, while Mary J. commented on a sky that was well adorned with billions and billions of brilliant, shimmering specs. "Do you ever wonder what keeps them all up there? You know, why they don't just fall out of the sky?" She shrugged at such a thought. "Isn't it beautiful out tonight."

"It sure is," he confessed, still looking at her bare legs.

She rolled her head sideways and realized he was looking at her. "I meant the stars, silly. I'm looking at a site that could never be captured on an artist's canvas, and you're—"

"Looking at a site that should be captured on an artist's canvas." Brian reasoned. Then he felt a tingle as he realized this was the element of intrigue she began introducing into their foreplay, after they had lost their third child, to put some spice back into their love life. So he continued to watch, spellbound, while she put the leftovers back into the picnic basket.

With the blanket now cleared, Mary J. stood up and, with a stripper's expert movements, let the skirt slip to the ground. Next, she ducked out of her blouse, exposing her nude body.

Brian realized for the first time that Mary J. wasn't wearing underwear. He stepped close to her and kissed her, then quickly removed his own clothes and felt a tingling sensation as their naked bodies touched. The champagne, the food, the stars, all of it came together to make this moment special, just as Mary J. had planned it out in her mind. It was perfect—until…

Something was there. Mary J. didn't know what it was, but she felt a presence, something—someone watching them. She bent over and grabbed her clothes and put them back on. As she did, something took control of Brian. She reached out to him, but a clawed hand swiped at her and she felt a terrifying sensation. Unconsciously, she reached for the lantern but knocked it over, and it rolled off the edge of the cliff. She then reached into the basket and pulled out a flashlight.

What she saw drove a stake through her heart. That was Brian's body, but that wasn't Brian. His face! What happened to his face? She took a step backward and covered her mouth with a hand that trembled. "Bri-Brian?" she screamed, her face a ghostly white. She wanted so much to touch him, to hold him. Dear God, what should she do?

"Brian!" she screamed again. He took a couple of steps toward her. She shrank into the darkness behind her. The creature raised and extended its deadly-looking arm toward Mary J. Suddenly, a disjointed voice said, "He's mine, now. And soon…you and your unborn child will be mine too."

The demon then turned and faced the cliff. It hesitated momentarily, looked back at Mary J., cracked a wicked smile, then fell face-first over the edge. Mary J. screamed repeatedly, then stepped quickly to the edge, wondering what she would see. She stared down at the water but could only make out dark forms. She remembered the flashlight, still clasped tightly in her hand. She shined it on the surface below.

Hidden in the shadows that danced on the still water was the body of Brian, his torso separated from the lower portion at the waist. Blood was spurting from the two halves and spreading over the surface of the cool, calm creek.

Mary J. sat up in the hospital bed and screamed.

A single hand covered her mouth, while the other extended out in front of her, as if she were reaching for something or someone.

The nurse quickly called for the doctor and then rushed into Mary J.'s room. She tried to lay Mary J. back down, but the frantic girl seemed to have gained unusual strength. They were locked in a struggle when the doctor arrived. Still screaming, Mary J. was winning the battle against the nurse. The doctor held her while the nurse injected a strong sedative into the IV. Dr. Williams was able to control Mary J. until the drug took effect. "I don't think she was awake," he suggested to the nurse.

"That was some nightmare," the nurse said quietly.

"Keep a really close eye on those monitors," he admonished her. The doctor shook his head and left the room.

"Yes, Doctor."

By the time Susie and Stoney arrived at Rockhole, it was a den of activity as officers and medical personnel swarmed around the creek below and the bluff overlooking it. The sheriff's department had the area cordoned off, so they couldn't get within a half mile of there.

Stoney pulled up and stopped in the middle of the low water bridge that crossed the creek on County Road 135. They started to get out of the car and walk the rest of the way when they were approached by a deputy sheriff. He recognized Stoney's car and held his hand in the air, a signal to stop. Stoney greeted the deputy and halted his approach. "Hey, Mike. What's going on?" he asked with an edge to his voice.

"Sorry," Mike replied, leaning against the car. "Can't say just yet. I haven't been here very long myself, and this is as close I've gotten. I was told to stick around here and not let anyone pass through." He glanced across the car and smiled at Susie standing on the other side. At one time, he had been sweet on her, but she was never interested in anyone other than Stoney. "Hi, Susie." He grinned sheepishly.

"Mike," she said politely. "You sure you don't know what they're doing?" she asked.

He shook his head. "Why? What are you all doing out here anyway?"

"We're looking for Brian," Stoney chimed in. "He and Mary J. were out here last night, and now Mary J.'s in the hospital all beat up and in a coma. So would you please ask around if anyone's seen him?" The deputy hesitated, but Stoney was insistent. "Come on, Mike. It's important. Please. Please!" he begged. They waited by the car while the deputy asked around about the crime scene. He was gone quite a while. Finally, when Mike returned, his demeanor told Stoney all he needed to know.

"Okay, guys, I still don't know much, but here's what I was able to find out." The deputy was taking his time, and Susie and Stoney were growing impatient. Finally, he blurted out, "You're right. It was Brian we found. And…" Again he hesitated.

"Mike!"

"I'm sorry, Stoney. He's dead."

The silence was deafening. Susie's hand flew up to cover her mouth. She quickly felt the sting of tears on her face. Stoney bent over at the waist and buried his head in his hands. He was shocked, and he was angry. His emotions were all over the place, and his mind whirled in several directions at once. How could this happen? It was supposed to be a simple night of romance and food.

"What happened, Mike?" he asked, the tremor in his voice evident to anyone listening.

"That's still not clear," Mike told him. "He was murdered. That much we do know. Look, Stoney, you have to leave. It's going to take a lot of time to figure this out."

"How did he die, Mike?" Stoney asked.

The deputy looked around anxiously. "I told you we don't know yet. Listen, I've got to get back to work and you need to leave. They won't let you anywhere near the scene. When they have enough facts about what happened, someone will be in touch. I really am sorry, Stoney, Susie." He tipped his hat at them started to leave and then pulled up suddenly. He put his hand on Stoney's arm and said, "If I can do anything, let me know. Okay? Either of you." This time he did walk away.

"Why Brian?" he asked no one in particular. "He was a good husband and father…and a great brother." Stoney didn't understand. He wanted to understand why his brother had to die. "Who would do such a thing?"

Susie had her legs pulled up to her chest, sitting on the car seat, still crying. She had questions of her own. What would Mary J. do now? Brian and Michele were her whole life—not to mention their unborn child. Oh my god!

"Tonight was the big night. Her sister had planned it ever since she found out she was pregnant. Some champagne, some food, and then the good news. Did she even get the chance to tell him? And now…Brian would never get to see their baby. Susie remembered the day Mary J. had told her and how excited she was. They had been through so much losing three children already. She wanted everything to be perfect when she told Brian. Now this. What would Mary J. do without him?

"Stoney."

The mention of his name out loud seemed to draw him from the quiet shock of Brian's death. Stoney's anger had seethed and boiled until it finally erupted. He doubled up his fist, drew his arm back, and hit the car window next to him as hard as he could. The window didn't break but cracked with hundreds of jagged lines running throughout the glass. His hand, however, did shatter. Susie recoiled at the shock of his violent outburst. She reached over and laid her hand on his shoulder.

"Stoney?" No response. "Stoney, pull over and let me look at your hand," she said softly. He pulled to the side of the road, and very gently she pried his arm away, exposing the hand he had bludgeoned the window with and gasped at the blood streaming down his fingers. "We have to get you to the hospital," she said, looking at the ghastly mess. "I'll drive." She slipped out of the car and went around to the driver's side. At first, he didn't move. Truthfully, he wasn't even aware of her presence. But at her gentle nudging, he finally scooted over just far enough for her to sit behind the wheel. She held him for a minute before driving away.

"I promise you I'll get whoever did this," Stoney warned with an icy stare.

"Don't you mean we?" she asked pointedly. Then she threw the car into gear and drove away.

"Sadie, Mary J.'s going to be fine," Daniel said, trying to sound convincing. "She just needs time to heal." Sadie knew he was right, but Mary J.'s health wasn't what bothered her. She was absolutely certain this was their fault. Now more than ever. First, their grandchildren and now Brian and Mary J. It was the Conners curse.

It was wrong! They knew it was wrong, and still they let those kids get married. Their family had lived under "the Curse."

The grandparents never believed there was anything wrong in what they did. It was never spoken of for generations. In fact, after Mary J. was born, they decided to keep a great many things secret. So not only was it not spoken of, but any proof of indiscretion from the past was put away for good.

"She looked so bad," Sadie whined. "I just wanted to take her in my arms and hold her like when she was a little girl." She smiled—out of the clear blue. *Strange*, Daniel thought. He was uncomfortable with her sudden shift in emotions.

"What is the matter with you?" he asked warily, afraid of pushing her too far.

"Do you remember that first time she fell out of the tree and got the wind knocked out of her?" She laughed as the memory floated through her subconscious mind. She noticed he too was grinning and snickering at the sight of that poor little girl trying to suck in air for all she was worth.

"She just knew she was going to die," Sadie murmured. "When she finally got a little dab of air in her lungs, she looked at me and said, 'I love you, Mama,' and then she just closed her eyes. She was so serene."

"And convinced she was dying." Daniel laughed so hard his eyes watered. "She was so sure that was her last breath here on earth. And if it was, she would use it to tell you she loved you." He continued laughing, and when he finally did stop, he said, "Never a dull moment around that one."

Sadie had a sudden thought. "Daniel, before we go home, let's drop by and look in on Michele."

He steered the car toward the shoulder, checked the traffic in his outside mirror, saw it was clear, and made a U-turn. Daniel headed back to Dala's, where Susie had left Michele.

Sheriff Rogers had been out here all night and was beginning to feel the effects of the sleepless night, but even more, the viciousness of this evil act. He walked over to where the coroner was loading the body for transport to the morgue. "When can I get an autopsy report, Doc?"

"The cause of death is obvious," the coroner stated. "Anything else will take more time. I should have that for you by late afternoon." He got into the meat wagon and drove away.

"Thanks, Doc," the sheriff shouted after the departing hearse. A thick, meaty arm came out the window and waved to Dan as it disappeared in the dust down the road. Rogers returned to the bluff, and his eyes were fixed on the water, still a red hue from the man's blood. He mumbled something unintelligible as Deputy Mike joined him.

"What's that, Sheriff?"

Only then did Rogers realize the deputy was standing right next to him. "Nothing," the sheriff remarked. "I'm still trying to figure this thing out," his hand made a sweeping motion over the area. "There's a lot of this that don't make sense. It just doesn't add up. Too many unanswered questions," he added.

"Like what, Sheriff?"

"At first, I thought the girl Delmer found on the road had something to do with this, but he said she was hysterical and talked like there was someone else here. I don't know," he said shaking his head. "I still think she's mixed up in this somehow."

"Dan, I know these people. And if Mary J. was involved, it was because she was a victim also. She couldn't do anything like this," he rationalized. "She was this guy's wife and they were happily married. I'm telling you, someone else did this."

"Let me play the devil's advocate for a moment. They came out here for a little romp under the stars and got into an argument, and she shoved him over the edge—maybe playfully, who knows—but then it turned deadly and she lost it. Okay, so maybe it was an accident," he said quickly when Mike started to object.

"For the record, I think you're wrong," the deputy concluded. "By the way, Stoney and Susie know about Brian's death. They just don't know how he died."

"You want to explain how they know?"

"They pulled up to the roadblock and started to come down here. I stopped them and explained the situation to them. Actually, they guessed that it was Brian," he replied. "They came out here looking for Brian and could have forced the issue if we didn't give them something. Besides, I think they'll be important to the investigation.

"I see your point, Mike," the sheriff agreed. Rogers fell silent and resumed his survey of the crime scene. *What a mess*, he thought to himself.

"I don't understand what's going on with Mary J.," Susie said thoughtfully. "Other people have lost a loved one, they didn't go completely bonkers like that. They were sad, yes, but Mary J. was completely hysterical, you know? There has got to be more to it than we've been told."

"Like what?"

"I don't know," she said pensively. "That's the problem." Susie slipped into her thinking mode. When she was like that, she was unaware of what was going on around her. Stoney had seen it many times. It wasn't so bad, though. It usually brought results. Call it woman's intuition, ESP, or alien influence for that matter. Regardless of what it was called, it worked.

"I think we better make sure Dala can keep Michele if we're going to spend time chasing down clues," Stoney said reasonably. "At least until we can make other arrangements."

Susie nodded as she concentrated on the road ahead. This was the first time since leaving Rockhole that Stoney made any sense. She was glad. But then she remembered his hand. "What about the hospital?" she asked. "Your hand?"

He had taken a cloth out of the glove box and wrapped it around the damaged paw. "It's all right. It's not as bad as it looks." To prove his point, he raised his hand and flexed his fingers. "See, not broken." He winced with pain but not where she could see.

Still not paying a lot of attention, Susie nodded. "If you say so. Head to Dala's then."

While driving to Dala's house, Stoney replayed the day's events in his mind. It began with their mad dash to the hospital. From there it went downhill. There were a lot of things that didn't make sense about this whole business. Singularly, each act held up just fine, but when you put them all together, they resulted in mass confusion.

What really happened to Brian at Rockhole? How did Mary J. get so bruised and battered? Why was she found on a gravel road… hysterical? Why didn't she get in their car and go for help and why was the sheriff being so secretive? Of course, a lot of things might be clearer if he knew what really happened to Brian—and to Mary J. *First things first,* he thought as Susie pulled into Dala's driveway.

"Curb service," he said dolefully.

"What?" Susie asked, confused by his statement. Then she saw Dala coming out of the house toward the car, but Michele wasn't with her. Maybe the baby was sleeping. For some reason, she had expected to see Michele with her.

"Have you guys seen Daniel and Sadie?" she asked tentatively as she approached them. They both nodded silently as she continued. "There was something peculiar about their behavior, and I couldn't make a lot of sense of what they were saying."

His own mind still somewhat clouded, Stoney shrugged off Dala's comments. "Let's go inside," he suggested wearily. We've got a lot to tell you and we're both tired."

"Of course, you are," she agreed. "You do look kind of ragged. Come on in. I've got a fresh pot of coffee on," she offered. They readily accepted and followed her into the house.

Stoney draped himself across the oversized chair that matched their sofa. It was massive for a chair, had immense arms, and was more the size of a loveseat. Susie chose the sofa where she could curl up in one corner and become invisible.

Dala brought coffee for them and then asked, "What gives?" as she handed each one a cup while listening to Susie.

"We don't really know yet, Dala," Susie spoke up. "All we know for sure is that Mary J. is in the hospital in a coma. She looks like she went through a meat grinder. And…" She faltered and broke down before she could finish, and tears sprang to her eyes. She set the cup down on the coffee table and bowed her head. It was evident from the terse trembling that she was crying.

Dala scooted over next to her and put her arm around Susie's shoulders. While she waited for the cries to subside, she thought about their years of friendship.

She and Mary J. had been best friends since the first grade. Mary J. was always popular with the boys and well-liked by the girls too, and Dala couldn't recall that even one person ever hated Mary J. She was always a friend to everyone. She had no enemies. Mary J. was the quiet one among the three girls. Susie was very popular in her own right but was more flamboyant than the other two. And Mary J. preferred being in the background. That was one of the reasons Brian fell so hard for her. That quiet reticence.

Dala, on the other hand, had a dominant personality. She was an imposing five feet, nine inches tall and had an enviable head of dark auburn hair and a cute little girl-next-door face. Her commanding height did sensational things for her trim figure. Instead of allowing it to eclipse her psychologically, she used it to her advantage. She sacrificed a lot to put herself through beauty school, and then after gaining some valuable experience working for another shop in town, she finally opened her own shop in a spare room in the back of their house. The same house she lived in now with her husband, Casey—which was located right next door to Brian and Mary J. They had planned it that way since they were kids. Casey and Dala bought their house first, and when the one next door came up for sale, Brian and Mary J. had jumped on it.

Dala knew the family as though she was born into it. And right now, as Susie sat there crying and Stoney wasn't saying anything, she knew something was desperately wrong. "Susie? Stoney?" She looked from one to the other.

Still nothing.

She grabbed a Kleenex from the end table and offered it to Susie, who took it and dabbed at her red tear-streaked cheeks. She regarded Dala for a moment, considering what she was about to tell her. Then she dropped it like a hammer.

"Brian is dead!" she cried, her words echoing through the room and her tears spilling anew.

Dala was visibly shaken and shook her head in disbelief. "No!" She too began to cry. The two girls hugged, crying on each other's shoulder. Dala was speechless. There had to be some mistake. This couldn't be real.

No wonder everyone was so despondent. "That certainly explains Sadie and Daniel," she said after finding her voice again.

"What do you mean," asked Stoney. "When did you see them?"

"When they came by earlier, they took Michele with them," she explained. "I guess they were trying to tell me about last night, but it sounded like they were mumbling and didn't make much sense. I finally gave them the baby and sent them on their way."

Susie glanced at Stoney and then back to Dala. "They don't know about Brian yet," she explained. "We just now came from Rockhole ourselves. Stoney practically threatened Mike before he would tell us. I don't think the sheriff wanted anyone to know, for some strange reason."

"Then I wonder what they were going on about?" Dala posed. "I've never seen those two act as odd as they did this morning. Anyway, they took Michele home with them? I hope that was okay?"

"Of course, it was." They both nodded at her.

"As soon as the kids are off to school, I'm going to the hospital to see Mary J.," she informed them. "What are you two going to do?"

"We're going to see if we can find out more about what happened to Brian," Stoney said quickly. "And I think the best place to start is with the sheriff."

"Why the sheriff? How did Brian die?" Dala asked, suddenly realizing they hadn't told her.

"That's what we intend to find out," Susie told her. "That's the big secret. They wouldn't let us near Rockhole. We weren't thinking too straight when we were out there, but we'll get some answers now, one way or the other," she said, fighting back the tears.

"Come on, Susie," Stoney coaxed her. "We'll catch you later, Dala."

Dala stood at the door and watched them leave. "God, how helpless they must feel," she whispered under her breath.

Sheriff Rogers was sitting at his desk, sipping his first cup of coffee since returning to his office. He had gone home and grabbed a shower and changed clothes after the night's gruesome events. The deputy on counter duty for the day meandered in and dropped a manila file folder on his desk. "The coroner's report on Brian Conners," he drawled. "Said to tell you it was brief, and he would give you a more thorough report in a couple of days—"

"Hello! Anyone home?" a voice called from the main room.

The deputy returned to the counter, gave Susie a once over then looked at Stoney and smiled. "What can I do for you folks?" he asked, still wearing a forced smile.

"We need to see the sheriff," Stoney demanded with a cold stare.

Deputy Wayne Barrows decided Stoney's tone could mean trouble. Silently he switched his focus back to Susie. He ran his eyes up and down her sleek body, then returned his gaze to Stoney. "Sheriff's busy with a case. He had a long night."

"Ours was even longer," Stoney replied evenly.

Wayne smiled. "Sheriff's still busy."

"Sheriff!" Stoney yelled out. "Sheriff Rogers!"

The deputy pointed his finger at Stoney across the counter, "Shut your mouth, or I'll arrest you for disturbing the peace."

Sheriff Rogers stood in the doorway leading to his office and watched as the deputy tried to control Stoney. He wasn't happy about the interruption, but he admired Stoney's spunk. "What in the hell is going on out here?"

The deputy turned to look at the sheriff and started to speak. He opened his mouth but was interrupted.

"We need to talk to you, Sheriff," Stoney blurted out.

"I told them you were busy, sir," the young deputy complained.

"Wayne, it's all right. Let them through," Rogers ordered. He turned and reentered his office. As he made his way around his desk, the sheriff indicated the two chairs in front of the desk have a seat you two."

Once they were all seated, Stoney opened the conversation. "Sheriff, we want to know what's going on with Brian and why you wouldn't let us go down to Rockhole this morning." Stoney tried to sound demanding without being belligerent.

"I knew you'd come. It was just a matter of time, though quicker than I expected," Rogers muttered, rubbing his eyes. "Sorry," he sighed. "I didn't get much sleep last night. You can't see him just yet."

"Why? Why is that?" Stoney inquired. He had wanted to know the truth about Brian's death, but what the sheriff just said gave him pause. But he was ready for it.

"What we took out of that water was nothing like your brother. I'm sorry you have to hear this from me—hell, I can't even believe I'm saying such things." He pounded his forehead with his fist a couple of times. "Look, this isn't going to be easy for me to explain or you to hear," he said with a note of concern. Susie gasped and braced herself for what the sheriff was about to tell them. Her eyes glistened with fresh tears as her emotions surged once again.

Stoney looked at his fiancé questioningly. She gave him a surreptitious nod, and he squeezed her hand tightly for a moment. "Go ahead, Sheriff. We need to hear exactly what you found," he instructed Rogers. The sheriff picked up Brian's file from his desk and held it in front of him. He opened the jacket and took out a single sheet of paper.

"Here, read this," he instructed them, extending it toward Stoney.

"What is it?" Susie asked cautiously. Dan looked at her, devoid of emotion.

"It's the coroner's report," he replied. "It's very brief at this point. A full report will be here in a couple of days.

They sat quietly in front of Rogers' desk and carefully read the report. As their eyes scanned down the page slowly, they finally landed on the cause of death. Susie lurched as the words jumped out at her.

Cause of death: an avulsion (complete separation) of upper body from lower body at the waist by a yet undetermined instrument.

Utter and complete shock spread over both their faces. Then Susie turned as pale as the driven snow—and fainted.

Sadie and Daniel had been home only a few minutes when they heard a car drive up. Daniel went out on the porch and watched as Seth and Sarah Baker crept along the driveway at a snail's pace. They waited until the dust settled before exiting their brand-new Lincoln Continental Town Car. It was a beautiful automobile, but Daniel couldn't see paying as much for a car as he had for his house. Of course, he bought his house and property long before cars were that expensive, but it was the idea of it. He was more than happy to stick with his Ford pickup. He had never even ridden in his uncle's expensive automobile, which was to be expected since they didn't get along all that well. Not since Elizabeth's death anyway.

"Uncle Seth, Aunt Sarah. What are you doing all the way out here?" Daniel asked, frowning but still respectful. "Or do I really want to know?" Lately, it meant trouble was brewing when they showed up.

"Sadie here?" Sarah asked curtly. Daniel knew instantly that it was another bitch session. Anytime Sarah started with "Sadie here?" he knew what was coming. "What's up your craw?" he asked sharply.

"We just got a bone to pick, that's all," she replied hatefully. God, he detested it when she was like this. "Well, are you going to just stand there?"

"Come on in," he grunted at her with dissatisfaction. He held the screen door open for them. If not for Uncle Seth, he'd have no problem telling Sarah what she could do with herself. "Sadie, we got company," he yelled.

Sadie appeared in the doorway between the living room and kitchen. She stopped when she saw who it was. She had never gotten along with Sarah. They couldn't even tolerate each other. It was more of a hate-hate relationship ever since Elizabeth had died and she married Daniel.

"Well, I hope you're happy with yourself," Sarah spat the words at her. "Because of you, that innocent little girl has ended up in the hospital."

"Aunt Sarah, what the hell are you doing?" Daniel demanded. "You come into our house with this crap? Sadie's been through a horrible ordeal. "We both have. Don't you have one ounce of compassion in you at all?

Sarah ignored him and continued with Sadie. "You and that Howard were related," she said accusingly, pointing an old, gnarled finger at Sadie. "Don't deny it? We all know it's true."

"Of course, it's true!" she snapped at the elderly woman. "But don't be too hasty in pointing that ugly ole finger at me, you dried-up excuse for a human being." Sarah inhaled sharply and straightened up as best she could. "My indiscretion isn't the only one this family has to deal with," Sadie said mockingly, looking at Daniel as she said it. "Your family isn't without its own skeletons." She hated to throw her husband to the wolves, but right now, she didn't have much choice.

Sarah looked at Daniel with an evil grin. "Still want to throw in with this bunch knowing the truth about her?"

"Aunt Sarah, I already knew it," he blurted out. As her jaw snapped shut, Daniel knew he had won a small victory over her. He walked over to his wife and put his arm around her waist. "You're not going to start any trouble here today. So why don't you go on home, okay? Uncle Seth, can't you do anything with her?"

"I'm not a puppy dog," she snapped at her nephew. Again, she pointed her crooked finger at Sadie and said, "Just remember that daughter of yours is in the hospital because of your wicked behavior. Mark my words, Sadie Conners," she still referred to Sadie as a Conners refusing to acknowledge her marriage to Daniel, "this isn't over."

"You get out of my house and don't ever come back here again," Sadie growled ferociously. She was desperately trying to hold back the tears until they left. She refused to cry in front of that despicable woman.

Seth and Sarah departed with Sarah in a huff and Seth shaking his head—saddened. *How had things come to this,* he wondered.

Daniel stood on the porch once again, but this time watching as the Lincoln disappeared down the road and thinking to himself, *It's just the beginning!*

Chapter Four

Dear God! What a nightmare.

How do I prevent this marriage from happening without ruining the lives of two very young and innocent people that I love with all my heart? Lila Clark sat in her living room amid the wreckage of her life feeling completely helpless for the first time that she could ever remember. She began thinking back over the events that led up to this unspeakable occurrence.

In the fall of 1860, a fire swept through the city of Bridgeport literally destroying everything in its path. Many left to resume their pillaged lives elsewhere. One of those who chose to remain and try to rebuild the city was the Baker family. Therefore, it was no surprise that they were greatly responsible for restoring it to its previously marvelous stature, as though the fire had never happened.

Besides the destruction of nearly every building and edifice in town, the thousands of lives that were lost, and nothing but a mountain of incinerated refuge to show for their historical past, it will forever be remembered as the day the Baker family suffered its greatest loss. Because Bridgeport was the county seat, all the county records had been lost in the fire. During the confusion, Lila Baker did as so many others around her had done. She left the city, but not before gathering up her two youngest children, Derek and Carlotta, and secretly whisked them away while the fire still raged wildly. She forsook her family leaving her husband, Carson, to raise their two oldest children, Curtis and Franklin.

The first thing Lila did to begin their new life was to change their last name to Clark. She never remarried choosing to live her remaining years in anonymity. She and Carson had never got on all that well ever since, well, from the very beginning, really. Admittedly, Lila only married Carson to get out of the house. She thought her home life was dreadful—until she became Carson's wife that is and discovered that this was worse. Lila endured the beatings, the loneliness, and the fear for seven long years before finding the courage to finally leave.

Derek and Carlotta were too young to remember that part of their lives. They grew up thinking that their father had been killed in an accident, and they had no reason to believe otherwise. The deceitful web Lila had entwined herself and her family in went along just fine until twenty years later when a simple twist of fate brought their past and their present crashing around them.

After she graduated from high school, Carlotta decided to go for a career, while Derek opted to go on to college. Carlotta had worked in a dress shop for five years. Originally, it was to help her mother with the finances, but during that time she discovered, as did many others, she had a real talent for dress designing. The proprietor, a lady of great conscience and a friend to Carlotta, took her under her wing and taught her everything she knew about design. They worked well together, which should come as no surprise since they were only about five years apart in age. And in fact, they had been best friends for the last three years. Occasionally, Carlotta's job took her to neighboring towns, and once out of state, in search of new and exotic clothing ideas and unusual designs. She was on just such a trip when fortune favored her with a chance meeting in Bridgeport.

While she was in the city, Carlotta had stopped at a local restaurant for lunch. During her meal, she noticed a rather handsome-looking man sitting at a table across the room from her. She was completely taken with him. He had sandy-blond hair, a fair complexion, and an eye-catching boyish grin. Carlotta couldn't help but stare. It was odd, though. There was something vaguely familiar about him. It was a strange feeling. She shivered noticeably and quickly looked around embarrassed.

After she paid for her meal, she was hurrying toward the exit door and chanced one last look at the handsome stranger, but he was not at his table. Much to her surprise, she crashed into a patron entering the establishment and dropped her parasol. Out of nowhere and to her delight, the sprightly, youthful-looking fellow she had been admiring was there to retrieve it for her.

Carlotta thanked him with an air of diffidence, smiling demurely. That was all it took to strike up a conversation and soon a budding relationship was begun. Franklin Baker and Carlotta Clark embarked on a journey that would eventually lead them to the altar. A perilous journey that would be filled with misfortune and end in tragedy.

Lila had been excited for Carlotta. It was rare when a young lady could find love so easily. And Franklin had been the perfect gentleman. It was almost too good to be true. In fact, she was beginning to believe it was. She remembered one day when Franklin had come to visit.

"Knock, knock," he called through the screen door. "Anyone home?"

Lila stuck her head around the opening that passed from the living room to the sitting room. "Franklin," she said, delighted. "Come in, please."

He entered and casually made his way into the sitting room. A brief inspection told him that Lila was alone. "Has Carlotta not come home yet?" he asked, some surprise evident. She was usually home from work by this time every day.

"No, dear. She must be running late today," Lila replied. "Can I get you something to drink? Something cool maybe? It's a little warm for this early in spring."

"Do you have any tea, by any chance? And cinnamon?"

Lila's head jerked around with great force. She hadn't heard a request for cinnamon tea since…no, it couldn't be. The coincidence was just too amazing. This surely wasn't—no. Absolutely not! She put the thought right out of her mind. "I'm sorry, dear. I'm afraid I'm out of cinnamon."

"Just tea will be fine." He smiled at her.

Lila disappeared into the kitchen, deep in thought. She couldn't shake the feeling of dread that had festered in her since Franklin's request moments before. She thought back over the past but couldn't put the two together—the child Franklin and this grown young man.

Lila had really wanted her only daughter to be happy. She wanted Carlotta to have a better life than what Carson had given her. They had been courting for two years and were just about to be married. Why, oh why, did this have to happen? Just once, God, couldn't things work in their favor?

Through eyes that stared into the distant past, Lila again recalled an incident that clued her to the possibility that there was a connection between this Franklin and the son she left behind.

Fourth of July was not a holiday that the Clarks observed with much enthusiasm. At least not since Derek and Carlotta had become teenagers. The last time they shot off any fireworks was when Derek, the younger of the two, was ten years old.

But this year, it was a special time, with Carlotta and Franklin ready to take the plunge into matrimony. So Lila decided it was a good time to celebrate their freedom as Americans.

The Clark's were not the only ones who had a special occasion to celebrate. The little town of Wakeford, where they had lived for the past fifteen years, was celebrating its centennial. The town leaders decided to have a citywide picnic and invite all its 133 residents and top the day off with a square dance that evening, ending with a firework show.

Lila thought it would be an excellent way for the whole family to celebrate the engagement of Carlotta and Franklin.

It was at the picnic that day, when Franklin exhibited a mannerism that caught Lila's attention.

The likeness was so striking that it caused Lila to do a double take. Franklin was over talking with a group of businessmen, and he appeared to be deep in thought. His stance was what captured Lila's attention. She stared intently, deep in thought, as she recalled where she had seen that posture before.

Suddenly, it came to her.

He held his left arm across his chest and rested his right elbow on the back of his left hand. Then with his right arm bent upward, he tapped at his lips with the first knuckle of his index finger. It was not a particularly common gesture, but one that was frighteningly like Carson's.

Lila remembered thinking she should ask Franklin about it later.

I should have just let it go. I should have just kept my big mouth shut, she scolded herself. *But how could I? It's morally wrong for a brother and sister to marry. If I don't intervene, then the outcome is my fault, and this sin is on my conscience.*

I will have to interfere, she decided. *But how? How do I break my daughter's heart forever? No matter what I say or how I say it, she will never forgive me. It will destroy our relationship.* "I'm going to lose my daughter," she cried aloud.

"Dear God, why? Have I been such a disappointment? Is my sin so great that I deserve to be punished so severely?" She cried openly for about ten minutes. "If I must do this, it will be in a letter. I-I don't have the courage to face her with it."

Lila wrote and rewrote her letter. It took her nearly two weeks to compose it. No matter what she said in it, it always came out wrong. She finally decided the letter itself didn't make any difference. There was only one line Carlotta would see anyway.

Franklin is your brother.

The rest was window dressing. But it needed to be written anyway. Her explanation about their sullied past was long overdue. Truthfully, she had hoped it would never need to be told. But now, the truth must come out.

So she sent her letter. It had taken her several months to come to the conclusions that brought her to this point. There were other clues along the way, too many to ignore, and in the end, they all pointed to the same resolution, write the letter. By the end of January, the dirty deed began. Her letter was dated on Valentine's Day.

February 14, 1896

My dearest Carlotta,

I have fretted over this for some time. As it may be the most difficult undertaking, I have ever attempted in my life. I ask you beforehand to please forgive me. Having said that, please know that I love you and Derek more than anything else in this world.

I gave up everything I ever knew and ever had to give you and Derek this life, you know. Nothing else mattered to me. Only my two beautiful children. What you think of me after this is not what's important. Just please, please, don't shut me out of your life.

Many years ago, we lived in another town and were part of a larger family. You had two older brothers and a father. Fortunately, he was more of a father to you than a husband to me. Our family enjoyed a position of stature in the community. We were held in high regard.

Then one day there was a fire that spread through the entire town. It destroyed all the county records, including the records of your births. So I took you and your brother and just disappeared. I changed our name and raised you two on my own. Until now, we have been very happy.

That brings me to the problem at hand. Your marriage to Franklin. That family I mentioned? He's a part of it too. I know this will be hard for you to accept, but it's the truth. Franklin Baker is your brother. Your name, before I changed it, was Carlotta Christine Baker.

I know this will come as a shock to you. And you have every right to be put out, but it is a serious matter that would best be served with levelheadedness rather than emotions.

To put it bluntly, you must sever your relationship with Franklin. It would be best if you did so without telling him why. Please consider my request carefully.

I love you dearly. Please, please forgive me.

Your loving mother,

Lila

"Dad, there's someone here to see you," Curtis called out to his father. He was the last of Carson's children left at home. Carson was glad, though. If Curtis moved out, he'd be all alone. Not a pleasant thought. He'd had his children around all these years and had never brought a woman into his house since his wife had left. "It's a woman," his son whispered, and then a little louder. "I'm going out for a while, Dad."

Carson was in the kitchen just finishing up the evening dishes. He shook out the tattered white dish towel and draped it over the back of one of the chairs. He couldn't imagine who had come to see him. He had never had a woman call on him. Carefully, he looked the kitchen over and then limped into the living room. He pulled up short and stared at the visitor, was she real?

"Lila," he breathed the name out softly.

"Hello, Carson." Lila smiled at him.

"Lila," he repeated in disbelief. "As I live and breathe. I didn't know if you were alive or dead. Well…Well…" Carson was suddenly at a lack of words and incapable of clear thought evidently. "I don't know what to say," he continued fidgeting while staring fascinated at something on the floor. "You look good."

"Thank you." She smiled at his obvious discomfort. "But how would you know? You haven't taken your eyes off the floor since you saw me." She figured if she was going to have the courage to do this, the best way was to be hardnosed. She was uncomfortable, as she was sure Carson was too. But it needed to be done. She couldn't just let it go and hope it would work itself out. She steeled herself for what was sure to be a verbal onslaught when Carson regained his faculties.

As though he could tell what Lila was thinking, Carson stopped his frivolous trifling. He was taken aback by her brutal approach. This was not the Lila he remembered. She had always been a cowardly thing. No backbone. She always did whatever he wanted, giving in to his rapaciousness. And he had fed on her weakness. Now, secretly, he would give anything to have her back. He had been wrong. Somehow, he needed to tell her. Maybe it wasn't too late. "It's good to see you too," he said in a respectful voice.

She could feel her defenses slowly dropping. She had come with a purpose, but she hadn't expected Carson to be so amicable. If the circumstances were right, she could probably live with him again. Lord knows she had been without a man for a long while. It was an entertaining thought. "Why don't you come and sit down, Carson. I won't bite. I promise," she replied with a charming smile.

Carson limped over to his favorite overstuffed—and in much need of repair—chair. He kind of fell back into it, which was one of the reasons it was in such a ragged condition. Since his accident, this was the easiest way for him to sit down.

"Lila, what brings you back here?" he asked indifferently.

"There is something very important I needed to talk to you about," she replied moderately. She could be just as callous as he was. "So unless you're in a hurry to get somewhere." Why was she being so incongruous suddenly? What happened to "I can live with him now"?

"What is so important that it brought you back here again?" Carson asked, his demeanor suddenly changed. He couldn't imagine anything serious enough to warrant the uneasiness she surely felt just being in his presence.

Carson smiled at her, hoping she would notice that the years had tempered him considerably, that he wasn't still that mean, self-righteous man she ran from all those years ago.

Lila returned his smile, her self-esteem growing as the moments passed.

"What do you want, Lila?"

"It's Carlotta," she said quickly.

"Carlotta, that little princess." He smiled inwardly at the thought of that beautiful little girl who could turn his heart of stone to putty until… "What? Is something wrong with her?" he asked, his face shrouded with emotion.

"No. She's fine," Lila informed him. "But she has met a young man and fallen in love. They are to be married next month."

"Is that so?" he replied with a huge grin on his face. "Does she want me to give her away?"

"I don't think you'll want to give her away to this particular young man," Lila said, her eyes twinkling in anticipation of dropping a bomb in his lap. She was enjoying baiting him. Something she had not had the pleasure of doing very often in the past.

"Why? What's wrong with him? He doesn't treat her right?"

"Carson, calm down," Lila admonished him as his temper began to surge.

"Well, what is it, woman? Are you going to tell me, or not?"

"It's Franklin," she said, happy it was finally out. His response was just as she expected.

"*Franklin?*" he roared so loud that she was sure people in the next town heard. "My Franklin?" he repeated but with less emphasis.

"Yes. Our Franklin," she confirmed, with special emphasis on the pronoun.

Carson acknowledged with a nod of his head. "Well, they can't do that," he stated with finality. "It's immoral, right?" he asked quizzically.

"Of course, it is, Carson. We cannot allow it."

"Well, what are we going to do then?"

Lila couldn't believe what she was hearing. For the moment, she almost wished there was someone lurking nearby listening to this so she would have a witness that Carson Baker had actually asked for her opinion.

He hadn't purposely planned on eavesdropping on his father's conversation with Carlotta's mother. Why was she here anyway? Did she think it was time to meet his family? He and Carlotta had never gotten their two families together. To tell the truth, they had never even talked about them. They had decided to keep their relationship a secret until they were sure of themselves. Carlotta was disturbed about that aspect of Franklin, but he had insisted. The only explanation she had managed to get from him, and it had been like pulling teeth, was that there was some bad thing happened to his father in the past and he wanted to be sure before he committed to an obligation with any woman.

His curiosity got the best of him, and Franklin propped himself against the side of the house under a window and listened in.

It was very blasé at first. They exchanged a few niceties, just general chitchat mostly, suddenly though the conversation took a sudden twist. His dad had never indicated that he knew the girl or her mother. Franklin was very confused about what they were saying.

He came out of his reverie and listened some more.

Whoa! If he didn't know better, Franklin would have sworn they were picking a fight with each other. This didn't make any sense. Not one bit.

Franklin glanced around the yard furtively, feeling a sudden sense of guilt at listening in on their conversation. He shifted his position—feeling somewhat uncomfortable his cramped muscles as well as his culpability—so he could better hear his father and his future mother-in-law.

He listened some more.

"Someone who wants to take advantage of my little girl," he heard his father say. *What does he mean his little girl? He doesn't have a daughter.* Maybe he was already starting to think of Carlotta like a daughter. But how could he? Franklin had kept their relationship a secret until now. All he'd ever told his father was that he had a girlfriend from over at Wakeford.

"It's Franklin," he heard Lila say, pulling him back to the discussion inside. Suddenly, the whole sordid thing made sense. They were saying that Carlotta was his…

Sister?

Franklin didn't wait to hear any more or hang around to be discovered. He hurried away from the window and began walking aimlessly through town.

"My sister," he repeated out loud. "Carlotta Christine Clark is my sister. I've got to see her now!" he shouted.

"Hello, Franklin," two girls crooned at him as they passed by.

He looked at them, startled, as he realized he had been thinking aloud. "Ladies." He tipped an invisible hat at them, and they giggled as they passed by.

He had walked for what seemed like hours with no actual destination in mind. By dark, he had arrived at the edge of town. He may have been walking aimlessly, but unconsciously he must have wanted to be here because this was the road to Wakeford. With any luck, he could catch a ride with someone going that direction and be there in no time. *Not many folks out today*, he thought, *but someone will come along.* He was going to have to be careful that Lila didn't see him. He didn't want her to know that he had listened in—at least not yet.

All he knew for sure was, he had to talk to Carlotta.

"Rebecca! Rebecca!" Carlotta shouted through the screen door. She stood peering in until her best friend entered the living room from another room in the house.

"Carlotta?" She crossed the room quickly, pushed the door open and stepped out onto the porch. "Honey, what's wrong? What's the matter? You look terrible. Here, sit down over here. I'm going to get us some nice cool tea and then you're going to tell me all about it," she said, leading Carlotta to one of the wicker chairs.

Rebecca Martin's house was substantial enough for a family of twelve, let alone her small family which consisted of two—her and her husband. She still insisted that they were going to have a big family someday, but Carlotta was pretty sure that her friend and employer was too involved in her career and business to have children. So Rebecca existed in the massive, lonely house.

The porch was representative of the house, as it wrapped around three sides and seemed to protect the enormous structure. There were double French doors opening onto the porch from each side of the monstrous home. Rebecca made sure Carlotta was snugly settled into one of the comfortable chairs on the front section before retreating into the house for tea. "You just sit there and catch your breath while

I'm gone and then you can tell me all about it." Her voice faded as she disappeared somewhere deep into the cavernous home.

Carlotta listened as her friend droned on and on until finally there was only silence—and her thoughts. She thought about the letter again, and again the tears started falling. Carlotta was sure that she had cried all her tears away, that there were no more left. But her face was wet, signaling a renewal of the flood that already had her face streaked red.

"Now, darling, what has got you all a buzz?" Rebecca asked again, setting a serving tray down on the small wooden table between the two chairs. "Why, you've been crying. It must be pretty bad," she said as she started to pour the tea. Then she thought better of it. "It looks to me like you could use something a little stronger. Wait just a minute." She hurried back into the house, returning within seconds, carrying a decanter of brandy. "Try this, darling."

Carlotta took the glass from Rebecca's outstretched hand and sat holding it just below her lips as though she were going to take a sip. Suddenly her hands shook, and her lips quivered as she tried to suppress the emotions that churned inside and threatened yet another wave of tears. Eventually more tears fell as she succumbed to her emotions. Rebecca took the glass from her and set it down.

"Carlotta? Please tell me what it is," she pleaded, holding the smaller woman's hand.

Carlotta took the letter from a hidden pocket of her dress and handed it to Rebecca. "This is from my mother," she cried, no longer trying to hold the tears back. When her hand was free of the letter, she reached into the pocket again and pulled out a handkerchief and dabbed at her eyes.

Rebecca sipped at her tea and read the letter, with each word her eyes widened even more until she was sure the skin had stretched over her face. It was painfully obvious what Carlotta was so distressed about. At one point she stopped reading and gazed at her longtime friend. She looked at her as though she were seeing her for the first time.

Carlotta stared straight ahead. She stared at nothing. But she didn't want to watch as Rebecca read the letter. Then with sudden astonishment, she realized she had given Rebecca a letter containing a dark family secret. What must her friend be thinking of Carlotta and her family now? She wished she hadn't given it to her. Maybe she should take it back and leave quickly. *Oh god, what have I done?* Her glazed eyes focused on some distant scene that only she could see. In that instant, her future was painstakingly clear. Everything would be different from now on. She needed to see Franklin. They needed to talk. God, how she loved him. Suddenly, the tears started afresh.

Rebecca had been watching Carlotta out of the corner of her eye. Suddenly, she didn't know this woman who had been her friend, who had been working with her side by side. Conscious of Carlotta's movement, she returned to the letter, which she held in her left hand. Her right hand was resting on the small wooden table that held the tray with the pitcher of tea and the brandy—and now her glass, untouched, forgotten as she concentrated on the dreadful letter with the shocking news.

Rebecca finally finished, folded the letter, and handed it back to Carlotta. What could she say to this? "Have you…have you talked to your mother?" she asked cautiously, choosing her words carefully.

"No," Carlotta responded quickly.

"Oh, darling." She frowned as she laid her hand on Carlotta's arm. "What you must be feeling right now. Now I understand why you were so distraught. Don't go thinking this is your fault. You had no way of knowing. Maybe this is just a mistake," she continued quickly. "You know, a mix-up of some sort." Rebecca bit her lip knowing what she just said was untrue. She was reaching for something, anything to explain this predicament. She felt ill at ease and wanted desperately to be alone.

As if sensing Rebecca's feelings, Carlotta rose to leave. "It's highly unlikely that this is a mix-up of any kind," she said, with no trace of emotion. "But thanks for trying." Years of wondering and asking questions of her mother about their past sprang to her mind quickly. Suddenly, a lot of things made sense. And just as suddenly, she had no desire to say any more about her family to Rebecca.

A distended, impassioned look dominated Carlotta's features. It frightened Rebecca. "What are you going to do now?" she asked hesitantly.

Carlotta stared at her with the most determined look in her eyes that Rebecca had ever seen. "I have everything to lose and nothing to gain," she replied resolutely.

"You could gain a father," Rebecca said hesitantly. "One you never knew you had." Carlotta frowned. What an odd thing to say. It was the only thing Rebecca had said so far that made any sense.

For a moment, Carlotta was intrigued by the notion. She had always wanted a father. She grew up without one and kids always made fun of her because of that. And all this time, she could have had one.

"I…have…to go," she said slowly. She knew what she had to do. It was all so clear. How could she have not seen it before? She had let too many bad thoughts cloud her thinking and impair her judgment. She looked like such a fool—but now she knew.

Now she knew.

"Carlotta, are you here?" her mother shouted as she walked in the door. She took her shawl off and hung it on the rack by the front door and then hung her parasol next to it. She shouted out again, "Carlotta, darling?"

Derek bounded down the stairs. "She's not here, Mom. What's the matter with her anyway? She stormed out of the house and wouldn't even speak to me."

Lila had done the best job she could raising her two children. It wasn't always easy by herself. But she wanted to think they had responded well to her guidance. Now, she wasn't so sure. "She didn't say anything. She didn't say where she was going?"

"No, ma'am. Just stormed out," he reiterated.

"Oh, dear. Where would she go if she were sorely troubled?" she wondered frantically. She snapped her fingers so loud Derek jumped at the sudden sound. "Of course, Rebecca's. Where else would she go?" She sighed with relief.

"Mom, what's going on?" he asked again.

"Honey, I'll explain it to you later. Lord knows I should have done this a long time ago," she said mysteriously. "Just bear with me a little longer."

"Yes, ma'am," he answered politely.

The hollow sound of footsteps as someone crossed the porch heavily, disrupted any further discussion. Carlotta stood, her expression accusing, in the doorway of the sitting room before the last echo had died away. Her mother waited expectantly but without confidence. Carlotta lashed out with fury that terrified even herself. She held the letter up. "This is the most terrible thing you could have ever done to us. How could you be so thoughtless, so self-serving? Do you realize what this does to me and Franklin? We are in love," she exploded. "Now what in the hell are we supposed to do? Tell me, Mother. What do we do now?" she yelled.

Lila had never seen her daughter like this. She didn't even know she was capable of it. She was completely caught off guard by Carlotta's outburst. "I…I…" She had no idea what to say. What could she say? Carlotta was right. She had no right to do what she did. But what about Carson? Did he have a right to do what he did to her? Was she supposed to just go on letting him beat her? Lila didn't know anymore. She just didn't know. Confronted with her misdeed, she saw it as she had never seen it before. And it was too much for her to handle. She covered her face with her hands, and she cried. Her body shook with enormous sobs.

Her children stood perfectly still—watching, shocked at her sudden display of emotion. They had never seen their mother a weak woman like this. She was normally the epitome of strength and fortitude, always remaining calm and composed in a crisis.

When it was evident that she was not going to stop, Carlotta took her by the shoulders and led her to the sofa. She gently guided her mother onto a cushion and then sat down beside her.

"Derek, bring a glass of sherry," she instructed her brother, who was pleased to have something to do. He had become very uncomfortable with the situation. "Mother, I'm sorry," Carlotta apologized.

Lila shook her head back and forth vigorously. "No!" she cried. "It's my fault. You have nothing to apologize for." She looked up for the first time since she had begun crying. Her eyes were red and swollen from the effort, and Carlotta was seeing her mother in a much different light than she had ever seen her before.

She looked at her mother's pretty eyes and was shocked at the depth of her pain and sorrow. She also saw, entrenched in the deepest part, her unmistakable love for her two children.

"Mother, what could have been so terrible that it forced you to separate us from the rest of our family?" she asked, feeling pity for the woman.

The long-overdue explanation poured forth as Lila told the sordid story of her past. A past that she desperately wanted to forget. Her two children listened in horror at the way their father treated her. How could he do that? Of course, she was justified in her actions. But that still didn't resolve Carlotta's present situation. "So you see, you have to end this relationship," Lila said in her most convincing tone. "You and Franklin are brother and sister. You can't continue," she pleaded, holding her daughter's hands. The look on Carlotta's face told her that her daughter had already made up her mind, even before she had arrived. They would not break up.

Now Carlotta felt the sting of tears in her own eyes as she looked away from her mother. "I love him," she sobbed, her face sparkling as fresh tears flowed.

"And I love her," a new voice added from the door. Franklin stepped through into the dimly lit sitting room. Somehow, he had slipped in unnoticed. They were so caught up in their troubles that they hadn't noticed the darkness slowly creeping in or Franklin's presence. Neither had they been aware of Derek standing just a few feet away the whole time. He was shocked and his face ashen at the discussion between the two women.

Lila took the glass of sherry her son still held. "Derek, would you put on some light," she asked, exhaling slowly. She was unaware that she had been holding her breath. "I suppose it's time you knew what happened too," she sighed, reaching over and patting Franklin on the knee.

"I already know most of it," he admitted to her. "I was outside the window, listening to you and father," he said, hanging his head, ashamed that he'd eavesdropped. "That's why I came tonight."

While Derek lighted the lamps, she began recounting for Franklin the same story she had just told her own children. It was a long arduous task for her, and often she had to stop to collect herself. But with three of her children around her, she was able to gather her courage and finish the saturnine tale. "And that brings us to now," she said, exhausted from the oppressive discourse.

As Lila's final words still echoed through the air, a thunderous silence ensued, while restless shadows danced around the walls. When the silence had become overbearing, someone moved. But no one noticed. As the silence grew, so did an uncomfortable chasm between mother and daughter.

Finally, mercifully Carlotta spoke. "I don't how you can expect us to just stop and forget it ever happened," she replied dolefully. "This isn't a summer fling, Mother. There are real people and real feelings here. I love him. I want to spend the rest of my life with Franklin. Can't you understand?" she cried. Carlotta turned her tear-streaked face toward Franklin. "I-I can't just stop. I won't."

"Neither can I," he added softly, wiping at the tears on her cheeks.

The finality of their statement was painstakingly clear to Lila. She sat in a stupor, staring at the couple. "Maybe when you've had some time to think this over—"

"I don't think so, Mother," Carlotta stated, interrupting her mother. "I'm sorry that fate has played such a dirty trick on us, but that doesn't mean we have to accept it. It's not our fault, so why should we pay the penalty for it?" She shot a look of disdain at her mother, who was crawling even further into her shell.

Lila couldn't believe this was happening. She certainly hadn't meant for it to. This was probably the worst that could happen, and she was powerless to stop it. But at the same time, she understood their feelings. Dear God! What would become of her children now?

Lila got up without saying another word and left the room.

Franklin and Carlotta sat on the front porch swing, the sweet scent of summer air wafting its way through the warm night, drugging them with its enchanting nectar. The swing rocked lightly from the occasional, gentle nudge of Franklin's foot. They had been sitting there swinging, holding hands since Lila had gone upstairs. Neither had spoken a word. Words weren't necessary. They had vowed their love to each other, and they had both sworn a long time ago that nothing, or no one would ever break those vows.

As the evening came to an end, they renewed their pledge of love once more. As they embraced each other, Carlotta could feel his strength piercing her shield of armor.

She needed his strength.

She needed his love.

She needed him.

Carlotta held him tight.

"Nothing in the world matters to me as much as you do," Franklin whispered in her ear. "I don't care what anyone else says. It's you I want for my wife."

Carlotta melted in his arms, wishing she could stay like that forever. "We may have to leave here to have happiness," she said solemnly. She began to weep at the thought of leaving all she had ever known.

Her mother.

Her home.

Her friends.

"If that's what it takes, my love." He pushed away from her and held her at arm's length. "If that's what it takes."

She forced a smile, kissed him lightly on the cheek, and went inside. Franklin waited until the downstairs lights had been doused before he descended the porch steps and strolled down the walk to the street. He was whistling softly, happy once again.

Carlotta, on the other hand, was unusually pensive as she climbed the stairs to the second floor. She entered her bedroom and undressed for bed using only the moonlight streaming in through the window to guide her movements. She moved slowly but methodically, removing her outer garments, and when she finally stood naked in the subdued light, she slipped on her cotton nightgown.

She knelt beside her bed and repeated the same bedtime prayer she had said hundreds of times before—except this time she added a small request at the end. "Could you please give me some extra help just this once? Please?"

Carlotta crawled into bed and cried softly as sleep eluded her. No matter what decision she made, she would lose someone she loved. She tossed and turned for what surely must have been half the night before a restless, unsettled slumber drifted over her. Her last thought before sleeping were Franklin's last words that night.

If that's what it takes.

Carlotta. Can you hear me? I have come to talk to you about your problem.

"Who are you? Where are you? I can't see you. All I see is a… cloudy mist. Are you hiding from me? Where are you?"

Look harder. You will see me, if you really try.

"I don't see—oh! There you are. Do I know you? You don't look familiar. But your voice has a pleasing sound to it, comforting—like I've heard it before. I like listening to it. Talk to me some more—who are you?"

I am the One you prayed to. Did you not ask for help in your prayer tonight? That is the reason that I am here. We only come when we are sent, to respond to a specific need. He is very adamant about that. We cannot interfere simply because we want to. So you need help with your little problem? That is why I came.

"That's nice, but I already know what to do about my problem. I have already made up my mind."

You have made a decision, Carlotta. It's not the same thing. A decision you must reconsider. It will only bring you heartache and unhappiness.

"That may be true, but my life would be even more unhappy if I didn't marry Franklin. Don't you see? We were meant to be together, or we would have never met. We met, fell in love, and are getting married. That's all there is to it?"

Just because you met fortuitously does not mean you were supposed to fall in love. You were supposed to meet and discover that you were brother and sister and that you had been kept apart because of your parents' selfishness. Falling in love was never a part of it.

"Just the same, we did fall in love, and you can't take back what has already happened. Maybe in the beginning this wasn't supposed to happen, but it did. Why doesn't anybody understand what I'm saying? It did happen! We…are…in…love! I can't make it any plainer than that."

I'm sorry you feel that way, Carlotta. I truly am. I came because you asked for help. Do you need my help?

"I don't know! I don't know!"

Then I have to leave. But I'll give you one more chance to back out—to say you'll stop this madness.

"Franklin and I are in love. We were lovers before we were brother and sister. Your words are meaningless to me. They have no depth. Nothing you can say will change my mind."

I'm sorry you feel that way. I must go now. I wish you all the happiness, Carlotta, though I truly doubt that will happen in your case.

"Wait! That's it? Where are you? Angel? Angel? Where are you? Where are you? Where are…?"

Carlotta sat bolt upright in bed and cried out, "Where are you?" She sat still in the dark and felt numb from the chilling dream. Even in her sleep, she was bothered by the ghosts of her and Franklin's past. Her face and hair were damp from sweating, and she felt cold. She pulled the covers up around her neck and cried herself back to sleep.

February 21, 1896

Dear Mother,

It seemed like my life had been very uneventful until Valentine's Day this year. It feels like there was a year's worth of living packed into the past week. But honestly, our lives were grand before that.

I don't remember those early years, as I was too young, although you have told us many times how we struggled right after moving here. But I remember when we first moved into this grand house. It seemed so…overwhelming at the time. To a little girl like I was back then, it would take a lifetime to explore all the rooms. I remember, too, being scared that I might get lost in some part of the house and you might never find me. Isn't it funny how our perception of things changes as we grow older?

I pray that I will have a pretty little girl to dote over like you did me. You raised me very well, considering you had to do it alone. I don't suppose I can ever give my daughter as much as you have given me, but I will love her, and she will be mine.

Listen to me. I'm rambling on carelessly. That was not the reason for this letter. But I did want you to know how I feel. You are still my mother. That will never change, thank God.

Franklin and I have decided to go ahead with our wedding plans. It's what we both want. I can't ever imagine life without him and wouldn't even want to try. We also believe that in so doing we cannot continue to live here. When word got out of our indiscretion—and it would; people talk—we would be persecuted relentlessly. We don't feel we could, in all good conscience, raise a family in such a hostile environment.

I know you will want to know where we are going, but I can't tell you exactly. Franklin was talking to a gentleman who was passing through, and he mentioned a place out west of here—the other side of the Mississippi, I think—called Crater Ridge. The way he, the traveler, explained it, it sounded absolutely beautiful. It is full of hills and trees. Well, anyway, I don't know any more than that. Not that it matters. You would never come to visit. That much is clear.

I will write to you when we arrive. My best to Derek in college. I love you both very much.

Your loving daughter,

Carlotta

Chapter Five

Both men stared at the crumpled pile on the floor. It was like neither man had ever seen a woman faint before. In one respect, Dan Rogers should have reacted immediately when Susie passed out. He was, after all, a public official who should respond quickly in emergency situations. But on the other hand, Dan was single, so he was inexperienced with the mood swings of a female. It was a flimsy excuse, but it worked for him—most of the time.

At any rate, he was timid about responding to Susie's episode.

"Should we call a doctor? Or take her to the hospital?" he suggested, bending over Susie with his hands propped on his knees.

Stoney looked hurriedly around. "Let's get her on the couch." Together they carried her to the old black leather sofa the sheriff kept in his office for several reasons. When he had worked too long, exhausted himself and just couldn't find the energy to make the drive home, or needed to stay close by because of a case he was working on. The couch was worn, the leather cracked and discolored, but it was still a serviceable couch in Dan's opinion.

"Is she going to be all right?" the sheriff asked, looking over Stoney's shoulder. It didn't really bother him what happened, but he was wondering now if perhaps he shouldn't have shown them the coroner's report. "Can I do anything?"

Stoney was brushing her hair out of her face. "I don't think so," he said warily. "She'll come around in a minute or so." Rogers thought he detected a note of doubt in Stoney's voice, but he kept his eyes on the girl.

"Maybe I should get her a glass of water…or a damp cloth."

That brought a smile to Stoney's lips and relaxed some of the tension that had filtered into the room. "I think that only works in the movies." He grinned at the sheriff.

Rogers forced a smile. He still wasn't convinced that this thing wasn't his fault. A good lawyer could make a sound case against him if they were a mind to. "Stoney, about that report." He paused long enough to be sure Stoney was listening. "Maybe I shouldn't have shown it to you two," he continued, with a worried look on his face.

As he looked closely at the sheriff, Stoney could see the deep lines of concern etched on the man's visage. "There's no need to worry, Sheriff. Really. See, she's coming around," he said thankfully when he heard Susie moan.

They both turned their attention back to the girl. Stoney helped her sit up while Rogers went for a glass of water, despite their earlier discussion about it. Suddenly, he felt very conscientious and needed something to do.

"Ohh," Susie moaned, grabbing her head.

"It's okay," Stoney reassured her. Rogers returned, holding a glass of water out to the slightly pale girl. Stoney took the tumbler from him and held it to Susie's lips.

She took a little sip and instantly jerked her head back as the cold water hit her mouth. "I'm all right. I'm all right," she insisted holding her hand up to ward off the offending glass.

Stoney set the glass down and took her hands. "Can you stand up?"

"Of course, I can stand up. I'm not an invalid," she snapped, embarrassed at pulling a stereotypical feminine stunt. He helped her to a standing position and held on to her hands as she wavered momentarily.

"You can go out this way," Rogers offered, unlocking a side door that opened to the parking lot. Stoney got her situated in the front seat of his car and then hurried around to the driver's side and jumped in behind the wheel. He backed out and was just pulling away when Rogers strode up to the moving vehicle. "Hold on a minute, Stoney."

"What is it, Sheriff?" he asked, perturbed. "I really should get her home."

"This won't take a minute," Rogers insisted, his hand resting on the door. Susie's head lolled about on her shoulders. "Are you sure you're all right?" he asked her again.

She smiled weakly at him. "I'm fine, Sheriff. I have a headache is all."

Rogers turned his attention back to Stoney. His demeanor suddenly took on a completely serious look. "You leave this investigation to me, Stoney. Do you understand? I'll find out what happened to Brian. And if I need your help, I'll ask for it. Okay?"

Stoney became obtuse. "He was my brother. You can't stop us from doing a little snooping around. Don't worry, we won't get in the way of your investigation," he replied. "Anything else, Sheriff?"

"No, that's all. But a word of warning. If you tamper with any evidence or do anything to hinder this investigation, I'll put you in jail. Both of you," he said, looking at Susie.

Stoney released his foot from the brake and pressed down on the accelerator a little harder than was necessary. The tires screeched as he pulled away from the sheriff's office. He braked to a halt at the street, then turned out of the parking lot, leaving the sheriff standing there, staring after them.

As Sheriff Rogers walked back into his office and sat down heavily in his chair, the telephone rang. Let the deputy get it, he told himself. He picked up his coffee cup and sipped on the lukewarm beverage. "Ick!" He spat it back into the cup. "Damn, I hate cold coffee," he growled in disgust.

"Sheriff, it's the coroner on the line," Wayne called through the closed door.

He grabbed the phone from its cradle. "What do you have, Doc?"

Dr. Grady Miles, county coroner and medical examiner, had been in this business for thirty years. He had seen every kind of death there was to see. He had seen the worst kind of agonizing death frozen on victim's faces as they breathed their last. Some looked like they were in dignified repose. Others—and this was most of them—just had a blank stare of death on their cadaverous faces.

But this one. This one was different. This he had never seen before in all his thirty years of service. "You had better come over here, Dan."

"What is it, Grady?"

"I'm not going to tell you over the phone," he grumbled. "You just come on over and take a look at this corpse."

"All right. Calm down. I'll be there in five minutes," he said, hanging up the phone. *What in the world could have gotten under that old man's skin?* he wondered. "Going to the morgue, Wayne. Be back in a few minutes," he told his deputy. "And try to be civil to people," he added balefully.

"Yes, sir."

"Now what?" Susie asked as they headed out of town.

Stoney thought about it for a minute before answering her. "I think it's time we visited Rockhole," he said thoughtfully.

"You think we'll see something the sheriff missed?" she asked, recovered from her fainting spell. Susie had never thought of herself as a detective, but it was a tantalizing thought. "I mean, he did tell us to stay out of it," she pointed out reluctantly.

Stoney knew she was right, but he had to try. Brian was his brother. He loved him, and besides, Brian would do the same for him. "He said don't mess with any evidence," Stoney pointed out. "You can never tell what we might uncover," he said thoughtfully.

Susie adjusted herself in the front seat of the car so that she was facing forward. This had been a nightmarish twelve hours that had passed, and somehow, she needed to try to put it all in perspective.

Just last night, they were watching Michele so that Brian and Mary J. could have a special night alone. It was going along perfectly—at least they thought it was. That's when the phone call came, and everything went to hell after that.

"Stoney," she muttered, swiveling sideways so that her left leg lay folded on the seat, her knee pointed toward him. "Did you read all of that report?" she asked curiously.

"No. I didn't get the chance," he replied honestly. She knew what he meant by that and chose to let it drop rather than suffer the embarrassment of talking about it.

"Very funny," she countered.

"Sorry," he rejoined. "Why do you ask?"

"Well, It's the way they say he died. It just doesn't make any sense," she said with a note of melancholy in her voice. "Brian is—was," she corrected herself quickly, "an excellent swimmer."

"Yeah, so what's your point?" Stoney asked, confused.

"My point is, how could Brian fall into the water from ten feet up and land in such a position that it split—" She couldn't finish it.

"Split him in half," Stoney finished for her. "Well now, that's the mystery, isn't it? The sheriff and I agree that there's something strange about the whole thing. It has to be something pretty extraordinary for it to happen that way." Suddenly Stoney realized that Susie must have a reason for asking the questions she was asking. "What are you thinking?" he asked derisively.

"Nothing really. Well…something," she added.

He gave her a discerning look. She could be so enigmatic at times. It was a quality he liked, but not in every instance. And right now, was one of those times. "You going to keep it to yourself?" he asked intrusively.

"I think someone attacked them," she stated firmly.

"What do you base it on?" he asked.

Her brows furrowed. "Oh, for God's sake, Stoney. Isn't it as plain as the nose on your face?" He didn't say anything, so she continued. "Brian is dead—albeit in a very suspicious manner—and Mary J. looks like she went ten rounds and lost. Do you think they did that to themselves?" she asked scornfully.

He didn't answer right away. She knew he didn't believe that. To tell the truth, he wasn't sure what he believed. One thing he did know. Susie had a valid point. Someone else was involved in this. And whoever it was, this was the person they were looking for. "You think you're pretty damned smart, don't you?"

He took her hand and pulled. She slid across the seat toward him. "Let's not fight, okay? We need to focus our energy on finding out what happened to our brother and sister."

Stoney put his right arm around her, and the fingers of their right hands intertwined.

They rode the rest of the way in silence.

Sadie had been in tears ever since her in-laws left. She had left Daniel to watch Michele and had gone into the bedroom to lie down. Daniel stood near the door of their bedroom for a bit and listened to her crying brokenly into her pillow. He walked away from the door shaking his head. She really believed that everything that had happened to Brian and Mary J. was entirely their fault. He wished he could convince her otherwise. But how? So far, she hadn't listened to anything he had said.

Daniel took the baby out on the front porch and put her in a playpen they kept for when their grandchildren came to visit. He had just sat down in his rocking chair when the front door opened, and Sadie came out of the house. He gave her chair a gentle rock, inviting her to sit. Her eyes were red and puffy, and he could have sworn that she had a permanent frown on her face.

Sadie sat down in the strong wooden rocker. She'd spent many a great moment in that chair, and it always seemed to make her feel better, no matter what she was facing. She doubted it could do that now. Nothing could undo what had happened. Nothing could bring Brian back. No matter whose fault it was.

Her firstborn was dead.

"Maybe Sarah was right," she said disdainfully. "We're all prisoners of our past. If ever there was anyone deserving of punishment, it's us," she lamented. "I just wish God would take it out on us rather than them."

"You think God is responsible for all this?" he asked, astonished.

"Well, don't you?" she countered.

"Not for a second, Sadie. I can't believe you would think that either," he gasped. "Sadie, I know we're not very religious people, but you can't possibly mean that. I'll grant you one thing, there's a spiritual force at work here, but it's not God. It's the devil," he said prophetically.

"I don't know what I mean anymore," she sighed. "Let's just forget about it, okay?"

Daniel leaned back in his rocker. "God help us," he muttered under his breath.

Sheriff Rogers strolled down the sidewalk on what was one of the nicest days they had seen all summer. He was glad he had decided to walk. It was a perfect day for it—and he needed the exercise.

The sheriff's office was in a separate part of town from the city and state offices. Primarily, it was to keep the prisoner's in the county jail as far removed from the public's eye as possible. He remembered one time when he had visited one of the large Texas cities. He was walking close to the downtown area and passed by the county jail. It was in such a way that the prisoners could see passersby on the walkway below. Most of the time their remarks thrown haphazardly from the windows on the fourth floor were harmless enough. But there were other times, especially when a young lady happened by, that it got rather ugly. So when the county had decided to build a new facility, he recommended they locate it in a remote area of town, thereby isolating the criminal riff-raff from the citizens.

It was a short walk, really, from his office to the coroner's office—eight blocks, which by his figuring was close to a mile. But it was a nice walk. The walk down Main Street gave him the chance to see what was going on in town and visit briefly with people on the way. Speaking of which, look who was coming down the walk toward him—two girls, both of whom had tried to get a date with him.

They were both pretty, and he supposed he should try going out with them, one at a time of course. He smiled at them. "Sandy. Debra. How's the world treating you?"

Sandy Barnes winked at him. She was twenty-six years old and still single. He was amazed at that. Particularly considering her gorgeous five-foot, two-inch, very petite frame. She was perfect for his short height. He smiled inwardly at the thought. He suddenly wondered why he had never asked her on a date. *I'm going to do just that*, he decided. "We're on our way to the tanning salon," she replied.

Rogers eyed her legs, which were accented beautifully by the white shorts she was wearing. "They look plenty tanned to me," he commented.

"Why, Dan. Thank you for noticing." She smiled demurely. "But that's not the only part we get tanned."

He blushed at her comment and decided he definitely wanted a date with this girl. "Well, I have to go." He smiled at them. "Don't overdo it in that fake sun."

"Don't you worry none. We're experienced at this. Goodbye, Sheriff," Sandy replied.

"Goodbye, Dan, Debra added. "I just love a man in a uniform. Don't you?" she asked her friend. Rogers smiled.

As he walked on, Rogers passed by Jake's Tire and Service, which was located next to the City Building. Jake had seen him coming and was waiting for him out front. He had been called on to tow the car left at Rockhole by Brian and Mary J. the night of the "accident."

"Sheriff? Anything on that murder the other night?" Jake asked.

"What makes you think it was a murder?"

"Well," Jake pressed, "wasn't it?"

"I don't know yet," he answered. "And you need to try and refrain from talking about this until I do come up with something!"

"All right, all right. I'm the soul of discretion," Jake assured him.

Rogers continued his march to the coroner's office glancing at his watch. "I'm already ten minutes late. Grady will raise holy hell over that," he said, talking to himself. He hurried into the building and up the stairs to the second floor where the coroner's office was located. "No time to wait for the elevator," he sighed, taking the stairs two at a time.

He stopped in front of the door marked "Coroner" and composed himself. He didn't want Grady to know he had been running. The old fart might expect him to hurry like that all the time. "Betty, my favorite secretary," he said, walking into the outer office.

"Dan, how're you doing today?"

"Oh, I'm fine. Is he fuming yet?" he asked, pointing at the door to Grady's office. "He's not in there," she informed the sheriff. "He's in the basement…and he's expecting you. I'll call down and tell him you're on the way." She picked up the phone from its cradle and pushed some buttons on the instrument. Dan heard her speaking into it as he disappeared out the door.

In the basement, he hesitated outside the door of the morgue. God, he hated to go in there. He wasn't bothered by the sight of corpses. They were something he had dealt with for years. But he had never gotten used to seeing one all cut up with a coroner's knife and saw. It turned his stomach. He hoped he died of natural causes so he wouldn't have to end up on one of those metal tables.

He opened the door and stepped through it.

"Well, it's about damned time," Grady Miles bellowed at him. "Did you stop to have lunch on the way?"

Rogers purposely averted his eyes from whatever it was that Grady was doing to the cadaver on the table in front of him. The sheriff stayed back about three feet from the table. His nose wrinkled at the pungent odor penetrating it.

"Here, put this mask on," the doctor ordered. "It'll filter out the smells for you."

"Thanks, Doc," he replied as he placed it over his face, covering his nose and mouth. "So what did you want to show me?"

Dr. Grady Miles wasn't much for showmanship, but he did like a grandstand every now and then. Particularly when it involved his friend, Sheriff Dan Rogers. He reached over and threw back the sheet covering the top half of Brian's body. "Look at his face," he directed the sheriff's attention to the uncovered head of the victim.

As soon as Grady reached for the sheet, Dan had automatically turned his head away. This wasn't something he enjoyed or could do with any enthusiasm. He slowly turned back to face the table, bringing his attention to focus on the face of what he assumed was Brian Clark's. "My god. What is that?" he asked shocked.

"Very prophetic," Grady nodded.

"What do you mean, Doc?"

He pointed at the face. "It may take Him"—he pointed upward—"to explain this because I sure as hell don't know. I've never seen anything like it."

"Is that Brian Clark?" the sheriff asked, shaken at the contorted images on the face.

"In a manner of speaking." Miles pulled on a clean pair of rubber gloves. "Try to focus on this, Dan. I know you have a weak stomach, so—"

"That's not it and you know it. I see mutilated bodies all the time. It's just that...what you do to them is what bothers me." He smiled ruefully. "Was that all you wanted to show me?"

Miles put his finger on Brian's face where the point of the cheekbone should have been and pressed. Instead of immediate resistance, his finger disappeared into the flesh past the first knuckle.

"Oh, Jesus! Oh, don't do that!" Rogers cried out in disgust.

Miles then placed the same finger on Brian's forehead and pressed. His action produced the same result as before.

"What happened to him?"

"He appears to have lost all bone structure from the neck up. And watch this." He pinched a small bit of flesh between his thumb and forefinger. The skin peeled off like it came from a ripe peach. Rogers started to raise yet another objection, but Miles silenced him with an uplifted hand. "Just watch," he strongly suggested.

Rogers stared at the injured spot, and within a minute it started to regenerate itself. After a few minutes, it had completely healed, leaving no scar or any indication that Miles had damaged the skin—or whatever it was.

"Son of a bitch!" Rogers exclaimed. "Is this an alien, Doc?"

"Doubtful. But it is something other than human," Miles confirmed.

"What do you make of the expression on his face? It's kind of mixed up, like a puzzle that was put together wrong."

"That's because it's more than one face," Miles concurred. "I took a sample of the six different sections and each one is a different epidermis, like there are strips of six different people's faces sown together—only, there are no marks or anything else to suggest that it's something other than a single visage. But there are six separate DNAs."

Rogers asked the obvious question. "Are any of these faces Brian Clark's?"

"Too tough to tell, Dan. Sorry."

This would cause quite a stir if it got out. Rogers pondered what the coroner had said. He was going to have to keep it quiet somehow. But how? Things like this had a way of reaching the public, especially if you didn't want it to. "What does all this mean, Grady? I mean, what am I supposed to do with this?"

"Let me see if I can confuse you even more," Miles said contritely. "That's him and it's not him."

"Well, that helps. Look...his face was normal last night at the creek." He suddenly backed away from the table. "What in the hell happened, Grady?"

"Don't worry. It's not contagious, or else I'd be in big trouble by now," Miles said evenly. He motioned at the rest of the body. "That's not the only thing that is strange. That fall wasn't enough to do this damage. I can't explain it yet, but I think you've got a real mess on your hands here." He stared at Rogers. Compassion won out. "You might try Father Pritchard. I really believe this is in his area of expertise."

"Thanks, Grady. I'll give him a call," Rogers decreed. "Anything else I should know?"

"Yeah. This whole thing is on videotape. Do you want a copy?"

Rogers nodded and left. He hustled down the corridor and climbed the stairs like a man running from an attacker. At the top of the stairs, he headed for the entrance to the building and threw open the door, gulping in the fresh air.

"You all right, Dan?" Mike Smith, the prosecuting attorney, asked as he approached the doors from the outside. "You look like you've seen a ghost."

Rogers held his hand out toward the attorney. "I'm fine," he told the PA. "It's nothing." He strode off down the sidewalk and headed back to his own office.

"Boy, it's sure a lot quieter out here today than it was last night," Susie observed offhandedly.

Stoney pulled over on the side and turned the motor off. "Didn't the sheriff say that someone found her out here on this gravel road?"

"Yeah, some farmer who lives around here," she replied. "Probably from that house over there," she said, pointing down the road at Delmer and Dora Matthews's house. "Maybe we should go talk to them while we're here," she proposed.

Stoney glanced toward the house and then back down the dirt lane in the direction of Rockhole. "After we take a look down here," he said, indicating the creek. As they approached the fence, Stoney started to spread the wires so Susie could climb through, but he suddenly jerked his hands back.

"What is it?"

He pointed at the wire that still held bits of Mary J.'s flesh and dried blood.

"Oh my god," Susie blurted out. There was no need to explain. They both knew instantly what it was. He moved down the fence away from the offending residual matter. Susie climbed through, trying not to touch the wire that had claimed so much of Mary J.'s flesh and blood. There was nothing on it where they had moved to, but the thought of it was enough to turn her stomach. Stoney quickly followed.

He searched the ground before they went any further and noticed a lot of footprints going in both directions. If there was something here before, it certainly would have been obliterated by all the traffic in and out. He spotted a circle of white paint on the ground and knelt to look it over. After a careful inspection of the area inside the paint, he noticed a trace of red on a rock sticking up out of the road. He assumed it was blood.

"What is it?"

"It looks like blood," he told her.

He stood up and continued along the dirt lane, his attention focused on the ground in front of him. Susie had remained behind staring at the speck of blood. Some twenty feet away, Stoney was kneeling again, inspecting the ground. "Susie, come here," he called out.

She hurried toward him and knelt to see what he'd found this time. There was another circle of white paint with a tree branch in the center of it. "More blood," he informed her. It was on the tree branch. "I'd say these spots of blood belong to Mary J.," he guessed. "Considering the condition of her knees and hands and elbows, it just seems to fit. She must have been in a terrible hurry or not conscious of what she was doing," he concluded.

"Poor Mary J.," Susie spoke for the first time since they started down the dirt road. "She must have been terrified. But from what? What in the world would have scared her that much?" she asked dolefully.

"Good question," he commented. "Come on."

Susie was right beside him as they made their way toward Rockhole. She reached over and took his hand in hers, clasping it tighter the closer they got. Her grasp was like a death grip. He should have been complaining about it. She gave him a furtive glance as they neared the incline descending to the bluff. Something was wrong with him. She wasn't sure what, but he wasn't himself. She shook off a feeling of dread that suddenly overwhelmed her.

They were at the beginning of the path leading to the swimming hole, but Stoney was not moving. He was as stiff as a statue, staring at the tree line—expressionless. Susie was scared. What should she do? Her mind raced, but she thought of nothing. It was a blank.

"Stoney?" He was barely breathing and not moving, not even a twitch. She thought maybe it had something to do with Brian's death. "You just wait here, baby," she said, patting him on the arm. "I'll go down and have a look around, okay?" No response.

Susie started down the slope. About halfway down she started to slide and grabbed a tree branch that hung just inches over her head, but it had a lot of slack and she continued to slide. Slipping and flailing down the path and unable to stop herself, she was slapped in the face and upper chest by the low branch. A wave of nausea swept over her, and she could feel the bitter bile creeping up her throat. By the time she regained her balance at the bottom, she had a split lip, a bloody nose and was throwing up. "Damn it! I hate that shit!" she yelled.

She looked around the spot where she stood but didn't see anything. Carefully, easing her way to the edge of the cliff, she took a quick look around in the water below. "Amazing," she thought out loud. Saline Creek was a clear, sparkling brook that flowed lazily through the countryside. Susie didn't see how something so beautiful and serene could have been the site of such a gruesome thing. "Well, I don't see anything!" she shouted back at Stoney. "It doesn't look like they left much for us. I've seen a lot of this in the movies and this just doesn't—"

"Ahh!" A sudden scream interrupted her.

Susie nearly jumped out of her skin.

"Stoney, what is it?" she cried, racing back up the slope. Even with branches smacking her in the face and her ankles bending sideways on the uneven ground, she still climbed the slope quicker than she descended only minutes before. She broke through the tree line above and stopped in her tracks.

"Stoney!" Susie rushed over and dropped to her knees next to him where he lay on the ground trembling. "What? What is it?" she shouted, grabbing at the air above him. "What can I do? Oh, God help me. *Stoney!*" she screamed at the top of her lungs.

Suddenly he stopped trembling and lay perfectly still. For a minute, Susie thought he was dead, but then she noticed his chest rising and falling as he breathed—barely noticeable—but enough to tell he was alive.

"Come on," she grunted as she lifted him to a standing position. "Let's get you out of here."

Slowly, with a great deal of effort, she helped him back along the dirt lane toward the car. It was more like she dragged him because he was hardly able to move. However, the closer they got to the car, the less she had to work. Whatever had happened, he was recovering from it.

It was a struggle to get him through the barbed-wire gate, but she finally managed it, only ripping his T-shirt once in the process. "What the hell happened?" he asked groggily. She sat him down in the front seat on the passenger's side and knelt next to him.

"You tell me," she said, breathing heavily. "Just as we got there, you went into a trance or something. Do you remember anything?" she asked.

"No," he gasped, rubbing his chest. "Not until we got to the fence." He winced at the lingering pain. "Boy, my chest sure hurts. Did you hit me?" he asked grinning. He gritted his teeth as a spasm of pain ripped through him.

"Stoney, you going to be okay?"

"Damn, that hurt," he exclaimed.

"Should we get you to a doctor," she asked fearfully.

"No, I'm fine," he chided, frowning at himself. "I've never had anything like that happen before. Don't really care to have it happen again."

"I think we ought to go home, Stoney."

"What about talking to the farmer?" he asked, relaxing as the pain finally passed.

"You sure you're up for it?" she asked plainly. "It's been a while since we've had any sleep."

"Agreed. But we should talk to him." Stoney got up to walk around to the driver's side, and a wave of dizziness swept over him, sending him crashing into the car door.

Susie grabbed him and sat him back down in the car. "You're not driving." She slammed the door shut before he could object and quickly darted around to the driver's side, hopping in behind the wheel. She started the motor but didn't put it into gear; she just sat there staring straight ahead deep in thought.

"What's the matter," Stoney asked.

"I didn't see anything," she replied, casting a glance his way.

If she was trying to confuse him, it worked. "I don't understand. What are you talking about?"

"Back at Rockhole," she said, gesturing down the dirt lane. "It looked perfectly normal, like nothing ever happened," she said thoughtfully.

"You had time to look around?" he asked, puzzled.

"Look, you didn't have your little spell until I was already down there," she retorted flippantly. She thought better of what she just said and reworded it. "Well…that's not exactly true. You were in a trance, but I thought you was just thinking about Brian and feeling bad about that."

"So you left me alone—"

"Stoney, I'm tired," she interrupted. "I can't think straight. Can we just go home? Please?" she practically begged. "We've both had a pretty tough day."

"Maybe you're right," he agreed. "I'm feeling a little tired myself. I guess we can come back and talk to the farmer tomorrow."

She smiled as she drove away, looking for a place to turn around. She finally ended up using the Matthews driveway.

Susie stood on the gravel bar on the opposite side of Rockhole. It was the first time she could ever remember standing on sharp rocks like this and not feel them poking through her shoes—except, she wasn't wearing any shoes. She looked down at her bare feet and watched her toes wiggling as if someone else was making them move. "This is really weird," she said out loud. "What's next? Wings and halos?"

That's not what I had in mind.

A deep, resonant voice echoed across the water.

Susie threw up her hands to protect her face, but it was unnecessary. The booming vibrations had stopped right next to her. They just hung in the air like a bad odor. She shuddered to think of what might happen if its fury was unleashed.

The voice mistook her shiver for fear and laughed. She looked around frantically for the source of the voice. She noticed an almost imperceptive movement, as a space on the cliff wavered. Was it possible she asked herself? Had the scientists finally figured out a way to bend space and time? That's what it looked like.

She forced herself to concentrate. If this was an alien invasion, she might—No! It's an image, she decided. It's like an image, and the light glowed from within it.

It became brighter. She drew in her breath sharply.

There was the barely perceptible outline of a person at the center of the image.

She couldn't tell if the image was supposed to be male or female. She gasped. What if it's neither? The image was of long, flowing hair. It hung to the ground. Or was that a hooded cloak?

Her analytical mind was interrupted by a voice.

"I brought you here to see something."

"What are you talking about? I came here on my own...didn't I?" she asked cautiously.

Ha! Ha! Ha! Ha!

"What are you laughing at?" she shouted up at the light. "At least I have the courage to show myself. Are you afraid of me?"

Two separate bolts of lightning shot from its eyes and pierced the darkness over her head. Susie ducked instinctively, a move that was completely unnecessary. It would not hit her unless it wanted to. And if it wanted to, ducking would do no good.

I am afraid of nothing!

Susie covered her ears and fell to the ground. Well, that wasn't true either. She was not touching the ground, she discovered. She was about six inches above it, as though she were on an invisible floor. She was lying in a fetal position, making every effort to keep the excruciating noise from penetrating her ears. She screamed. The voice was so loud, she couldn't hear her own screams.

Suddenly it stopped—and so did she.

It's time we got on with our business. Stand up!

Susie raised herself to a kneeling position. This could get ugly she told herself.

"Why should I?" she asked belligerently. Another lightning bolt from the creature. This time it landed at her feet, causing her to take a step backward. "Who the hell do you think you are?" she shouted at the apparition.

I don't know if you are courageous or just stupid.

"Go to hell," she said, defiantly.

Too late, bitch!

The image raised an arm—at least she assumed it was an arm—and held it extended, pointing at Susie.

Now what? Another lightning bolt? Susie stood erect now, ready to make whatever move was necessary to defend herself. She was a bundle of nervous tension and very skittish. She was fidgeting with her hands when she suddenly felt herself being lifted into the air. "Oh my god! Oh my god! What's happening to me."

Shut up, bitch!

She didn't know why, but Susie refrained from saying anything further. She was sure this being, whether immortal or alien, meant what it said. She also didn't think this was the time to test her mental fortitude.

Susie watched in horror as the image on the bluff was replaced with a different scene. There was Mary J. She was in the hospital but not in the same room. What was happening to her? Oh, she's in labor. Susie smiled. Suddenly something went wrong. Mary J.'s pain turned to fear. She could see the terror in her sister's eyes. Eyes that were focused on her own stomach. Susie looked and gasped at what she saw. She covered her face, but it didn't help. She could still see.

Mary J.'s abdomen had suddenly turned transparent, and they could see the baby. It was struggling. Why was it doing that, she wondered. She continued watching. The baby's struggles became frantic. Then it disappeared. Mary J. wasn't in labor anymore. She was no longer pregnant. "What happened to the baby?" Susie asked, dismayed.

It is with me.

Susie looked on the cliff. There was Mary J.'s baby and the image. Only now it was a person.

It was covered with a heavy black cloak that did a good job of hiding its features. But the face was visible. It was the most terrifying, frightening thing she had ever witnessed. Susie wasn't sure she could find the words to describe what she was looking at. It was like every kind of evil imaginable. Every hideous, vile creature all rolled into one.

Susie should be afraid of this horrible creature. Instead, there was a calmness about her, and it came from those penetrating eyes and the soft, musical voice that surrounded her with its untroubled serenity.

Suddenly, the eyes were looking down at the water.

She directed her own gaze to follow that of the creature's. "*Oh my god! Oh! Oh, God help me! Nooo!*" she screamed and screamed until her voice was a mere screech. Somehow, she forced her eyes from the scene in the water and looked at the creature. "Why?" she whispered in a hoarse voice. "Why did you show me this?"

So that you would remember. This child is mine!

"Nooo! I won't…I won't…I won't…"

"Susie, wake up! Susie! Susie!"

She sat bolt upright in bed. Sweating. Trembling. "I won't!" she shouted one last time. She suddenly realized she was in the familiar surroundings of her own bedroom. She burst into tears while Stoney held her close.

"Honey, what is it?"

"It…it was a nightmare," she stammered. "Oh, Stoney, it was awful. It was so real," she remembered, her terror returning along with her tears.

"Okay, okay. It's all right, baby. You're safe, everything's fine." He held her close and patted her back. "You're safe now. It's okay."

"Oh my god!" she said suddenly. "Stoney, something's going on." He laid his hand on her bare leg and slid it slowly up her thigh as he began to fondle her.

"Yeah, you could say that—"

"No! I'm serious," she blurted, quickly pushing his hand away. "Listen to me! I think something happened out there. Something—I don't know—something alien." He snickered. "No, Stoney," she cried, pulling away from him. "I'm not crazy. You have to listen to me." She explained her nightmare to him.

He listened, intently at first, then smiled at her story. "Come on, Susie. It was just a dream," he replied, unmoved by her tale.

"Why do you want to try and explain away something that might help us figure out what happened to Brian?" she asked, puzzled. "Don't you want to know the truth? Or was all that just talk you were spouting off earlier?"

Stoney finally realized that he wasn't going to get anywhere and reclined back against the pillows. "Of course, I do. But what you're saying is so bizarre."

"That we agree on," she conceded. "But then, this whole thing has been bizarre—not just what happened to Brian, but there's something else," she said with a strange look in her eye. "I think it has something to do with our past."

"Wow!" Stoney stared in amazement at her. "You should be a writer. What does your nightmare have to do with anything?" he asked officiously.

"That's what we have to figure out. That's the mystery that awaits us," she said amorously.

Suddenly feeling better about her nightmare, Susie decided the best way to forget about all that was to make love to her fiancé. She stood up on the foot of the bed.

"What are you doing?" he asked coyly.

In answer to his question, she slipped off her nightgown and stood stark naked in front of him. She dropped to her knees, reached up and pulled his shorts off. Then running her tongue along his thigh, she had just reached his groin and...the phone rang.

"Aw, crap," she cursed the interruption.

"Let it ring," Stoney said, breathing heavily.

"It's too late. The mood is broken," she replied, reaching for the receiver. Stoney fell back on a pillow and stared at the ceiling. "Hello?" Susie answered harshly.

"Uh-oh! I interrupted something," Dala guessed correctly. "I can call back later."

"No, that's all right," Susie replied. "What's up?"

"We need to talk," she said cryptically. "I was going to the hospital to see Mary J. Can you guys meet me in the cafeteria? We'll have some breakfast and talk."

"Both of us?"

"Yes. This concerns Stoney too," she said cryptically. "See you all in half an hour?" Dala asked.

"Half an hour," Susie agreed. She hung up the phone as Stoney disappeared into the bathroom.

She followed him in, and they finished what they had started before the phone rang.

Chapter Six

June 21, 1896

Dear Mama,

This will be a short letter. I don't really feel up to writing, but you have a right to know that our dear little Solomon left us a few days ago. The doctor says he died in his sleep and didn't suffer. I know he thought it was a helpful thing to say, but I felt like scratching his eyes out. I wouldn't have, of course. I was just very upset.

I don't think I can ever be happy again. I feel like someone has torn the heart right out of my chest. It hurts, Mama. I wish you were here. No mother should ever have to go through this. I can't believe God intended for us to suffer so terribly.

Joshua has done his best to be a vessel of solace, but there's nothing like having your mother near at a time like this. Please tell me—just once—that you still love me and that you forgive us.

Well, I better close for now. I tire easily these days. There just doesn't seem to be much reason for living anymore.

With deepest regrets,
Joshua and Jenny

"I was wrong about that weather," Solomon said derisively. "This is the coldest day so far this year, and it looks like it's going to hang on for a while. It's supposed to stay like this for at least a week."

Elise was sitting at the kitchen table listening to her husband ramble on about the weather. But that was not what she was concentrating on. She had made her mind up earlier, after struggling with the decision for some time, to approach Solomon again about the children. He had made it his feelings quite clear and she usually followed his lead. But not this time. She simply couldn't bring herself to agree. They were her children. She was the one who had carried them for nine months in her womb. She was the one who fussed over them, changed their dirty diapers and clothes, bathed them, and saw to it they had everything they needed to grow up healthy and happy.

So this time, she made up her own mind. This time, she would try to turn the tables on her dear husband. She had been receiving letters from Jenny since shortly after they had left here. She had sent only one letter, though. It was to tell her daughter to send any future correspondence to Grace and Francis. She needed time for Solomon to get over what had happened. Receiving letters from their children would only cause the situation to escalate.

Elise didn't know why she had not written any more letters. Each one she read from Jenny tore at her heart. She supposed that deep down, in places where she chose not to frequent, she also felt as her husband did. But a little closer to the surface, where she lived her life, she didn't care what Joshua and Jenny had done. She just wanted her children where she could be a mother to them—and a grandmother to Solomon. Her husband still didn't know that he had a grandchild named after him, she thought sadly. And so far, she hadn't been able to tell him. If she did, she would have to admit to receiving letters from the children. But finally, this morning, she had decided to tell him.

It was long overdue.

So here she sat, her decision made. All that was needed was the courage to carry it out.

"Elise! Elise! Have you even heard a word I've said," Solomon railed at his wife. "I've been going on and on, and all this time you were sitting there daydreaming."

"Solomon, could we talk?" she pleaded with him. "Please?"

"We are talking," he said cautiously.

"Not about the weather," she complained. "We need to talk about something a little more important than whether it's hot or cold or cloudy or clear."

He gave his wife a suspicious look. He could usually read her pretty good, but this time he was clueless. "What is it, Ellie?"

Now that she'd opened the door, now that she had his attention, she was unsure how to proceed. She could only sit there and stare. The longer she hesitated, the staler the air became. At first, she was just scared. But then her lower lip began to quiver. Unable to contain her feelings, tears slowly wound their way down her wrinkled face and fell onto the sparkling clean white tablecloth.

"Ellie?" Solomon walked over to the stove and poured himself a cup of coffee before sitting down across from his wife. He reached over and took her hands, which she had been twisting and wringing constantly. It was about the most affection he had shown his wife in a long time.

"So, Solomon," she started but was unable to finish.

"Whatever it is, we can talk about it," he assured her. "Come on now. What has got you so upset?"

She pulled one of her hands loose and patted his with it. "All right, dear." She reached into her apron pocket and pulled out an envelope. She held it for a minute before commencing. "This is what we need to talk about," she told him, laying the letter on the table where he could reach it. She had purposely laid it facedown, forcing Solomon to pick it up and look at the name on it.

He stared at it, sure he knew what it was. Finally, he picked it up and turned it over. He stared at the return address on the envelope and quickly dropped it. He was correct. He scooted his chair back to get up.

"Solomon. Read the letter. Please!" she begged him, almost in tears again. "I need you to talk to me about it."

"You know my feelings about this," he said, disgustedly and stood up. For some reason, he forced a glance at his wife and what he saw caused him to reconsider. He had never seen her so emotional about anything. Something must be wrong. "All right Ellie, we'll talk," he told her. He picked up the letter and took it out of the envelope.

Most of this battle is won, Ellie told herself. Just getting him to read that letter was the biggest hurdle. *I really think the letter itself will do the rest*, she thought with an obvious optimism. She knew her husband well enough to know his own emotions were swiftly changing as he progressed through the letter.

Elise had expected more of a fight than what she got. She needed to pause and regroup. After all these years, Solomon could still shock her. It was amazing—and one of the reasons she loved him. He could be an impossible person sometimes, plum irritating as a matter of fact. But moments like this was what drew her to him.

When he had finished the letter, Ellie thought she had actually seen a tear in the corner of his eye. "Well?" she asked timidly.

Solomon laid the letter on the table, not putting it back into the envelope. He walked over and put his coat and hat back on. Just moments after reading the letter, all bundled up, he opened the back door to go out. Just before stepping across the threshold, he looked back at his wife. He stared at her for a few seconds and told her, "I have to check on the livestock."

Elise gave him a knowing smile. If it were anyone else, she wouldn't know what to think. But she had known Solomon for so many years, she knew him as well as he knew himself, maybe better. He was going to consider what he had just read. That didn't mean he would change his mind, although she hoped he would eventually, rather it meant he would give it every due consideration. His decision would be dependent on how he worked through it. It was a big step for him. One she hoped would work in her favor this time.

Elise prayed that night. More earnestly than she could ever remember praying.

Sometime before, while he was still working at the bank, Joshua had taken the traveler's advice and invested in a farm at Crater Ridge. He had made the purchase sight unseen but had seen an artist's drawing and a thorough description of the farm and believed it to be more than enough for their purpose. Little did he know that it would end up being their principal home.

Fortunately, it would be sufficient for their current needs. Unknown to either Joshua or Jenny, family of the previous owner had made standing arrangements to have the house cleaned on a regular basis. So in the summer of 1896, when they were run out of their home and made their move to Crater Ridge, Tracy just happened to be in the middle of her routine cleaning.

As they approached the cottage, Jenny couldn't help but remark on its beauty. "Joshua, this is fabulous!" Jenny shrieked. "Some cleaning and some work outside, it will be the envy of the entire area."

They pulled up in front and Jenny jumped from the wagon and hurried to the front door. She opened it tentatively and was surprised at the presence of a strange woman inside. The woman looked like she was about the same age as Jenny but quite a bit heavier. She noted that Joshua liked pretty petite women. "Who are you? What are you doing here?" she asked, stopping short, obviously startled.

The woman came toward her, her arm extended in greeting. "Hello. You must be the new owners," she said, shaking Jenny's hand vigorously. "I'm Tracy Cross."

"Hi," Jenny replied, momentarily taken aback at the woman's aggressiveness. She quickly began to warm to the unexpected friendliness of her new acquaintance. "I'm Jenny Conners and"—she paused, waiting for him to enter—"this is my husband, Joshua." Tracy gave them a cordial smile and motioned for them to come in. "I'm glad to meet you both. I'm in the middle of cleaning the place," she informed them.

Jenny glanced at Joshua and he shrugged at her. "We weren't expecting anyone to be here," she replied.

Tracy nodded as she turned and began picking up some of her cleaning supplies. "It was an arrangement I had with the previous owner. I came in and cleaned on a regular basis. When he told me he had sold it, I agreed to clean one last time for him. It's part of the contract," she pointed out.

"It's a...pleasant surprise," Jenny acknowledged. "I'll help you finish."

"Thank you," Tracy replied, accepting the assistance graciously. "Well, we'll be neighbors. I live just down the road. The next house to the east. You can't miss it. Just look for the one with a hundred kids running around," she said jokingly.

"Oh! O-okay," she stammered helplessly. Suddenly, Jenny turned and ran out of the house.

Tracy stared after her. "Oh my goodness. What did I say?" she asked helplessly, spreading her hands in total confusion.

Joshua looked first at the door that Jenny had just run through and then at Tracy staring at it. "It's all right, Tracy. It-it's not your fault." He needed to go see about Jenny, but he also needed to explain to Tracy. "We lost a baby on the trip here," he said by way of explanation before going out the door himself.

"I'm sorry," was all she said. Ever since that incident they had become the best of friends, with the unfortunate circumstance of their meeting soon forgotten.

Joshua had been down to the pond to see if it was frozen over. It was. Being frozen solid meant he didn't have to worry about his cows wandering into the pond and drowning. He couldn't afford to lose any. It had taken him a long time to build up his livestock. As he came in the door, he began talking to his wife. "Well, the pond's still frozen. It should stay that way for quite a while. We're not supposed to have a warm up for at least a week." He was stamping the snow off his boots and suddenly realized he was talking to himself.

He shed himself of the heavy outdoor gear, swept the remaining snow from his boots, and started through the house in search of her. "Jenny? Where are you, honey?"

There was no response. When he had searched through all the rooms on the main floor of the house, he started up the stairs. One step at a time at first, but then he began to grow concerned and picked up the pace, taking the steps two at a time.

"Jenny?" he called out, still only halfway up the stairs. There was a note of panic in his voice. It had only been a short time since they lost little Solomon, and he was unsure of what she might do. She had been in quite a funk since that fateful day.

"Jenny? Jenny?" he called again. At the top of the stairs, he looked all around quickly and then sprinted for their bedroom. He gave it a hasty inspection and then headed for the bathroom. Just as he was about to enter, he heard someone singing a song softly.

It was coming from the nursery. Joshua screwed up his courage and took a couple of steps toward the baby's room. As he drew closer, he could make out the tune she was singing. It was the song she used to sing to Solomon when she rocked him to sleep.

Dear God, please don't let her go crazy, he prayed silently.

He had reached the door of the nursery and leaned forward, peering into the darkened, desolate, memory-filled room. At first, he didn't see her. He stood still for a minute letting his eyes adjust to the dim light.

There she was! Sitting in the rocker. Her posture was like it would be if she were holding a baby and gently rocking it. She was even making little gestures and noises, as if…as if Solomon was really there. "Jenny?" he called out softly.

She looked at him briefly and crossed her lips with her finger. "Shh! He just went to sleep," she whispered.

"Oh my god!" It had happened. She had finally slipped over the edge. He had wondered about it. She had never cried. Not when the doctor had pronounced Solomon dead. Not at the wake. Not even at the funeral.

Joshua approached her slowly, not because of her shushing, he just didn't know what to do about this kind of thing. He didn't want to see her end up in a sanitarium. There must be something he could do. "Jenny," he murmured, resting his hand on her arm as he knelt beside her.

"Isn't he a beautiful little boy," she said, just a shadow of sorrow on her face.

Joshua caressed her face with his other hand. She kissed it as a sigh escaped her half-parted lips.

Regardless of the situation, she was content. "I love you," she said.

"I love you too," he said mournfully. "Jenny, you have to stop this." He was reluctant to bring her out of her reverie, but she needed to come back to reality. "He's dead, Jenny. Nothing you do will bring him back."

"Stop!" she cried, clamping her hand over his mouth.

"Jenny! You must face reality. Solomon is dead. Our baby is gone, and no amount of insanity will bring him back." Tears were beginning to stream down his weather-beaten face. "Jenny, I love you and I can't bear to see you like this. Please, please come back to me." His head fell to the arm of the wooden rocker and hit it with a resounding crack.

Jenny had been sitting perfectly still. Something he said had made its way into her subconscious mind. She wasn't pretending anymore. It had really happened. Her little baby boy was dead. The shock of that devastating event suddenly gripped her with a hand of steel. It was more than her mind could accept at the moment, and she cried out in agony.

"*Nooo!* Oh god, no!" She stood up, took one step toward the crib, and fell to her knees. She lifted her arms toward the ceiling. "*Nooo!*" she screamed again. She was about to fall forward when Joshua caught her up and held her in his arms.

"You go ahead, darling," he whispered in her ear. "Let it out."

Jenny tried to wrench herself free of his grasp, but he held on to her, afraid that if he let go, he might lose her forever. She finally gave up and fell into his arms, crying and crying. She cried until she was sure there were no more tears left—and then she cried some more.

The whole time, Joshua held her, comforted her, reassured her. They stayed that way for a long while. But time didn't matter. This was an event that was as timeless as the earth itself. From the very beginning, people had wept for departed loved ones. When it didn't seem to matter anymore, she separated herself from Joshua's grasp.

He continued to hold her at arm's length, peering into her eyes, trying to see past the hurt and the pain that filled them. He felt guilty for being the one who had to tell her. It hurt him, like it was happening all over again.

"He's really gone," she said with a hollow emptiness to her voice.

Tears sprang to Joshua's eyes, but for a different reason than Jenny's. He realized that he had her back. He pulled her close and hugged her until he was sure she would break in half.

"He's really gone," Joshua echoed her.

The harsh realities of winter had given way to the pleasant brightness of spring. The death of their son was but a painful memory—certainly, it lingered still, and more certainly, it was unpleasant—that was shuffled into the dark recesses of their minds with the move and making of new friends.

Tracy had been a valuable resource during Jenny's adjustment period. True, it was a rather clumsy beginning, but one that both women were able to put aside for the sake of a new friendship. Tracy understood Jenny's feelings, though somewhat limited, in that she had suffered a miscarriage with her first child. It was never discovered what the cause was, but it never happened again. In fact, she had become extremely fertile and resilient. She and her husband had managed five boys and three girls, in a somewhat mixed-up order.

Joshua had plowed through his feelings with the strength of a man who rarely showed emotion, especially in front of others. And when he did, it usually had to do with Jenny. He was very protective of her. Ergo, the incident with Reverend Weeks. So suffice it to say, he was overjoyed at the closeness Jenny had found in Tracy's friendship. It allowed him to pursue what he had determined was his new life's work.

Cattle farming.

Joshua had started out with one cow and one bull. He had nursed them through the winter—and done a pretty good job of it, evidently—feeding them plenty and taking special care of them so that with the advent of spring, they had produced a calf. Now their livestock numbered three. Joshua had it all worked out. If the bull did his job correctly, they could have a small herd by the time they had to think about raising a family.

The birth of the calf was news he had to share with Jenny immediately. He busted through the back door, stomping and wiping his boots on the old braided rug that they kept there for just that purpose. The spring rains had been plentiful so far. The barnyard was nothing but a mud hole. Of course, the hogs he raised for food did plenty to add to that situation, but he never complained about the circumstances. Always laughed about it.

"Jenny!" he shouted, still stomping and wiping. Realizing disdainfully that he would never get all the mud off, he removed his boots—Jenny would kill him if he got even one trace of mud on her clean floors—and raced through the house in search of his wife. "Jenny, where are you? I've got some great news." He had looked in every room downstairs and started upstairs, when he was suddenly overcome with that same nagging feeling of foreboding as before. This had a familiar ring to it.

Joshua slowed his pace, hesitating as he cleared the top few steps. "Jenny?" he called out softly. This time he didn't bother to search the other rooms on the second floor. He started immediately, if not hesitantly, toward the nursery. He was sure that was where he would find her. The reason for the feeling was unclear, but it was a definite feeling. "Jenny?"

He approached the door casting an occasional glance beyond the room, as though he expected her to emerge from a different room down the hall. However, he knew where she would be. He just didn't know what to expect from her. Maybe this time she had gone over the edge. Maybe this time she—he couldn't think about it. The possibility of losing her would be more than he could bear.

Joshua stepped through the doorway of the nursery. "Jenny?" She was sitting in the rocking chair, moving back and forth in a gentle rocking motion. She didn't cradle an invisible baby as before. Instead, she was looking at her stomach and rubbing it with her left hand. Just inside the door, Joshua stood and delivered his good news. "We have an addition to the family," he told her, trying his best to make it sound exciting. "A calf just born, late this afternoon."

Jenny raised her head and stared at Joshua. It wasn't the blank, meaningless stare he expected. It was more of a satisfied, contented look. He was caught off guard. "Jenny? What is it, darling?"

She smiled. "Our family is going to grow even larger."

Now it was Joshua's turn to stare blankly. "What do you mean? I don't understand," he said slowly. "Are you trying to say that—"

"That I'm going—that we're going to have another baby," she finished for him.

Joshua hadn't moved. He couldn't believe it. Was this for real? "Jenny, don't tease me," he said, his cheerful mood swiftly vanishing.

"Honest!" she exclaimed, her own excitement bubbling over now. She got up from the chair.

"Really?" he asked, still not completely convinced.

Jenny couldn't believe his reticence. She was sure he would be as happy about the news as she was. "Joshua? Don't you want another baby?" she asked, her heart sinking momentarily. Suddenly, he grinned at her and she knew he was funning with her. "Sometimes you can be so irritating." But she too was smiling.

Joshua sat in the rocker with Jenny in his lap. "When I couldn't find you, I thought maybe you had regressed," he began in a subdued voice. "I thought that finally…the presence of Tracy's children had gotten to you, that it had pushed you over the edge. Then when I saw you in here, my heart sank. I didn't know what to do." His shoulders slumped, and his head lowered until it rested on her breast. A slight jerking of his head was the only indication that he wept. Finally, he continued in a voice so quiet, Jenny struggled to hear him. "I couldn't go on if I lost you. You are my whole life. I'm nothing without you. Do you know that?" He raised his head and stared at her through tear-filled eyes. "I won't live without you."

Jenny turned so that she cupped his face in her hands, wiping the tears away with her kisses. "I will always be right here with you. Joshua? Always." She pressed her lips against his, kissing him long and lovingly. It seemed to strengthen him.

"I love you," he said fondly, laying his head once again on her breast. She stroked his hair as he gently, lovingly moved his hand over her abdomen. "I can't believe we're going to have another baby. It's like a miracle. A miracle from God," he said in a faint but unmistakably distinct tone.

"A miracle from God," Jenny readily agreed.

March 13, 1898

Dear Mama,

Even in the face of disaster, things manage to work themselves out. We will have another child to fill the void left by our dear departed Solomon. Even though it's been nearly two years, it seems like it was only yesterday that we laid him to rest.

We are both very happy and look forward to the birth of our next child. I hope this will bring you some measure of happiness as well. God knows no one can replace little Solomon, but this child will surely brighten many of the darkened moments

I wish you would write. Has our baby's death burdened you so much? If so, I'm sorry about that. I wish I could have offered you some comfort. It must have been very hard for you too.

Please write and tell me you still love us.

All our love,

Joshua and Jenny

"Tracy! You in there somewhere?"

"I'm in the kitchen. Come on in," she shouted over the din of playing children.

Jenny made her way slowly to the kitchen stepping over toys and artfully dodging other debris and paraphernalia, as though she was experienced with years of child-rearing. Now, however, it had a much better result than before she found out she was with child again.

"Looks like you could use some help digging your way out of that jungle in the living room." She laughed as she walked through the kitchen doorway.

"Now don't you make fun of my disordered life," she pointed an accusing finger at her friend. "It took me years to get my kids to that level of training." Tracy joined her neighbor to alleviate some of the strain of daily child-rearing. "Have a seat," she said, indicating the kitchen table, "I'll get you a cup of coffee."

"What were you busy doing when I rudely interrupted?" Jenny asked.

"I was in the middle of planning a couple of things," she answered. "One was what to fix for supper, and two was whether or not I wanted to clean up that mess you stumbled through in the other room. Neither of those, by the way, is very appealing to me."

"Well, why don't you grab a cup yourself and join me," she coaxed her friend.

Tracy poured them both a cup and handed one to Jenny. She sat down slowly as she eyed her friend with a thoughtful contemplation. "You've got something on your mind. What is it? What's going on?"

Jenny had been simply bursting with the exhilarating news of her newest secret. She was able to control her tongue, but her bubbly spirit had long since overflowed. Something Tracy had picked up on immediately.

"I'm going to have a baby."

"Oh, Jenny. I can't tell you how happy I am for you." She got up and went around the table to give her friend a hug. "When? When is it due?"

"September."

Tracy did some quick figuring in her head. "You're already three and a half months and you're just now telling me?" She sat back down and did her best to look pained. She took a quick sip of coffee and then pushed her lower lip out as if she were pouting. For all her efforts, she might as well have done nothing at all. They had been friends long enough now that Jenny knew it was a ploy.

"I only found out today myself, silly."

"Have you told Joshua yet?"

"To be sure. He was the first to know," she admitted. "Oh, Tracy, you should have been there. It was the best surprise I have ever given him."

"Tell me how you did it. And don't leave out one scrumptious little detail, you serpentine devil," Tracy said with an evil grin on her face. Jenny had told her right after they became close that if she ever got pregnant again, she was going to break it to Joshua in a completely unorthodox manner.

She spent the next several minutes detailing the extravagant way in which she fulfilled her promise. "I really had him going," she finished with a flair.

They talked and giggled on and on for most of the morning like a couple of schoolgirls carrying on about some boy. They told each other everything. All their secrets. It was as though they grew up together and had been lifelong friends.

All their secrets—except one. Jenny never divulged the truth about her and Joshua. And never would. That was one secret she would take to her grave. They had made a pact to keep it just between them. Never to allow what happened before to ever happen again.

Their past was locked up forever. Only they could unlock it.

There was an insistent knocking. It started with a few quick raps. Then it turned into a series of rapid-fire strikes. No beginning. No end. Just one long continuous irritating knock.

Grace was in the sitting room reading. Francis was just returning from carrying some magazines upstairs. They both arrived at the door about the same time.

"What on earth?" Grace gasped, clutching her dress just above the heart.

"Elise? Are you all right?" Francis asked hurriedly.

Elise jerked open the screen door. "May I come in?" she asked, shoving her way into the foyer. "I have to sit down. I ran all the way over here."

"Elise, what on earth has happened?" Grace pressed for a response. "Francis, get her a glass of water."

"Of course." She scurried off toward the kitchen while Grace steered Elise to a chair.

"No, I'm all right," Elise assured her. "It's Solomon." She was still breathing heavily from her jog to Francis and Grace's house. Francis returned with the water and she gulped it down quickly.

"Solomon? Something has happened to Solomon?" Grace asked hastily.

"Yes!" she almost shouted.

"Oh my god!" Francis gasped, covering her mouth with her hand. "What is it? What has happened to him?" she asked in a half whisper.

"I showed him a letter from Jenny," she began excitedly. "He wouldn't look at it at first, but then he finally picked it up, and when he realized what it was, he read it. When he was through, he threw it down in disgust but not before I saw what it truly did to him. It had an amazing effect on him. He actually had a tear in his eye. When he's had some time to think about it, I know he'll come around. Isn't it great?" she finished even more excited than when she began.

"I would never have believed it," Grace said with brutal honesty.

"Truly amazing," Francis added.

"Oh, by the way," Grace said as she got up and went toward the fireplace. She took something from the mantle and handed it to Elise. "This came yesterday," she offered.

"Oh. It's a letter from Jenny." She took it in her hands, holding it gingerly. Afraid it might vanish into thin air if she treated it roughly or took her eyes off it. "Can I read it here?" she asked.

"Please," Grace indicated.

Elise removed the letter from its envelope. Carefully, she unfolded it, caressed its edges, and turned it over and over in her hands. Eventually, she began to read. It was short and concise. By the time she finished, her face was tear streaked, but she was smiling. It was several minutes before she was able to say anything. Grace and Francis were beginning to get worried. "Jenny is with child," she finally spoke.

"Praise God," Grace murmured.

"Yes, praise God," Francis agreed, nodding.

"I have to go home now. Thank you both for everything you've done for me," she muttered. "You'll never realize what stalwarts you've both been to me during this time." She gave each of the sisters a hug. "Thank you," she said again.

The months passed by with the brilliance of eras that stood out in history. They eclipsed each other, engulfing and arousing their occupants, like the words of a splendid book. Their lives were as busy and colorful as the changing leaves on the trees that dotted the hillsides. The melancholy days of their past were soon replaced with the joyous anticipation of their future. Those days were mere shadows on the horizon. Gone—but not forgotten, installed in the dark recesses of their minds, where they would continue in repose, collecting dust, until some unfortunate, deplorable event caused them to surface again.

Then one morning in late September, it was time.

Joshua ran down the road to the Crosses' house and beat on the door with a vengeance. "Tracy! Tracy!"

"Whoa, Joshua. What's the matter?" she asked.

"It's…Jenny." He huffed and puffed, grabbing breathes between words. "It's…it's time," he finally blurted out. "Would you go stay with her? I'm going after Esther. She's going to midwife for us."

"Let me grab a jacket and I'm right with you," she said, stepping up her pace.

Solomon was born in the clinic before they had moved here, where there were adequate medical facilities. But here in the country, where towns were far apart and much smaller, facilities found in the big cities didn't exist here. There was old Dr. Pogue, but he was eight miles away in town. He would never make it in time for the actual birth. Esther would send for him later. It was customary for the mother and child to be examined by a physician after the delivery. But most of the work was up to the midwives.

So this was a new experience for Joshua and Jenny. And one in which Joshua was extremely tense. He hitched the horse to the wagon in record time and disappeared down the road.

Tracy did everything she could to make Jenny comfortable. She wasn't an experienced midwife and prayed Joshua would return with Esther before the baby decided to make its entrance into the world. Of course, she had given birth to eight babies herself, but it wasn't the same as helping another woman with hers. She just didn't want anything to go wrong.

"Ahh!" Jenny screamed as another contraction hit. "God, it hurts," she roared through clenched teeth. "Tracy, this doesn't feel right." She grabbed her friend's hand and squeezed it with the might of a woodsman. "Oh, God! Please don't let anything be wrong with my baby," she prayed as the pain subsided.

"Jenny, you're going to be all right," Tracy said without much confidence. "And so is this baby. You just relax now."

Jenny tensed again as another contraction hit. She squeezed Tracy's hand with one of hers as her other hand beat ferociously on the bed. When the pain became too much to bear, she let out another scream.

"Breathe, Jenny. Come on now. You know how to do this. Breathe. In and out. In and out," she coaxed as she took deep breaths herself. "Jesus, I'm going to pass out if I keep this up."

Again, the pain subsided. Jenny relaxed her grip on Tracy's hand as her body relaxed on the bed. She just lay there for a few seconds. "How long between contractions?" she asked with a breathy voice.

"You're down to a minute," Tracy said, smiling down at her. "Think you can hold on until they get here?" Tracy quizzed her friend. "I don't have any experience at this, you know? I'm usually the one doing what you're doing. The one taking the advice," she said, hopeful that Jenny would understand.

"Tracy. I'm scared. I don't like the way this feels," Jenny cried.

Tracy gave her hand a consolatory squeeze. It was the only thing she could think of to do. She hoped it was enough. She looked down at the face of her newest and dearest friend. It was a face wet with perspiration and tears, but it was more than that. She thought she detected—well, it was really strange, but she thought for a second it was—a darkness. Like a shadow creeping along the ground as the sun sets. This was ridiculous. Jenny just had her skittish with her talk of something going wrong. But still—

"Tracy, if anything happens to me, promise me—"

"Now that's enough of that. In the first place, nothing's going to happen. Like I told you before, you and the baby are going to be fine. Now, relax."

"What was the second place? Ohh!" Jenny screamed as a contraction hit. "*Oh! Oh! Oh!* Tracy, do something," she yelled. And then suddenly she let out a bloodcurdling scream that was heard a mile down the road where Joshua and Esther were traveling as they approached the house.

"My god," Esther said aloud.

"What? What is it?" Joshua asked, desperation creeping into his voice.

"Hurry! Hurry!" she admonished him.

Joshua didn't wait for anything further or to ask any more questions. He grabbed the whip and snapped it over the heads of the two horses. "Hiya! Hiya!" he yelled, snapping the whip again.

Jenny had her feet pulled up like they were in stirrups. She was holding her abdomen now and yelling with excruciating pain.

"Hold on, Jenny," her friend urged her. "I can hear the wagon coming down the road. Esther will be here in a moment." She was almost crying herself now. Here her friend was writhing in obvious pain, and she couldn't do a thing to help.

Suddenly she heard Joshua and Esther as they burst through the front door and clambered up the stairs. "Esther, thank God you're here. Something's wrong," she reported to the midwife.

"Jenny, what is it. What do you think is wrong?" Esther asked softly. "Talk to me, Jenny. I need you to tell me some things." She glanced over at Joshua and motioned toward the door. "You, go make some coffee or something."

When he had gone out the door, she told Tracy, "We need to get her underwear off. Then I need you to get me some rags and a bowl of warm water."

When they had removed Jenny's undergarments, Esther checked her for dilation and position of the baby. "Oh my god!" she exclaimed.

"What is it?" Tracy asked quickly.

"The baby is breeched. It's turned the wrong way," she whispered. "This is not good. Quickly, get me the rags and water." She continued to work with Jenny after Tracy left. "Young lady, your baby is breeched. It is coming out wrong. I'm going to see if I can turn it. It will be painful, but you must endure, okay?"

"Just do something," Jenny urged through gritted teeth.

Joshua had been sitting at the kitchen table for what seemed like forever. He had gotten up several times and started for the stairs, but each time he returned to his seat to wait some more.

He stared into his coffee cup while sitting at the table. Suddenly, he became still. His surroundings disappeared, and the darkness returned. The calm musical voice was calling him again.

Joshua.

"Who's there?" he asked flatly.

You know who it is, Joshua.

The voice completely wrapped itself around him and filled him with its warm, euphonious inflection.

Your time is coming—

"Not yet!" Joshua shouted. "Please. Our baby is being born, at this very instant."

No. Not yet, Joshua. But soon, very soon.

The darkness disappeared. The kitchen returned to its normal state, and everything was right again.

Just when he thought the baby was never coming—he heard it crying. He bolted from his chair at the table and raced up the stairs. At the door, he didn't know whether to knock, or go on in, or wait to be invited. "This is stupid," he said to himself. But evidently, it was loud enough for Tracy to hear.

"Come on in, Joshua," she said, pulling him by the arm. "You have a beautiful baby girl."

"Is she all right?" he asked as he looked at Jenny. He walked over and knelt next to her, taking her hand in his. He brushed back her wet, matted hair and bent over to kiss her.

Esther had finished cleaning the baby, for the moment, and brought her over and laid her next to Jenny.

"Isn't she beautiful?" the new mother asked.

"She's gorgeous. And so is her mother," Joshua replied. He was smiling, but at the same time, he was crying.

"Joshua?"

"I thought you was going to die," he muttered through quivering lips. He raised her hand and kissed it gently. "I thought I was going to lose you," he whimpered.

"Oh, no. No," she consoled him as best she could. "I would never leave you," she promised.

"Speaking of leaving," Esther interrupted. "I have to get back. You are not the only one expecting a baby this week." She smiled at Jenny. "The baby is fine. I sent for the doctor. He should be around soon. You rest," she said, pointing at Jenny. "And take good care of that baby."

"Don't you worry," Jenny replied. "That is one thing you can count on."

"Joshua, I need a ride."

"Of course," he apologized. "I'll be right there." He stood up and kissed both Jenny and the baby.

"I'll stay with her till you get back," Tracy vowed. "Now, go on. Get out of here," she said, pushing him out the door.

"Yahoo!" he yelled as he descended the stairs to the ground floor.

September 30, 1898

Dear Mama,

I finally have some good news to tell you. We are the proud parents of a beautiful baby girl. Her name is Diane Elise. She was born last Thursday morning at ten forty-five. She weighs seven pounds, four ounces and is nineteen inches long. Her hair is so light it's hardly noticeable, but it's thin and silky.

Joshua simply beamed at the news that this was a girl. She was a breech birth, but we had a very good midwife. She did an expert job of bringing our little girl into the world. It started out a very difficult delivery but ended up well.

Although we were devastated over the death of our first baby, they say time will heal all wounds. But somehow? I don't think this wound will ever close. It still oozes with the poison of a wasted life and remains severely bruised when the subject is broached. Maybe someday it won't hurt as much, but for now, we will make every attempt to enjoy our little evening star.

Well, guess what. It's feeding time. I'll close this for now and hope to hear from you soon. I look for a letter every day. Please, please write. I need to hear from you.

Our love to you both,

Joshua, Jenny, and Diane

Basically, Elise was a chicken at heart. She would rather do just about anything to avoid an argument. It had always been easier to ignore a problem than to deal with it. She had to work very hard at approaching Solomon about anything that had to do with Joshua and Jenny. But somehow, some way, she had to bring it up again. They had to talk some more.

Elise waited until they were through with supper before broaching the subject. She had planned on it all day. And she had been as nervous as a cat in a room full of rocking chairs, thinking about nothing else.

Solomon went into the living room after supper, which was his habit, to sit and read awhile. Elise finished the dishes and joined him. She picked up her knitting and just sat with it on her lap. This was as good a time as any, she figured. "Solomon, it's time we continued our conversation from before."

"About what?" he asked, distracted by what he was reading.

"About Joshua and Jenny," she said anxiously. And then she moved on quickly before he could interrupt. "We never really finished our conversation. I'd like to continue."

Solomon had known this was coming, but he hoped it would somehow be forgotten. "I've given it some thought since we talked," he said evenly. And then he stopped. What more was he supposed to say? He had been totally against this thing. But he loved his kids and missed them. So what should he do now? He had taken a position, and Elise knew it. If he backed down now, he would appear to be a man with no principles. But then, that was what she wanted. She wouldn't care if he looked good or bad, firm or indifferent. She only cared about those kids. And he couldn't blame her. Deep down, he did too. So maybe he should just give in and, what, forget about his values? Forget his religious beliefs? God, what a dilemma.

"You have?" Elise asked shocked. This was not the response she expected. She had prepared herself for an argument. She had thought of all the right answers. She had even worked out an answer, readied herself for every contingency. So now what should she do? Just let it go? Pursue with more questions? Dear God, life was always so complicated.

"You sound surprised," he said in a small voice, not his customary booming bass.

"I-I…I am," she finally managed to eke out. This was ridiculous. "Solomon, I know what you thought about Joshua and Jenny when this thing happened. And I confess, to some degree…I felt the same way—at first. But, Solomon, they're our kids. And I miss them—terribly!" She spat those last words out as her tears began to fall.

Solomon sat in his chair across the room. Paralyzed. How would he ever resolve this? How would he ever make the right decision?

He returned to his reading.

CHAPTER SEVEN

Dala arrived at the hospital ahead of Stoney and Susie. She decided to look in on Mary J. while she was waiting for them. As she walked down the long hall toward her best friend's room, she thanked her lucky stars that she had never had to spend any time in a hospital. They were the dreariest places she could imagine. What she had seen on TV was enough to keep her away. But that wasn't the reason for her dislike.

When she was a young girl, her mother had been in a terrible car accident. In the remaining days of her mother's life, which were spent in the intensive care unit at the hospital, Dala practically lived there. After that, she had made a solemn promise to herself not to go to the hospital unless they carried her in on a stretcher—unconscious.

One twenty-one. Mary J.'s room.

Dala pushed the door open and peeked around the edge of it. She could see the foot of Mary J.'s bed. She leaned a little further into the room. It was empty except for her friend, who lay on her back, two pillows under her head so that she was slightly inclined.

She just looks like she's asleep, Dala thought with nervous curiosity.

She wasn't sure what she expected, but she didn't think this was it. Except for a few bruises and some bandages, which she figured were cuts or scratches, she looked fine. Except, of course, that she was oblivious to her surroundings.

It was hard to believe that someone so sweet and kind as Mary J. did anything to deserve this kind of treatment. Why did God allow such ghastly things to happen to good people? You know? Why couldn't stuff like this happen to bad people, people whose "I don't give a shit" attitude and "I'm an ignorant bastard" behavior merited such callous tragedy in their lives?

Mary J.'s right hand had an IV hooked to the back of it. Dala picked up her friend's left hand and held it for a while. It felt cold, lifeless almost. At that moment, Dala desperately wanted to wrap her hands around the neck of the person who had done this. She wanted to give tit for tat. An eye for an eye. She wanted to clamp her hand on the bastard's balls and cut 'em off. And then stuff 'em down his throat. She stiffened at the callousness of her own thoughts. It was not like her to talk or think that way. She needed to clear her mind of the evil that filled it. Dala stood still with her eyes closed and let her mind drift to a time of more pleasant events. She thought of the fun she, Mary J., Brian, and Casey had had in the past. She thought of the time they all went canoeing on the rapids. They had wound up drenched because of their inexperience at the sport but then busted out laughing at the comedy of their situation. Still she held on to Mary J.'s hand as a single tear rolled down her cheek to her chin and dropped onto the cold, almost lifeless flesh of her best friend.

"Please be all right," she said out loud. "Please, Mary J."

Stoney picked up the tray of food he had bought for himself and Susie and walked a few feet from the cashier, where he stood and searched the room for Susie. He saw her waving her arm and headed in that direction.

"I thought Dala would be here by now," he said, setting the tray down on the table. Susie helped him clear the tray, after which he slid it over onto the table next to them.

"Yeah, so did I—there she comes," Susie proclaimed, pointing at the hallway outside the glass partition, which separated it from the cafeteria. She waved at Dala until she got her attention. Dala walked in through the exit door and ambled over to their table.

"Sit down and tell me what you want to eat," Stoney ordered, kicking a chair out from under the table. "I'll go get it for you. My treat." She gave him her order and then picked up his coffee cup and started drinking from it. The two women exchanged informal chit-chat while they waited for Stoney to return.

While he waited his turn to pay the cashier, Stoney let his gaze wander around the room settling on the two gals he was having breakfast with. Susie, he knew very well, since they had been seeing each other for—what was it now—six years? And engaged for two years? He liked her a lot. She took care of herself; she didn't overeat. Still had the slim, gorgeous figure she had in high school. He loved just touching her. It sent electric sensations down his spine—not to mention the other affected parts.

Dala, on the other hand, was also a striking woman. She was probably one of the most beautiful redheads his eyes ever had the pleasure of seeing. Her hair wasn't flaming red. It was more of a deep, glistening auburn. She was a year or so older than Susie, but unlike his fiancé, she was tall and slender. At five feet nine, she carried herself very well. *Very well indeed*, he thought as he stared at her. Stoney admired beautiful women. He wondered if that was the reason, he and Susie hadn't gotten married yet. Maybe, subconsciously, he still wanted to be single. But he did love her.

"Sir!" he was suddenly aware of the cashier calling to him. He moved forward and paid for Dala's breakfast and then joined the women.

"Okay, what's so important?" he asked Dala as he began munching on his pancakes.

She swallowed the mouthful of toast and coffee and then looked around like someone might be listening to their conversation. "Remember yesterday when Daniel and Sadie picked up Michele?" They both nodded. "Well, I didn't think much about it at the time, but there was something Sadie said that stuck in my mind. I woke up this morning thinking about it. Anyway, I thought you two should know." She took another sip of coffee.

"Well…you've certainly got my curiosity aroused," Stoney said, urging her to continue. *That's not all that's aroused me*, he thought silently. *But unfortunately, she's a married woman.* "What should we know?" he prompted her.

Dala glanced around again with an air of conspiracy and then leaned in toward the middle of the table. "Among all their bickering and carrying on, I heard the word incest mentioned."

Susie frowned at Dala. Stoney's expression never changed, even when he finally spoke. "I don't understand. What does that mean? Were they talking about someone in our family?"

"I can't answer that," Dala replied. "Sadie was so distressed, she didn't make any sense. And Daniel kept telling her to shut up. At one point, I thought he was going to hit her. Anyway, they went back and forth for quite a while. And then in the middle of this big argument they were having, Sadie let it slip that, it was their fault. The incest, she said. I started to ask her what she meant by that, but Daniel changed the subject and then I forgot all about it until I woke up this morning." She shrugged. "That's what I wanted to tell you."

Stoney and Susie peered at each other across the table. Susie was the first to speak this time. "Do you suppose they would give us a straight answer if we asked them a direct question?"

"I don't think they'll tell us a damned thing," Stoney proclaimed loudly.

"Stoney, keep your voice down," Susie admonished him. "We don't need the whole hospital knowing about our family problems." Even without her reprimand, Stoney knew he had spoken a little too loudly. He glanced around to see if anyone had noticed. But everyone seemed concerned with their own conversations.

No sooner had she scolded him than Susie regretted it. She reached over and clasped his hand. "Sorry. This whole thing's got me on edge."

Dala stood up. "I've got people coming for appointments. I'm going to have to leave."

"Thanks, Dala," Susie sighed. She stifled a yawn but not before Stoney caught a glimpse of it. "If anything comes of this, we'll let you know."

The tall redhead walked away. Stoney waited until she was out of sight before he spoke again. "You look tired. Why don't you go home and get some sleep? I'll be home later." He fully expected a battle from her. Normally, she didn't like being slighted in anything important. But today she relented.

Susie stifled another yawn before it too was noticed. "Where are you going?" she asked wearily.

"I think I'll pay Mom and Dad a visit," he said thickly.

She gave him a casual glance and said, "Yeah, I think I'll go see Mary J. for a while and then go home."

Stoney walked as far as Mary J.'s room with her and then started for the main entrance doors. "Susie," he called after her. "How are you going to get home?"

"I'll get a cab." She waved and disappeared into Mary J.'s room, thinking to herself that she'd just walk home. Stoney waited until she went into the room before leaving.

Driving out of town on Highway 38, Stoney found it hard to believe that on such a nice day like this, his family was facing such tragic circumstances. Brian was dead, Mary J. was lying on a hospital bed in a coma, and then to top it all off, he found out there may be some deep, dark family secret that could break their family apart. At the very least, it would tear at the seams.

He didn't think he stood a chance of getting any information from Daniel or Sadie, but he had to try.

The wind blew through his hair as he rode out of town with his car window down. It was kind of a blustery day but a great one to be outside. He slowed to make the turn off Highway 38 onto County Road 135. The county road was graveled, compared to the paved state road. It was also rough and dusty, but Stoney enjoyed the ride on that road, basically because of the way it skirted the ridge, following the base all the way around the hill. It was a nice drive with plenty of view and trees along the roadside.

Daniel and Sadie lived around on the south side of the ridge, on a spread across the road. After thirty minutes of driving, he turned into their driveway and crossed a cattle guard. Stoney wasn't a farmer and never wanted to be one, but he liked living in a farming community like Crater Ridge. Simple things like crossing a cattle guard, with the rumble they made when the tires contacted the metal bars was music to his ears.

He pulled up in front of the house, already dreading the confrontation that was imminent. Daniel waited on the front porch, as Stoney got out of the car. "Son, what brings you all the way out here? You just need to get out of town for a while?"

"Hi, Dad," Stoney greeted his father. "No, I've been doing some snooping around, trying to figure out what happened to Mary J."

"Any luck?"

"Not much yet," he said casually. "Mom inside?" Stoney hated what he was about to do. But it had to be done—and he had rather it was him than the sheriff or a deputy. Sadie came to the door at the mention of her name.

"Stoney," she said cautiously. "What brings you out?" She still hadn't opened the screen door.

Stoney fidgeted around for a minute, unable to bring himself to deliver the bad news. He opened his mouth, but nothing came out.

Daniel was growing tired of his son's silence. "Stoney, if you've got something to say, just get on with it." Stoney nodded in agreement with his father. That was the best approach. Just get it over with quick.

"Brian is dead." He heard Sadie gasp and Daniel only stared. Somehow, he got the feeling that this news was not what they expected.

"How did it happen?" Daniel asked, keeping his composure.

Stoney sat in one of the rocking chairs on the porch and gave them a blow by blow of the events that brought Mary J. to the hospital. He covered everything except what Dala told them she had overheard. There was plenty of time for that later. He also had spared his folks the gruesome details of Brian's death. It just didn't seem necessary that they know about it.

In the country, every sound is magnified. And in the silence that ensued when Stoney finished his lengthy explanation, the only sounds that could be heard were those that nature provided. But among the sounds of nature, Stoney could hear his stepmother sobbing. He went into the house and brought her a tissue.

"Thanks, Stoney."

The uncomfortable silence was broken when Daniel finally spoke. "Brian was a good swimmer. How could he drown in a shallow creek like the Saline? It doesn't make any sense," he said, shaking his head.

Stoney didn't feel right about not telling them the circumstances surrounding Brian's death, but he wouldn't feel right telling them the gruesome details either. "The sheriff didn't say, but he could have hit his head and been knocked out," Stoney offered as an explanation. "It's hard to say..." He trailed off, drifting into a reticent silence rather than keep talking and complicate things.

Hoping to evade any further questions, Stoney decided the best way to do so was to steer the conversation in another direction. The only thing he couldn't figure out was how to broach the subject. He had turned it over in his mind several times, but no matter how he looked at it, it always came out the same—clumsy. And besides that, how would he keep them from discovering it was Dala who had given him the information?

Tact. Stoney decided to be tactful in his approach. "There's a lot about our family that us kids don't know," he said, hoping he was being reasonably discreet.

Daniel and Sadie cast a despairing glance at each other and asked the silent question with their eyes. It was Sadie who finally spoke. "What...what do you mean, Stoney?" She tried to keep the fear out of her voice that she was suddenly feeling.

"Oh, I don't know exactly," he said offhandedly. "I was just wondering. You never really talked about anyone other than Grandma and Grandpa."

"Not much to tell," Daniel declared, determined to keep their secret a secret.

No family was that uninformed. Parents and grandparents always passed down family history by telling stories to their children and grandchildren. That way they managed to keep the past alive through the generations to come. "Well, maybe Grandma or Grandpa will know something about our ancestors," he declared.

"I don't know. I really doubt it," Sadie said hesitantly. "Why all the sudden interest?"

"Oh, no particular reason. I was just curious." Stoney stood up and stretched. He was pretty sure they were being closemouthed about it. He just couldn't figure out why. What was all the secrecy about? He decided to leave it alone for now and try again later. Daniel and Sadie were probably in shock over Brian's death. They probably needed some time to deal with it. After all, he had known for one full day now. "Well, I'm going to take off. Are you going back to the hospital today?"

"Probably later," Daniel said hollowly. Sadie only nodded.

As he drove back along County Road 135, Stoney mulled over the conversation with his folks. There wasn't much to think about really. They refused to tell him anything. *No sense worrying over it,* he mused. It wasn't something that would clear up Brian's murder. Mary J. had the key to that mystery. And it was locked up inside her mind. They might not find out for sure what happened until she regained consciousness.

He decided to review what he knew about the case.

The first thing was the awful condition Mary J. was in. To begin with, she had several nasty cuts and horrible bruises over her entire body. She looked like she had gone through the windshield of a car. That alone was enough to cast suspicion on what happened. Then there was the coma. What in the world could possibly have been so terrible to put her in a coma? Stoney had seen enough people in comas to know that it took a traumatic incident to throw a person into a coma like this.

Third, what did Sadie mean when she said this was her and Daniel's fault? Damn! He wished Dala had caught more of their parents' conversation. Somehow, he believed there was an important clue buried in all that gibberish. He just wished he knew what it was.

Most importantly, was someone after Brian and Mary J.? Were they involved in something he didn't know about? Something that brought this trouble on them? That was ridiculous. He worked with Brian; he saw him all the time. If there was anything wrong, he would have known.

"Damn it to hell!" he yelled, thumping the steering wheel with his hand. "There are too many questions and not enough answers." The uncertainty of the events surrounding Brian's death and Mary J.'s condition created a seemingly impenetrable wall. How in the world would he find the answers? Maybe he should leave the investigating to the experts. "Bullshit! I'll find out one way or another," he shouted, still taking his frustration out on the steering wheel.

Where to start. The farmer. That was the most logical choice. He would pass right by there. Might as well stop off and see what he can find out. It was just possible the old man might know something that would help. He needed to keep in touch with the sheriff too. Any new developments would be funneled into the sheriff's office. The coroner was another source he needed to visit. Not one he was looking forward to but one that was necessary.

Stoney was thinking he should have another talk with the doctor at the hospital. Surely there were some medical facts that would have an impact on, at the very least, Mary J.'s problems.

As he pulled into the farmer's driveway, he noticed the name on the mailbox read "Delmer and Dora Matthews." He vaguely remembered the doctor mentioning those names.

As Stoney was getting out of his car, he saw the farmer coming out of his barn. He bypassed the house and went out to greet the old man.

"Can I help you?" Delmer called out.

Stoney waited until he had closed the gap between them and greeted the farmer with a handshake. "Morning. I'm Stoney Clark. The girl you found on the road the other night is my sister-in-law."

"Oh, yes. Of course," he replied. "I'm Delmer Matthews. It's a pleasure to meet you. I'm sorry it had to be under these circumstances. It's a shame what happened to that young lady. Is she all right? I never heard any more after Doc Williams took her to the hospital."

"She's in a coma," Stoney informed him. "They don't really know what's wrong with her or what happened to her. That's why I stopped by. I was hoping you might know more about what went on that night other than what we've heard so far, which isn't much."

Delmer scratched his chin and was thoughtful for a minute. "I don't know what I could tell you that I haven't already told the sheriff." Stoney's hopes were momentarily dashed. But then he latched onto something the farmer had said.

"You might have told the sheriff everything that happened that night, but would you mind going over it again for me?" He hoped the farmer had a humanitarian side to him. Otherwise, his chances of getting any information were sad. "I really need to satisfy my own mind about what happened."

Delmer didn't have to think about it. He wasn't told not to say anything. Besides, the family had a right to know about their loved one. "I don't suppose it could hurt anything." He described again the odd occurrence of two nights ago. He didn't get very far, when he came to the part about finding Mary J. on the gravel road.

"She was on her knees on the road when I found her." He related the scene, as though it were happening all over again. "She was crying for help, but when I tried to help her, she became…well, sort of crazy. I was afraid she would hurt herself more than she already had. Anyway, when I tried to take the flashlight from her, she said, 'No. You won't get me too,' and then she shouted 'Get away! Get away!' Then she got even crazier and then…well, she passed out." Matthews went on and explained the rest of the night, but it was all incidental after that.

What did she mean by "You won't get me too"? Stoney wondered to himself. Then he voiced his question to the farmer. "What did she mean by 'You won't get me too'?"

"You got me," Delmer said, shrugging and chuckling at his humorous response. Stoney figured he had got as much as he was going to get. They shook hands and he left. On the drive into town, he tried to figure out what Mary J. meant by that cryptic statement.

You won't get me too.

Who? Who won't get her? This really opened all kinds of possibilities. Susie was right. Someone was after them, but who? And for what reason? Stoney had hoped to come away from this visit with a clearer picture of what happened. Now, it was murkier than ever. "Crap, all this does is make more questions." As he drove into the parking lot at his and Susie's apartment, one thing he was certain of was *the coroner was next.*

All she remembered about the nightmare was the evil-sounding voice. Susie couldn't remember what it said or anything else about it, but she remembered it was terrifying. She also remembered it was the reason for her nap being cut short. She checked the clock on her nightstand. "Crap!" A perfectly fine nap interrupted by a scary nightmare. Two hours of sleep.

Still feeling sluggish, she crawled out of bed and lumbered toward the window that overlooked the street. When Susie took this apartment three years ago, she was adamant about having a unit that faced the street. If she was going to be forced to live in a multihousing establishment, she wanted one with a decent view.

Her one-bedroom apartment was large by most standards. It was a thousand square feet, which included a gigantic living room with a huge bay window that contained a large picture window in the center section. Although it was meant only as a decoration, Susie used the sill as a window seat. It was wide enough to accommodate the cushion she had specially made to fit, and it had become her special place. She often sat there, surrounded with throw pillows, and stared out at the activity on her street and the park across the street. The kitchen was probably the smallest room in the apartment. It contained the basics for comfortable living; stove, refrigerator, double stainless-steel sink with disposal, dishwasher, plenty of cabinet space, and a convenient bar between kitchen and dining room. The appliances were upgraded from normal furnishings in an apartment. The refrigerator was a side by side and the stove was a Jenn-Air. Those two, along with the sink, were designed to form the kitchen triangle.

The only thing about the bathroom that was worth mentioning was the tub. It was sunken and contained a Jacuzzi. The bedroom was twice the normal size of most apartment bedrooms and had a fireplace on one wall. The closet was big enough to be a small bedroom, and she needed every inch of it, especially since Stoney had moved in with her a year ago. They figured he might as well. They were together most of the time anyway.

Susie went into the kitchen and fixed herself a cup of hot chocolate. She then retreated to her favorite place in the apartment, the window seat. She curled up and watched the whirlwind that had formed in the yard. Some kids were playing on the grass and tried to follow the whirlwind around, but it was much too fast for them and soon disappeared into the park across the street.

About halfway through her cup of chocolate, still staring out the window, she saw Stoney turn into the parking lot from Wood Street. She continued gazing out the window while she waited for him.

She suddenly recoiled as she remembered something else about her nightmare.

Stoney entered the apartment, still puzzling over the strange remark that Mary J. made to the farmer. He noticed Susie sitting on the window seat. He slipped his shoes off and joined her. "Get some sleep?" he asked as he slipped his arms around her waist.

"A couple of hours." She buried her face in his chest, and he could feel her body tremble as her muted cries vibrated against his frame.

Stoney gathered her closer, his arms offering the solace she desperately needed. He could feel her tears wetting his shirt front. Gradually, as her sobs subsided, she removed her head from his chest. "What's wrong?" he asked softly. Susie dried her eyes before answering.

"I-I had another nightmare," she said. "Stoney, it was awful." He felt her shivering and hugged her tighter.

"Want to tell me about it?"

Susie didn't say anything for the longest time. Stoney was beginning to think she had fallen asleep. "I don't know if I can do this," she finally replied. She was crying again, but not as bad as before.

"All right. It's okay," he assured her. He let her cry it out.

When she had calmed down enough to talk, she slowly began telling him about her nightmare. It took a while because she had to stop and cry a few times as she recalled the horrible things she had seen.

Stoney was patient with her, letting her tell it at her own pace. When she was finally finished, he had to agree that it was absolutely horrible.

"What is happening to me?" she cried. "All these nightmares must mean something. Stoney, I'm afraid. What is wrong with me?"

She was on the verge of hysteria and Stoney wasn't sure what to do about it. So he just kept holding her. "I can't get that out of my head," she cried. "Over and over I keep hearing that horrible laugh and the words 'so that you would remember.'" She looked at him, and her eyes reflected the fear that she felt.

"Stoney, I don't want to remember, but now...I can't forget. This is the second time I've had the same nightmare. Stoney, help me," she cried.

What can I do? he wondered. *I'm not a doctor. I'm not even sure a doctor could do anything about this. And I'm not a priest.* Suddenly, something clicked. "That's it," he said aloud.

"What?" she asked, her sobs subsiding.

"We'll go talk to the priest. This sounds like something he would know about."

She looked at him quizzically. "My nightmares?" she asked.

"No," he scoffed. "The whole thing. Don't you see? This whole situation reeks of satanic stuff. Anyway, what would it hurt?" he commented dryly as she frowned.

He spent the next several minutes telling her about his stops that morning. After he finished telling her about his talk with the farmer, she became excited, forgetting all about her nightmare.

"That's great, Stoney. At least we're getting somewhere," she exclaimed. "What now?"

He recounted for her his earlier ruminations of the case. "I think we should go see the coroner," he replied. "Are you up for that?"

"Just the coroner?" she asked, a queasy feeling rumbling through her stomach. Susie wasn't sure she could hold up to seeing a dead body, especially Brian's.

"Well," Stoney said hesitantly. "The ultimate purpose is to see Brian's body. You know, to satisfy ourselves that he's..." He still couldn't bring himself to say it out loud. If he did, then Brian really was dead. "You don't have to go with me," he said dryly. "But I have to know. And I think the coroner's report can only do so much." He left the rest up to her imagination. Stoney got up from the window seat, gave her a quick kiss, and headed in the direction of the bedroom, pulling off his shirt on the way.

"You want me to make some coffee?"

Stoney had already disappeared into the bedroom. "That'd be great," he yelled back to her. "I'm going to grab a quick shower."

Susie heard the water running as Stoney turned the shower on to regulate the water temperature. She suddenly realized she had not taken a shower herself since coming home from the hospital. She quickly finished throwing some coffee grounds into the coffee maker, filled it with water, and switched it on.

When she walked into the bedroom, Stoney was already in the shower. Susie began peeling off her clothes. She hadn't taken the time to undress. When she got home, she just fell into bed. Tired—physically and emotionally. The two-hour nap wasn't enough by a long shot but would get her through to that night.

She walked softly into the bathroom. Through the clear shower door, she could see Stoney as he leaned against the wall, his head under the running water. Very gently, she pulled the shower door open, slipped in, and carefully eased it shut so it wouldn't click. Then she wrapped her arms around him, snuggling up to his back.

Stoney turned around and became lost in the magnetism of Susie's wanting embrace. Their kiss went on for a long time, neither conscious of the running water. His hands moved down her back and came to rest on her small, tight buttocks. Susie responded by pressing her hips into his and moving in a circular motion. She could feel the rigid stiffness of his erection pushing against her abdomen. In one swift motion, she lifted her legs up as Stoney cupped her behind in his hands. She slipped her hand down and guided him into her. The water pelted them from above, keeping rhythm with their movements.

Stoney turned, placing her back against the wall and their passion consumed them.

Dr. Miles stood in the doorway that separated his office and the outer office. He looked at the young couple through narrow slits. He'd been expecting this. Relatives were bound to show up sooner or later. He still didn't know what to tell them. Nothing had changed in Brian Clark's case since the sheriff had left. He wasn't even sure the sheriff wanted him talking to anyone. The hell with it! There was no reason to keep quiet.

He cast a despairing glance at Stoney. Their eyes met, and he knew immediately this young man would not be put off. "Come on in," he sighed, holding the door for them.

They entered an office that could belong to any doctor—not necessarily a coroner. Susie had been expecting something much more dramatic. She wasn't sure what that was exactly, a coffin or two braced against the wall, a couple of bodies suspended from the ceiling, but definitely not one as normal as this.

Bookcases lined two walls and were filled with books and magazines that spilled over to the floor. There were stacks of magazines that probably hadn't been gone through more than once—and some of them not at all. The credenza behind his desk was covered with assorted medical items. Most of which were replicas of human anatomy used, she was sure, as visual aids for describing various problems to people like her and Stoney.

It was a small office. At least it was smaller than what she expected. Besides the two chairs in front of the doctor's desk, there was a maroon leather sofa occupying the remaining wall. She didn't see how it could be of any service, though. It was literally covered with a miscellany of items, strewn about in a disorderly fashion. A collect all, she surmised. Like most people's dining tables.

The two amateur investigators sat down slowly in the chairs facing the desk, neither wanting to get too comfortable. Dr. Miles filled his expensive leather desk chair with his bulk and fiddled with some papers on his desk.

"Doctor..." Stoney suddenly realized they hadn't been introduced. He noticed the name plaque on the desk and continued after a brief hesitation. "Miles. I'm Stoney Clark, Brian's brother. This is

Susie Conners, she's his sister-in-law." Still no acknowledgment, not even a courteous nod.

Stoney glanced quickly at Susie and then back to the doctor again. This wasn't going well. He wished the doctor would be a little more congenial. It was hard enough doing something like this, notwithstanding the normal difficulties. "Well…we would like to know more about what happened to my brother."

Dr. Miles sat stiffly, reclined in his chair. His posture said he wasn't going to be much help. After what seemed like an eternity, he finally stirred. "Your brother was the victim of a diastasic avulsion." *They'll have to think about that for a while*, he thought, chuckling to himself.

But Stoney would not be predisposed, at least not easily. "What does that mean?"

Miles sighed but resigned himself to the fact that he was going to have to say something they would understand. However, he should tread carefully. "It means, his body was split in half and he died as a result of that."

Stoney was becoming frustrated. "You haven't told us anything that we didn't already read in your report." Why was he being so secretive? What was all the mystery surrounding Brian's death?

"You read my report?" he asked, surprised.

Stoney smiled inwardly. Now he had the upper hand. "Of course. The sheriff let us read it." He decided to take another line of attack. "Doctor, we know how he died, but what we don't know is what caused it. There was no mention in your report that his body was water-logged. So drowning is out. I've never heard of anyone reacting so violently, in such a short distance. Have you? It's not far enough from the top of that cliff to the water to split—split"—as much as he wanted to be strong, it was affecting Stoney to think that this discussion was about his brother—"a person in half. What caused him to end up there in the first place?"

"I don't have an answer for you. Now wait a minute!" he said hurriedly, when Stoney started to interrupt. "I didn't find any signs of foul play. There were no wounds to his head or any other part of his body that might indicate foul play." He paused, waiting for Stoney's question. "That is what you wanted to know, isn't it?"

"Yes, but I don't see how it's possible," he retorted. He was sure he already knew what the answer to his next question would be. "Can we see him?"

To his surprise, the doctor didn't disagree. "Are you sure you're ready for that? I mean, it's not exactly a pretty picture." Stoney nodded his assent. Susie indicated her agreement.

Dr. Miles got up from his desk and led them out of a different door from the one they came in. They exited into a hallway, where they walked the short distance to the end and then down two flights of stairs. The door at the bottom opened to another hall. Their footsteps echoed in the long, empty corridor. About halfway down, they came to a door on their left. He opened it and flipped on another switch. The room flooded with light, illuminating the assorted tables, which Stoney knew were used in performing autopsies.

He cringed when he suddenly remembered that Brian had occupied one of those recently. The thought of his brother lying there on one of those cold metal tables was almost enough to make him turn and run. But he had to know. He had to see for himself what happened to Brian. In his numbed state, he managed to feel Susie pressing against him. He put his arm around her and held her tight.

The chubby doctor walked over to one of the stainless-steel doors on the wall and pulled the latch, opening the door. The contents inside rolled out easily. Susie gasped as the slab with Brian's body on it almost hit her. She quickly stepped aside and glared at the doctor. Inside the bag was Brian. Suddenly she wasn't so sure anymore. She stiffened as Miles reached over to unzip it, but Susie stopped him. "Wait! Wait...please?"

"Did you change your mind?" Miles asked, his stubby hands poised over the sinister-looking bag. He looked from Susie to Stoney and then back to Susie.

"No," she breathed out the word. But her response was barely more than a whisper.

Stoney returned his gaze from Susie to the doctor. "I think what she means is, we'd like to be alone, if you don't mind."

The doctor looked from one to the other. He finally backed away from the slab where the dead body lay. "I'll be outside."

Stoney regarded the black bundle in ominous silence. He knew he needed to do this, but now that the time had come, he was filled with doubt. He reached for the zipper, his hand trembling.

Susie drew her breath in sharply.

"What is it?" Stoney said, jerking his hand back.

Her words were muffled as she spoke with her hand covering her mouth. "It didn't seem so bad when the doctor was in here." She paused while summoning the courage to follow through. "I-I thought I was ready," she murmured. After she took a moment to collect herself, she nodded. "Go ahead."

Stoney finally unzipped the menacing bag down to the chest. He couldn't bring himself to bare anything below that. He slowly uncovered Brian's face. Susie was prepared to react violently. She had never seen a dead body before, but she had seen a lot of movies and was sure Brian would look much like those dead people. His face bloated, his eyes bulging out and, of course, bloodless. But that is not the way it was.

On the contrary. It wasn't even Brian.

"Who's that?" she asked.

Stoney never broke his gaze from the corpse before them. "I don't know, but that isn't Brian. It couldn't be."

"Oh, that's him all right," Dr. Miles replied, coming back into the room.

They both stared at the strange-looking face again. It was a study in multiplicity, but at the same time, there was something very familiar about it. Stoney couldn't put his finger on it, but he was sure it would all become clear in time.

"We don't have an explanation for this phenomenon," he said, indicating Brian's faces. "But I have sent for some experts. Perhaps they can shed some light on this enigma. Until then, we will have to do what we can to solve some of the mystery on our own." They looked at him, chagrin spreading across their faces. "I'm sorry for this, but if we're to get anywhere at all, I must ask it."

Stoney indicated his approval, that they would do what they could to know the truth.

Dr. Miles smiled his thanks. "Are any of these faces Brian's? I mean, do any of them resemble his normal face?" Miles felt clumsy asking the question. Truth be known, there wasn't any proper way to ask. No matter how he approached it, it would appear awkward. At the very least, Miles felt awkward.

Stoney and Susie looked carefully at the freakish object. To Susie, it was like looking in a broken mirror. A mirror that had several slivers running up and down and as you look at yourself in it, you see many sections of your own face. Only, it wasn't her face she saw in the mirror this time—it was other people's faces. And she didn't recognize any of them. There was a myriad of people staring at her. All strangers. She shook her head violently.

"I don't see any that I recognize," she told him.

"Me either," Stoney agreed.

The doctor nodded as though that was the answer he expected all along. "I figured as much. But we needed someone close to him to make the actual comparison. I'm sorry it had to be you two," he apologized, beginning to feel some sorrow for the young couple. "Do you need to see any more?"

"No," they said in unison. It was obvious, they had seen enough. They left the building, feeling extremely heavyhearted—and even more convinced that something supernatural was involved.

Within minutes they were back at their apartment. Unlike a couple of hours earlier, when they were feverishly embroiled in lovemaking in the shower, now they sat dejected, sipping on a cup of Irish Creme International Coffee. Stoney was lazing on the sofa with his feet kicked up on the coffee table.

Susie was in her favorite spot, soulfully ensconced in the window seat with pillows all around her. The day had become overcast, which was a perfect match for their mood. The dreary gray sky lent itself ideally to the shadowy gloom of their visit to the coroner's office.

Susie sat up abruptly, nearly spilling the contents of her cup on the unmarred white pants she wore. They were a gift from Stoney.

He didn't give many gifts, so she sure didn't want to stain them with coffee. She focused her attention on what had caused the near accident to begin with. She thought she had seen an old woman on the sidewalk below. But it wasn't so much that she saw her, as it was that she felt her. But there was no one there. The sidewalk was empty. *It must have been my imagination*, she told herself. *Too much spooky stuff today.*

There she was!

Coming out from behind that giant oak tree. The one Susie admired so. She stared at the elderly lady and suddenly had the feeling she knew her. The woman was turning first in one direction and then in the other. But she had stared in each direction, as though she was looking for someone.

Suddenly, she was looking right at Susie.

Susie leaned back against her pillows and averted her eyes, but she was sure the woman had seen her looking. How impolite that was. But it was the woman's fault. She shouldn't have been looking in Susie's window in the first place.

Her discomfort made her feel even edgier. Hell! She's an old woman and probably lost. You should be ashamed of yourself, Susie Conners. But still there was something odd about their brief meeting of eyes. Susie couldn't quite get it straight in her head. What was it? That's it. Now she knew why she had felt so uneasy.

That woman was an inculcator.

She was putting thoughts in Susie's mind. What was that she said? Said! Like it was words that were placed there. But they weren't words. They were thoughts. It was impressions, made with the woman's own mind. What was she trying to tell her? To cur—no, damn it! To cur-curse. That's it. To curse? Why would the woman want her to curse? Hell, she did enough of that as it was. Suddenly she knew.

The Curse!

She tore her eyes away from the old woman and glanced quickly at Stoney. He sat sleepily on the sofa. "Stoney! Come here."

He snapped his head up and begrudgingly got up and sauntered over to the window. Susie felt sorry for him as she took note of his exhaustion. "What is it?" he asked, his voice laced with sleep.

"Look at that woman," she cried, pointing at the sidewalk below. "Where is she? Shit! She's gone," Susie cursed violently. "I really wanted you to see her. It was the oddest-looking woman I've ever seen."

"What was odd about her?" he asked, a yawn slowly working its way through his tired body. Susie began to explain what had happened, or at least what she thought had happened. When she was through, it didn't sound quite as plausible as it had felt moments before.

"She said, 'The Curse,'" Susie repeated what had been implanted in her mind.

Stoney looked at her confused. "What does that mean?" he asked, his weariness giving way to curiosity.

"I don't know. But it might have something to do with what Dala was talking about this morning. Remember? She said that Mom and Dad were talking about this whole thing being their fault, like there was some big family secret or something. I don't know," she blurted at him. "But it means something."

Stoney looked doubtful at her.

"I'm not making this up," she said indignantly. He could be so frustrating at times. It really pissed her off. "Stoney, this is me. I don't live in a looking glass."

"All right," he said, grinning at her. "I believe you. But what does it mean? There's been some god-awful curse put on your family? Everyone is going to turn into a vampire or some crazy shit like that if we don't kill the main guy?" He stopped when he saw the baleful look in her eyes. "What is it?"

"Not my family, *our* family," she replied evenly.

A cold chill swept over Stoney. The kind you got when someone walked over your grave.

Chapter Eight

In the spring of 1896, Franklin and Carlotta left their homes, their families, and their lives behind. They packed up everything they owned, arranged for its shipment, and went in search of their future. They hoped they would find it in a place called Crater Ridge.

As they neared the small midwestern town, Carlotta realized for the first time just what she had left behind. This place was so small, it was more like a village than a town. There were very few businesses to speak of. Outside a general store, post office, bank, and restaurant/boardinghouse, there was little else it had to offer.

She was surprised at the way it was laid out, as well. Carlotta guessed she had an entirely different picture of what it would look like in her mind.

It was primitive but friendly.

Franklin had stopped in front of the bank. "I'm going to get this business out of the way before they close for the day. Do you want to come in with me?" he asked.

Carlotta had been gazing around at the strange little town. Without looking at him, she said, "You go ahead. I'll be fine." Painfully, as she stared at the weather-beaten buildings, the dry, dusty street that was lined with wooden walkways on both sides, she thought of the home she had left behind.

While reminiscing about her recently discovered tainted past, it dawned on Carlotta that the streets seemed awfully deserted. There was a couple walking away from her on the opposite side of the street and an elderly man just going into the general store. There were two men sitting on a bench in front of the store, and some kids were racing down the street holding crudely fashioned sticks in their hands, chasing a hoop, desperately trying to keep it in the middle of the street, right and rolling.

There were those few, but somehow it still felt deserted. A cold chill swept over Carlotta. She was just thinking of climbing down from the wagon and investigating this strange place, when Franklin came out of the bank.

She waited until he had sat down beside her before saying anything. "Franklin, where are all the people?" she asked bewildered.

He looked up and down the street, even twisting in his seat to peer at the other side of the street behind them. He shrugged. "At home, I guess." He untied the reins but left the brake on and then looked at his wife. "Why?"

Carlotta surveyed the town again. "Oh, I don't know," she sighed heavily. "I just wondered."

Franklin retied the reins and took his hand off the brake. He looked intently at his wife for a minute. She was still staring intently at something down the street. He had never really considered what she might expect, or what her feelings were really. She would quite naturally have questions and most certainly have ideas about this strange new place.

It occurred to Franklin that they really hadn't talked about it. They knew they had to get away from their families and the places where they were known so well, but they hadn't considered too much beyond that. "Darling, is there something wrong with this town? Now is the time to decide," he pointed out, weary from their trip.

"No," she said, gently patting his arm. "Here will do fine. It will do just fine." She turned to face him, and Franklin thought he detected a sad, broken expression before she smiled at him.

Franklin was unconvinced and suddenly filled with uncertainty. "Let's not make any hasty decisions," he said, squeezing her hand. "The fellow I spoke with in the bank says there is a farm for sale not too far from here. We'll go look at it tomorrow, and then we'll decide. Is that all right?" he asked hopefully.

"Yes, of course," she replied, not paying too much attention.

Franklin picked up the reins, released the brake and slapped the horses on the rump. They started down the street toward the boardinghouse. He tried ignoring his wife's strange attitude by pretending everything was going the way they wanted. But he was troubled about her sudden gloomy disposition. When they left Bridgeport, he could have sworn this was where they wanted to go. This was where they wanted to live.

When he stopped the wagon in front of the boardinghouse, Franklin confronted his wife again. Her eyes had cleared, her features were hardened and sharp. She acted like nothing had ever happened.

Franklin shook his head. Peculiar. Very peculiar.

The next morning, Carlotta awoke early. She got up and stood in front of the window, gazing at the early morning predawn light which was enough to let her see the spectacular view overlooking the hills behind the little town. She could see far enough to tell that there were hills as far as she could see.

The farther away the hilltops were, the darker their shade of gray until the last one she could see looked black. Amid the hills was an early morning fog that sifted in and out of the trees.

Carlotta didn't realize she was holding her breath until she gasped for air. She raised the window and took in huge gulps of the crisp, fresh scent. The light breeze that wafted its way across the treetops and into her room gently stirred her hair. She closed her eyes and bathed in the moist air that accompanied the breeze washing over her.

Suddenly, she felt Franklin's presence behind her.

He had noiselessly gotten out of bed, joined her at the window and wrapped his arms around her, holding her hands in his. "Morning."

"Isn't it fabulous?" she remarked without ever taking her eyes off the placid scene that stretched for miles. For the first time in her life, Carlotta felt at peace. And for some reason, the tranquil beauty of this natural phenomenon completely hypnotized her.

"I want a house that has a view just like this," she said, finally stirring from her somnolent state.

Franklin gave his wife a bear hug and told her, "You will have it. I promise. The property we're going to look at is in those distant trees." He pointed at a hilltop far away.

The first rays of the morning sun bathed their faces adding its pleasure to his promise.

Carlotta was fidgety as they rode out of town toward the east. The bank president had given them directions to the property he had mentioned to Franklin the day before. She had accompanied her husband into the bank and, at the first opportunity, mentioned her desire to have the kind of place that offered a view like the one she had witnessed only a couple of hours before.

"I think you will be very pleased to discover it's even better than that," Mr. Lacey, the bank president, told her. He was a squirrely little man who precisely fit her image of a small-town banker.

Carlotta had thanked him with a tremendous show of gratitude and left the rest of the proceedings to the men.

"Mr. Lacey said the property is up on that ridge," Franklin said, his voice trembling slightly thanks to the rough road. "He said there is a bowl-shaped depression on the top of the ridge that looks like a crater but isn't really. He doesn't know how it got there but swears it's not from a meteor." He shrugged at the explanation. "Anyhow, that's how the town got the name of Crater Ridge." Franklin was thoughtful for a minute. "Oh! He also says that is the best piece of property in the area."

Carlotta looked at her husband and wrinkled her nose in a smile. Maybe this wouldn't be such a bad place to live after all. She hooked her arm around his, and they rode the rest of the way in silence.

The little dirt road leading to the old Miller place was nothing more than two wagon wheel tracks with a patch of grass between them. The road wasn't rutted, which was a miracle. The rains that frequented this hill country often caused the dirt tracks to rut from the wagon wheels. But of course, it had not been used since the Miller's left six months ago. That accounted for the good condition of the road. The dry summers afforded most farmers in the area the chance to beat down the ruts that formed in the winter and spring.

Ergo, the smooth, dusty dirt lane that led up to the old farm.

Carlotta drank it all in, as though she had been blind and was seeing everything for the first time. As they rode slowly up the lane, she was particularly taken with the way the trees lined both sides of the road. Their tops reached toward the sky, towering high above the ground and swaying with carefree indifference. The lower limbs curved inward in a gradual arc toward each other, meeting in the middle and completely swallowing the insignificant wagon and its inhabitants.

Carlotta was breathless as they continued at a snail's pace, twisting first one way and then another. She inhaled the aromatic fragrance of the spring flowers whose assorted perfumes drifted through the air, blending together, and dulling the senses with their provocative, intoxicating odors.

This was one ride Carlotta wished would never end. But end it did, at the abandoned Miller farm. Even so, the unbelievably gorgeous surroundings seemed to go on forever. As soon as Franklin brought the wagon to a stop, she climbed down without waiting for his customary help.

Forget the inside of the house and other outbuildings that had patiently stood the test of time. They showed their age in the weather-beaten clapboard siding and cedar shake shingles. But they looked as sturdy as the day they were built. Instead, Carlotta went straight away to a shaded grassy area under a hundred-year-old oak tree.

This tree had a thousand stories it could tell. Some were happy. Some were sad. But all of them had one thing in common. They took place right here, in one of the most beautiful spots in the country.

Carlotta could sense the shadowy phantoms of some of the more vibrant loves that had met in the shade of this aged tree. A shade that each lover slipped on with the ease of an old shoe.

As they sat or stood, bathing in the coolness of the tree's penumbra, every eye gazed on the same fabulous view. There might have been some minute differences in everyone's perception, but the view had been the same for ten thousand years. Natural. Untarnished. Undiminished.

"Darling, are you going to look at the house?" Franklin asked, walking up behind her and bringing her out of her reverie.

Carlotta took his proffered hand and felt a twinge of electricity pass between them as they both looked out over the neighboring hills. "Isn't it beautiful," she breathed out slowly. "Isn't it absolutely ravishing?"

"Yes, I agree. It is a nice view, but I really think you should see the house," he said reasonably.

The Bakers—Carlotta thought it was ironic that she had her real last name again—entered the house through the back door. It opened into the kitchen, which was modest in size and furnishings, and somehow felt right coming in that way. The room was light and airy, even though it had not been used for some time. Even the curtains looked fresh. Carlotta found herself hoping the rest of the house was just as luminous and cozy.

However, as she stood in the kitchen, she was overwhelmed with a sudden feeling of melancholy. She staggered under an invisible force, rapaciously grasping to crush her, to strangle her with the emotions of every person who had ever lived in the ancient dwelling.

Carlotta thought she would surely collapse under the callously cold and cruel weight that pressed down on her. The radiant easiness of the room was suddenly turning dark and sinister. She was sinking further and further into the depths of the old house. Carlotta was flailing about, grasping for anything she could cling to until help came.

What was happening to her?

Franklin was standing right there, just a few feet away. Why wasn't he helping her? What was wrong with him? Couldn't he see that she was in trouble? "*Franklin!*" she shouted, reaching toward him.

He just stood there. Looking at the kitchen, pointing out some of the features to her—like she couldn't see them for herself. But she wasn't interested in those things now. She needed help before it was too late—before she disappeared into the bowels of the earth.

The room was growing darker. She could hardly see Franklin now. Her desperate attempts to free herself had failed. Carlotta felt alone, detached from everything she had ever known. She began to weep softly, sure that she was on the verge of dying—if she wasn't dead already.

She stopped crying and listened carefully. A noise caught her attention. It sounded a lot like a voice. She craned her head in the direction she thought it came from. There it was again! "Who's there?" she called out.

A brief silence ensued. Carlotta continued listening, silently terrified at what was happening to her. She huddled in the darkness, quivering with fear. Aghast and trembling uncontrollably, she was about to give up when she detected a dim light not too far away. She watched as the light got brighter but was still dim by most standards.

You have nothing to fear. The time is coming soon.

"What—" she started to exclaim, but suddenly the darkness gave way to light, and the room returned to normal, as if nothing had ever happened.

"These floors. You won't ever have to do anything to them. They shine like a new silver dollar," Franklin was saying.

"What are you talking about!" she demanded, exploding at him.

Franklin tensed at her abrupt outburst. "I was just talking about these beautiful hardwood floors," he said, pensively. "They look like…like red oak," he stumbled over the words, confused by her odd behavior. "Honey, are you all right?"

"I-I just…I don't know." She suddenly felt weak. "I need to sit down." Carlotta went out the back door, crossed the porch, and sat on the edge of it, propping her feet on the top step. She was trembling.

"Darling, what is it?" Franklin asked, sitting down beside her. He put his arm around her shoulders. "Why, you're shaking like a leaf. Tell me what's wrong," he urged his wife.

"I can't explain it," she said in deference to his questions.

"Can't explain what?"

Carlotta didn't answer right away. How could she? She didn't understand herself what just happened. If she tried to explain that to Franklin, he would think she was senseless, that she didn't have a sane thought in her anymore. No! Best to not say anything at all.

"It's just that—I'm just tired from the trip," she said with a quiet confidence. "I'll be fine in a moment." She shook off any residual effects from what she was sure now must have been insanity. Within seconds, the incident had begun to fade from her memory.

"Are you sure that's all it is?"

Carlotta searched her memory but by now could not remember what she was looking for. "Yes. Yes, I'm sure," she said with finality. "Let's look at the rest of the house."

Franklin and Carlotta went about inspecting the house and grounds without further incident. It was amazing, but they couldn't find anything wrong with the farm, except that it needed some basic attention from sitting unattended.

The yard had mutated from a soft, grassy green carpet to a field of brown weeds that needed haying. There were boards broken and some missing around the corral. Many of the outbuildings were in disrepair. But overall, there was nothing that couldn't be quickly repaired. All they needed to do was come to an agreement with the bank.

They were emerging from the barn, chatting excitedly about what they were already calling home, when they realized they weren't alone anymore. Coming out of the house were a man and a woman about their same age. Franklin finished closing the barn door, and they walked over to meet the couple.

The man was slightly taller than Franklin, six feet, two inches, Carlotta guessed. He had jet-black hair that was combed back with no part. He had a medium build, set on a strong muscular frame that she was sure came from farming.

Of all his features, however, the most telling one was his beard. It was dark, like his hair and dominated his appearance. The beard was close-cropped and reminded her of a teddy bear. It generally brought a comment from everyone who crossed his path.

The woman was probably a foot shorter than the man. She was thin but not bulimic. In sharp contrast to the man's dark hair, she was a flaxen blond. Her eyes were such a pale shade of blue, they were almost transparent. But there was no doubting the twinkle in them.

Carlotta would later recall that the flashing brilliance of the woman's eyes was what made her like this pretty petite girl so much.

"Hi. We're the Warrens," the woman smiled at them. "I'm Kelly, and this is my husband, Michael. We live on the spread that you passed right next to this one," she explained after seeing the look of confusion on their faces.

"I'm Carlotta Baker, and this is my husband, Franklin. We were just…looking around," she said haltingly.

"Are you interested in buying?" Michael asked after they had exchanged formal greetings.

"This is a great place," he said, casting a wistful eye around the property. His eyes had a pleasing smile as they came to rest on Franklin.

"I'm kind of curious," Franklin said, puzzled. "Why hasn't this place sold already? It really looks like a great piece of property."

Michael was nodding, even before Franklin had finished his question. "Figured you'd want to know about that. It only came on the market a couple of weeks ago."

"But Mr. Lacey, at the bank, said it had been empty for six months," Franklin recalled.

Michael and Kelly looked at each other. They hadn't really wanted to get into that, but it didn't look like they could avoid it now.

Carlotta thought she detected a strange expression pass between them. It was almost like they had a secret and didn't want to share it. Suddenly, she found herself thinking, maybe they didn't really want to settle here after all. She certainly did like it though, especially the view. She wondered if she should be so bold as to ask what was going on.

"I suppose you have a right to know since you're interested in it," Kelly stated flatly.

Well, I guess I won't have to worry whether I'm bold enough, Carlotta thought silently. *Thank goodness I didn't speak too quickly*, she congratulated herself.

"Six months ago, the Miller family was found dead in the house," she continued mournfully. "Murdered in their sleep. They had all been shot at close range with a shotgun, except for Mr. Miller. His throat was slit." She halted and took a couple of deep breaths. It was amazing, but after all this time, she still got sick thinking about the senseless deaths. The Millers were a nice family and didn't deserve such cruel, appalling treatment.

Kelly suddenly felt uncomfortable. She could feel their eyes staring at her. It wasn't her fault what happened to the Millers, but somehow, she felt responsible for just telling the story.

"Those poor people." Carlotta felt the sting of tears. She didn't know them, but she suddenly felt very sorry for what happened to them. "It must have been absolutely terrible for you," she said, giving Kelly's arm a light squeeze.

"I had nightmares for months," Kelly readily admitted. "I wish there had been something we could have done to help or to prevent it from happening. They really were good people. Anyway, the family finally put the farm up for sale at the end of last month." She and Carlotta had begun to walk away from their husbands, as they headed toward the friendly old oak tree.

Michael and Franklin wandered over by the corral and leaned against the weather-beaten boards, each one propping a foot on one of the lower wooden runners. Their conversation covered several different topics, but the main one had to do with farming.

Michael's experience with it and Franklin's lack of it.

Besides the friendships that formed that day, the most important thing that came out of the visit was Michael's assurance that he would help his new neighbor with anything he needed to know about farming and being a farmer.

The women's dialogue leaned more toward child-rearing. Neither had any children, but both were looking forward to starting a family. The rest of the day was wasted on meaningless chitchat.

With summer not too far away, Franklin decided to use this first year as a learning experience in farming. Admittedly, he would have his hands full for a while repairing the buildings and generally cleaning the old Miller place up. What he didn't know was how helpful the folks around Crater Ridge could be to new neighbors, and the Bakers were no exception.

So the very next Saturday after they moved in, a group of folks showed up early in the morning, ready to work. Ben and Anna Wright, who lived on the road coming out of town; Eugene and Carol Sheridan, their neighbors on the east of them; and Sarah Robbins, who owned the boardinghouse they had stayed in. There were others, including Michael and Kelly.

"Sarah, I don't want to take you away from your business." Carlotta sighed.

"Oh, please," she said loudly. "Take me away. You wouldn't believe how boring it is just sitting there doing nothing, day after day. Crater Ridge is not exactly a hub of activity, in case you hadn't noticed." Carlotta remembered the day they had arrived and how deserted the streets had been.

"Well, if you're sure it's not an imposition."

"Believe me, young lady. I would much rather be here today than there." She smiled at Carlotta reassuringly. "Now, let's get started, shall we? Are we ready to work?"

Kelly came over to where Carlotta and Sarah were talking and steered her new friend to a secluded corner of the room. "There's something you need to know about the folks around here," she stated flatly. "They will help you do anything in the world, but don't ever make the mistake of turning down their help. Not with any regularity. Or else, they won't offer again." She noticed the frown that crinkled the skin between Carlotta's brows. "It's just the way they are," she concluded.

"Well," Carlotta said uncertainly, "I don't want to offend anyone."

"Then accept their help and let's whip this place into shape." Kelly giggled.

Carlotta couldn't believe the energy that the town people had in welcoming a new family to Crater Ridge. This would never have happened back home. Folks back there were too private. The children were whitewashing the fence, while the ladies were either cleaning or fixing lunch.

Michael Warren and Eugene Sheridan brought horses and plows. Together they plowed up the field for spring planting, while others cleared the weeds and other trash out of the yard and raked it up.

Not everything was done on Saturday. Sunday after church, everyone returned along with a few new faces. The afternoon started with a huge outdoor dinner, which was provided by the church. By sunset that evening, the only thing left for Franklin and Carlotta to finish was the unpacking.

With a sudden feeling of disparity, Carlotta realized she hadn't written her mother since before their arrival here. She decided to write a letter that evening and post it the next time they went to town.

On Monday, what furniture they had and the rest of their belongings that they couldn't bring with them arrived from Bridgeport. Everything had been stacked in the rooms on the lower floor. Carlotta stared at stack after stack of boxes. The remnants of their separate lives before they knew each other. Reminders of their past. Some of it they would keep, and some of it would be given away or thrown out.

"This will take forever," she cried, a disheartening cloud filling the room.

Undaunted by the task before them, Franklin was the soul of optimism. His cheerful confidence was enough to emit a smile from Carlotta. "I'm sorry," she apologized to her husband. "After all that was done for us, I have no reason to complain."

"Can't say that I disagree with you," he retorted.

By Thursday, they were down to the last box. Franklin had long retreated to the field, sowing his row crops. He had picked up a used, but sturdy plow from Ben Wright. "It still has a lot of life left in it," Ben claimed heartily.

Franklin couldn't believe how little he wanted for it. "Are you sure?" he questioned his new neighbor. "That doesn't seem like very much for such a useful tool."

"I've got two. Can't use but one at a time," Ben conceded. "Do you want it?"

"Yes, of course," Franklin replied. "I'll put it to good use."

That afternoon, with the sun already hot like it was midsummer, they were sitting on the front porch, trying to cool off with the aid of a gentle breeze blowing from the southeast and a pitcher of cool tea on the little wooden table between their chairs, when Kelly and Michael stopped their buggy in front of the gravel walk, got out, and sauntered up to the porch.

"You two look like you could use a glass of this," Carlotta called down to them, holding her glass aloft for them to see.

"It would certainly hit the spot right now," Michael said as they ascended the steps to join the Bakers. "This heat is just a preview of what to expect this summer, you know. Although, it usually stays a little cooler up here on the ridge."

"Please tell me this is abnormal for March," Franklin moaned.

Michael looked thoughtful as he contemplated his response. "Abnormal, yes. But not out of the question. We get these kinds of spring days every few years or so."

"Here, drink some of this," Carlotta said, handing him a tall glass of tea spiced with a slice of lemon. "Maybe it'll take some of the agony out of the heat."

Franklin waited until everyone had settled into chairs and then asked, "What are you two up to? You certainly didn't come all the way over here in this heat to inform us that it was out of season."

Michael tipped his head back and let a swallow of the cool nectar trickle down his throat before he answered. "Ahh. This really hits the spot, Carlotta." He looked from one to the other and then suggested, "We thought you both might like a cool, refreshing swim after a long week of hard work."

"And where would we go swimming around here?" Franklin asked, his curiosity aroused.

"There's a great little swimming hole just down the road a piece," Kelly informed them. "It's on Saline Creek. We're not really sure how long it's been around, but folks round these parts call it Rockhole. The name will become obvious when you see it," she explained at Franklin's wrinkled nose.

I've been waiting for you. This is just the perfect opportunity. Tell them, Franklin. Tell them, Franklin, tell them, tell them...

"In a creek?" Carlotta asked. She could imagine a stale, tepid pool that was fit for nothing more than the cattle's bathing place.

"Oh, don't worry. It's safe," Michael countered, nodding.

Kelly couldn't believe they wouldn't want to cool off in the refreshing creek water. "Come on, you'll love it," she said, her face lighting up with a charming smile. When she smiled like that, it was captivating the way her eyes twinkled, and her nose wrinkled up real cute. Michael found it was hard to resist her then. She often used it on him when she really wanted something and needed an edge to tip the scale in her favor.

"Well, what the heck. It sounds like fun," Franklin suddenly decided. Was it the hopeful smile on Kelly's face? Or was it something else? Franklin shuddered as a peculiar feeling swept over him. "What do you say, darling?"

"I say, let's go," Carlotta chimed in.

"Good, grab some swimwear and come on," Michael announced heartily. "And don't worry about supper. We have a picnic basket full of food."

Franklin and Carlotta disappeared into the house only to reemerge within minutes attired in swimsuits under their outer garments. The two couples hopped into the waiting buggy and headed for Rockhole.

"Careful going down that slope. The footing is loose, and it can get a little tricky," Michael warned, looking back at the newcomers.

He was carrying the picnic basket and leading the group. "I should tell you about the time when Kelly—"

"Don't you dare, Michael," his wife cautioned him.

"But it's such a funny story," he whined like a child. Kelly thumped him on the back a warning. "Now, you know I wouldn't without your approval," he confessed.

"Do you get the feeling we're being shunned?" Carlotta said good-naturedly, speaking to Franklin but looking at Michael. "I think we, as friends and neighbors, should be included in this little nodule of a lover's tale-bearing."

"Oh, I agree, darling," Franklin said, jumping on the bandwagon.

"If you all are through," Kelly finally spoke up, "can we get on with what we came down here for?" During the exchange, she had been subtly positioning herself so that Franklin was between her and the cliff. With surprise on her side, pushing him into the water should be easy, even given his larger size and weight.

As she and Michael both knew, it would be a chilling experience. This time of year, the water temperature would still be extremely frigid compared to the temperature of the air. It would feel good on a hot day like this one—once your body became accustomed to it. They usually eased themselves in from down below and jumped off the bluff only after they were conditioned to the chilly temperature.

"Okay, how do we do this?" Franklin asked, looking down at the crystal-clear, slow-moving water below.

"Like this," Kelly laughed, placing her hands in the middle of his back, and with a loud grunt, she pushed him into the creek. Michael was standing a few feet behind her and watched as she playfully shoved their new friend into the creek. He was grinning as Kelly turned her attention to Carlotta and raised her hands like she was going to do the same to her.

But Carlotta figured she would beat her new friend to the punch and jumped in after her husband. Both surfaced in the shallow water, yelling and shivering.

Thus began a close and intimate friendship between the two neighbors.

The rest of the day came off without a hitch. The four adults romped and swam for about an hour before finally calming down enough to eat. They spread a blanket out on the bluff and quietly laid their food out while listening to the crickets and frogs serenade them.

Just before sunset, they packed up to leave. Michael and the two women were headed up the slope to the wagon trail above, when Michael noticed Franklin wasn't with them. He discovered him kneeling at the edge of the rock ledge, staring intently at something below. "Franklin, are you coming?"

"Go ahead. I'll catch up to you in a minute," he called to them. "I'm watching this snake work its way across the water. It's fascinating," he murmured softly.

They disappeared on the trail above, leaving Franklin alone to stare at the reptile, which was disappearing as well. He got up to leave, and suddenly everything started going black. He looked all around him, but the trees and the creek—everything around him was slowly fading away to be replaced with total darkness.

Within seconds, it was pitch dark. He couldn't see a thing.

Franklin, I'm glad you're here.

It was strange. It was almost like the voice was coming from inside his head, but that was impossible. He needed to hear it again. He wanted to hear it again. "Where are you? Who are you?"

That's not important. What is important is that you are here...and I am here. I just wanted a minute for us to get acquainted.

Now he knew it wasn't inside his head. It was all around him. It filled the void and closed in on him from every side. That must be what made it seem like it came from his own head. The voice was very pleasing to the ear. It almost had a calming effect.

"What do you want with me?"

It didn't answer right away. It didn't have to. Time was suspended. Franklin was perfectly happy to wait however long it took to get an answer.

Nothing in particular. We will meet again.

"When?"

Again, the voice took longer than normal to answer, or was it just his imagination? Time just didn't seem to matter here. Franklin found he was anticipating the response. He was intensely desirous—thirsty even—to hear the voice again.

Soon.

"How will I know—"

He didn't have to wait for an answer this time as the voice interrupted him.

You will know, Franklin. You will know.

As quickly as it had come, the darkness disappeared. Franklin stood on the rock, intrigued by what had just happened to him.

"Franklin." He stirred at the sound of his name. It came from far away and with it the image had faded into his consciousness.

"What was I doing? Oh, the snake." He focused his attention on the water again and then remembered that the snake had disappeared. "I remember. I got up to leave and…Michael was shouting my name. Why would he do that?" Franklin wondered aloud. "I was leaving already."

He started up the incline. "Coming!" he shouted back. Franklin stopped and looked back at the bluff. "Fascinating!"

The months passed quickly for Carlotta. She had plenty to keep her busy. The house still needed, well, a personal touch. It wasn't because it had been sitting empty such a long time, it had only been six months. It was more that Carlotta wanted it to reflect their personality, rather than the Miller family who lived in it before.

Once that decision was made, she decided to take on the responsibility, teaching herself to do some things she had never tried before. Such as wallpapering every room in the house, refinishing the kitchen cabinets, and making new curtains. She was pleased, of course, with the help the neighbors had given them, but a different wallpaper would make it seem more like theirs.

She would also tend to the yard, which was where she spent most of her time.

The folks who had pitched in and fixed their place up had put in a lot of hard work. But they had only done the basics. The rest was up to her and Franklin.

Carlotta had made up her mind early on to have a beautiful yard. She sowed grass, planted flowers, fertilized, and watered all through the summer, and her hard work had paid off. She had what Kelly referred to as a comfortable, cool yard.

The only thing that was missing were children to run and play in it. Carlotta had looked forward to having children ever since she and Franklin first began courting. My, that seemed like such a long time ago. Always before, when she wanted to escape the problems of today, she would simply fall into a daydream, traveling back in time to her and Franklin's early days together.

But not lately!

Something was wrong this time. And she couldn't quite figure out what it was. She should be one of the happiest people on earth because she had just discovered she was with child—Franklin's child. Just the way she had always dreamed. But for some queer reason, she felt sad. It was hard for her to put into words; she had tried several times already. Mostly to Franklin because he had a right to know.

Maybe Kelly could help her figure it out. It was like a spell had been cast over her, one so strong she couldn't tear herself free of its hold—

Carlotta.

The call had come softly to her ears. Who would be calling her name? No one was allowed in her mind but her.

"Who is that?" Did she say the words, or did she just think them? Nothing seemed real anymore. How would she ever know—

Carlotta.

Again, someone called her name softly. I have to get out of—

Carlotta!

She was shaking. Why was she shaking? "Leave us alone!" she screamed.

She tried to stop her body from its helpless quivering, but it was useless. Suddenly she felt herself falling…falling…

"Ohh!" She started involuntarily and grabbed the table. She was okay. She wasn't falling; it was just a dream. But in the middle of the day?

For the first time, Carlotta noticed Kelly standing beside her. Her hand was on Carlotta's shoulder, shaking it gently.

"Carlotta? Honey, what is it?"

Carlotta's mind still wasn't clear. She gazed at Kelly, her face expressionless, her eyes glazed over.

Kelly drew her breath in sharply, removing her hand from Carlotta's shoulder and taking a step backward. The emptiness in her friend's eyes was overwhelming. "Carlotta, honey, you're scaring me," she said, still staring at the vacant but captivating expression, powerless to pull her eyes away.

With unrealized determination, Carlotta turned her face away from Kelly. Her eyes began to clear, as did her mind. Her body relaxed, and once again Kelly laid her hand on the bewildered woman's shoulder.

"Kelly? When did you get here?" she asked, surprised.

"I've been here for about a while. I stood at the front door, knocking for the longest time. When you didn't answer, I got concerned and came on in. You were sitting here…"

Carlotta waited for Kelly to finish her sentence. But after a few moments, it was evident she would not. "What? What was I doing, Kelly?" A note of panic crept into her voice.

Kelly kept her eyes on her friend. "I-I don't know. It was like you were having a dream or something." For a fleeting moment, she wavered, then summoned the courage to continue. "Then you screamed, 'Leave us alone!' Carlotta! What were you dreaming?"

An amazing transformation took place as Carlotta switched first from the tormented emptiness to the uncertainty of skepticism and finally to one of fear. She had a sinking feeling that she might have betrayed their family secret while in her unconscious state.

"I can't remember. What else did I say? Anything else?" she asked, petrified and feeling exposed.

"That's…all I heard," Kelly said hollowly. She sat down at the table next to Carlotta. "I had something I wanted to tell you," she whispered, tears beginning to moisten her soft blue eyes. "I'm going to have a baby."

Carlotta's brows flew up, and her melancholy spirit disappeared. "So am I," she cried in return. They fell into each other's arms, crying tears of joy now, the terror of moments ago forgotten.

The two friends sat at Carlotta's kitchen table, drinking coffee and making plans, the trepidation of the earlier incident an unimportant memory. An hour later, all their plans for the next five months seemingly made, a look of pure astonishment crossed Carlotta's face.

"I haven't even told Franklin yet. Well, obviously I have even more to tell him," she said, indicating Kelly's stomach.

"Listen," Kelly said, suddenly inspired with a touch of romanticism. "Why don't you fix him a special supper this evening and tell him then?"

"That's a great idea. I'll do it," she replied full of determination. For the first time in a long time, she felt good about herself.

"Ohh, god, it hurts." The screams were the loudest when the contractions first hit, but the pain lasted during the whole contraction hadn't counted on this part during her pregnancy. After nine months of hell, this was what she had looked forward to with such great expectations.

Carlotta's screams faded as the pain released its grip. "Honey, if you keep this up, I'm going to be looking for a bottle of whiskey when my time comes," Kelly teased her friend.

Her breaths coming in short, heavy gasps, Carlotta peered through sweat-drenched eyes. "Sarah, you make sure she gets to enjoy…every waking moment…of this wonderful experience." Then another pain hit. "Ahh!"

Sarah Robbins had done a lot of midwifing in her years. But she had given it up a few years before. With Kelly's help, the two pregnant women had begged, pleaded, and made promises until Sarah finally caved in. "Don't you worry none. She'll get her fair share of everything you're getting," Sarah promised. "Now, you pay attention to this baby. The next contraction, I want you to push, really hard. Do you hear? Really bear down." Her voice was raised above its normal tone to be sure Carlotta heard over the agonizing screams. She had been in labor all day, but they didn't send for Sarah until the pains were closer together.

"*I hear you!*" Carlotta shrieked through clenched teeth. "*Ahh!*"

Kelly braced herself for another onslaught at Carlotta's sudden outburst. "All right, here it comes, young lady," Sarah bellowed. "Now, push!"

Carlotta's fierce reply was brutal enough to penetrate even the thickest of skin. "*I am pushing!*" Kelly patted her hand, even as Carlotta was about to crush every joint in her other one. Yet she managed to rinse out the cloth with her one free hand and continue mopping Carlotta's brow.

All things considered, though, it was a relatively easy delivery. Everything went along fine, just the way it was supposed to, until…

As the baby's head began to clear the birth canal, Carlotta gave one final push. It was at that instant—just as the last ring of Carlotta's shrill cry died in her throat—that Kelly shocked everyone, including Carlotta, with a piercing scream of her own.

"Oh my god!" she exclaimed. She glanced at Carlotta, a startled look on her face. Suddenly, she grabbed her stomach. "I think it's my turn."

Sarah came into the living room holding a bundle wrapped in a small blanket. "Franklin, meet your daughter." She smiled at him. She uncovered the baby's face and showed the beaming father a tiny replica of its mother, its skin still glistening from the recent birth.

Franklin took his newborn daughter's miniature hand in his and cooed at her. "Isn't she beautiful? I swear, she's the spitting image of her mother." Sarah let him fuss over the infant a few more minutes before she interrupted.

"Franklin, I need for you to go get Michael."

"I'll do it right now," he offered. "Should I tell him why?" he wondered if there was something wrong.

"Yes," she replied. "Tell him he's about to become a father."

Franklin blanched at Sarah's explanation. "You mean—"

"She's in labor too," Sarah finished for him. "Yes, I do. Now get on with you. Scat! Oh, Franklin."

He stopped just short of running out the door. "Stop by and see if Carol Sheridan can help me, will you? I just ran out of helpers. Now go on, git." She didn't wait for Franklin to exit before she disappeared up the stairs to get Carlotta settled and then begin on Kelly.

CHAPTER NINE

The next morning, Stoney and Susie sat in his car on the side of County Road 135 adjacent to the dirt lane that led to Rockhole. They had been there for an hour and still hadn't convinced themselves that they wanted to do what they came for. Stoney was remembering the last time. It wasn't the kind of experience that prompted one to return for more.

"Well, the choice is yours," Susie declared. "If you want my opinion, it's not worth it. Personally, I don't think we're going to find anything there anyway."

Stoney thought about it for a little while. "I think I'm more interested in what will happen to me than in finding any clues," he proclaimed. "Whatever it is, is directly related to your nightmares and Brian's death. Let's just look at it like an experiment." He smiled. "Ready?" He got out of the car and started for the barbed-wire gate. As he was about to climb between the two upper strands, he noticed that Susie was still in the car. "Are you coming?"

"Yeah, I'm coming," she said sourly. "I can't very well let you go alone, can I?" She slipped out of the car and climbed through the wire while he held it for her, then she did the same from the other side of the fence for him. They trudged along the dirt lane silently, each with their own thoughts.

Had she not been so preoccupied, Susie would have noticed a gradual change coming over Stoney. At first, he was engrossed with thoughts of Brian and this being the last place his brother was alive. But then his silent contemplation slowly gave way to an altered state. He still managed to put one foot in front of the other. But it required a great effort on his part. *Left foot, right foot, left foot.* He said over and over in his mind, as though he had to be reminded which came next.

By the time they arrived, Stoney was transformed into a living statue. Something that Susie had yet to discover. "Well, we're here," she said without any emotion. "How do you feel?" She looked at her fiancé. Susie couldn't believe it. She had just looked at him, and he seemed normal. How could it have happened so fast? "Stoney?" she said timidly, grabbing for his arm. But her reaction was too slow. He had already lost consciousness and fell to the ground. He had gone into convulsions. "*Stoney!*" Susie dropped to the ground beside him. She started to turn him over onto his back when she suddenly realized…

They weren't alone.

Mary J. couldn't remember her last dream. She knew it hadn't been that long ago. But for some inescapable reason, the dream eluded her. She thought maybe Brian was in it, but it was vague, and…She shook her head. It was just too hard to recall.

Her mind wandered aimlessly. She floated from one image to another.

Suddenly, Brian's face appeared to her. He had the look of death, pale and drawn. His eyes were accusing, penetrating. Mary J. lowered her own eyes, averting his visual attack.

"Why did you leave me? You left me to face that monster alone. As long as we're together, we can do anything…but you left me… alone."

"I-I'm sorry, Brian. I don't know why I left. I was scared. Brian? Do you hear me? I was afraid. I was afraid. I was afraid!"

Don't worry about that, Mary J.

She jerked her head around, trying to find the soft, smooth voice that spoke to her. It sounded like an elderly woman's voice.

That's all behind you now. There are more important things to worry about.

"Who are you? Where are you? I can't see you—"

Suddenly the woman appeared. She stood squarely in front of Mary J. and didn't try to hide her appearance. Mary J. gasped as she stared at the beautiful, ancient woman. "Are you a nurse? Where's Brian?"

It is not important what I am. That I am here, is. I have come to warn you about the Curse.

"Are you a ghost?" she asked desperately, not hearing what the old woman said.

Mary J., you must pay close attention to what I'm saying. You need to understand what is happening to you and your family and why. The only way is to heed my warnings. It is imperative that you listen and understand.

"I know. You're an angel. You've come to take me home."

Mary J.! Clear your mind. I can only tell you this once. Your family is in danger. It is the Curse. You must do something about the Curse. Heed my warning, Mary J., heed my warning.

"But how? What do I do?" she asked, puzzled.

You must face the demon that curses you. You must go to the place where the demon lives and face it. When the time comes, you will know what to do.

"The demon?" Mary J. was frightened. "What demon? Why does it have to be me?" She looked around, but the woman was gone. "Hey, where are you? Come back." She was disturbed by what the woman had said, but then her thoughts quickly returned to Brian. Was that really him she saw? Maybe he was fine, and nothing happened. She imagined it? Was he all right?

Mary J. drifted back into a fitful slumber.

At first, Susie couldn't make out who it was. Frantically, she thought about running away and hiding in the trees—but only briefly. She had to stay with Stoney. She focused on the figure coming toward them, wondering how she would protect herself and Stoney. She was madly searching about for a rock, a stick, anything to defend herself with. Then she recognized the intruder.

It was Sheriff Rogers.

Thank God. He could help her with Stoney. She cried out to the peace officer. "Sheriff! Hurry! There's something wrong with

Stoney." She tried to make Stoney a little more comfortable. He had stopped convulsing and was lying perfectly still. She straightened his arms and legs out.

By this time the sheriff had closed the distance between them. "What's wrong with him?" he asked suspiciously, kneeling beside her.

"I don't know," she cried loudly. "We were walking toward Rockhole, and he suddenly collapsed." An overwhelming sensation swept over her. Wait a minute! Why was he here? Susie wondered silently, when suddenly it dawned on her. He followed us! But why? Or maybe it was just coincidence.

Sheriff Rogers checked Stoney's pulse. "Pretty rapid," he commented. "But it doesn't seem to be life-threatening. I suggest we try to get him back to the car." Together they managed to lift Stoney up and prop him between them, half carrying, half dragging him toward the road. After a few hundred feet, Stoney began to come around. He moaned, sluggish at first and then his eyes opened.

"What happened?" he whispered in a harsh, raspy voice.

No one spoke for a minute. Then Susie stumbled under his weight. "Just hang on, Stoney. We're almost to the car. We'll talk in a minute." She was laboring under his weight but tried not to think about it. She kept stumbling along, trying to keep up with the sheriff.

"Can you stand on your own?" the sheriff inquired.

Susie doubted he could. She was out of breath and her muscles ached. She let Rogers hold Stoney up as she walked over to the barbed wire. "We're at the fence. Can you climb through?" she asked.

She stepped on the middle strand with her right foot and pushed down, while lifting the top strand, thereby spreading them apart. Sheriff Rogers held on to Stoney's arm while the younger man climbed through, but Stoney stood up too soon and snagged his shirt on the barbed wire. Susie heard it rip and lifted the wire a little higher. The fence released its bite on the material and Stoney passed on through, stumbling toward the car. He slammed up against it but managed to stay on his feet.

Rogers quickly followed and grabbed hold of Stoney before he could fall. Susie climbed over the fence and joined them. She opened the car door and helped Stoney sit down. "How do you feel?" she asked.

Stoney looked at her with the silly, lopsided grin of a person who was about to throw up. "I don't feel so good." He winced, holding his stomach. She put the back of her hand on his forehead and quickly took it away.

"My god, you've got a chill and you're still white as a sheet. I'm taking you to the hospital," she said firmly. She put his seat belt around him and fastened it, something she wouldn't have bothered with if the sheriff wasn't there. She slammed the car door shut and started around to the driver's side. "Thanks for your help, Sheriff." He followed them out here to find out what they were up to. He had warned them to leave the investigating to him, but it was evident they hadn't listened. He had decided to try again and had followed them out here. But with Stoney getting sick suddenly, he decided to wait.

"Maybe I should follow you in," he suggested. "You know, give you an escort."

"Oh, I'm sure it won't be necessary," Susie said as she jumped in behind the wheel. Then as she hooked up her own seat belt, she said, "It's probably just the flu. There's a bug going around, isn't there?" The sheriff shrugged.

"I better get him in there before he throws up in the car." She turned the steering wheel all the way to the left and rolled the car forward until the front right tire was almost in the ditch. Then she backed up, turning the wheel all the way to the right, bringing the car to a stop at the edge of the opposite ditch. Once more, she put the transmission in drive and took off toward town, completing her three-point turn.

Still wanting to warn them off the investigation, Rogers decided to follow them anyway. There was plenty of time to come back and get that second look at the crime scene, he reassured himself.

By the time they arrived in town, the air flowing in through the open car window had completely revived Stoney. He was lucid and his color had returned. "It's really weird, don't you think?"

"What is?" Susie asked, distracted. She had been watching in the rearview mirror and a couple of times she thought she noticed the sheriff following them. "Damn it! I was going to go back to our place, but now I'm going to have to take you to the hospital like I told him."

"Who? The sheriff?"

"Yes, the sheriff. Who do you think?" she replied scornfully. She was mad but not at Stoney. "He's following us."

Stoney turned in the seat so he could see behind them and watched for a while. After a minute or so, he finally turned back around. "I didn't see him. Are you sure?" She threw him an amused look. "Anyway, why would he want to follow us?"

She shrugged and drove on in silence. A few blocks from the hospital, Stoney said again, "That was weird, wasn't it?"

"What?" she asked again.

He laughed and then realized there was nothing to laugh at. "I'm talking about what happened to me back there. That's twice it's happened." He looked at her, but she was concentrating on her driving. "Every time I get close to Rockhole, I pass out."

The hospital parking lot was nearly full. Susie made two passes at it before finding a spot that she was satisfied with. "Passing out was not all you did." She hadn't really thought about it, but he probably didn't remember what happened to him. "You had convulsions too. Your heart rate was really high, and you turned pale, as white as a sheet." Her brows furrowed into a frown as she tried to remember if there was anything she had forgotten. "Oh, yeah," she suddenly remembered. "You had chills."

"Damn! It's a wonder I survived," he said mockingly.

"Let's go in and see Mary J. since we're already here," she suggested. They walked hand in hand into the main entrance of the hospital. As they rounded the corridor where it turned to the left, a doctor hurried past them and into Mary J.'s room. A feeling of consternation gripped them as they picked up their pace.

When they went into the room, Mary J. looked like she was asleep, but the monitor they had hooked to her was sending out a plethora of erratic signals. Besides the doctor that had gone in just ahead of them, there were two nurses and a resident working on their sister.

Susie desperately wanted to ask what happened to Mary J., but she didn't want to distract anyone from helping her sister. So she tried to be patient and contented herself to watch until they were finished. At one point she buried her face in Stoney's shoulder, convinced that something terrible was wrong. The medical team worked with Mary J. for the better part of an hour before they pronounced her out of danger. Other than a nurse who would stay and monitor the patient's vital signs, the doctor was the last one to leave the room. When he noticed Stoney and Susie looking on and the tears in Susie's eyes, he stopped and asked them, "Are you family?"

Considering Susie's state of mind, Stoney decided it better if he spoke for them. "This is her sister and I'm her brother-in-law," he informed the doctor. "What was wrong with her?"

"Can't say for sure," he replied. "Since she's in a coma, anything we might deduce would be guesswork at best. Her vital signs escalated to a dangerous level. We had to bring them down to a more manageable rate, or she could have gone into cardiac arrest."

Susie had trouble accepting the doctor's vague explanation. "So what caused her heart to do that?" she asked hostilely.

The doctor ignored her angry outburst, shrugging it off as grief, something he had to do often in his business. "My guess is she had a nightmare, and that's what set her off. I'm afraid I can't do any better than that. Excuse me please." He departed quickly, leaving two confused people behind.

Their minds on something other than the room's occupants, they marched toward Mary J.'s bed. Susie halted suddenly, catching her breath when she noticed Dala standing in one corner of the room. She appeared to be in a stupor, heedless of their presence. Susie went over to the distraught woman and lightly touched her arm. "Dala? Were you here during the whole thing?" she asked, surprised that she hadn't noticed the girl before. She was sure the redhead had been there for a while, attested to by the fact that her eyes were red and swollen. A sure indication that she had been crying.

When Dala finally looked at her, Susie could see that she was on the edge of collapse. Her emotions were raw thanks to witnessing the medical teams reviving of Mary J. She couldn't believe they had let her stay in the room. Must not have realized she was there, Susie deduced.

"Yes, I was," Dala replied hollowly. "It was awful. I thought, for a minute there, that she wouldn't make it." She couldn't be sure, but Susie got a distinct impression that Dala's words were mechanical. She lacked the normal enthusiastic emotion that was so much a part of her vibrant personality. At any rate, she didn't seem to be herself. "I think, we should go to the cafeteria," she advised them, nodding in the direction of the nurse. What she wanted to talk about should be done in more private quarters.

The somber trio made their way silently to the cafeteria where all three ordered coffee. It just so happened that their clandestine meeting coincided with the noon lunch hour and tables were at a premium. Stoney, the taller of the three, gazed gloomily around the room and, after his eyes made three scans of the area, detected two nurses finishing their meal and were about to leave. He signaled the girls to follow him and hurried toward the vacant table before someone else claimed it.

In a short time, they had installed themselves into various seats around the table. Stoney and Susie waited expectantly for whatever important news or question Dala had for them.

She didn't waste any time. "Does the Curse mean anything to you guys?"

Stoney didn't catch the significance of Dala's question immediately, but Susie sat in startled silence. Dala's glance passed over each one in turn and then settled on Susie. A satisfied smile spread over Dala's face. "Ho-how?"

Dala noted Susie's indecision. "You know something, don't you?" she asked accusingly. The younger girl's demeanor told a lot, but unfortunately, it did not explain what was meant by the Curse. Dala was confident she had touched a soft spot, but she wasn't confident that Susie would tell her about it. She was becoming angry at herself for her belligerence. It clouded her reasoning. "What does it mean?" she asked suspiciously.

An indiscreet pout played at the perimeters of Susie's mouth. She wondered why Dala was being so hateful. "I don't know," she muttered quietly, still feeling the sting of Dala's remarks.

Dala was suddenly complacent. Not only was she her old self, but she seemed unaware that she'd been hateful. "You must know something about it," she said in disbelief.

Stoney was thoughtful for a minute. Susie was pensive. Dala was beginning to wonder what in the hell was going on. She thought she knew this family. Mary J. had been her best friend for several years, and Daniel and Sadie had treated her like their own daughter.

"I wonder if this has anything to do with what happened to me a while ago," Stoney said, reflective of the freakish affair at Rockhole.

"What are you talking about?" Dala demanded.

The whole bizarre incident was recreated for Dala as Susie told her not only about today's odd occurrence but the previous one as well. Of course, none of it made any sense. And she wondered silently what it had to do with the Curse.

"I don't see the connection," she said warily.

Next, Susie launched into a dissertation about her own nightmares. She told Dala what she could remember about them, which was very little. But the one thing she did remember was the old woman talking about the Curse.

Dala didn't say anything.

"Well?" Susie prompted. "Am I crazy?"

"Certifiably," Dala kidded. "How in the hell did we progress from Mary J. having a nightmare to all this?" She pointed an index finger at Stoney. "You pass out at Rockhole and go into convulsions—not once but twice." She then aimed the pointed digit at Susie. "You have two similar dreams where some old lady visits you—probably from the past—and warns you about the Curse. "Then you have a nightmare where some evil creature takes control of your body and shows you some really gruesome stuff." She was either trembling from fear or shaking from anger—probably anger, Susie decided. This was all unbelievable and sounded made up.

She placed her hands on the table as though she were going to get up and leave. "You are both crazy," she said, not trying to hide her cynicism. She stared into her coffee cup.

"Dala, we're not making this up. I know it sounds...kind of out there," Stoney said, searching carefully for the right words and not finding them. "But if you have another explanation for all this—we're listening."

It suddenly dawned on Susie that there was one fact that Dala didn't know about yet. "You didn't see Brian's face," she said, her own face lighting up.

"Yeah, you didn't see that," Stoney agreed with her.

"That was real...and unreal," she said, remembering the horrible-looking collection of evil faces. She shuddered, filled with a sudden dread.

"You know, if you put it all together, it does make some sense," Stoney argued. "This whole thing started with Brian dying at Rockhole and Mary J. ending up in a coma. And I think her coma is due to something other than the shock of Brian's death." He noticed the look of uncertainty on Dala's face but continued anyway. "I think she saw something that caused her to have such a traumatic reaction that it put her in a coma," he replied, pleased with his powers of deduction.

"I don't know," Dala drawled, still not convinced.

Stoney's head dropped, but he was determined to not give up. "All I know is, something is going on at Rockhole. Brian died there. Every time I get close to it, I black out. Mary J. has a nightmare that nearly sends her into cardiac arrest. Susie has not one but two nightmares that are probably, and the key here is probably, related to Mary J.'s. This old woman shows up warning us of a curse—not saying what it was you understand—and you don't think there's something strange going on?"

"I see what you mean?" Dala's anger abated under his emotional outburst. "So tell me about Brian's face. What do you think happened there?"

"Hard to say. But I think it's at the heart of the thing. One thing is certain, Brian may be de-dead." He paused.

"Stoney," Dala sighed at the anguish on his face.

"I'm all right." He smiled at her and then continued. "But his death has provided the strongest clue yet. Other than that, we have mine and Susie's incidents to go on—until Mary J. wakes up that is. And then, like the doctor says, she might not remember anything."

It was a somber-looking group sitting around the table in the hospital cafeteria. "I think it's time to go see Grandma Rachel," Susie said blankly.

"What good would that do?" Dala asked.

"Mom and Dad know something about all this, but they're not talking. I think Grandma might know something about it," Susie added. "All I do know is, something is going on and considering what's happening to us, I think we have a right to know. Someone's going to have to talk eventually."

The party broke up after that with Dala returning to Mary J.'s room and Stoney and Susie heading out to their grandmother's farm.

Unknown to them, they still wore a tail. Something was definitely going on with these two, and Rogers was determined to find out what it was and what it had to do with his case.

Robert and Rachel Clark were never told by Carlotta or Derek that they were first cousins. After marrying her own brother, Carlotta didn't figure marrying your own cousin was all that bad. Derek, Carlotta's youngest brother, was confused over the entire situation anyway and decided to stay out of it. He gave his youngest son, Robert, and his fiancée, his blessing and went about his business. Rachel and Robert had been happily married for seventy years until he passed away in his sleep one night six years ago.

Rachel sat in her padded rocking chair on the front porch of their seventy-two-year-old log cabin, holding her cane and listening as a car progressed slowly along the winding driveway that came to an end at the front porch of the ancient home. Rachel had been blind for ten years, but at the age of ninety-two, she still got around well.

She heard two car doors slam, so she deduced that there were two visitors. "Who's there?" she called out in a tottering tone. Her voice may be faltering by deteriorated vocal cords, but you could hear the trenchant mind projected through the scratchy utterances.

"Hi, Grandma," Susie called out cheerily. "It's me and Stoney. We just came by to see how you were doing." They climbed the rickety steps to the porch, careful of the worn planks, especially the third one, which could give at any time. Everyone in the family had been after Rachel to let them fix things around the cabin, but she declined, saying, "I can't see it anyway, so why bother?"

Stoney leaned over and gave her a quick kiss on the cheek. "Hi, Granny. How are you doing?"

Regardless of the physical problems she might have as a result of old age, Rachel Clark had no problem with her hearing. Fortunately for Stoney and Susie, her memory was another area unaffected by her advanced years. "I'm nearly a hundred years old, and I don't feel a day over eighty," she said, a big smile on her face. "You kids don't usually come out here just to chitchat. What's on your minds?" she asked, rotating her head from one to the other, as though she could still see.

Susie glanced at Stoney. At the same time, he looked questioningly at her. She shook her head vigorously, declining the offer.

"You kids figure out who's going to speak first?" she smirked, self-satisfied.

Stoney chuckled. "Nothing gets by you, does it, Granny. We have some strange questions, and no one seems to want to talk about it or give us a straight answer. Do you think you could help us out?" he asked hopefully.

She smiled at her grandson, with an impish twinkle in her eye. "Not if I don't know the questions."

"They're not tough," he said hesitantly. "They're just...well, they're strange."

"They have to do with me, Stoney, Brian, and Mary J," Susie added quickly.

Rachel winced at the mention of Brian's name, feeling his loss tremendously. She had never accepted death well, recalling the stories her mother had told her about the untimely deaths of her brother and sister and then the mysterious death of her father. "How is Mary J.?" she asked, her manner suddenly bleak. Rachel was devastated at the loss of her three great-grandchildren, but she knew why it had happened.

The Curse.

Something she had been trying to forget for a great many years.

The two youngsters looked at each other. Susie finally spoke. "She's still in a coma, Grandma." Rachel's question opened the door for their first question. "That's one of the reasons we're here."

"I'm listening."

Susie explained what happened at the hospital before coming out. She then described her own experience and encounter with the old woman. "The really strange thing about it was, I didn't hear her say the words out loud. It was like they were in my head, like a feeling, a sensation," she tried to explain. "I just knew they were there, even though I didn't actually hear them." Susie had a distinct feeling she was rambling and not making much sense. But Rachel didn't seem to notice.

"What words?" Rachel asked so quietly Susie almost didn't hear.

"The Curse."

Rachel drew her breath in sharply. A gesture that didn't go unnoticed by Susie. "Maybe we can finally get somewhere," she said, but no one heard her. And then a little louder, "What is it, Grandma?"

That was something no one had breathed a word about since Carlotta's death. The rest of the family had made a pact to let it die with her. She had been hopeful that beginning with Daniel and Elizabeth, their family would be able to return to normal. But evidently, such was not the case.

Why couldn't it let them be?

Why couldn't the mistakes of the past loosen their grip and remain in the past? Then maybe this family could get on with living. Suddenly she had an appalling thought. What if the Curse had started all over again? Could that be what was happening to Brian and Mary J.? Rachel wished more than ever, she could undo what was done before more harm came to her family. Dear God, why couldn't this nightmare end?

Susie was concerned with the elderly woman's silence. The only sounds that could be heard was the constant chirping of the birds in the trees surrounding the old homestead. Somewhere in the distance an old pickup with a bad muffler rumbled by and backfired. It was the only sound within hearing to remind them of the outside world.

That was one reason Rachel liked it here so much. She had moved away from the ridge after her mother had died. And never regretted it for a minute.

"Grandma?"

Rachel was snapped from her reverie by Susie's persistent voice. She wished more than ever that she could escape the next few moments as she looked at her granddaughter. "Honey, why don't you go in the house and get us all something to drink. Then we'll talk about it." She found the young girl's knee and patted it gently. "There's some sodas in the refrigerator, honey." She waited until Susie had disappeared into the house and then frowned at Stoney. "You've had a rather odd, unexplainable experience, haven't you?"

He looked surprised at his grandmother. "Yes, I have. How did you know?"

Her frown deepened. "Tell me about it." Stoney recounted the two incidents for the elderly matron. By the time he had finished, Susie was back with three glasses filled with ice and Coke.

"Did I miss anything?" she asked suspiciously. She knew she had and wondered why her grandmother waited until she was in the house before talking about it.

"Not much," Stoney admitted. "I was just telling granny about my little problem at Rockhole." Susie cast a curious eye at Rachel, wondering what was going through her mind. "I think that if we're to get anywhere with this mystery," Stoney continued, "we need to turn over a few rocks." He turned his attention back to the elderly woman. But she was staring straight ahead and thinking about the questions that both wanted to ask.

Rachel gave the matter a lot of thought before answering. She loved her grandkids, and the last thing on earth she wanted to do was hurt them. She and Samuel Conners, Susie's grandfather on her mother's side, had long ago decided to keep the whole messy quagmire from the rest of the family. They were in hopes that it would go away.

And here it was again.

After sixty years, it had surfaced once more. It should never have plagued Brian and Mary J., though. It should have died with Carlotta. She didn't understand why this was happening. Rachel allowed her thoughts the pleasure of drifting back over the past, her mind sifting through the events that brought their family to its present state. Of course, most of the damage was done before she was born, but there were still some mixed marriages after that. The most recent, she now knew, had been dealt its blow.

"I'm afraid I'm not going to be much help to you," she said to both. "But in answer to your question, no. You're not going crazy."

Their crestfallen visages told a more exacting story than words ever could. They were glad, of course, that they were not going out of their minds. But they also believed that if anyone would know whether they had a sordid past, Grandma Rachel would. She always seemed to know more about their family history than anyone else in the family. They had always been able to count on her before. It had been up to her to keep the family together after Grandpa Clark had died a few years ago.

"What do you know?" Stoney asked abruptly. "I mean, somebody has to know what in the hell is happening to us. It's really becoming scary. Do you understand what I'm saying?" His voice had risen so much he was almost yelling.

Rachel gave her grandson a patronizing smile. "I have been listening," she replied in a low, soft voice in deference to her grandson's loud, obnoxious tone.

"No! I don't think you understand at all," he continued in the same intonation. "You didn't see Brian's face. It-it was the most horrifying thing I've ever seen. It wasn't even his. It was like his face had somehow been removed from his body and replaced with several strips of..." His sentence trailed off unfinished, not really knowing how to explain it. He stared at her, steadfast in his stance, his gaze never wavering. "Granny, I don't scare easily, but this thing has me terrified. Please! If you know anything about this...curse, you've got to tell us. Please," he begged, finally lowering his voice.

Whether it was her love for her grandson or his sense of urgency, Rachel wasn't sure, but she knew they would be happy with nothing less than the truth, or at least some part of it. After all, at this point they didn't really know what the truth was, or how extensive it was.

So I need only be selective, she told her herself. *But how do I decide what morsel of truth is the right one? It has to be something that will aid them in their confused state. But it cannot be such that it impacts them beyond their acceptability.* She searched through the vast library of her mind. She kept coming up empty and finally decided on something she believed would satisfy their insatiable curiosity.

"How much do you know about your great-grandfather and great-grandmother?" she asked Stoney, looking him right in the eye.

"Great-Grandma Carlotta and Great-Grandpa Franklin?" he asked, surprised.

With a nod, she acknowledged his question. "The very same." Rachel hesitated before going on. What she was about to divulge would not come easy. It was a secret she had carried ever since her childhood and thought she would never have to tell. "You must promise me you won't reveal any of this to anyone. Promise me," she demanded. They both said yes in unison. "Before they were husband and wife, they were brother and sister," she said quickly to get it over with. She launched into a long explanation of how the family was split up, how their relationship developed, and the subsequent events that led to the family curse.

Stoney and Susie listened spellbound to the story as it unfolded. They had heard the story about the big fire that destroyed the city and were always amazed at how their family had all survived and then rebuilt the city, making it even better than it was before. Never had the story been told quite like this, though. It was so bizarre, they didn't want to believe it at first. But Rachel assured them it was true.

My god, it was true.

Their family did live under a curse. And it all started over a hundred years ago, when a brother and a sister fell in love—not knowing they were related. And of course, it was too late then. They were already in love, and for the two young people, nothing would deter them. Like Romeo and Juliet. But unlike Romeo and Juliet, this young couple did not take their lives; instead, they got married.

They lived happily ever after—until the Curse.

Sheriff Rogers hurried up the sidewalk that led to the building which housed the county offices. No sooner had Stoney and Susie turned into the long, winding driveway that led to Rachel Clark's house than his car radio came to life. He picked up the microphone and responded to the call.

It was his deputy. "Go ahead, Mike. I'm listening," he said into the handheld microphone.

"Sheriff, Grady Miles called a few minutes ago and wants to talk to you. Over."

What in the world could Grady want with him today, unless it was something to do with the *Clark* case? "Did he say what he wanted?" the sheriff asked, foregoing the formal radio lingo.

"No, sir. He just said to get hold of you, that it was very important that he see you—now. He seemed pretty excited, Sheriff," the deputy's voice came back over the radio. Mike had been his deputy for two years and had done a pretty good job. Besides that, he knew most people in town, and he knew Grady Miles well enough to know if the call was important. "What do you want me to do, Sheriff? Over."

Rogers thought about it briefly. If it had something to do with the *Clark* case, he needed to be there—and quick. He pushed down hard on the accelerator and watched as the speedometer needle jumped. He loved the way this car responded to his touch. "Call him back and tell him I'm on my way. ETA is ten minutes." The sheriff got a kick out of listening to Mike on the radio. He still used it like they did in the old days, very polite by signing off each time he ended his transmission.

"Roger, Sheriff. Base out."

The drive back into town was long enough that it gave Rogers some time to think. And what he thought about was the fact that the *Clark* case had never been solved. For that matter, the one after that, the Baker case had never been solved either. Both men, Joshua

Conners and Franklin Baker, had died at Rockhole over a hundred years ago, and the case files had never been closed. Every now and then he pulled them out and went over them again just to keep them fresh in his mind. The most recent time had been yesterday. As he sat at his desk going over the files, he discovered one irrefutable fact. There were similarities between each of those and Brian Clark's. His counterpart from back then, Sheriff Eason, didn't have the modern techniques and equipment at his disposal that Rogers enjoyed today. He hoped more than anything that he could solve this case and then maybe, with a little luck, solve those two cases as well. Thereby, ending a bloody nose the sheriff's office wore, not to mention a century of unanswered questions.

He rolled into the parking lot and skidded to a stop in the spot reserved for official cars. Rogers checked his watch. Four minutes on the dot. Damn, he was good.

By the time Rogers entered the coroner's office, Grady was pacing the floor. "Oh, good. You're finally here. I was afraid it would be finished before you got here. Come on, follow me. I've never seen anything like it," Miles rambled on.

Rogers ignored everything he said after that. One of Grady Miles' favorite saying was "I've never seen anything like it." Of course, he was usually right. Most things were a first in his line of work. It was unique in that no individual's death or reaction to it was exactly the same. So most of the time, the good doctor was correct.

They had arrived at the morgue, and Miles was pulling the door open that housed the body of Brian Clark. He slid the slab out and unzipped the black bag part of the way down. Rogers took one look and knew immediately what the coroner had called him for.

Brian Clark's face was returning to normal.

At least three of the sections had reverted to the young man's own countenance. "Jesus Christ, look at that!" Rogers shouted emphatically. He took a step backward, as though it were contagious.

Miles had gone over to one of the cabinets on the wall and taken out a video camera. He began taping the change as it took place. Within a few minutes, it was complete and now, half of Brian's face was back to normal.

"What do you make of that, Doc?"

Grady Miles thought it over a while. The conclusion he came to, that this was way over his head. "I think it's time we brought in an expert," he said, putting the camera down. "Remember what happened when I poked his face the last time?"

"Jesus. Don't do that again," Rogers cried, recoiling at the thought.

Miles smiled at his queasiness. "It's all right. Look." He poked at the normal side of Brian's face, and it reacted like a normal dead person. A slight depression in the skin but solid enough in death that it didn't give.

It made no difference that the dead body was back to what Miles called normalcy, the sheriff still didn't like that kind of thing. He thought he'd change the subject before his stomach did a complete flip-flop. "So who's the expert your calling in?"

"Father Pritchard," Miles answered. "I think he can shed some light on"—he gestured at the corpse—"what's going on here. At least, I hope he can." He shoved the slab back into the wall and closed the door. As Rogers left the building, the coroner told him, "I'll let you know what happens about…you know."

"Thanks, Doc. See you later." Rogers left the building shaking his head. Another mystery to add to an already mounting heap, he sighed with resignation.

"How much do you think they know?" Sadie asked apprehensively.

Daniel was beginning to think the past would never leave them alone. He wished he didn't know as much as he did about their family. He wasn't meant to, that much was certain. The things he and Sadie found out were intended to remain secreted from ever being seen again. They were to be buried with the family's storied past. It was most definitely an accident when Daniel stumbled across the old chest full of letters, pictures, and other reminders of the once proud Clark tradition.

A great deal of agony went into Daniel's decision to keep the shocking discovery from the rest of the family. He had every intention of concealing it from Sadie too but soon found that to be an impossible task. They rarely kept secrets from each other, and Daniel was unable to do so then. Their horror was indescribable at what they read in the letters.

"We surely weren't meant to see these," Daniel uttered quietly. He pointed at the outside of the chest. "See the burn marks around this thing? It was supposed to have burned with the rest of that old house, and I'm sure that's what they thought had happened. But it didn't. It survived the fire and has lain here, undiscovered, all these years covered over by the debris. I wouldn't have found it myself, except that I saw the sun glinting off something in the pile. When I got to digging around, I stumbled across this," he hissed, slamming the lid down hard.

"Do you think Rachel knows about any of this?"

He had to think about it. The letters only told part of what happened back then. "Rachel was born afterward from everything I can tell." He shook his head slowly. "The only way she could know was if her mother told her. It's hard to say for sure."

"She's never talked about it. Never said much of anything about the family outside of good memories—except for that distant look she gets in her eyes when she talks about her father," Sadie remembered.

"We have to find a safe place for this until we can dispose of it," Daniel confided. "But I want to keep it until I have time to look through it all." Sadie gave him a brief nod. The only sign that she had heard him. So on top of their own indiscretion, which was bad enough, there was this to add to it.

"Where will it all end?" she asked of no one and of everyone. "Where will it all end?"

Chapter Ten

April 2, 1901

Dear Mama,

Just once I would like to be able to write and ask some ordinary questions or give you and Daddy some normal news of our lives here. But nay, it seems that lately everything I write about is terribly depressing. So once again, my letter arrives with heartbreaking news.

I would rather an affliction had come to me than to have to suffer this burden. I don't think I can live another day. I feel like the weight of the world has been dumped on my shoulders, and every person on the planet is pushing down as hard as they possibly can. What did we do so terrible that it deserves such a severe punishment? Have we not been subjected to enough tragedy in our lives already?

It has been a year since Diane disappeared. She was just a baby, barely two years old. She was playing alone down by the brook below the house. She was in my line of sight all the time, except for a moment. I was hanging up laundry and was wrestling with a sheet. The wind was blowing and making it difficult. By the time I finally got it hung, I glanced down toward the brook and she was gone. It was only a few moments.

She would often go there and sit with her feet dangling in thc water. And just that quick—she was gone. Vanished. It happened so fast. I still can't believe it. I have replayed it over and over again in my mind. Mama, it was my fault. I should never have let her go alone. I could have taken time out to spend a little time with her. Oh god! This is my punishment for falling in love with my brother, isn't it?

She didn't come home, Mama. I couldn't find her. We looked until it got dark. Then the sheriff called out a search party, but nothing turned up. He said most likely she was taken by a stranger passing by, and he would check with neighboring counties and send out some reward posters.

I don't think we'll ever see her or hear from her again. Why has God brought this torturous issue on us? How are we supposed to bear the pain of such a heavy burden—a second time? Of this much you can be sure. I don't plan on letting such a thing happen to me ever again. Losing two children is too much. It is more than any human being should be asked to shoulder in a lifetime.

I still await a letter from you—to know if you will ever forgive us—to know if you still love us. Please write. Please—please!

Our love to you,

Joshua, Jenny, and Baby Diane

Tracy hated death.

She always had. It scared her more than anyone would ever know, and basically, she refused to talk about it. It had always been her little secret, and it always would. She avoided anyone or anyplace that had anything to do with death. It was one of the reasons why she didn't go to church. Instead of talking about life, which they should, they talked about death and hell.

Tracy hated funerals.

Especially funerals for little children. She attended the funeral of Diane Conners simply because she was Jenny's best friend. And a mother needs her friends around her at a time like that. It was a small gathering since folks were scattered in a rural area like Crater Ridge—especially in an area like Crater Ridge.

Right after the funeral is usually the worst time for most people. It's an adjustment period—a time when the most devastating event in your life suddenly swarms over you like a thief in the night. It is a quintessential being that sucks the life out of you until all that's left is an empty shell that once was recognized as the individual you were. One who loved and gave love. A person who was known in the community, individualized by his or her particular traits. Generous, caring, trustworthy, respectable, honorable, and dependable. All this was what formed the nucleus of what was now an abandoned, barren, lifeless void.

That was when Jenny needed her the most. Tracy just hoped she could hold up her end of the deal—that of being the best friend of someone who just lost their second child in three years. These would be trying times for Jenny and Joshua. She too for that matter. Other than having a miscarriage, she had never lost a child. What would she tell her friend that might soothe her deadened feelings? What words could she possibly say that had not been said before that would make some difference in how Jenny felt. What great truths could she utter to keep this childless mother from becoming another charter victim for the doctors of the feared sanitariums? A place where only those who were completely crazy themselves would go.

Somewhere, somehow, she would need to find the right thing to say. Jenny needed her. And she would not desert her in the greatest hour of her need.

Once her mind was made up, she had only to act on it—for her, the hardest part.

Tracy had been sitting at her own kitchen table drinking a cup of coffee, while reflecting on these past several months. Thinking about the events that led up to the funeral of little Diane. Until they came to Jenny's door with the horrible news of the discovery, there was still hope. There was always a chance that Diane was still alive. Jenny was so hopeful, she had even become pregnant again. That good news had preceded the bad news of Diane by a couple of days.

Tracy had been there the day the sheriff came. Having finally worked through her feelings, she was doing what little she could to brighten Jenny's days—and for a while, it was working. They were visiting back and forth, just like old times. Apparently, time can heal old wounds—not make them go away, just scab them over, so the softness underneath wasn't exposed to everyday life. And then the sheriff came.

He dispatched his morbid bit of news with a dispirited effort. When he was finished, the house itself groaned like a morgue. It echoed and re-echoed as the daggered words forced themselves through Jenny's heart, tearing it, even ripping it out and putting it back, just to rip it out again, several times in the space of a few seconds. Dead! Dead! Dead!

She is dead. Diane is dead.

Jenny could only cry.

The silent tears flowed down her cheeks, caressing her throat, and met at the juncture of the first button on her dress. They searched out and found the cleavage between her breasts and then disappeared.

Tracy shook her head violently to clear it of the unwanted memories that coursed through her. It wasn't the first time. Every time she found herself alone like this, her mind would conjure up those ghosts of the past. If it was this bad on her, what must it be like for her friend? She decided to pay Jenny a quick visit—if only to ease her own conscience.

Joshua threw a bucket of slop in the hogs feed trough. It was amazing. He had started out with two calves and then later with two pigs. He had amassed a small herd of twenty-one cows and an even smaller group of six hogs. He would have more hogs, but they butchered one each year to put up for food.

Jenny used to keep a good garden, enough to keep them in vegetables for a whole year. But recently, with the tragedy in their family, the garden suffered at first. She still worked it, but it just wasn't quite as good or productive. So among all his other chores, Joshua had began helping her with it—unbeknownst to her. Finally, she quit it altogether.

Actually, Jenny spent most of her time sitting in her rocking chair and staring at nothing. Staring out the window. She didn't do anything or say anything. She just rocked…and stared.

Joshua seemed to spend more and more time away from the house lately. It wasn't totally unproductive. He was accomplishing a great deal with his property and his livestock. Fences were finally mended. Outbuildings were repaired. The only problem was, his marriage was in disrepair. Jenny was turning into a recluse. And he was losing interest. It appeared they were headed on a downward spiral with no hope for recovery.

Joshua was repairing a loose step on the front porch when Tracy walked up. "Good morning," she said cheerily.

"What's good about it?" he grumped.

"Uh, oh." She clucked her tongue at him. "Somebody got up on the wrong side." She stood and watched him until he finally got up to let her pass. She placed her weight carefully on the bottom step and then lifted her other foot over the step he was working on. Just as she made contact with the wooden plank above it, Joshua grabbed her arm and pulled her back down to the ground.

"Tracy, can I talk to you for a minute?" He started to move away from the house and turned back to face her. "Walk with me, would you? Please?"

She followed him in the general direction of the barn. Tracy was beginning to feel a little uneasy. She wasn't sure why. Joshua was a good friend. He had never tried anything with her. He was so devoted to Jenny that such a thing would never enter his mind. "Joshua, what's going on? Why are we out here?"

He gave her a blank stare. "I wanted to get out of earshot of the house," he confided.

Now Tracy was concerned. There was something obviously wrong. She came a little closer and put her hand on his arm. "What is it? Has something happened to Jenny?" she asked, anxiously.

"Yes, you could say that."

A look of sudden fear crossed Tracy's face. "Tell me, Joshua. What's going on?" The alarm she first felt was passing.

"I'm scared, Tracy." He paused before going on. His silence made her uncomfortable. "I'm afraid she'll try something."

"What do you mean, Joshua?"

Continued silence. He cast his eyes at the ground and traced patterns in the dirt with the toe of his boot. Tracy hated to see either of them like they were now. Jenny was becoming almost catatonic, oblivious to anything outside her own mind. Joshua was in a dilemma unfamiliar to him. He knew how to make her happy, how to make her laugh. He could fix a cut or a scrape. He could even turn an unhappy tear to a sparkle in her eye. But this—this was different. It was hopeless in his case.

"Joshua, what do you mean she'll try something?" she demanded loudly.

"Tracy, keep your voice down," he cautioned her. "I don't want Jenny to hear us."

"I don't think she would hear anything you say right now," Tracy continued in a raised voice. "She doesn't exactly respond to anything anymore. Come on, Joshua. Wake up. She doesn't even know when we're around her. She doesn't say anything. She doesn't do anything. She just sits there in that chair and rocks—all day." Her voice had risen another octave. "Go ahead and tell me what you started to say a while ago," she demanded.

"Of course, you're right," he said apologetically. "I'm just concerned she may try to kill herself."

"No! Why do you think that?" she cried in amazement. She hadn't known Jenny but a few years, but she thought she knew her well enough to know she wouldn't try suicide. At least she thought she did.

"You didn't see her after Solomon's death," he pointed out. He began to explain what had happened that night. How close he believed she was then. "I think this might just send her over the edge. I was hoping you could talk to her and, I don't know, do something."

"Oh, I don't know, Joshua. What if it backfires on us?" she cried, disheartened.

"Tracy, you have to try," he pleaded. "I don't know where else to turn."

The look in his eyes told spoke volumes of truth. The hurt and despair were so obvious, she couldn't help but feel sorry for him. "All right," she finally agreed. "I'll try."

He walked back toward the house, leaving Tracy behind in the barn. By the time she had sorted through her feelings and walked back to the house, Joshua was working on the step like nothing had happened. It was like watching the whole thing being replayed. She lifted her foot over the step he was working on. As it made contact with the wooden plank, she half expected him to grab her arm again. She was hoping he would grab her arm again, but nothing happened. She proceeded up the steps carefully, crossed the solid wood porch, and disappeared into the house.

Joshua finished the step he was working on, gathered up his tools, and headed for the toolshed. The last thing he wanted to do was get in the middle of Tracy's conversation.

He had just finished putting his tools away, when he heard a voice in his head. It called him repeatedly. He felt it mysteriously draw him away from his farm. Time was unimportant. He continued listening to the voice. It told him to come to Rockhole.

The day was young and there was still work to be done, but Joshua was hypnotized by the voice that continued to drone on in his head. He worked his way across the pasture behind the barn and down the hillside that dropped off, gradually at first, then steeper the closer it got to the creek.

When he reached the tree line at Saline Creek, Joshua turned west and followed it until he came to the spot everyone called Rockhole.

You're here.

"You brought me here," Joshua pointed out. "I didn't think I had a choice." He looked around at the area. "Why am I here?"

This is where it will happen. I just wanted you to see it. You are free to leave at any time.

Joshua worked his way back along the creek, following the tree line until he came to the place where it joined with his property. He climbed, without effort, up the hill until he came to the barbed-wire fence that marked the beginning of his pasture. Within minutes he was back in the toolshed.

"Joshua, where were you?" Tracy asked, stepping through the shed door and coming up behind him.

"What? I've been right here since I finished working on that step," he said smugly.

"I looked for you. I called and called you. You weren't anywhere around."

"I told you. I was right here all the time. Don't you believe me?" he asked in a strange voice.

"Well…I'm going back up to the house," she said distantly, edging toward the door. "I-I'll be with Jenny." She turned and left quickly before he could say any more. That was very bizarre she said to herself, walking hurriedly toward the house. She cast a wistful eye at the shed before going through the door.

"Jenny," Tracy called softly. She pulled a straight chair over next to the rocker and sat in it. Jenny wasn't moving. She sat rigid in the living room chair, her eyes fixed straight ahead. Her arms were resting on the chair arms, but her hands had a viselike grip on the wooden frame. "Jenny, it's Tracy. Honey, can you hear me? I know this has been hard on you, but you still have a lot to live for, you know? Joshua loves you so much. And there's the new baby coming." She paused to see if there was any reaction from her friend. Nothing. "Jenny, I love you too. You've been a good friend to me. I don't want to see you do something you'll regret later. Please, please come back to us."

Tracy could see no apparent change in her. "Dammit, Jenny, don't do this to us," she cried. Her own tears began to fall. She grabbed her friends' arm. "You can't just shut yourself off like this and leave the rest of us wondering what in the hell is wrong. Do you hear me?" she shouted. She shook the catatonic woman harshly. Still no response. "I want an answer—please?" she cried.

Suddenly she stopped. There! In the corner of Jenny's eye—a tear!

Tracy's head fell to her friend's arm, but it didn't stay long. Jenny began to tremble. Tracy raised her head to see what was happening and was shocked to see this sudden reaction. Jenny's tears were flowing freely now. Her lips were quivering.

Suddenly everything changed. Tracy scooted her chair back as she watched the metamorphic change pass through her dearest friend. Jenny clenched her fists so tight, Tracy was sure she would cut her hands with her fingernails. Then the despondent woman began to rhythmically pound the chair arms with both hands. It began just a light, moderate tapping at first but was soon hard, bruising blows.

Just when Tracy was sure Jenny would cause permanent damage to her small hands, the pounding stopped. She could only watch as the violent action continued with Jenny pulling on her hair with both hands. She pulled and snatched and yanked, only coming away with small strands of hair each time. After repeated attempts, she was finally successful in extracting a handful of her pretty blond locks. Tracy came alive.

She grabbed Jenny's arms to prevent her from further hurting herself, but the result was not what she had expected. The grieving woman's strength was greater than normal, and Tracy was not prepared for what happened next.

Jenny stood up and, with little effort it seemed, threw her friend across the room. Tracy landed against the secretary that Jenny had sat at so often to write her mother letters. She could have sworn she heard some wood cracking. The secretary might have given under her weight, but somehow, she knew—it wasn't the desk. It was her ribs.

She lay on the floor, gasping for breath.

Jenny chose that particular moment to return to reality. "Tracy. Oh my god!" she exclaimed. "What happened? Are you hurt?" She was surprised to find her friend lying there, gasping for breath. She sat down on the hardwood floor and gingerly took Tracy's head in her lap.

Tracy was whimpering. Jenny stroked her hair as though it was the most natural thing in the world for her to be doing.

Joshua burst into the house. "Tracy, what the hell—"

"Josh, I think she needs a doctor," his wife said innocently. "I don't know what happened, but she seems to be hurt. Tracy, what's wrong?" she asked again.

"Jenny," her husband breathed her name out slowly. He knelt beside her and looked from one to the other.

"Would…someone…please get a…doctor," Tracy winced in pain as she spoke. "I think…I have…broken ribs."

Jenny looked up at her husband. "Joshua? Are you going to get the doctor?" she asked, amazed that he still hadn't left. "She needs medical attention." Her smile took some of the sting out of her sarcastic tone. She looked back down at Tracy. "It'll be all right. The doctor will be here soon," she confirmed, seeing her husband disappear out the door. "Can you sit up?"

"I think…so. If you…help me," Tracy stammered over the words as the pain shot through her chest. Jenny did the best she could to help the injured woman struggle to her feet. She slowly, painfully walked her to the sofa and eased her down and finally into a reclining position, propped up with several pillows.

"Did you fall?" Jenny asked, still ignorant of her violent behavior only moments before.

Tracy laughed, which brought on another round of unbelievable pain. She had both her arms wrapped across her chest and tightened her clasp as she clenched herself even tighter. She erupted into a fit of coughing, from which the pain was so intense that she lapsed into unconsciousness.

"Tracy! Tracy! Oh, dear God," she gasped. There was a trickle of blood coming from the corner of Tracy's mouth. She ran into the kitchen for a wet cloth. "Please hurry, Joshua. Please." She stood over the kitchen sink and prayed silently for her friend.

She returned to the living room and wiped the blood from Tracy's mouth. Jenny sat beside her close friend and talked to her. But Tracy never regained consciousness. Why was it taking so long to get the doctor? "Tracy, please don't die. You're going to be fine." An hour passed before she heard their wagon stop out front.

When Joshua came in with Dr. Pogue, Jenny got up and moved so he could attend to Tracy. She stood next to Joshua, trembling at the thought of her closest friend lying there, hurt and unconscious. "She started coughing and then passed out just before you got here," Jenny explained to the doctor. "Oh. She also had blood coming from her mouth," she held out the hand cloth so he could see.

"Hmmm," the physician snorted. He took something out of his black medical bag and held it under her nose. In a second or two, Tracy jerked back to life trying to escape whatever the doctor was holding there.

"*Ohh!*" she cried out in pain.

"Okay. Okay, young lady," the doctor said soothingly. "I just need to know what's going on inside of you." He pushed gently on Tracy's chest just under her breasts. First one side, then the other. Each time she screamed in pain, but when he depressed her left side, she screamed even louder. Again, she began coughing and bleeding at the mouth. He took out a stethoscope and listened to her breathing. After a minute or so of listening, moving, and listening some more, he removed the stethoscope and replaced it in his bag. "She's got some broken ribs all right. But she also has a punctured lung," he explained.

"What does that mean?" Jenny asked. "Is it bad?"

"It means she'll need surgery," he confirmed. "She's bleeding internally. I need to stop it, or she'll bleed to death." He turned his focus from Jenny to Joshua. "We'll need to get her into your wagon and take her to my office," he suggested. "Can we put something in the back to make it comfortable for her?"

"Yes, of course," Joshua replied. "I'll lay some hay down."

"And I'll get some blankets and pillows to put on the hay," Jenny offered quickly. She hurried up the stairs, and they heard her clomping across the wooden floor.

Within a few minutes, they had Tracy loaded into the wagon and as comfortable as possible. The ride was certainly easier on her since she was unconscious. But Jenny was all in a dither, still ignorant of what she had done.

She held Tracy's hand and prayed softly—so that only she and God could hear.

Joshua and Jenny sat in Dr. Pogue's outer office waiting for some news of Tracy's condition. Still unaware of what had transpired, Jenny questioned her husband. "Joshua, do you have any idea what might have happened to Tracy?"

He looked at his wife with some surprise. It was difficult to believe she didn't have any memory of her recent brush with insanity, which could have resulted in a tragic end for Tracy—and still could for all they knew.

"Jenny, Diane is dead," he said instead of answering her question.

Tears welled up in her eyes as she slowly rotated her head until she faced her husband. "I know," she cried openly.

"We buried her three days ago, and you have been in some kind of a trance ever since," he began. "I can't even begin to tell you what these past days have been like. You never did anything or said anything. You just sat…and rocked. Stared all day…at nothing. I did everything I could think of. I talked to you. I sat with you. I touched you—I even kissed you. Jenny, I was scared. I didn't know what to do, where to turn. I finally asked Tracy to talk to you. It was my only hope," he whispered hoarsely.

"You mean, I did that to Tracy?" she asked in disbelief.

"I don't know what you did," he said, shrugging. "I came in after it had already happened. I had been working on that loose step on the front porch. You know, the one that you've been after me to fix forever? Anyway, I had finished and was taking my tools back to the shed. Just as I was walking back toward the house, I heard a scream. By the time I got there, it was over. You were sitting on the floor holding Tracy's head in your lap."

"God help me. What have I done?" she breathed rapidly. She began to whimper and shake. Her breathing became even more rapid.

"Hey, slow down, darling," Joshua fretted. "You're going to make yourself sick."

"I-I didn't mean to-to hurt her," she cried.

"I know, darling. I know." Joshua held her close, patting her on the back. It was about the only thing left he thought he could do to console his wife. "She knows that too," he reassured her.

He was still holding her when the doctor came out. "Joshua, Jenny." He came over and sat opposite them, still wearing his surgical gown covered with Tracy's blood. It wasn't what Jenny needed to see at that moment, but she did her best to keep her eyes on the doctor's face and off the imbrued smock. The doctor continued, "She had a punctured lung all right, as well as three broken ribs. Luckily, we got to the lung before it collapsed. The bleeding has stopped, and she'll be fine. You two can go on home," he said tiredly.

"What about Tracy?"

"I'm going to keep her here overnight." He sighed. "I need to keep an eye on that lung for a while. You go on now. She'll be all right," he assured them.

"All right. Thanks, Doc," Joshua said relieved. "Come on, darling, let's go." We better find Doug and tell him." He helped his wife up from the sofa, and they left the doctor's office.

March 16, 1902

Dear Mama,

It has been a harrowing week. I couldn't even begin to explain it all. But somehow, I will try. I only know this, I don't want to ever have to live another one like it. I know why we must stay away from you and daddy, but I miss you—both.

It's times like this past week when I really, really need you around.

Two days apart we received good and bad news. First, we learned that, in fact, I will give birth to my third child. I can't imagine how that happened. What I mean is, I can't imagine how this horrible thing happened with all the precautions I took. Nothing seems to work in my favor anymore. Well, anyway, I am, I reluctantly admit, with child again.

Then just two days later, we learned that our precious baby girl was found. A nearby farmer was plowing up a stretch of land that he hadn't touched for some time, and he dug up some bones. He notified the authorities, and they say it was our little Diane. She had been molested, murdered, and then buried in a shallow grave in the next county.

Dear God, I can't go on. Please forgive me. I must stop now. We await word from you. It has been so long since you've written. Why have you been silent for so long? Have we lost your love completely? Please, please write.

We love you still,

Joshua and Jenny

It was one of those unseasonably hot summer days that start out already warm in the early morning hours. By midmorning, the temperatures had already reached what should have been their afternoon high. The air was humid and sticky. The heat buildup continues until it's just plain hot—unbearably hot. So instead of waiting for late morning or early afternoon to do any gardening, the outside work begins at daybreak.

The early bird gets the worm, so to speak.

Grace and Francis had been out weeding and watering flowers for hours by the time Elise arrived. She strolled up the walkway, her eyes silently admiring what the two ladies had accomplished. She could remember when the only flowers they had were those that bordered the path leading to the house. Now, they had such a wide variety of colors and types and so tastefully done that it caught the eye of nearly every passerby, generating frequent compliments to the delight of the two sisters.

"I just can't get over how beautiful your yard is," she said by way of greeting.

"Good morning, Elise," Grace said cheerily.

"Good morning," Francis joined in. "How are you this warm summer morning?"

"Ladies, I feel like I'm on top of the world today." She practically floated down the walkway. "Solomon and I had another talk about Joshua and Jenny, and I believe he's finally starting to come around. He even admitted to me that he misses the kids too. Isn't it wonderful?"

"It sure is," Grace admitted. "Oh, speaking of which, you got a letter yesterday. You all get comfortable on the porch, and I'll bring us some tea and get you your letter."

Moments later they were all settled in well padded, porch chairs, sipping on iced tea. Elise had opened her letter from Jenny and was beginning to read to herself. Soon after, she shared a bit of good news with her nieces. "She's with child again."

"My goodness, that girl is as fertile as the Nile," Francis proclaimed.

"Oh, dear God!" Elise gasped. She covered her mouth with her hand. "They found the baby," she cried as tears began to cascade down her cheeks. "Ohh! Oh no!" she exclaimed as her eyes continued to scan the letter. "She's dead. They only found her bones," she said, her voice taking on a hollow, desperate note. Her tears flooded down her face, wetting the paper as she stared at the ghastly letter. Finally, she got up and descended the porch steps. At the bottom, she turned and thanked the sisters for the tea.

"That poor woman," Francis said, softheartedly. "She has had more than her share of tragedy. I can't even imagine what she's going through."

"Nothing good can come of this," Grace said emphatically. "Absolutely nothing!"

Jenny was taking more walks these days. She was of the firm belief that exercise was the best thing for a pregnant woman. Eat and drink right, exercise, and for heaven's sake—stay busy.

For her, the latter was the best advice anyone could give her. The last thing she needed to do was dwell on the future of this baby. She had already replayed in her mind the events surrounding the deaths of her first two children. So much so that she nearly lost her mind, all over again. At least once every day.

Now, it had been eight months since this baby was conceived and walking was the only thing that helped her to keep her sanity. She always found, though, that her walks ended up at Tracy's house. She would spend much of her day visiting with her friend and helping her with her housework. In fact, it was bordering on becoming a tradition.

"Knock, knock. Anyone home?" Jenny called through the screen door.

"Now, where else would I be?" Tracy asked lightheartedly.

"My, someone's in a bit of a snit this morning," Jenny noted, hesitating as she opened the door. Was she beginning to wear out her welcome already? If she did, there would be nowhere else to turn. Tracy was the only real friend she had made here. If she lost her friendship—well, she might as well die.

"I'm sorry, Jenny. Come on in," she apologized. "Don't let my mood bother you."

"What's wrong?" Jenny asked cautiously.

Tracy didn't answer right away. She was sorry now that she had even opened this can of worms. "Oh, it's nothing," she said casually, waving her arm in the air.

"Tracy, I can read you like a book," Jenny said accusingly. "Tell me what's bothering you, or—" She had no idea what she would do if her friend didn't talk.

"Or you'll what?"

"I'll find another godmother for this baby," she finished lamely. She and Joshua had made the decision from the beginning that Tracy and Doug would be the godparents of their next child. She smiled at her friend. "Come on. What's bothering you?"

"Are you sure you want to have this baby?" she asked out of the clear blue. Already she was wishing she could take it back.

"What? What are you saying, Tracy? That's a mean thing to say," Jenny said, her voice filled with the obvious pain of her friend's question. "Where in the world did this come from?"

Tracy clumped down on one of the kitchen chairs. She laid her elbows on the table and cupped her head in her hands. She just sat there like that, shaking her head. Jenny was beginning to think she wasn't going to say anything. She closed the space between them and laid her hand on Tracy's shoulder.

Tracy began to cry softly.

Jenny couldn't think of anything to do, so she lumbered over to the stove and poured them both a cup of coffee. As she sat down at the table opposite of Tracy, she scooted the cup and saucer toward the distraught woman.

Maybe the best thing to do in a circumstance like this was—to do nothing.

So they both sat there. Jenny sipping on her coffee. Tracy weeping gently, her face still covered with her hands.

"I…," she began but quickly aborted. She wiped her eyes with a rag she had been toting around all morning.

"Tracy, I'm your friend," Jenny said, breaking the awkward silence. "You know you can tell me anything."

"I-I thought I could," she managed to stammer through her tears. She took another swipe at her eyes with the rag. "But…this is hard. I don't even know where it came from," she cried, still dabbing at her eyes.

"Well, I'm not going to know what it is unless you break down and tell me," Jenny said, chuckling at her little spurious innuendo.

Tracy laughed at the ill-timed bit of humor from her friend. "Break down is absolutely correct. I just—Jenny, I'm sorry if this hurts you in any way. I certainly don't intend for it to. Do you understand?" she asked quizzically, her head tilted sideways.

"Whatever it is, we'll deal with it. Okay?"

"Okay," Tracy said smiling. But then her smile faded just as quickly as it had come. "I had a dream last night—no, that's not right. I had a nightmare last night," she quickly amended. "In fact, if there was a word that described what I had better than the word nightmare, I would use it."

"Strange," Jenny muttered softly.

"It was about you, Jenny. The whole nightmare, or whatever it was, was about you. When I first woke up, I thought it might be an omen, but it was just too…unreal," she finally blurted out after searching for the right word to explain her feeling of it.

"Now you've got me worried."

"See, I told you. I should have just kept my big mouth shut," Tracy said, her tension mounting. "You're not in any condition to be hearing this. I'm sorry—"

"No, go on," Jenny insisted. "You have to tell me now."

"Are you sure?" Tracy asked, her voice laced with just a trace of suspicion.

"I'm sure," she said matter-of-factly, shaking her head for emphasis. "Out with it you rogue."

"As I said before, I had a nightmare and it was about you." Tracy spoke with more confidence this time. "I dreamed you had your baby, but it was evil and ugly." She shuddered at the memory of it. "It came out with its eyes open and they were a real bright red. They looked like they could bore right through you if you looked at them for very long. And its hands weren't the hands of a baby. They looked like they belonged to an eighty-year-old man. There was no meat on them, just skin that hung like wet paper over the bones. And the fingernails were at least an inch long. They were yellow with red stripes running down them." She shuddered again as she began to remember more about the dastardly nightmare.

"Its hair was long and thin. It hung down to the middle of its back, and it was a charcoal gray." She paused for a moment to check Jenny's reaction. The pregnant woman was sitting, rooted to her seat, holding the coffee cup tight enough to shatter it. Tracy got up and poured them both another cup of the black broth before resuming her tale of woe. But not before forcing Jenny to set her cup down.

"There was no doctor holding the baby," she continued in a soft drone. "It just came out and stood at the foot of the bed and stared at both of us. Suddenly, the lights dimmed to almost nothing, and we were plunged into near darkness. The only light in the room came from its eyes. They cast a terrible red tint to the whole room. And then…" She shivered unmistakably at the scene that only she could see in her mind's eye.

"Go on," Jenny squeaked the words out in a strained voice.

"And then—oh, Jesus," Tracy breathed the words out slowly as she suddenly remembered what had happened next. She covered her mouth with her right hand as though she were going to throw up.

Jenny nodded at her, encouraging her to continue the unbelievable yarn.

"And then," Tracy finally resumed, "it started eating the afterbirth. It ate until it was all gone." She gagged and covered her mouth quickly as she headed for the sink. After a few minutes of retching violently, she leaned on the counter top. "Jenny, it was the most awful thing I have ever seen, real or imagined. It had rolls and rolls of extra skin that hung and overlapped. It was—I didn't—" She began to cry again.

Jenny went over to the counter and put her arm around her friend. "I don't know why you had this terrible nightmare either, Tracy. Come on, now. It was just a nightmare and nothing more," she said rather unconvincingly. "You were probably tired or something. You've been working too hard. I tried to knock you silly not long ago, remember? All that weakened you and caused you to have this nightmare. Okay?" she said, comforting her friend.

Tracy went back to her chair at the table. "What in the world could it possibly mean?" she asked, a little calmer now.

"I don't know, Tracy. Can you remember anything else about it? I mean, do you remember anything besides the baby itself? Anything about the circumstances surrounding the whole episode?"

"That's all I remember," she stated flatly. "Jenny, I don't even want to remember that much. It was the most dreadful thing I have ever seen. And it was so real. I-I don't know," she said shaking her head as though that would clear the images from her mind.

"Well, I better get home," Jenny murmured, getting up from the table and starting to clear the dishes.

"Leave those," Tracy ordered. "I'll get them in a minute."

Jenny picked up her parasol and pushed open the screen door. She was just about to take a step down when she grabbed her stomach and groaned.

"What is it?" Tracy said excitedly. "What's wrong?"

"I-I think it's…time," she said, gasping for breath. With Tracy's help, she waddled back to the table and sat down heavily in the same chair she had occupied moments before. She started to breathe in and out rapidly. "Go get Joshua and tell him to bring the wagon," she commanded her friend.

"Jenny, you can lay down here," Tracy suggested.

Jenny grabbed her arm and pulled her closer. "I want to have this baby at home. Now, go," she ordered, shouting this time.

"Oh god, Jenny! Oh god, this is my fault. It's all my fault," she sobbed.

"No, it's not. Now go, Tracy." She gasped as another pain hit. "*Gooo!*"

Tracy flew out the kitchen door.

Solomon took out his handkerchief for the hundredth time today and chased another bead of sweat down his face. It was only ten in the morning, and already it felt like it was a hundred degrees in the sun. Like every other day in his life since he was eight years old, Solomon Conners had begun working well before sunup. He believed the day was wasted if you didn't get at least three hours of work in before breakfast.

"It'll be a scorcher before this day's over," he said aloud, wiping another trail of sweat that had run down his neck and joined with another trail forming a wide band. In all actuality, he was sweating profusely. So wiping the sweat from his brow, from his face and from his neck was a wasted effort on his part.

"A little rain would be just the ticket," he said, continuing his one-sided conversation with his dog Sammy since there was no one else to talk to.

Solomon worked alone.

He always worked alone. He had never had a helper or even a relative to him. He wasn't vain about anything; it was his work. It had to be done to suit him, and no one could do it as well as he could.

So at an early age, he had developed the habit of talking to himself while working. But he soon grew tired of the loneliness and found a dog that would follow him around while he did his daily chores.

Sammy wasn't the first dog he chummed around with. He was the fifth in a long line of faithful friends in the field. In his early years, Sammy would answer with a resounding bark, sometimes two, when his master said anything to him. But in these later years (he was thirteen years old), he mostly gave a flicker of the eye but, on special occasions, would utter a weak groan.

Sammy uttered a weak groan now in agreement with his owner.

"No need to be so blasted talkative, Sammy," he said, winking at his faithful companion. "Aren't you hot?" The aged collie opened his eyes wide and looked briefly at Solomon before lowering them and swiping around his mouth with his long tongue. He opened his mouth and continued panting.

"Yeah, I thought so," Solomon nodded in agreement. He wiped his brow one more time before replacing his dirty, worn straw hat on his head. He got up from where he had been reclining against the trunk of a ninety-year-old walnut tree, taking his morning break and stretched his tired limbs.

"Arrghh," Solomon groaned as he limbered his arms and legs. "Come on, Sammy. Time to get back to work."

He limped over to the fence that separated the barnyard from the pasture behind it. He reached down with one hand and lifted his leg up and placed his foot on a fence board. The view from here was fabulous. "You can stand right here—in this very spot where I'm standing now—and see nearly all the way to the back of my property. If it weren't for the tree line at the creek, you probably could see the property line. I've always loved just standing here and looking at it," he said, rubbing his knee and leg.

Out of the clear blue, Solomon's next statement surprised even him.

"I miss my kids." He suddenly turned his head and looked in every direction. *Thank goodness*, he said to himself. *No one heard me*. He looked at Sammy, who was lying next to the fence. "Who would hear me anyway? There's no one here but you and me." Solomon painstakingly took his leg down from the fence and squatted down, petting the tired old collie.

"I do miss them, boy. I think I have all this time. I just couldn't admit it to myself—and especially not to Ellie. I hate what they did you understand. But...they're my kids and...I love them." He grew quiet for a while.

"They gave me two grandchildren, you know," he said, stirring from his reverie. Then just as quickly, he returned to his silent meditation. "But they both died," he said sadly.

Solomon thought back to that first letter announcing the death of their first grandchild. At that age, David would have been such a tiny little thing. And to die so young, never to learn to crawl or to walk. He would never have the chance to say Daddy or Mommy. Life was so unfair, Solomon thought to himself.

So unfair.

Chapter Eleven

Father Pritchard sat at his desk, mulling over the astonishing story Dr. Miles had told him. It was like something out of the Dark Ages. In eighteenth-century New England, this would have been normal stuff, but in the twentieth century—almost the twenty-first—it was unheard of.

Witchcraft was a thing of the past.

True, the church still had its problems with Satan and his henchmen. Christians were by no means safe from the ongoing war. But it was a spiritual war that was fought on a spiritual plane. Human beings were treated more like pawns as an endless barrage of numinous bullets were fired back and forth in a realm that cannot be seen. So he had told the coroner he would come. There seemed to be a note of anxiety in the doctor's voice; therefore, he consented to come right away because he had appointments that afternoon.

After checking his calendar and finding nothing conflicting or that couldn't be rescheduled, Father Pritchard readily accepted, his curiosity aroused.

He pressed the intercom button on his phone. "Sister Catherine, would you come in here."

A few seconds later, the door to his office opened, admitting a well-rounded, pleasant-smiling nun dressed in the traditional attire of the Roman Catholic Church. She brushed into the room, her habit rustling with the sound of a freshly starched garment. As was her custom, she strolled up to the front of his desk and stood, waiting for him to speak.

His finger still pointing at some entry in his appointment book, Father Pritchard could sense the good sister staring down at him. He was well aware that she had entered the room. Her noisy skirts were hard to miss. And he had tried, hundreds of times over the last several years, to convince her to say something or sit in one of the chairs in front of his desk or do anything to break the annoying habit she had fallen into early in his ministry here. She insisted that she handle herself properly in the service of God and that she was neither a secretary nor an associate.

He looked up while still marking his place in the book. "Sister Catherine, sit down a moment." He glanced down at his book again and started to speak. His sixth sense, and good hearing, told him she was still standing. He slowly lifted his eyes until they met her stolid, emotionless stare. "Sister, are you going to sit?"

Her stance never wavered. "It wouldn't be proper to sit and slovenly banter words back and forth with someone of your position," she stated firmly and devoid of sentiment.

Father Pritchard returned her stare and then finally broke into a grin. "Even if your priest requests it?" he asked curiously. He decided to try one more time to loosen the steellike girders that bound her jaws too tight to smile. "Sister, do you really think I would do anything to place either one of us in jeopardy with our Lord? When you stand at attention like that, you make me feel like a guard in a concentration camp. All I'm asking for is a little less tension when you come into my office. Relax, Sister. God will not condemn you for such a menial pleasure while still on this earth. And neither will I."

Slowly, very slowly, Sister Catherine backed up two steps and sat rigidly in one of the chairs. "What do you need, Father?" she asked in a crisp, businesslike voice.

He laughed.

The priest rarely amused himself at the expense of others, especially those he worked with. But Sister Catherine...well, Sister Catherine was Sister Catherine. What else could he say? He finally got around to the matter that brought her into his office.

"I have to go over to the coroner's office for a while. It appears to be a matter of some importance. I need you to call these people and reschedule their appointments for another day. But this one… with the monsignor, try to set it for later this afternoon." He looked at his watch and pulled at his lower lip, which was a flaw in his mannerism. "I should be back in an hour. Be sure he gets the change in our meeting time right away."

He got up from his chair, signaling the end of his instructions.

Sister Catherine stood also and followed him through the door carrying his appointment book.

Late afternoon and early evening were her favorite time to sit in her special place. Susie could sit in the window seat all day long, but those were her favorite times. It faced east, so the building blocked the afternoon sun, which created a shadowy hue over the grounds, a diffused lighting. As a result, the silver leaf maples glistened in the subdued light. The flowers almost danced in the eerie setting, reaching toward the sheltering tree limbs above. If she let her mind run free, she could almost imagine herself there among the delicate flora, stretching as they did, toward the protective arms of the trees.

"Do you think it's true?" Stoney asked, intruding into her private thoughts.

Susie was jolted back to reality by the sound of his voice. She glared at Stoney while dabbing at the coffee she'd spilled on her blouse when he startled her.

"Well, do you?" he asked again, light agitation sneaking its way into his tone. He wasn't upset with Susie. But that's where he always seemed to take out his frustrations. And then later, after it was over, he was always sorry. He could see he had gone too far again. She was beginning to show the effects of his malicious manner.

Stoney went over to the window seat and sat down beside her, wrapping his arms around her quivering body. Neither spoke until Susie had calmed down. "You're talking about what Grandma said a while ago?"

"The very same."

Susie returned to watching the evening light. "I don't know why she'd lie about a thing like that," she responded solemnly. "She's got nothing to gain by lying."

That was true. And Stoney knew it. Granny Rachel had never lied about anything important in her whole life. He turned over in his mind everything that had happened to this point but was still unable to put the puzzle together. There were still so many pieces missing. "All right. For the sake of argument, let's say it really happened. What does that have to do with Brian and Mary J.?"

Stirred with sudden interest, Susie spun back around to face the room. Her mind was working feverishly, collating all the facts they had gathered so far, ready to expose some mental image of what really happened.

"You all right?" Stoney asked, concerned at her sudden diversion from the view outside.

She still looked thoughtful. "Grandma knows more than she's letting on. You don't just drop a bombshell like that and then say no more." Stoney's face was screwed up in an odd, questioning look. "Well, don't you see? It's just not that simple," she said eagerly. "They fell in love. They got married. They had children." Susie paused to let him think it over. When he still didn't respond, she continued. "Stoney, that's not the end of the story. Somewhere along the way, they found out they were brother and sister. That's when all the trouble started."

She was right, and he knew it. There had to be more to it than that. But how in the world would they find out the truth? It was evident that Granny wasn't going to say anything more than she already had. "Okay. Okay," he laughed, holding off her onslaught. "I agree with you. There is more to it than we've been told. But where do we go from here? Granny is the only person who would know anything about what happened back then."

"Maybe not," Susie said, with a twinkle in her eye. "Maybe not."

Thelma peered over the rim of her glasses, shifting her attention from the typewriter long enough to see who had entered the office. The nondescript gesture consumed no more than half a second of her time. After thirty-five years of minor interruptions like this, she had become very proficient at removing her eyes from her work for a hasty glance at the door, and then returning to the typewriter, never missing a stroke.

She completed the sentence she was working on and then reached to her left and picked up the telephone receiver on her desk. She punched a number on the dial and spoke in a low tone. "Doctor, Father Pritchard has just come in," she informed the coroner.

"Good! Good," he responded enthusiastically. "Send him into my office. I'll be right up." He was still in the morgue studying the strange countenance of Brian Clark, which had completely returned to normal. He took off the green gown, removed the mask from his face and picked up the videotape.

Father Pritchard was sitting in the doctor's office enjoying a cup of Thelma's coffee. He rarely had coffee, at least not as far as Sister Catherine was aware. She had determined that the dark liquid with the acrid smell was not good for him, and so she quit making it at the church office. Thank God—literally—he was still able to enjoy it in the rectory. Somehow, he believed that if the sister knew about it, she would pitch a fit.

He was determined to retain at least one bad habit that was—maybe, it hadn't been proven, at least not to his satisfaction—physically disabling to a person. After a bout with breathing difficulties three years ago, he had given up cigarettes. It was a nasty habit anyway. But come hell or high water, he would have his coffee.

Dr. Miles entered the office from his private entrance. He strode over to the desk and greeted the priest with a handshake. Miles wasn't Catholic, so he didn't try to involve himself in any of the rituals associated with their religion. "Father Pritchard, I'm glad you could come," he said quickly before sitting behind his desk. "This thing has me completely bamboozled. I sure hope you can make some sense out of it because frankly I'm stumped."

He picked up the videotape, which he had lain on the desk. He swiveled his chair around to face the credenza behind him and told the priest, "I apologize for the brutality of this. It's extremely grotesque, but it confirms everything you've heard. I'm showing you this because I believe you to be an expert in the field."

"I must say, you've certainly got my curiosity aroused," Pritchard replied.

Grady Miles inserted the tape into the VCR and pushed play on the machine. He picked up the remote and leaned back in his chair so that the priest could view uninterrupted. He explained to Father Pritchard, as the tape began playing, that it was a time lapse and the pictures were taken over a longer time span than what they were watching.

And then he shut up and let the Catholic priest watch in silence.

At first, Father Pritchard was skeptical about doing this. But the doctor was so insistent, so he finally relented. The brief explanation over the phone did not adequately prepare him for what he was about to see. It looked like a picture of someone on a book cover that contained a story about a schizophrenic person. His first inclination was to ask what they were supposed to be looking for. After all, he was a priest, not a psychologist. But then, just as he was about to speak, the picture changed. Instead of six separate images on the face of the individual they were watching, now there were five.

The sixth was blank.

It contained no features whatsoever.

Father Pritchard had seen enough. "Is this a preview for a horror film?" he asked, not sure exactly what it was or why the doctor wanted him to see it.

"I can assure you, this is real. I have this individual in my morgue, downstairs," he replied gruffly. If it weren't so important, Miles believed he would stop right then. But he needed the man's help right now, so he bit his tongue and continued. "When the next section blanks out, the first one will begin to take on a different image. It will be completely different from the original. I'll fast forward to the change," he offered to conserve some time for the impatient priest.

Just as the doctor had explained, the blank strip began to mutate into an image with even different features than the others. Miles began fast forwarding through the slower parts and then resuming normal speed during the transmutation periods. Once the process was completed, they were staring at the picture of a normal human being.

A dead human being, the priest concluded.

"Do you want to tell me more about this?" he asked courteously but firmly. If this were in fact a real-live case—he shuddered to think of the implications.

Miles began a lengthy explanation of the circumstances surrounding the discovery of Brian Clark's body and the subsequent events, leading right up to the moment he first noticed the change taking place with Brian's face.

Father Pritchard was thoughtful for a long while. Somewhere, embedded deep in his memory, was a fact that had something to do with this family, but it eluded him for the moment. When he finally stirred from his reverie, the doctor sighed with relief. "I should know something about these people," he told the doctor, "but I can't quite put my finger on what it is." He shook his head in obvious displeasure at the elusive fragment.

"Well, it will come to me," he said disdainfully.

"I hope it comes to you soon. We could really use a break in this case," Miles replied in disappointment.

"Could I borrow that tape?" the priest asked as he was about to leave.

Miles ejected the tape from his VCR and handed it to the priest. "You can have this one," he offered. "It's a copy. Just let me know as soon as possible if you come up with anything. The sheriff is waiting for a report from me."

Father Pritchard had a sudden thought. "I'm meeting with the monsignor," he glanced at his watch, "oh my goodness, in a few minutes. May I have your permission to show this to him? I think he might be of some help."

"Yes. Yes, of course. Anything to expedite this matter and thanks for your help."

Father Pritchard hurried out of the office. He could just make it and not keep the monsignor waiting. Unless, of course, the monsignor was early, which he never was. The priest marched into the rectory just minutes ahead of Monsignor DeGuardo. He quickly dismissed Sister Catherine for the rest of the day and hurried into his office. When he was sure she had left, he went into the tall oak cabinet in one corner of the office and unlocked it. He made sure he was the only one with a key to that cabinet since it contained only his many personal items. Among them, a coffeemaker and coffee. He reached in and pulled out the automatic drip coffeemaker and began throwing a pot together quickly.

He had just finished turning the machine on when he heard the outer door to the rectory open and close. He stepped through his own office door and knelt in front of the monsignor, kissing his ring.

"Andrew, I hope the change in our meeting time wasn't an inconvenience," he said hopefully.

Andrew DeGuardo had been a friend of his ever since their seminary days. His friend was the one responsible for getting him appointed to this parish when it became vacant. Their friendship was renewed once again with his arrival here. However, only in closed quarters dared they act and talk like the close friends they were. In public, their relationship was nothing less than professional.

"On the contrary, it worked in my favor," he assured the priest. "But tell me, my friend, what was so important that it drew you away suddenly?" Father Pritchard sighed as he thought about the disturbing video. His eyes came to rest on it, lying on his desk a harmless thing. He put it aside, as the coffeemaker finished its gurgling and sizzling, signaling the conclusion of its assigned task. The priest crossed the room and poured two cups of the fresh, hot, and pungent liquid. Both men still drank their coffee black, having never developed a taste for cream and sugar. Not until they had taken a couple of sips of the steaming coffee did Father Pritchard begin explaining the unusual events concerning Brian Clark's death. He started back at the beginning, hurrying through most of it until he came to the phone call from the sheriff and his subsequent meeting with the coroner. When he had finished, Monsignor DeGuardo sat with his lips pursed, his brows furrowed into a thoughtful frown. Father Pritchard began pulling at his lower lip while he waited for the elder church official to sift through the bizarre happenstance. When DeGuardo finally stirred back to life, the priest produced the videotape.

"What is that?"

Pritchard smiled at his friend. "Proof! It is documentation of the story I just told you," he confirmed. "It is even more bizarre than the oral account. But I think you should see it. It's very descriptive." He popped it into the VCR and told the monsignor, "I'll fill our cups while you start watching this."

The priest refilled their cups and sat one on the coffee table in front of the monsignor. Father Pritchard didn't sit right away. Instead, he stood off to the side and watched with a satisfied smile at the reaction of his friend and superior to the gross images on the TV screen. When the tape was finished, he stopped it and switched the two machines off.

"Give me your impression before you have time to sit and think about it," Father Pritchard suggested.

"At first glance, it appears to be a manifestation of Satan in the young man's face. Did I see that? Is this real? It's beyond belief!"

Father Pritchard smiled a wary thin smile. They were in full agreement. "That is what I believe it to be," he said heartily. He was relieved that his old friend saw the same thing he did. It would be a hell of a limb to climb out on by yourself, if you tried to convince the nonreligious world of such a religious phenomenon.

"But why?" Monsignor DeGuardo asked suddenly. "Why now? Why here?"

"I believe this family has some very guarded secrets that would explain the recent occurrence," the priest offered. "There is an irritating fact floating around in the back of my mind that I can't seem to put my finger on. It has to do with the Conners family and would explain some things. But it will not explain the manifestations in their present state. There has been no activity of this type from the satanic cults in hundreds of years," he continued. "Everything has been of a spiritual nature in recent history."

The monsignor sighed, letting his breath out in one long, distinctly audible sound. "This has trouble written all over it," he mused. "How are you involved in it?"

"The coroner felt it had religious overtones and asked for my help in trying to understand its meaning. He feels that the answer to the mystery surrounding this case hinges on one's knowledge or understanding of this particular event." He was beginning to feel the monsignor's reluctance in the church's involvement or Pritchard's personal involvement. The priest decided to prod his superior for permission to resolve this issue. He felt compelled to provide a resolution. And—the mystery intrigued him.

"I really believe the church should take a stance on this, Andrew," he began. "We are highly regarded in matters like this. Image comes into play here." Timothy Pritchard decided to play his trump card. "We are not on very solid ground in this parish. This could give us a huge boost in the community," he confided.

It was enough. "Okay, Timothy, you have my permission," Monsignor DeGuardo responded. "As long…as long as it doesn't end up giving the church a black eye. We certainly don't need that." He rose as if to leave.

"Are you going back tonight?"

The monsignor deliberated a short time. "Yes, I think so." Then he looked his friend in the eye. "Call me if you discover anything worthy of the church's attention." Pritchard detected a glimmer of a smile on the corners of the monsignor's mouth. He kissed the monsignor's ring and noted silently that he was willing to take the glory if the outcome was positive.

He returned the almost smile and bade the monsignor good night, closing the door behind him.

Stoney was getting more and more frustrated with everything about this case. With each clue he uncovered, another, more puzzling one took its place. He couldn't believe how complicated this whole mess had become. He had sent Susie on to bed but had stayed up himself to try to make some sense of this riddle. All it had given him was a huge headache. He headed for the bathroom to get some aspirin from the medicine cabinet and paused at the foot of the bed when Susie stirred in her sleep. She tossed first one way then the other. Stoney hoped she wasn't having another nightmare, but the way she was tossing and turning he decided she probably was. For a fleeting moment, he considered waking her and, against his better judgment, decided to let her sleep. A restless sleep would be better than no sleep at all. He continued into the bathroom, retrieved the aspirin, and returned to the living room.

While the aspirin was working, he decided to make yet another mental list hoping something would strike a chord in his seemingly nonfunctional brain.

Mary J. is in the hospital in a coma. Brian is dead. Susie has had two horrible nightmares. She has also dreamed about an old woman, who evidently was related, with a warning. I've gone into convulsions twice when I neared Rockhole, and then lapsed into unconsciousness. Brian's face. Granny Rachael's twisted tale about our great-grandparents incestual relationship. The Curse.

Have I forgotten anything? he wondered. *Oh, yeah! The mysterious statement that Dala told us she overhead Sadie saying. What was it? It's all our fault. What in the hell does one of these things have to do with the other?* He went over the list again, searching for a common denominator. Searching for anything that could tie it all together.

Suddenly, he thought he saw a trend. Excited about the prospect, he looked for a paper and pencil. If he was right, it would show up when outlined on paper. He found what he was looking for in Susie's rolltop desk. Stoney sat down at the desk and made two lists side by side. When he was finished, he had two columns with four entries in each column. The column on the left he headed "Rockhole." The column on the right he headed "The Curse." So his list looked like this:

Rockhole	The Curse
Mary J. in coma	Susie's dreams of old woman
Brian's death	Brian's face
Stoney's convulsions	Great-grandparents incest
Susie's nightmares	Sadie's cryptic remark

Finally, something made sense. Each of the items under Rockhole were on that lest because they happened at Rockhole, or Rockhole was involved in some way. Likewise, the list under the

Curse was there because each of those items was related to the Curse in some way.

There had to be a way to tie all this together, and that's where Stoney drew a blank. That plus the fact that all these things had one other thing in common—well, two if you counted the fact that he couldn't prove any of it. But the one thing they had in common was that none of these events were ordinary: the reason for Mary J.'s coma, the way Brian died, Susie's nightmares, and even his own reaction when he got close to Rockhole. None of these things should have happened the way they did. Something had to cause them to happen, something extraordinary, something out of the normal.

And what about the Curse? That was even more unbelievable than the Rockhole list. He got up from the desk and stepped back a few feet. No way! This was like vampire shit. It made good movies, but it wasn't real. There was no way any of this stuff could be real.

Stoney went over to the window and sat down on the window seat. He could understand why Susie liked this spot so much. But he doubted it could help him any with his current dilemma.

An earsplitting scream from their bedroom shattered the late night, quiet in their apartment. Stoney jumped, startled by Susie's high-pitched wail. "Jesus! Not again," he whispered silently while racing for the bedroom.

CHAPTER TWELVE

Imogene Lucille Baker was quickly approaching her sixth birthday. She was the most active toddler Carlotta had ever seen. And although she wasn't an expert on children, she was pretty sure that her little girl walking at nine months old must have been a record of some kind. And the hyperactive girl hadn't slowed one little bit.

Little Imogene had completely skipped the crawling stage and advanced, without hesitation, to walking. And in the five years since, she had discovered the great outdoors and wasted no time exploring.

She still seemed awfully small to her mother and father to be such a gadabout. Carlotta feared that something terrible would happen if they weren't able to keep Imogene on a much-tighter rein. She was a free-spirited little girl and circumstances became even direr when Kelly brought Kimberly over.

Kimberly Sue, who was born the same day as Imogene, had waited a little longer to start walking. She didn't take her first steps until the age of fourteen months. But when they were together, those differences didn't seem to matter. They somehow managed to create new ways of getting into trouble.

Such was the case on this particular day. Three days prior to Imogene's sixth birthday.

Kelly and Kimberly came one spring morning to visit. The day had started off cool but warmed nicely until by noon the temperatures were in the sixties. Carlotta and Kelly had begun fixing lunch while the girls were playing in the backyard. The two mothers were chatting away when it suddenly grew very quiet outside.

Carlotta craned her neck to listen. "Do you hear anything?" she asked suspiciously.

"No. What am I supposed to be listening for?"

Carlotta didn't answer right away. Instead, she walked over and swung the screen door open. She looked about the backyard for a minute and then called out. "Imogene." There was no reply. On the contrary, she was met with a deafening silence. She called out again. "Imogene Lucille Baker!"

A hushed stillness—except for the wind that suddenly gusted out of the southeast.

"Kimberly?" By this time Kelly had become concerned also. She stood next to Carlotta and looked over her shoulder.

After a couple of more calls and no reply, she told her friend, "I think we better go look for them. Imogene has a bad habit of disappearing, but she usually answers when we call her." Kelly was beginning to worry now. Carlotta might be used to this, but she wasn't.

As they crossed the backyard, calling out the girl's names, there was still no response. Carlotta suggested they split up and check all the outbuildings. "You take the cellar and the outhouse. I'll look in the corn bin and the barn."

They separated quickly and began their search. After fifteen minutes of frantic searching, they had found nothing. "You go get the men, Kelly."

"What are you going to do? What about the children?" she asked anxiously.

"What do you think I'm going to do?" Carlotta asked with surprise. "I'm going to keep looking." No sooner had she said the words than she wished she could take them back. She bit her lip in regret. "Kelly, I'm sorry," she said, taking the other woman's hands in hers. "I'm scared too. I didn't mean to snap at you. You know that?"

"I know," Kelly sobbed.

"All right. I'm going to look some more. You go on and get Franklin and Michael," she said, patting her friend on the arm. Kelly hurried away, while Carlotta stood and watched her go. As soon as she disappeared out of sight, Carlotta started her search again with a renewed vigor.

She went first to the cellar and pulled open the old wood-framed door that was barely holding it together. It lay at a fifteen-degree angle to the ground and swung on rusty, squeaky hinges. The creaking door alone made entry into the dark, dank underground shelter a frightening experience.

Carlotta descended the steps into the subterranean shelter, stopping on each step and listening for any sound from below. By the time she reached the bottom, she was certain the missing girls weren't down there, but she needed to see with her own eyes. What if they were hurt? What if something had happened to them and they were injured and unable to call out to her? She had to go all the way in. She had to know for sure.

At the bottom, she stepped onto the ground and advanced into the cellar a couple of paces. The only light in the room was the light that came in from the open door. She stood still while letting her eyes adjust to the darkness. All the time, she could feel the moisture seeping from the dirt walls into her bones.

Carlotta suddenly felt something crawling on her arm. She bolted back into the light from the door and started jumping around, brushing herself off. She never did see what had landed on her but figured it was probably a spider or a granddaddy longlegs, neither of which she had much affection for.

She turned and crossed to the other side of the room and checked over the entire area. Feeling a little safer and a little more confident than before, she checked the side of the room she had just escaped from. Still nothing. Carlotta checked all around the cellar, under shelves, on shelves, in every corner. She even moved some of the things on the shelves, knowing how ridiculous it was. Thank God they weren't down here. She quickly abandoned the cellar for the safety of the light outside.

The next place she looked was the outhouse, but it was a quick once over. There wasn't much of a place to hide there, except for under the toilet seat. She had even checked there—just in case.

The corn bin beckoned to her. She pulled open the door and cast her eyes about before crossing the threshold. There was a pile of corn in one corner of the small building that looked like it had been there for a long time. The pile was about three feet deep and crawling with various rodents and insects. Carlotta flinched when a rat ran across the floor at the back of the room.

Separating the partially filled bin from an adjoining bin, which was empty, was a solid board wall. Evidently, the partially filled bin had been full sometime in the past because the boards that formed the barrier between the two bins were bowed so that they projected into the empty bin about six inches.

Across the room was a workbench with various tools and several tins—some of which were empty and some which were partially filled with an assortment of nails, screws, and a collection of odds and ends. Hanging on the wall around the workbench was an array of miscellaneous saddle and tack items.

Carlotta called out to the children. "Imogene? Kimberly? Are you in here, girls?" She glanced up at the rafters but saw only vacant space. Her shoulders sagged with the realization that she had come up empty in her search so far.

She left the corn bin and stopped under a silver-leafed maple tree. Carlotta was beginning to sense the initial stage of desperation setting in. She stood in the shade of the maple and wept softly beneath the comfort of its rustling leaves. After a minute or so of shedding senseless tears, she turned her attention to the barn. The only outbuilding she hadn't scoured yet.

With resolute determination, she marched toward the towering relic. The closer she got, the larger it loomed, and the greater the task before her seemed. There were a hundred places to hide in there. At the moment, Carlotta felt awfully small and inconsequential. It was almost enough to reduce her to tears yet again, but she steeled herself, remembering the two little girls that were missing. One, her own little Imogene.

When she searched the barn earlier, Carlotta remembered that the door was swinging open in the wind, a wind which was blowing even stronger now than when they first started searching. She had made a mental note of it but had forgotten until now.

"Why would the door be open?" she wondered aloud.

She grabbed the door before the wind could rip it off its hinges and hooked it shut. She stood just inside the closed barn door and surveyed the surrounding area while listening to the wind outside. It seemed to be crying for the lost children in its own way.

"Must be a storm coming in," she said offhandedly. "Imogene! Kimberly!"

"Come on, Kimberly," Imogene said, running ahead of her friend.

Kimberly was still in the tree swing, and as it started its ascent, she jumped out when Imogene started running away. Less experienced at jumping from the swing than Imogene, she shot out of it as the swing started its upward climb. The motion caused her to lose her sense of direction, and she came down on one foot.

She felt an instant bolt of pain but was determined to not be left behind. Kimberly started limping after Imogene, calling out to her. "Wait for me. I can't go very fast."

Imogene slowed up and turned to wait for her. "Come on, Kimberly. Hurry up." Seeing that her friend was limping along slowly, she darted back to her side and helped her along. "Is that better?" she asked.

"Yeah, it is. I'm glad you came back for me."

"You're my friend, silly. Of course, I'd come and help you," Imogene squealed in delight. "Don't worry. When we get to my secret hiding place, you can sit down and rest. You'll really like it. No one knows about it but me," she bragged.

As they approached the barn, Imogene left Kimberly to stand alone on one foot while she quickly went to open the door. She gave the heavy door a big push and swung it wide open, then returned to help her injured friend.

They entered the barn at a slow pace, nursing Kimberly's sprained ankle along. "I'm sorry about your foot," Imogene said, an unusual note of sincerity in her voice.

"Oh, it's okay," Kimberly sighed. "It doesn't really hurt that much, especially if I don't step on it." She leaned on Imogene, putting most of her weight on the other girl's shoulder. They walked through the open, center of the barn toward the back wall, where there was a smaller door.

Kimberly figured they were heading for that door and kept her sights on it as they progressed through the gigantic building. She gazed at the loft high above them, yearning to climb up, to run and jump in the vast playground of hay. Falteringly, she lowered her eyes back to her own level, focusing again on the door at the end of the barn.

Just as they were a few paces away from the slightly ajar door, Imogene steered the wounded girl to the right. They moved parallel to the back wall of the barn until they neared a stack of hay bales. The hay was in uniform stacks about ten bales across and nearly touching the floor of the loft.

They stopped right smack in front of the monstrous mountain. Kimberly tilted her head back and looked up at it, a knotted wrinkle on her young brow. She looked from the mass of hay to her friend and asked, "Are we going to climb it? I can't climb, Imogene. My foot hurts." She was whimpering as the pain got worse.

"No, silly. Watch and I'll show you." She dropped to her knees and reached for a bale of hay in the center of the stack on the very bottom. She grabbed hold of the wire wrapped around the bale and pulled with all her strength. Slowly, it started to move outward.

Kimberly gasped at the sight. "Imogene, what are you doing?" She eyed the immense heap, taking a cautious step backward. "Imogene, it'll fall," she cried in a shrill voice.

"No, it won't, silly," she laughed. "I've done this a million times. It's never fallen yet." She continued pulling on the hay bale until it was halfway out of the stack, resting at a forty-five-degree angle. She peered into the opening and then looked back at Kimberly. "Come on. Follow me." And they disappeared into the small hole.

Kimberly edged forward timidly until she was directly in front of the opening. Gingerly, she went down on her knees and stuck her head just inside. It was at that moment that Imogene decided to play a joke on her friend. Partially hidden in the darkness of the small tunnel by lying against one side, she could hardly be seen at all.

Imogene waited until Kimberly's head was in and then yelled, "*Boo!*"

The frightened girl screamed and fell backward. Imogene laughed and laughed until she realized Kimberly wasn't laughing with her. "What's the matter?" she asked, tears streaking down her face from laughing so hard.

"You scared me," Kimberly cried.

Imogene realized her joke had been cruel and tried to soothe her best friend's feelings. "I'm sorry," she apologized. "I didn't mean anything by it." She took Kimberly's hand and started to lead her back to the opening. "I won't do it again. I promise."

The sullen look from Kimberly was enough to convince Imogene. Finally, though, the trembling girl's fear gave way to Imogene's much stronger personality. "All right, as long as you promise," she replied sheepishly.

They crawled into the hole made by the removed bale of hay, and then Imogene pulled the hay bale back into place and concealed their entryway. Then they inched their way along on their stomachs until they came to a large open area in the middle of the huge stack of hay.

"Imogene, I'm scared," Kimberly cried. "It's dark in here. I want to leave."

"No, Kimberly. Don't leave," she pleaded. "Look, I'm lighting a lantern." It took a couple of minutes to locate her lantern and matches in the dark, but finally, with Kimberly beginning to tremble, the light came on. Suddenly it wasn't so bad after all.

"Isn't this great?" Imogene shrieked. "And no one can find us in here."

"How come?" Kimberly asked innocently.

Imogene sighed heavily as she cleared a space on the floor, free of hay, and traced designs in the dirt with her finger. "Because…I'm the only one who knows about it," she announced triumphantly. "And…" She deliberately hesitated for effect. "No one can hear us in here."

"How do you know that?" Kimberly asked.

Imogene sighed and busied herself with playing. Finally, when she realized her friend wasn't joining in, she answered Kimberly's dumb question. "Because I tried it." There was a look of disbelief on her friend's face and so she explained her answer.

"I hid in here one day and screamed real loud for a while. Nobody came looking for me. That's how I know." She nodded, self-satisfied with her explanation.

Convinced that Imogene knew what she was talking about, Kimberly joined her in playing house. They played until they got tired, and then both girls laid down in the soft, warm hay and fell asleep.

Sometime later—time was irrelevant to the girls in this secluded haven—they awoke from their nap and began playing again. There was no day or night in Imogene's secret hideaway. The only light was provided by her dad's lantern she had taken from the barn. So they played on for hours. Unaware of the frantic mood of the adults on the outside, or the storm that raged around them.

Carlotta had searched every inch of the barn and found nothing. She stood in the middle of the floor and shouted the girls' names several times until the shouts turned into screams. Eventually, her screams died down, and the only noise that could be heard above the whistling wind was her sobs, which were mixed with freshly fallen tears.

She emerged from the barn as Kelly and their husbands were arriving in Michael's wagon. She fell into Franklin's arms but only for a few seconds. "Have you looked everywhere?" he asked anxiously. She shook her head.

Taking turns, each slipping into the conversation easily, Kelly and Carlotta explained the circumstances leading up to the present moment. "After Kelly left to get you, I searched every building again. I couldn't find them anywhere," she cried brokenly.

"All right, Carlotta. Calm down," he urged her. "You won't do them any good if you're hysterical."

The four adults stood in a circle. No one spoke.

Franklin looked up at the sky, his frown deepening at the sight of the dark clouds approaching quickly. "Well, we better do something fast, or this storm is going to erase any signs of where they went. Michael, any suggestions? You know this country better than we do."

Michael nodded in agreement. "I think we better split up. We can cover more ground that way." He cupped his chin in his hand for a moment, stroking his beard. It was obvious he was concentrating on something. "Kelly, you and Carlotta take a wagon and search the ridge. Franklin and I will head down to the creek. We'll meet back here in half an hour."

The ladies took the wagon and departed for the crater. The two men saddled a couple of Franklin's horses and took off for Saline Creek. When they arrived, a few minutes later, they slowed to a trot and Michael gave Franklin some quick instructions.

"You swing around to the north side. We'll search both sides at the same time. Can't travel much more than a mile before we run into brush too thick to ride in. Then we'll double back and sweep the pasture between here and the ridge. There are some gullies and other hazards those young'uns can get hurt in."

"Okay, let's get started, then," Franklin said, impatiently.

After a careful and arduous search of the area, neither group was able to find any sign of the girls. That's when Michael suggested they get some help before the storm got any worse. "I'll go get the sheriff and round up a group of volunteers. Franklin, you go over to the Wrights and have Ben bring his bloodhounds over," Michael proposed. He turned his horse around to leave and then thought of something else. "Kelly, you and Carlotta get something that belongs to the girls for the hounds to use to pick up their trail." And then he rode off at a dead run, whipping the horse's behind with the reins.

Time is usually inconsequential when you're only six years old. You think about playing. You think about creating your own little world of fun and fiction. At times like this, the outside world doesn't exist. Children live in a fantasy world anyway. And they don't worry about those irritating schedules that adults try desperately to keep them on. As a matter of fact, there wasn't much they needed to keep track of the time for—except for one thing. Their growling stomachs.

Imogene and Kimberly had already missed lunch, and it was nearing suppertime. "My tummy hurts," Kimberly complained. "I'm hungry." She rubbed her stomach and groaned as the hunger pains grew even worse.

"Yeah, so am I," Imogene agreed, rubbing her stomach as well. "I think we should go get something to eat." She put out the lantern and then crawling on her stomach led the way back through the narrow tunnel to the loose hay bale and shoved it a little at a time until the opening reappeared. Kimberly followed close behind, creeping along slowly.

After Imogene had carefully replaced the loose hay bale so that no one could detect it, she helped her injured companion limp to the barn door. The wind was howling with the fierceness of a lion, and it fought against her as she opened the massive wooden door. Once it was opened a little, the wind caught it and threw it back against the barn.

Imogene pulled it around with difficulty but couldn't get it all the way shut. She leaned against it and pushed with all her might. Kimberly tried to help but couldn't do much because of her injured ankle. Between them, they almost had the door shut, when a great gust of wind screamed around the corner of the barn. It was accompanied by blinding, streaks of lightning that spread across the darkened sky, followed soon after with an explosion of crashing thunder.

The two girls had the door under control until the lightning and thunder scared them. They let go of the door and closed their eyes and covered their ears. The wind whipped against the door, nearly ripping it off its hinges and grabbed the girls with its invisible fingers. Frantically, their hands clawed at the air as they tried to grab hold of something to hold on to. However, their momentum from the swinging door tossed both girls into the air like they were a couple of rag dolls. That brought on a chorus of high-pitched screams as they landed on the ground five feet away.

Following an exhausting all-out search, everyone involved had met at Franklin and Carlotta's house. The storm had grown even more in intensity, but the worse of it was yet to come. The search party was gathered in the Baker's kitchen, throwing down some much-needed coffee and donning raincoats and other rain gear.

"If that wind switches around to the north, we'll have a real problem on our hands," Sheriff Eason informed the group.

Grabbing a lantern from the supply on the kitchen table, Franklin started for the door. "Then I suggest we get going. We have enough to contend with—" His statement went unfinished as he was interrupted by a bloodcurdling scream from outside.

The whole group, led by Franklin, scooted out the door and streamed off the back porch. They stood riveted to the ground as they stared in disbelief at the two girls they had been searching so diligently for all afternoon. Kelly was the first to recover. "Kimberly!" she shouted and broke into a run toward the barn.

Kimberly got up and limped toward her mother, aided by her best friend. Kelly grabbed her daughter up and clung to her, crying. Imogene released her friend's hand and ran to greet her own mother and father.

The children were quickly carried inside and out of the weather. Franklin and Michael remained outdoors to offer thanks and see their friends and neighbors off who had come to help.

Imogene was afraid they might dismantle her secret hiding place, so she refused to divulge its location. But she did promise to check with her mother occasionally and not be absent for so long at a time. Imogene glanced at her friend and winked so that only Kimberly could see her.

They had kept their hiding place a secret.

Springtime was the most beautiful time of the year to Carlotta. A lot of people favored the fall season when the leaves started changing colors showing off nature's beauty, but she preferred the birth of the new green leaves to the dead brown ones that followed in winter. She would rather walk on soft, cushioned green grass than the ugly lifeless brown grass. And of course, there was no comparison in the fall season to the bright, colorful flowers that found new life in the spring.

Yes, sir, she definitely preferred spring to any other season.

But eventually, it would end and give way to the strife of summer. Such was the case this warm summer morning when Kelly and Kimberly came calling. Everyone had pretty much put behind them the ghastly event of a few months before. And the two little girls were a lot more careful about spending time in their secret hiding place.

"Thought you two might like to take a ride into town with us today and then stop over at Rockhole on the way back for a swim," Kelly proposed.

Carlotta fanned herself with a paper lying on the table beside the sofa. "That's an easy decision, considering this heat," she replied with brutal honesty." She got up from the sofa and started for the stairs. "Come on, Imogene. Let's get changed and go for a ride. What do you say?"

"Yes, ma'am," she answered politely.

Imogene took her mother's extended hand and hopped up the stairs one at a time.

The ride into town was always an adventure. The road followed the crest of the ridge for a couple of miles and then began a downhill course that wound back and forth descending in a snakelike fashion until it reached the bottom. It then followed the base of the hill, winding around to a low water crossing at Saline Creek.

Carlotta liked the ride down the hillside. It wasn't so steep that it made the ride dangerous, but if a wagon or carriage got out of control, it could have tragic consequences.

Across the creek, their road joined with another road which came from the direction of town and continued east. It was a long but interesting ride to Crater Ridge. During the trip, Kelly pointed out some of the more interesting families whose homes dotted the landscape on both sides of the road all the way into town.

Carlotta tried to keep them separated, but it was impossible to do. Kelly had done this more than once on their excursions into town. To this day, however, it was all still a jumble of names and places.

Imogene and Kimberly were content to sit on the boardwalk out in front of the general store and sip on a ginger ale. These trips into town, which were occasional at best, were the only time they got to enjoy a cold drink right from the bottle. It was probably one of the best solutions to quell a young girl's mischievous nature that Kelly could conjure up.

On this day, however, it wasn't enough.

These two troublesome little gals had already proven that when together, they could be a nightmare. Something that Kelly had not considered when she and Carlotta walked away, admonishing them against leaving that spot. "In other words," Kimberly said, with just a teeny-tiny bit of rancor, "stay here and be bored."

"Exactly!" Kelly replied, pointing a finger at her daughter—and then smiled.

No sooner had the two ladies disappeared into the new mercantile, then both girls hopped up and took off in the opposite direction, in search of adventure. They began walking along main street until they came to the last building and quickly ducked around the end of the building. There was a trail leading into the woods directly behind the barbershop, which they decided to follow.

The dense trees and brush created a darkness in the woods that caused the trail to vanish from sight almost immediately when standing in the bright sunlight. After advancing a few feet into the woods, the girls halted to allow their eyes to adjust to the subdued light.

"I know a fun place to play back here," Kimberly bragged to her friend. Ever since Imogene had shown her the secret hiding place in the barn, she had wanted to reveal one of her own. This was as close as she could come. "Do you want to see it? It's really special." She tried to make it sound as best she could, like the most wonderful place in the world.

"Bet it's not as special as my secret place."

Now Kimberly was beginning to get a little upset. "It is so!" she pouted. "Anyway, you won't know if you don't see it. And I'm not so sure you should see it."

"Why not?" Imogene wailed. "Aren't I your best friend? Don't best friends show each other everything?" She didn't want to miss out on the chance to see a special place. It might really be special. Imogene decided to try another approach with Kimberly rather than waste this opportunity.

"I didn't really mean it wasn't as special as mine," she said by way of apology. "I'll bet yours is better than mine."

It worked, she thought silently. She could already see Kimberly's eyes light up.

"Come on, I'll show you," Kimberly shouted, running deeper into the woods. Imogene darted after her. She had to run at full speed, which wasn't all that hard since they were going downhill, to catch up with the smaller girl. Just as she did, Kimberly stopped in a level clearing. To one side of the clearing was an opening in the hillside.

Imogene stared at it.

"It's a cave," Kimberly cried excitedly.

Imogene frowned at her friend. "I know what it is. I'm not an idiot you know." She looked at the cave again. "Have you been inside?"

"A couple of times. But not very far. It's really dark and hard to see." Imogene started in, followed by a hesitant Kimberly. The opening was large but got smaller after a few feet. She got down on her hands and knees and crawled further in.

"Can you see?" Kimberly called from where the tunnel telescoped.

"Not very well at first. But after a while, you can start to see a little better," Imogene called back to her friend. Suddenly, she realized Kimberly wasn't right behind her. "Are you coming?"

Kimberly thought about it for a minute and then yelled into the tunnel. "No. I think I'll wait here." She sat down in the large opening and leaned back against the rock wall. After what couldn't have been more than a couple of minutes, she heard a terrifying scream echo through the cave and bounce past her and fade into the thickness of the woods.

"Imogene!" she shouted into the cold, dark passageway. There was no response. She called out again, but there was no sound except her own scuffling. What should she do? She needed to go get help, but she hated to leave her friend alone. Kimberly reasoned in her mind that the best thing to do was get help, so she shouted into the tunnel, "Imogene, I'm going for help."

And with that, she took off at a dead run.

Carlotta and Kelly entered the general store, fully expecting to find the girls inside trying to talk another soda out of the storekeeper. But in fact, the store was empty. They looked around but didn't see the clerk either. "Hello," Kelly called out.

The store owner shuffled out of the back room and took his customary place behind the counter. "What can I do for you, ladies?"

Kelly spoke first. "We left our two little girls on the walk outside drinking a soda while we went to the mercantile," she replied. "But we didn't see them anywhere when we came in. Have you seen them?"

"Haven't seen 'em since you all left earlier," he stated indifferently.

They thanked him and hurried out of the shop. Then they walked down both sides of the street, looking in every store and shop, asking everyone they came across, but no one had seen them. The last place they looked was at the land office across the street from the barbershop. After still another disappointed, they stood on the boardwalk discussing what they should do next.

"Excuse me, ladies," an elderly, bearded fellow grunted, breaking into their conversation. He had been sitting on the bench in front of the land office. "Did I hear you say you're looking for two little girls?"

"Yes, have you seen them?" Carlotta asked, anxiously.

He scratched at his beard for a bit and then said, "Yeah. 'Bout thirty minutes ago, I saw them go lickety-split around the corner of the barbershop there. Haven't seen 'em since," he finished lamely.

"Oh, thank you—" Carlotta's response was shattered by a series of bone-chilling shrieks.

"Oh my god!" Kelly tensed, recognizing her daughter's voice. She bolted for the barbershop, followed by Carlotta and the elderly gent. People were coming out of stores all up and down the street, looking for the source of the screams.

The three adults had just reached the beginning of the trail, when they were almost run over by Kelly's frightened daughter. "Mama! Mama!" She pulled up short at the sight of her mother, out of breath and white as a sheet.

Kelly got down on one knee and placed a hand on each of Kimberly's shoulders. "All right, honey. Take a deep breath and… and then tell me what happened."

The dark-haired little girl was petrified but took several quick breaths. "You gotta come. It's Imogene. Something happened to her," she shrieked.

Carlotta's face quickly became ashen. She knelt too. "Kimberly, honey." She drew a deep breath herself. "I want you to tell me exactly what happened. Okay? It's all right. Just start at the beginning."

Sobbing and trembling, Kimberly retraced her and Imogene's steps. She brought them right up to the point where Imogene screamed and then stopped.

"Well? Did she say if she was hurt?" Carlotta asked. Kimberly started sobbing again. For a minute, Carlotta didn't think she was going to say any more. The silence was uncomfortable, and for a brief second, she felt like throttling an answer out of Kimberly. "Well?" she prompted.

"I don't know," the little girl cried.

Carlotta could tell Kimberly was visibly shaken. She grasped the frightened girl's shoulders and swung her around to face her. "Honey, it's okay. Nobody's going to be mad at you. But Aunt Carlotta really needs you to answer a couple of questions, okay?"

"All right," she bawled.

"Did she say if she was hurt?" Kimberly shook her head back and forth. Carlotta drew a quick breath. She was afraid to ask the next question. "Did she say anything at all?"

Kimberly shook her head no. "She only screamed. That's all!"

By now a small crowd had gathered, and they could sense there was something terribly wrong. A couple of the men suggested they go to the cave and see what they were up against. Kimberly led the way and when they arrived the smaller of the two men, Earl Hampton, who had been in the barber's chair when he heard the little girl's shouts, crawled into the tunnel, holding a lantern in front of him to light the way.

After about fifteen minutes he returned. He looked Carlotta straight in the eyes and told her, "She's lying at the bottom of a shaft. It's about twelve to fifteen feet down. I couldn't tell if she was hurt or not or even if she was breathing. It was too far down, and the light wasn't good enough to see clearly. I called to her several times, but she didn't respond and there was no movement."

Much to the surprise of everyone, Carlotta's eyes rolled back in her head and she fell to the ground. Jack Wilkens, the barber, tried to catch her, but he was a little too far away to get a good hold and came up with nothing but air. She had no sooner slammed into the ground before Kelly was at her side.

"Jack, I'm going for some rope and other supplies," Wilkens told him. "There's a small room carved out around the shaft. I think that two of us can work in there together without too much problem." He took off while Jack Wilkens and Kelly tended to Carlotta.

"Bring Doc Pogue with you," Wilkens shouted to him. Earl nodded while he kept his attention on the trail in front of him.

By the time Earl returned with Dr. Pogue, Carlotta had regained consciousness. She was sitting up with Kelly and Jack's assistance. Earl pulled Jack away to help him with the rescue attempt, while Dr. Pogue attended to Carlotta.

She held the doctor off with one hand and clasped her head with the other. "Kelly, would you go get Franklin? Please?"

"Of course, I will," she replied, patting her friend on the arm. "You don't worry. She's going to be fine. Okay?" She stood up to leave. "Come on, Kimberly." Kelly started back toward town and noticed her daughter hadn't moved.

"Kimberly."

"I want to stay here, Mama," she cried. Kelly walked back to where her daughter sat staring sadly at the ground.

"She'll be all right, Kelly. We'll look after her," Carlotta assured her friend.

The cave was a nest of activity. A large group had gathered once word had gotten out. It was one of the most intense local events to come along in years, and no one wanted to miss it. Be that as it may, Carlotta wasn't sure if these people were here because they were concerned or if they were just looking for something interesting to pass the time of day.

Jack and Earl were still the primary rescuers, but now there were several people outside the cave entrance and along the tunnel to offer their help. Carlotta and Kimberly stood quietly by, merely spectators in this unfolding drama. The distraught mother was gradually beginning to feel detached from the activity. Almost as if she were watching it from afar off. However, she steeled herself in the face of this crisis. Anything else would have to wait until she had her baby back.

Carlotta was like a statue, caressing Kimberly's hair while waiting for some word from inside the cave. The unsettled mother was the picture of courage. That bothered Pogue. He had been in the medical profession long enough to know that emotionless mothers usually meant shock had set in. She should be worrying her hands, a deeply embedded frown creasing her forehead, maybe even a trembling lip, some tears—but alas, there were no outward signs to indicate her inward feelings.

Dr. Pogue, who was standing by trying to appear casual about the unfortunate occurrence, was keeping a close eye on Carlotta. He was sure she had all the symptoms of a woman going into shock. Probably, the only thing that kept her upright was the need to know about her daughter.

"Carlotta!" She turned in the direction of the voice and saw Franklin approaching on the trail from town followed by Kelly and Michael. She stopped playing with Kimberly's hair and fell into her husband's arms.

Finally, the reality of the situation hit her, and the flood of tears that should have already come were released. She cried openly, her small frame wracked with sobs. Franklin did his best to console her, then realized it was probably the best thing for her, considering. Dr. Pogue was glad to see her crying.

"There, there," Franklin said soothingly. "She'll be all right. She's going to be fine."

Carlotta looked up into his face. He wiped the tears from her cheeks and smiled at her. "Do you know what happened?" she asked softly.

He nodded. "Kelly told me the whole story on the ride in." He pulled her head close to his chest again and held her close. Somewhere in her mind, it registered that Michael was there also. He and Kelly were talking quietly off to the side.

"They've got her," someone at the front of the crowd, close to the cave opening yelled. Franklin and Carlotta weaved their way through the mob of concerned citizens until they were at the opening. "They're bringing her up now." Carlotta stared at the man who stood bent at the waist, his hands resting on his knees, staring into the tunnel. It finally dawned on her that it was Ben Wright who had spoken.

A couple of men started backing out from the tight quarters of the tunnel. Ben helped them, pulling out equipment and clearing their way, while Sheriff Eason turned to face the crowd and raised his hands in the air. "All right, folks, let's back up and give them some room here. Come on, now. Make some room," his voice boomed through the clearing in the woods.

The men had made a pallet with ropes tied to the ends forming a soft basket to lift Imogene from the shaft. They were slowly, gently pulling it through the tunnel. Carlotta thought the process was moving much too slow. "What's taking so long?" she asked anxiously.

Ben supplied the answer. "The tunnel has a couple of turns in it," he explained. "They have to guide it through, or it'll get hung up on those turns."

Franklin could hear his wife whispering a silent prayer. "Dear God, please let her be all right." She uttered the same words over and over again. He tried to offer comfort to his nervous, distraught wife, but her state of mind surrounded her with an impenetrable shield. His words fell on deaf ears.

Suddenly, the end of the bed appeared in the wide opening. And then the whole bed was in view. There, wrapped in a wool blanket, was their daughter. She lay on her back, her arms at her side, her eyes closed in silent repose.

Carlotta couldn't wait any longer. She broke free of her husband's grasp and dashed for the injured child. Falling to her knees, she held Imogene's head in her hands. "Honey," she cried softly. "Imogene, can you hear me? Imogene?" Her tone had increased an octave.

Franklin began pulling her back as Dr. Pogue knelt beside the child. He listened to her breathing first. Satisfied that she didn't seem to have any internal injuries, he felt her arms and legs for broken bones. Again, he came up empty with injuries and moved to her head.

As he placed his hands under her head to rotate it and check for a broken neck or collar bone, he felt something warm on the fingers of his left hand. He removed his hand, and his fingers were covered with blood. Pogue curled his fingers under her neck and felt around for a minute. Finally, after what seemed like an interminable period of time, he stood up and faced the parents.

"The only thing I found is a head injury. Mind you, it's just a cursory examination at best," he said quickly. "I need to get her to my office and examine her more thoroughly.

"How bad is her head, Doc?" Franklin asked cautiously.

"I can't be sure until I get her back to the office." What Dr. Pogue discovered—and wouldn't say yet—was that Imogene had a severe head injury that brought on a coma. Physically, she was all right, but the trauma to her brain was his main concern now. The length of the coma, he told them, pretty much depended on Imogene. The only thing they could do was keep an eye on her, and hopefully someday, she would come out of it.

Six months later there was no change in Imogene's condition. She had been lying in her bed since they brought her home, never moving. The only indication she was alive, her shallow breathing and soft heartbeat. Carlotta spent most of her waking hours with her daughter. She flew through her chores as quickly as she could in order to maximize her time with Imogene. She tried to keep her schedule as fixed as she could so that Imogene could get used to it.

She bathed and clothed her each morning and then read to her from Imogene's favorite book. Carlotta only hoped that something she was doing would break through her daughter's unconscious mind and tickle her memory.

Dr. Pogue came by every day at first. His visits soon dropped to every other day and then, eventually, to once a week. Friends and neighbors dropped in occasionally to check her condition and ask if Franklin and Carlotta needed anything. But there was no change, and her parents only needed for her to wake up.

Kelly and Kimberly came over often too. They hoped that hearing her best friend's voice might turn on some hidden switch in the dark recesses of Imogene's awareness.

Carlotta and Kelly had gone downstairs to have a quick cup of coffee soon after they arrived one morning, leaving Kimberly to read a story to her friend. They had poured a cup and sat down at the kitchen table, when the sudden outburst came from upstairs.

"Mama! Aunt Carlotta! Hurry, hurry." The heightened screech alarmed Carlotta. Her blasé attitude rapidly shifted to fear as she cast her eyes toward the ceiling. She quickly came to her senses and dashed for the stairs with Kelly right on her heels.

They burst into Imogene's bedroom, and Carlotta stopped so fast, Kelly ran into her.

"Look," Kimberly said, smiling brightly at them and holding Imogene's hand. "Isn't it wonderful?" she beamed at them.

Imogene was smiling too. Her eyes were open, and she was lucid. Suddenly she stretched her arms toward her mother and said in a voice that was hoarse and sore from lack of use, "Mama." Carlotta forgot about everything that had happened over the last six months. It was like it was only yesterday when they pulled Imogene out of that hole in the ground. Suddenly, six months of crying, of praying and constant attention to every detail in her daughter's life melted away.

"Imogene, honey," she cried, gathering her child into her arms. Carlotta held her tight, and they rocked back and forth for a minute. Her hardened demeanor that she wore constantly over the last six months finally gave way to a quivering mass.

After a few minutes of frenzied crying together, Carlotta pulled back from her daughter to look at her. However, she kept a tight hold on her shoulders as though Imogene might regress if she didn't.

There was so much to talk about, so much time to make up for, but she preferred to start with the announcement that soon Imogene would have a brand-new baby brother or sister. That seemed to remove some of the sluggishness in Imogene's eyes. She had waited a long time for a brother or sister and was beginning to think one would never come.

Suddenly, she looked at her mother with the oddest expression on her thin pale face and asked, "Mama, how long have I been asleep?" Everyone burst out laughing.

It's wonderful to hear laughter in this house again, Carlotta thought to herself. *Thank you, God!*

CHAPTER THIRTEEN

They were supposed to be there.

The chest with the letters in it was supposed to be at the old family homestead. The old woman had told her it was there. Why would she lie? A dead person had nothing to gain by deceiving them. Unless this whole thing was a hoax. And if that were the case, she would be the laughing stock of the community. Shit! She hated to be made fun of.

But it had to be true.

The dreams were too real to not mean anything. Susie went back over what the woman had said in her mind. She searched for something she might have missed, anything that might clue her to where the letters were. She relaxed in the seat and tried to order her thoughts.

The Curse!

The old woman talked about a curse on their family. It must have something to do with what Grandma Rachel told them. About their great-grandparents being brother and sister and getting married. Yuck! Susie shivered at the thought of being intimate with a brother or sister. That was the grossest thing she had ever heard of. Although, she did know some people who had done that. They lived over on Southtown Road. It split off from Highway 54 and came out on the south side of town by the old Baptist church. Anyway, there was a family who lived about two miles back down that road named Little. Two of those kids had married. She remembered the town's reaction. It had really gotten ugly. They were never run out of town or anything, but it was so terrible that they couldn't show their faces in town. So they might as well have left.

You must figure it out soon!

That's what the old woman had said. So not only did they have to solve her puzzle to solve their own mystery, but they had to do it quickly. What else did she say? Susie replayed the dream in her mind, as much as she could remember, and seemed to recall something about Mary J. What was that—*Oh! Mary J. understands, she said. That means she has spoken to Mary J. too.*

The last thing the old woman said was about the letters. *They will help you understand what your great-grandparents went through. Before you form an opinion about them, read the letters. It must be important for us to not condemn them,* Susie thought silently. But she had found it to be almost impossible to do. Everything about their lives demanded that they follow certain paths. Not traditions, particularly. Forget traditions. She was thinking more along the lines of ethical and moral behavior today. There were certain standards that people were expected to live by. If you didn't, you were labeled and looked down on by the greater part of the population. Heretics, prostitutes, and homosexuals were the immediate ones that came to mind. But none of those were hardly given a second thought anymore.

The problem with the old woman's request about not forming an opinion was that the conviction was already there. That's what society does for you. It brands you with tags and fills your head with preconceived ideas before you barely get out of elementary school. By then, it's too late unless you have the courage to stand up for your own beliefs. That's what Susie wanted to do. She wanted to do what the old woman had said. Read first, and then form your opinion.

Look for the letters in a small chest in the old family house.

That's what they had done. They went out to the old family home. It was nothing more than a pile of debris, but there was no chest, no letters. Why did the old woman say to look for them in the old family house anyway? It wasn't even a house anymore. Susie was really confused—unless! Maybe she meant Great-Grandma and Great-Grandpa Conners. Joshua and Jenny's house. It was still standing.

"Of course!" she cried out loud. "That's got to be it."

"What are you talking about?" Stoney asked. They had arrived at the hospital to check on Mary J. and was pulling into a parking slot.

Susie was sure that she'd figured it out. That's why they didn't find the letters. They were looking in the wrong place. She told Stoney what she figured out. "We need to go out to Great-Grandpa and Great-Grandma Conners' house," she told him. "We'll find the letters there."

"How can you be so sure?" Stoney asked suspiciously. After this last escapade, he wouldn't be so quick to run off on another wild-goose chase. He loved Susie, but he wasn't so sure but what she was buckling under the stress of Brian's death and Mary J.'s condition.

"Because it's the only thing that makes sense," she said, satisfied with her skills of deduction. "Come on, Stoney. Please?" she begged him. "If you don't go with me, I'll go alone," she said, unyielding in her determination to discover the truth. Susie could be stubborn when she wanted to be, and right now, she wanted to be.

Stoney gave in. "You are so much like your mother. As bull-headed as the day is long," he said, backing out of parking space. They left the hospital and headed out of town again.

She stared at him, grimacing painfully at his obdurate attitude. He surely didn't know how much that comment hurt. How could he know the anguish she suffered at her mother's constant refusal to acknowledge her presence? She had never told him about it and wasn't sure if he even had a clue.

It hurt.

It hurt so much, sometimes she wished she were dead. Except for Stoney, she had thought about it before. "How rude," she finally said.

"Sorry. I didn't really mean that," he confessed, reaching over and pulling her across the seat to his side. She slid across the seat easily and snuggled up against him. They rode in silence.

Rogers sat at his desk, staring at the two files that had plagued the sheriff's department for many decades. They were the unsolved cases of Joshua Conners and Franklin Baker. He had pulled them out of the dusty old box in the basement where they stored their old files, solved and unsolved, and read and reread them several times since the Clark kid had died. There had to be a connection between the three. They had all died at Rockhole. True, Joshua and Franklin were not related. As far as he knew, they didn't even have any ties with each other when they were alive.

But in death they did.

They were joined together by the marriage of Brian Clark and Mary J. Conners. Of all things, it was that one innocent act that dissolved the vagueness of that past, bringing it storming into the present. Now all Rogers had to do was figure out what it all meant.

That was why he had called in the priest. He still believed it would take someone with ties to the world beyond the grave to resolve them. After seeing Brian Clark's face at the morgue and rereading the old files, he was surer than ever that it was a supernatural phenomenon they were dealing with. What he didn't know was why, nor how to resolve it. Perhaps Father Pritchard would have those answers.

He picked up the manila file folder on Joshua Conners and studied it again for the hundredth time today. He was buried deep in its contents when the jingling of the phone drew him away. He picked up the receiver and put it to his ear. "Hello," he called out gruffly.

The caller paused, momentarily ruffled by the curt opening. "I'm sorry, Sheriff. Did I call at a bad time? This is Father Pritchard."

"Oh, Father. Good," he said eagerly. "No, it's just this case. It has me twisted in knots." He thought he detected a sigh from the other end of the line. "Do you have some news for me?" he asked hopefully.

"I wish the answer was yes," the priest replied guardedly. "You obviously are not making any progress. But I'm afraid I have nothing to report. I met with the monsignor last night. We discussed this at great length, but unfortunately, we could not agree on the church's involvement."

Rogers considered the priest's statement. He feared he was becoming used to the feeling of rejection as he accepted the brief explanation, no questions asked. "Thank you, Father. I would appreciate you letting me know if you do come up with anything."

"Yes, of course, Sheriff. I'm sorry," he apologized, hearing the heavy sigh come over the phone.

"No. No, need to apologize. Goodbye, Father," he said ruefully.

"Good day, Sheriff." He hung up, pleased that he didn't lie, but feeling guilty that he didn't tell the sheriff the whole truth. He only neglected to mention that he was going to try to deal with the demon himself. He knew that evil spirits were involved, but was he ready to take them on? If he did, he knew also that he stood to lose his life. It was a chance he was willing to take. The church had to take a stand, or else evil would rule.

Although he was ill-prepared for a confrontation, he had to summon the diabolic being to see what he was up against. Father Pritchard went into the sanctuary and prayed. He exited the church thirty minutes later, a glum but determined look about him, got into the parish car and drove away.

He drove in the direction of Rockhole.

The old Conners house guarded the ridge like a surviving soldier after a well-fought battle on a barren hilltop. All about were strewn the ravages of its victory. Trees stood as sentinels on the worthless piece of ground, surrounding a house covered over with vines so that it was almost hidden. Weeds rushed to the doors and windows, begging to enter to the safety of the inside. The shutters barely clung to the ramshackle siding, having long ago given up any attempt to keep intruders out.

"Still want to go in?" Stoney asked, dreadfully.

Susie opened the car door and stepped out. "More than ever. Are you coming with me?" she asked, slamming the car door a little harder than was necessary.

"Shit, Susie!" he blurted out. "You know I don't like places like this." But he got out of the car and joined her. He couldn't let her go in alone.

They walked slowly to the front porch, their eyes glued to the half-opened door. Suddenly, Susie screamed as a snake crawled across her foot. She jumped backward into Stoney. "It's just a little garden snake," he whispered.

She kept her eyes on the snake until it disappeared under the porch. Then she stared at Stoney with the same contempt she had for the harmless little reptile, before resuming her march.

They climbed the steps, testing each one before placing their full weight on it. The creaking boards reminded Stoney just how much he didn't want to be here. Susie was amused at his childish fear but kept her attention focused on the gloomy interior of the house as they drew closer.

As she stepped across the threshold, taking care not to open the door any more than it already was, Susie wrinkled up her nose when several decades of dust, decaying rodents, and rotted wood invaded her nostrils, as well as some odors she couldn't identify. She crossed through the foyer and stood in the doorway leading into what must have been the sitting room.

Susie shivered as a chill trapped inside the house worked its way into her bones, even though it was warm outside.

"Well?"

She was startled as Stoney's voice shattered the eerie silence and echoed through the vacant building. "Damn it, Stoney!" she spat at him.

"What's the matter? Afraid we'll wake the dead?" he chuckled at her. Susie shot him a scornful look. "Sorry," he apologized. "Just trying to ease the tension a little."

Susie looked around the room. Where should they start? All the furniture was still here. Some of it had been covered with sheets, the larger pieces like the sofa, chairs, table, and so forth. And everything had a coat of dust an inch thick on it. She lifted one corner of a sheet and peeked underneath.

"This is impossible," Stoney said sarcastically. "We'll have to look under every sheet in every room. Susie, this is like looking for a needle in the haystack," he complained loudly.

She came back over to where he was standing. "I know it seems like an endless task, but we have to do this. Look, I'll go upstairs and look around. You keep looking down here, okay?" He nodded and she started for the stairs.

"Watch those steps," Stoney warned her. "There's no telling what condition they're in." Susie left him to wander the lower floor, while she climbed up the ancient stairway. She tested each step, but it wasn't necessary. The only thing wrong with them was they creaked badly like the front steps outside. She noted that she left perfect footprints in the dust which had gone undisturbed for several years. Silently, she wondered about the old house's previous occupants.

At the top of the stairs, she hesitated while trying to get her bearings. The hall went an equal distance in both directions. There appeared to be more doors to the left than there were to the right. She reasoned that the master bedroom would be larger than the other rooms and would take up more space, allowing for fewer doors. It made sense to her anyway. So she chose to go the right based on her survey. Halfway down the hall she stopped and opened the door to the room on the left. Susie couldn't believe it.

This was obviously the master bedroom.

She was sure this was how it must have looked the day Jenny Conners died. And even more unbelievable, it was almost completely free of dust. "This is beautiful," she observed, breathing the words out slowly.

She roamed the room, finally coming to a stop next to a lonely wooden rocking chair that sat idly in front of a dormer window. She had noticed when they drove up that the old house had several gables protruding from the roof. She fell in love with it immediately.

The chair seemed to carry her back through the years to a point in time where she could feel the presence of her great-grandparents, as they moved through the room, having a conversation, while getting ready for bed. Susie hadn't realized that she had sat in the rocking chair.

She jumped up.

Suddenly, she was dizzy. She must have stood up too fast. She grabbed the back of the chair for support and realized for the first time that the sensation of the past was gone.

The chair. It must have been the chair.

It beckoned to her.

Susie thought she must be losing her mind, but it had been too strong, that feeling. She sat down in the chair again but slowly—unsure of herself. As soon as she touched the chair, that same feeling returned. This time Susie didn't get up. She sat there and let the past flood over her. All the emotions that were trapped in the house came crashing in on her. It was wonderful, electrifying. She felt such a surge of power.

She felt like she could do anything. It was so…heavenly.

She relaxed and let the feeling completely wash over her. The light from the window disappeared as she was surrounded by darkness. And in the darkness, she saw a different kind of light, subdued but well lit. In that light, coming toward her, was the old woman, then she heard her speak.

You came. I was beginning to think you weren't going to come.

"I went to the wrong house first. I thought you meant my other family's old home. But when I saw it burned to the ground, and nothing but rubble remained, I knew there was something wrong."

I'm sorry. I should have given you better instructions. But you still made it in time. I wish I were still alive to see you, to talk to you.

"That would be nice," Susie told her. "But you probably lived in a much better time than now. Things have changed so much, the world is not such a nice, safe place to live anymore. You probably wouldn't like it. Even the people are different. Used to be that a person was believed when they told the truth but not anymore," she said, thinking about her mother.

Susie, your mother does love you, you know. She doesn't show it, but deep down in her heart where it counts, she loves you. You should give her a chance. You haven't exactly told her that you love her, either. Just…give her a chance. Have a long talk with her.

"How did you know about that?" she asked astonished. "How do you know so much about me?"

It'd not important how I know, dear. It's only important that I do know and that you find those letters. Inside that large chest at the foot of the bed is a smaller chest. You'll find what you're looking for in there. Susie, have a good life.

"Thank you. Thank you. Thank—"

"Susie? Who were you talking to?" The darkness fell away to be replaced with the sunlight streaming through the window. Stoney was standing over her, his hand on her shoulder. "Are you all right? I thought you were up here looking for the chest? What happened?"

She smiled up at him. Then she got up and walked over to the foot of the bed. "It's in here," she told him. Stoney looked from her to the chest and frowned. He lifted the lid and right inside, where the old woman had said, was the smaller chest.

"How did you know?"

Rather than answer him, she bent over and gingerly picked up the little box. She held it in her hands like it might fall apart if she wasn't careful. They stared at it. Now that they had it, they were uncertain what to do, it seemed. Stoney noted that it was made from cedar and didn't look like it had aged at all. In fact, it still had a fresh cedar smell to it. Suddenly, it dawned on him. "You had another dream, didn't you?"

"While I was in the rocking chair," she admitted. "The old woman came to me again. She told me where the chest was and…" She paused.

"And what?"

Susie was undecided about telling the rest of the conversation she had with the old woman. It was private and not relevant to finding the letters. She didn't want anyone else to know about it. She finally made up her mind to not say anything—for the moment. "Oh, nothing really. We just talked, that's all."

Their eyes met. Stoney felt there was something there but chose not to pursue it for now. "Let's take this home and look at it there," he suggested. As they left the bedroom, Susie gave the rocking chair one parting glance. And for a second, she thought she saw her great-grandmother sitting in the chair…rocking.

Susie smiled at the chair—and Jenny smiled back.

Father Pritchard had never been to Rockhole, but it was easy enough to get directions. Nearly everyone in the Crater Ridge knew where it was. He drove out State Road 38, following the directions he had been given. When he came to County Road 135, he turned off, crossed the low water bridge, and parked on the side of the road.

The priest sat in the car for a while, staring down the road that was really nothing more than a wagon trail. Down there, not too far, is where the young lady had lost her husband, and where he had undoubtedly had his encounter with the satanic creature.

Those two young people had no idea what they were up against, he thought to himself, getting out of the car. He crawled through the barbed-wire fence and proceeded along the trail. As he walked along, he couldn't help but wonder what things that young woman had seen that night to put her in the state of mind she was in. He had a pretty good idea. And he had a heavy heart for her.

As he neared the swimming hole, he could feel the stirrings of the demon. It started as a weight on his chest, much like the first symptoms of a heart attack. But he trudged on. Soon, he came to the trail that descended through the trees to the rock cliff below. It dropped no more than four feet from top to bottom.

He started down the slope, and almost immediately the weight on his chest became heavier. Then his lungs began to burn, again symptomatic of a heart attack. Father Pritchard tried to tell himself that it was all in his head, completely psychological, but the pain felt so real.

When he had descended to the rock surface, he stood in the middle of it, his eyes closed. "I know you are here," he called out to the invisible creature, his arms held straight out from his sides, palms up.

The priest had to wait for quite a while before the creature finally responded.

What do you want, priest? You have no business here.

"As a matter of fact, I do," he retorted sarcastically. "You have been tormenting some poor souls in this area for a hundred years. It's time for you to leave." His statement was very matter of fact.

Ha! Ha! Ha! Ha! And who is going to make me leave? You? You are nothing to me. A mere coincidence. You are but a lowly priest. Why don't you toddle on back to your despicable little church and leave me alone?

"That's what you would like for me to do, but I'm afraid it's not that simple. We have business, you and I." Father Pritchard steeled himself for the onslaught he knew would come. He had challenged the demon and the beast would not take it lightly. He decided to fuel the fire some more. He needed to know more about this particular demon. "You have pilfered and ravaged the fine people of this community long enough. You are *nothing! Nothing!*" he shouted at the still unseen creature.

He was quickly rewarded for his insolence. Suddenly the whole area was lighted with a glowing, subdued illumination. He focused his gaze—when had he opened his eyes, for he didn't remember doing that—on the center of the light, knowing that was where the creature would be. Soon, he detected two points of stronger light at the nucleus of the object. The eyes, he thought to himself.

Time to ignite that fuel. "Your power is *nothing!* I laugh at you. You are a disgrace to your kingdom."

Suddenly the beast hurtled a ball of energy at the religious leader. The priest was ready for the assault, however, and had knelt in prayer, calling on the name of Jesus at the same instant the creature made its move. The wave of energy passed over and around him, dissipating into a harmless void.

"You will leave this place, or I will destroy you," Father Pritchard ordered the demonic creature.

We will meet again, little one. The next time, you will not be so fortunate. Your God cannot protect you forever. This is not over, priest. A word of warning, if I am destroyed, you will come with me.

The light disappeared. "That may very well be," said the priest, shaking his head sadly. There would be another confrontation. And he feared the outcome could very well be as the creature had said, but he was certain God would be victorious. Of that much he was sure. He rubbed his chest over the place where his heart was located. Although he would not admit it to the demon, he was suffering a heart attack. He could feel the immense pressure on his chest. The priest had never had any heart problems, but that didn't matter. This was not the result of a human medical problem. He left the immediate area and started toward his car. Halfway down the dirt lane, he fell to the ground grabbing his chest. "Good must win over evil," he said softly.

"God must prevail!"

Just as Stoney and Susie neared the edge of town, an ambulance roared past them headed in the same direction they had just come from. With nothing more than a cursory glance in its direction, they continued to their apartment.

When they walked in, Susie noticed the light blinking on their answering machine. She pushed a button to activate the messages, while Stoney sat down with the small chest on his lap. He had just lifted the lid of the chest when the sound of Dala's voice came from the machine. "Hey, you guys, you home?" A pause. "Hellooo. Pick up. Pick up." Another pause. "Well, I guess you aren't home. When you get home, come to the hospital as soon as possible. Mary J.'s awake. See ya."

Stoney dropped the chest on the coffee table. Susie shut off the answering machine, and they fled the apartment in a hurry.

They made record time to the hospital. Stoney screeched to a halt in an empty parking space. Susie had her door open before the car came to a complete halt. They ran from the car to the entrance of the hospital and then dashed hurriedly through the halls to Mary J.'s room. When they got there, the room was already crowded. Between the doctor, the nurses, friends, and family, the room looked like a press conference. Sheriff Rogers and one deputy, Mike, were also there asking questions.

But the only thing Susie saw when she bolted through the door was her sister sitting up in bed, her eyes open. She flew to Mary J.'s bed and threw her arms around her sister. Both girls broke into tears. "I didn't know if you would ever wake up again," Susie bawled in Mary J.'s ear. "I'm so happy you're awake."

Between the tears, her sister replied in kind. "Me too. I'm glad you're here, although you are kind of late. Where the hell have you been?"

"It's a long story," Susie said, choking back more tears. "I'll explain it all later."

The sheriff cleared his throat. "Excuse me, ladies. I know you have a lot of catching up to do, but I really need to ask a few more questions—and then you can get back to your reunion," he added. Susie looked at Mary J., her eyes asking the question her mind couldn't accept. With just one look, the answer was obvious. *Yes,* Mary J. said without speaking. *I know about Brian.* The sadness in her sister's eyes tore at Susie's heart.

Stoney leaned over and gave his sister-in-law a hug and then stepped out of the way. Susie remained on the edge of the bed, holding one of Mary J.'s hands, while the sheriff continued asking questions.

"Mary J., I know this is tough on you, and I'm sorry. But there are a few things we need to clear up. We're getting absolutely nowhere on your husband's...well, you know," he finished clumsily.

She smiled at his awkwardness. "It's all right, Sheriff. I know you're just doing your job. I don't have anything to hide."

He returned her smile and then continued from where they left off. "Okay, the last thing you said was that the two of you ate supper." She nodded. "What happened next?"

"After that, Brian and I were just starting to..." She paused, embarrassed. "To make love," she said shyly. "That's when I blacked out. I don't remember anything after that. And now...I can't believe he's dead," she cried. Susie pulled Mary J.'s head to her shoulder and held her.

"You go ahead and cry, sugar. You just go ahead and cry." She patted her sister gently on the back like she would a little baby to calm it down.

After a few minutes, Mary J. pulled away and apologized for her behavior. "That's all right, young lady," the sheriff replied, uncomfortable at having to ask her these questions in front of her family.

"No need to apologize. Do you remember the farmer finding you on the road?"

She frowned at him and shook her head no. Her look apologized again to the law enforcement officer for her apparent lack of information. "I think Mary needs to get some rest, Sheriff," the doctor told him. "She's weak and not yet fully recovered. Perhaps you could continue tomorrow."

"Thanks for your help, Mary J.," Sheriff Rogers said, dismissing himself. He and the deputy left the room.

"I have to go too," Dala chimed in. "My kids are probably driving Casey crazy." She gave Mary J. and Susie a hug, jabbed a playful knuckle at Stoney's arm and left. The doctor and nurse were checking Mary J.'s vital signs as Susie got up from the bedside and headed for the door. When she passed Sadie, she whispered something in her ear and then went out into the hall.

A few seconds later, Sadie exited the room also. "Well, what is it?" she asked gruffly.

Susie forced herself to remain civil as she remembered what the old woman had said to her. Suddenly, she did feel calm. She felt different. She smiled at her mother. "I-I love you," she said unsteadily. "I should have told you a long time ago, but then somewhere along the way, I thought you stopped loving me, so I stopped saying it. I'm sorry, Mama. I never did stop loving you." By now, her eyes were full of tears.

So were Sadie's. "Oh, baby. It was when you stopped saying it that I thought you stopped loving me. I was so hurt, I couldn't even bring myself to look at you. Oh god, it's my fault," she cried. "It's all my fault. For everything." She wrapped her arms around her daughter, and they cried on each other's shoulder. It was much more than Susie could have hoped for. She wished at that moment that she could see the old woman and thank her. She had been right.

"Hey, what's going on out there," Mary J. called from inside the room. The doctor and nurse came out of the room as they walked in.

In the distance, somewhere, a siren wailed.

Monsignor DeGuardo had asked the cab driver to let him out a couple of blocks away from the hospital. He strolled along slowly due in part to his age, but at this moment due more to the fact that he wanted some time to think before confronting Father Pritchard. When he arrived in town, he went to the rectory, expecting to find the priest there, but instead, he received the message that his friend and subordinate had been taken to the hospital, apparently suffering a heart attack.

He was sure it had something to do with the topic of their discussion the day before since Father Pritchard was in excellent health and had been discovered near a creek, out of town. But somehow, he hadn't anticipated such an immediate response. Of course, he realized this was his old friend he was talking about. Timothy never did anything with less than the greatest enthusiasm, nor did he back down from a confrontation because there might be an element of danger involved. Obviously, what his friend needed now was his support, not chastisement.

He turned up the walkway to the hospital, his stride much more purposeful than it had been moments ago. After consulting the directory and satisfying himself as to the location of the intensive care unit, he marched down the long hall to the elevator and took it to the second floor. With signs posted directing him to the appropriate area, it didn't take long to find ICU.

The monsignor was escorted to Father Pritchard's bed by a young nurse. She was more than glad to do anything to help. This was her priest lying in that bed. He noticed she wore a concerned frown, and now he understood why. She lingered for a moment before leaving them alone.

DeGuardo stared down at his old friend. He looked dead. As if the priest could read his thoughts, he said, "I'm not dead yet. Don't look so forlorn."

"You have always been the most stubborn man I've ever known. See? You even refuse to die when you've had a massive coronary," he teased. He took his friend's hand and said a quick prayer before discussing it further. "How did this happen? You want to tell me about it?"

Father Pritchard managed a weak smile. "I would not presume to tell you something you already know. It was just as we expected. The only problem is, I was ill prepared for the encounter." He swept his arm in a wide gesture. "I've been too long in an easy assignment like this I suppose. And have become soft. Blind to what is really going on around me." Suddenly he had a thought. "They sent for you? How long have I been here?" He started to get out of bed. "The creature is still there. My work is not finished."

Monsignor DeGuardo restrained his friend. "You're not going anywhere. You would never make it out of the hospital." As his friend started to protest, he interrupted. "It will wait until you have healed. The creature will still be there. Now, do I have to call the doctor to knock you out, or are you going to cooperate?"

The priest fell back onto the pillows, letting a huge sigh escape his lips. He reached out and clasped the monsignor's suddenly finding renewed strength. "Andrew, this isn't finished. That was only the beginning," he rasped.

"That's one hell of an introduction from the creature," the monsignor replied, smiling ruefully. "Give your guest a heart attack. Maybe he won't come back."

But I will go back, the priest thought silently. Then he remembered his condition. Squeezing the monsignor's arm, he pleaded his case further. "Will you go out there and finish what I started? If you don't, the curse will never end. It will strangle this community and darkness will rule forever."

"Timothy, I am not the right person to be asking," he scoffed. "Such a thing is completely out of my realm. Besides, I'm not convinced that this isn't anything more than…" He paused, searching for the right words. "Some deviant's attempt at skullduggery. Pure and simple," he stated with finality.

The priest squeezed his friends arm even tighter. "You think I'm making this up?" he shouted. "You think I don't know the difference between evil sorcery and pranks?" His voice had risen steadily as his anger increased. "Andrew, I thought you knew me better than that!" He was already thinking to himself that the task would remain his.

Somehow, he would have to find the strength to finish what he had started.

Father Pritchard let go of his friend's arm, and the monsignor unconsciously took a step backward. "They told me I could stay only a few minutes. I think I have overstayed my welcome," he declared in more of a superior's tone than a friend's. "I will look in on you tomorrow. Is there anything I can bring you?" he asked. Pritchard thought the question sounded much more businesslike than one that would come from an intimate friend.

He shrugged off the monsignor's offer and watched as the elderly church leader departed. When his friend had disappeared through the automatic doors that sequestered ICU from the rest of the hospital, he had but one thought.

He would have to finish what he had started—tonight.

Monsignor DeGuardo hadn't been gone five minutes when Sheriff Rogers walked in. He stared down at the priest, who didn't seem aware of his presence. In fact, the priest's face was a study in anger. "I take it your visit with the monsignor didn't go well," he chided.

Father Pritchard glared at him. "Well, I guess you've figured out by now that I didn't exactly tell you everything. But you can't exactly put me in jail for lying, can you?" he scoffed.

Rogers smiled at him. "You want to tell me what's going on now?"

"That wouldn't be my first choice," the priest replied. "But I suppose you have a right to know." He shifted his position, sitting up a little more. After a brief pause, he told Rogers about his suspicions and subsequent visit to Rockhole. "As you can see it was all for nothing. I'm not in a position to do much now."

The sheriff felt sorry for Father Pritchard. He had guessed correctly that the priest was very passionate about his work and this time was no exception.

"When you get out of here, we'll get together and start over."

Pritchard nodded.

"Well, anyway, I hope you do get to feeling better," Rogers said. He walked off feeling depressed about his conversation with the priest. He had almost reached the doors when Father Pritchard called out to him. He turned and looked back.

"Thank you for coming."

Rogers nodded and then left.

Room 122, earlier the center of a great deal of activity, was remarkably toned down. The only remaining visitors were Mary J.'s parents, sister, and brother-in-law. And Daniel had decided that it was getting late and, therefore, time for him and Sadie to leave as well. It had been a nice evening, with the reconciliation between Susie and her mother.

As they stood to go, Sadie glanced at Susie and suggested, "Why don't you and Stoney come by later and let's talk."

"Sure, Mama," Susie responded. "If that's all right with Stoney."

She looked at him for confirmation. Stoney was about to agree when he suddenly remembered the letters. "Can't do it. We've got those letters to read," he reminded her.

"Oh, damn! I forgot about those in all the excitement."

"Letters?" Sadie asked, her brow knitted in a frown and panic etched in her tone. "What…what letters?" Her terrified response wielded a sudden chill to the air. They stared at her.

Stoney decided it was time for total truth. He started back with the first encounter Susie had with the old woman and finished with their finding the chest containing the letters in the old family house.

Sadie was horrified, but Mary J. was the first to speak. "I had the same dream," she said, her face turning ashen. Suddenly, a lot of things made sense to Susie. Things she hadn't understood before.

"That's what the old woman meant by, I think Mary J. understands. She had me really confused with that," Susie informed the group.

"It's odd, but I do understand," her sister replied. "But I didn't remember until you guys said something about the letters." Her eyes glazed over as she seemed to be concentrating on something the others could not perceive. Suddenly, everything came flooding back.

The picnic. Her pregnancy. The lovemaking. Oh god! She and Brian were making love when they were interrupted—by it.

Her terror was reflected in her face. It happened so fast, and everyone was so startled by the abrupt shift of emotions that it took a minute for someone to respond. "Mary J.," Susie said, dismayed by her sister's expression. "What is it? What's wrong?"

But Mary J. didn't hear.

The only sounds she heard were those of her own heartbeat pounding in her head. She relived the horrible sequence of events again as the vivid reality of Brian's death overwhelmed her. "Mama," she cried. "Mama, Brian's dead." She held her arms out like a small child waiting to be picked up by its mother and protected from the horrible monster.

Sadie moved over to the side of the bed and took her oldest daughter in her arms, pulling her to her bosom. She stroked Mary J.'s hair and repeated over and over, "I know, baby. Mama's here... Mama's here..." It seemed to soothe her some and after a while, her body wracking sobs were reduced to a few low and occasional wails and, eventually, to just sniffles.

"I-I remember everything," she said sadly. "I thought it was all a bad dream. But it's true, isn't it? He's really gone. I'll never hold him again. He'll never get to see Michele grow up, or her first day of school, or learn to dance. He won't be there to hold me at night when I'm cold, or if I have a bad dream." She had tried to be brave and not cry anymore. But the more she talked, the more her lips quivered, and the tears returned. Even though she tried, hard as it was, she couldn't prevent herself from collapsing into a trembling heap of heartbreaking sobs.

Suddenly, she thought of their unborn child. "What...what about...our baby? Oh, Mama. He'll never get to see our baby," she wailed even louder.

Then Sadie could see a transformation taking place in her daughter. Her momentary grief was gradually replaced by an unbidden anger. This was something different for Mary J.

It was like she was being manipulated by an outside force. She climbed out of bed, finally free of the monitor and IV, and shuffled over to the window. She stood there, her reflection staring back at her, and saw herself for the first time since that tragic night. She looked drawn and haggard, not at all like herself. "Why did you do this to us?" she screamed at the night. Everyone was startled by her outburst. They stood by silently and watched. Mary J. raised one hand and lashed out at the window. "*Why! Why!* Why, Brian?" she shouted as her words bounced back from her own reflection in the darkened glass. "He was a good…he was…" She couldn't say it. Susie had recovered from the shocking moment and put her arm around her sister. At her gentle nudging, Mary J. left the window, the image still imprinted in her mind.

She led her troubled sister back to the bed and when the distraught girl was settled again, she told her, "We'll find the person responsible, Mary J. No matter who it was, with your help, we can find him."

Mary J. was shaking her head. "It's not a person. It's a demon… or something," she proclaimed, her eyes glassy and staring. "It wants my baby." She put her hands on her stomach, protecting the unborn infant.

"What is in those letters?" Sadie asked.

All three of her children looked at her. They had forgotten about the letters when Mary J.'s memory returned, and she had suddenly remembered everything that had happened—including Brian's death. "We haven't had a chance to read them yet," Stoney answered. "We were just about to when we got the message about Mary J." He started to say something else, then decided against it.

"It's not very late," Sadie said, looking at her watch. "Why don't you call or come by when you finish reading them. We need to talk."

Stoney glanced at Susie. The look that passed between them confirmed what they both already suspected.

There's more here than meets the eye.

Chapter Fourteen

Elise drew the back of her hand across her forehead. When she brought it away, it was covered with the sweat that had popped up on her brow. Her dress was wet across the neckline, and her eyes were stinging as some of it strayed down through her brows. She did the best she could at keeping the seething body fluid out of her eyes, but alas, it was a lost cause.

She bent down and scooped up the basket of clothes that was sitting on the ground next to her feet. As she straightened up clutching the basket under her left arm, a wave of sweltering heat washed over her, nearly taking her breath away, but was followed immediately by a gust of cooling wind.

"Thank you, Lord," she said, looking up at the sky.

Elise made her way to the clothesline through a constant barrage of heat but with only an occasional gust of wind. Devoting her full concentration to her task, she didn't notice the voice at first. It was close by, but she had to strain to hear what it was saying. It sounded like a conversation, but there was only one voice.

Elise continued hanging up her clothes but kept one ear to the wind. Finally, as she was finishing with the last garment, she decided to look for the voice.

It was coming from behind the barn.

She quickly put the clothes basket on the back porch and made her way toward the barn. It had been a nice barn when it was new. She could still picture, in her mind, the bright yellowish wood and the brown circular knots. It was a sight to see. Of course, in time, the yellow wood had turned brown with age. And although Solomon had been faithful with repairs on it, there was only so much repairing that could be done before it needed to be leveled and started over again.

As she approached the barn, the voice grew louder. Now she recognized it as Solomon's. Who in the world was he talking to, though? Probably that mangy old dog that followed him everywhere. Her curiosity temporarily overshadowed her better judgment of eavesdropping.

She sidled up to the barn and edged her way along the east wall until she came to the end. Then she leaned forward and peeked around the corner. There was Solomon leaning against the fence that surrounded the corral, his left foot resting on one of the middle boards.

He was talking to Sammy, his dog.

So she had been right. He did talk to that broken-down, scruffy-looking dog. She had thought so for several years but had never really known for sure.

Wait a minute! What was that he was saying? Something about the children? Something like I do miss them. Elise strained to hear what Solomon was saying. She was barely breathing.

"I just couldn't admit it to myself—and especially not to Ellie. I hate what they did you understand. But…they're my kids and…I love them."

Elise wiped the tears from her eyes with the back of her hand. *I knew he would come around*, she told herself. I just knew it. She was so happy, she almost cried aloud. She heard him say something about grandchildren and they died before she stepped from her hiding place.

"Solomon."

The elderly farmer recoiled at the sound of another person's voice. He had checked and was sure he was alone. God, he felt foolish at getting caught talking to no one.

"How long you been there, woman?"

"Just a few minutes," she admitted, embarrassed. It was completely out of character for her to eavesdrop on her own husband.

She continued her approach at a slow, resolute gait. "I didn't mean to listen in. Really, I didn't," she confessed wholeheartedly.

"Just what did you hear?" he asked in a gruff manner.

Elise bowed her head as she admitted her guilt. "I heard you talking about the children. Oh, Solomon," she cried suddenly. "Could we please get in touch with them? They have been through so much, and we should have been there for them. It would mean so much to both of them if we just let them know that we cared." She stopped talking as she realized that she was babbling.

"Whoa, just hang on a minute," Solomon said, dismayed. "I can't believe you did that."

"Solomon, I'm sorry," she apologized quickly. "I didn't do it on purpose. It's just that I heard some talking and came over to see what it was…and then I heard you say something about the children, and I just didn't have the heart to interrupt you. I'm sorry," she said again, taking in a deep breath.

"Oh, it's all right," he said in a slow drawl. "It's probably something you should have heard anyway—and would have eventually." His mouth curled slightly at the corners.

"Oh, Solomon, I don't know what to say," she blubbered.

They walked back to the house, Elise clinging to Solomon's arm, chattering on and on.

Joshua and Jenny were expecting Doug and Tracy for dinner. They didn't get together that often, but it was getting close to Jenny's delivery date, and they knew it would be a while before they could do this again. So to prepare for such a special occasion, Jenny had spent most of the day cleaning and cooking.

But not alone.

Tracy simply would not allow her to attempt all that in her present condition. She had spent the day helping her friend with the chores and dinner preparation. Even if Jenny were not with child, Tracy would have helped. It was their way of doing for each other. It also gave them an excuse—as though they needed one—to spend time together and catch up on any local gossip that might have missed one or the other's door.

Life in the small community of Crater Ridge was boring enough without the simple pleasure of chatting about one's neighbors. And Tracy and Jenny were not about to miss one single chance of contributing their part in the local color.

Instead of waiting for help, or at least waiting for someone to be present while attempting such an awkward maneuver, the stubborn woman that she is, Jenny had climbed up on a chair and was stretched out as far as her petite little frame would stretch trying to reach a dish in the space above the cabinets. It was one she didn't use much but would need for tonight.

It was actually going pretty well, all things considered, until Tracy entered the kitchen and saw what her friend was doing. Without thinking of the possible consequences, she scolded Jenny rather loudly, and then all hell broke loose.

"What in the name of sanity do you think you are doing?" Tracy chided the pregnant woman.

Jenny turned her head just enough to see Tracy watching her movements, and as luck would have it, that was all it took to unbalance her. She teetered on one leg for a moment before the chair slipped sideways and she went in the opposite direction. Tracy closed the distance between them but not soon enough. Jenny was already falling by the time she got to her. She caught Jenny awkwardly, and the pregnant woman's weight and momentum sent them both crashing to the floor.

Jenny rolled off Tracy like a ball sailing down a hill and slammed into the cabinet. She grabbed her stomach and groaned. "Tracy—ahh!" Jenny started to sit up but fell backward as the pain grew worse.

It took a minute for Tracy to shake off the effects of the fall but was soon at her friend's side. "Are you in labor?" she asked excitedly.

"I-I don't know." Jenny shuddered as another wave of pain shot through her body and then subsided. She began to breathe normally. "It doesn't feel like labor," she cried, grimacing.

Tracy got behind her and cradled her arms under Jenny's and lifted her to a sitting position. "We need to get you to bed, but I'm going to need help. I better get Joshua," she grunted. "Where is he?"

"I'm right here," a deep male voice boomed from the kitchen door. "What happened?"

"Quickly, Joshua. I'll explain in a minute. We need to get her to bed. I think she's in labor," Tracy explained.

As they both lifted, one to either side of Jenny, she suddenly felt an unusually warm sensation between her legs. She screamed. "Joshua, something's wrong. There's something wrong with the baby!" she shrieked, horror replacing her pain.

"Come on, let's get you to bed and then I'll go for Doc Pogue. Tracy will be right here with you, won't you, Tracy?"

"You bet I will," she said, glancing at Joshua. "I'll be right here beside you, honey. Anything you need, you just ask, okay?" Tracy's eyes narrowed, and her brows furrowed as she remembered her dream. She turned away before Jenny could see. She had a bad feeling about this. But it wasn't anything tangible. It was just a feeling.

"You go on, Joshua. We'll be fine," she assured him.

Jenny was just coming out of another round of labor pains. She had a death grip on Tracy's hand and finally relaxed her hold with the fading of that last agonizing pain. She looked at her friend. She remembered too. "Tracy, your dream."

Tracy looked at her friend with horror. "Now, you just forget that. That was just a dream and nothing more," she said, trying to sound commanding.

The only problem was—she didn't believe it herself.

Joshua led the doctor to the foot of the stairs and then up to the second floor. They could hear Jenny moaning and screaming from her pain as they pulled up out front. Now, it was louder than ever the closer they got to the bedroom.

While the doctor went in to attend to Jenny, Joshua remained at the door, watchful. Tracy was still at the head of the bed, holding his wife's hand and offering words of encouragement. The doctor was at the foot of the bed rummaging through his bag. He pulled out a stethoscope and put the two hooked ends to his ears and the large shiny discus end to Jenny's stomach.

He listened for a minute and then took the apparatus off and laid it aside. "Help me get her legs up and move her closer to the foot of the bed," he instructed Tracy. "Joshua, get me a pan of warm water and some rags. I need a sheet also." He and Tracy pulled Jenny's legs up and then gently scooted her toward the foot of the bed. The doctor set the pregnant woman's feet on the bed rail for her to use as a brace for her feet.

As soon as Jenny was ready, he stepped away from the bed and took off his hat, pulled off his jacket, and rolled up his sleeves. He took the sheet that Tracy offered him, unfolded it, and threw it over Jenny's legs covering her from the knees to her waist.

Tracy helped him straighten the sheet and then turned aside from her friend and asked the doctor. "Is there anything wrong with her? Or is she just in premature labor?"

"It doesn't look good," he said kneeling at the foot of the bed. "Did she start bleeding immediately?"

"No. The pains came first, but the bleeding started a short time after that," she replied. "It wasn't very long between them. Just a few minutes."

He nodded at her and then turned his attention back to Jenny. Suddenly, she went into another fit of pain. Tracy moved the chair she had been sitting on closer to Jenny's head and took her hand again.

"You're going to be just fine," she reassured her. "And so is the baby."

But Jenny wasn't convinced. "Are you telling me the truth?" she asked suspiciously between pains. "You wouldn't lie to me, would you?" She gave Tracy a nefarious glance. Right now, in this condition, Jenny wasn't sure of anything. Nor did she think she could believe anyone.

Joshua eased his way into the room a little at a time. He tried to be as nonchalant as possible, not wanting to disrupt any of the rhythm of the birthing.

Suddenly, Jenny looked over his way and asked, "You'll tell me the truth, won't you?"

"Young lady, you're going to have to help me if you want this to go at all smoothly," the doctor informed her gently. "The next time you have a contraction, I want you to push. Hard," he ordered.

They didn't have to wait long for the next pain. The doctor had no sooner given them instructions when the next contraction hit. And it hit hard.

Jenny yelled and squeezed Tracy's hand with her left hand, while her right hand grasped first at air and then a fistful of bedspread. Tracy gave Joshua a quick look that said, *Get on the other side of the bed and hold your wife's hand.*

His furrowed brow showed his uncertainty, but he moved over to take Jenny's free hand in his. "I'm here, darling," he murmured in her ear.

Just in time as it turned out.

She clenched her hands into fists as the next pain hit and bit back the urge to scream. Jenny didn't know if she was becoming accustomed to the pains or if she was just numbing. But whatever it was, this time it didn't hurt as much. However, it did seem to last longer than the previous ones.

"All right, now push," the doctor said loudly. "Come on, Jenny. Push, harder. You've got to help me out here. Push," he said again.

Jenny was half sitting with the aid of Joshua and Tracy while emitting an awful gurgling sound through gritted teeth. And then the pain subsided. She relaxed her grip and lay back down on the pillows Tracy had placed under her head when she was moved.

"You're doing just fine," the doctor informed her. "Just fine. It won't be long now. Take some quick, deep breaths and try to relax until the next one comes.

"I'll try," she puffed through labored breathing.

And then the worst pain hit. Jenny thought she had experienced the ultimate in pain—until now. She had never felt such awful pain in all her life and couldn't believe that childbirth was ever meant to be so horrible.

Scream after scream escaped her lips. Jenny felt nauseous like she was going to throw up. She didn't think she could continue and, in fact, felt herself beginning to lose consciousness. She was about ready to give up when she suddenly felt the baby slip out of the birth canal. Exhausted from her efforts, she fell back on the bed and closed her eyes.

Joshua spoke to her softly while Tracy brushed her wet, matted hair from her face. She saw the doctor hold the baby up and heard the resounding smack of flesh on flesh as he spanked the infant on its bottom.

Her baby made no sound.

Tracy was rinsing out the rag she had been using to wipe Jenny's forehead. She held it aloft as the excess water dripped into the pan, when it suddenly dawned on her that the baby should be crying but wasn't. She had given birth to enough children that she knew the routine as well as she knew her own name. Why wasn't it crying? She gaped at the tortured soul that refused to draw its first breath.

Whack!

A second try by the doctor yielded no change in the baby's condition. He tried a couple more times without success. Still nothing. He depressed the infant's chest over the heart with no results. It was useless. The baby's heart would not beat. When the doctor wrapped the newborn in a small blanket, Tracy shielded Jenny's eyes from seeing any more. But from the stricken look on her friend's face, she could tell it was too late.

Jenny's head rolled back and forth on the pillows, as she looked at Joshua first and then at Tracy. "My baby's dead?" she cried, hysteria knifing its way into her sane world. "I want my baby." She began to struggle but was too weak from the delivery effect much. "I want my baby," she cried over and over.

Tracy had gotten a good look at Joshua and Jenny's stillborn baby while the doctor worked feverishly to vivify it.

It was blue.

It was cold.

It was dead.

Jenny's baby was dead. What was this going to do to her? She had already lost two children. What in God's name would this do to her? She chanced a look at the parents. Jenny was still crying, but her eyes were closed. Joshua was staring at the empty doorway, where the doctor had just walked through.

He knew, she thought silently. He knew.

One minute, Joshua was sitting next to his wife, holding her hand after the birth—and death—of their child. The next, he was walking through the pasture behind his barn. He heard the voice in his head again, willing him to go to Rockhole.

He followed basically the same path as before. Through the pasture to the tree line beside the creek and west until he came to Rockhole.

Joshua stood alone on the bluff that overlooked the clear, calm water of Saline Creek. He stared into the pristine pool and watched the fish swimming around lazily. Then he turned his attention to the reason he was here.

"I'm here."

As am I.

The smooth, musical voice filled him with ethereal tranquility.

Always before, it was just a voice in the darkness, a sensation that replaced the loneliness he felt from the loss of his children. He didn't blame Jenny. He loved her. It wasn't her fault, but she couldn't take away the pain. It could. However, today was different. His pain was still there.

The darkness gave way to a shaft of energy, dim at first but gaining brilliance as the seconds passed. After a short space of time, Joshua was staring at a translucent being. It wasn't a form, like that of a human, but it was alive. He could feel it.

"Is it time?" Joshua asked, his voice lacking concern.

It is very close.

Joshua couldn't believe what he was hearing. He had just lost another child. He didn't even care if he lived now. "Why not now?" he demanded. "It's a good time." There was no hesitation when it answered.

There is one more. There must be one more.

The words seemed to pass through him and then grip him with understanding.

You will know.

"How will I know?" Joshua asked. But before there was an answer, the light began to dissipate.

"*No!*" he shouted. "How will I know? How will—"

Joshua was still in his bedroom, sitting next to Jenny, holding her hand. Tracy was still on the other side of the bed, mopping her brow with the damp rag. For a moment, their eyes met. There was something there he couldn't recognize. Her stare chilled him, and he wondered if she knew about him and Jenny. But that was something they both promised to never tell. She wouldn't have told. He shook it off and looked again at the empty doorway where the doctor had just passed through.

Tracy preferred to do her mourning in private this time. They didn't have a real funeral. Joshua buried the baby, which they named Paul, in a plot near a huge oak tree up on the ridge. It was just a small affair with Joshua, a minister, and Doug. Jenny was in no shape to attend. She had reverted to her comatose state.

The doctor said the baby was developed enough to have lived, but it was what he called a blue baby. It never really stood a chance, according to the learned physician. The heart gave out as soon as Jenny started into labor.

Tracy figured she would give Jenny some time to recover from her dreadful experience before visiting her. It wasn't that she didn't want to, as a matter of fact, she had to force herself to stay away. She just thought it was better for Jenny to kind of work through it herself. "God knows she's going to have a difficult enough time getting through this," Tracy commented.

"Who you talking to, honey?" Doug asked his wife.

"Oh!" She swatted at her husband missing him by a mile. "You gave me a start," she fussed at him. He smiled at her and grabbed a coffee cup from the cabinet.

"I was talking to myself," she said agitatedly. She was immediately sorry for her remark. After all, it wasn't Doug's fault. No need to take it out on him. "I'm sorry," she apologized. She got up from the table and gave him a kiss.

"What's gotten into you?" he asked, returning her kiss. "You've been pretty moody here lately."

After Doug poured himself a cup of coffee and sat down at the table, Tracy tried to explain what was bothering her. "It's Jenny," she began slowly. "I want to go and see her, but…I don't know what to say."

"Maybe you don't need to say anything," Doug pointed out. "Maybe she just needs someone to listen to her or someone to just sit with her."

Tracy tilted her head sideways and looked at her husband. Just when you think you know a person, he throws you a curve. "That's very good, sweetheart," she admitted. "How did you get to be so darned sensitive," she asked, puzzled.

"Well…" He paused, trying to think of just the right thing to say. "I guess because I've been married to you for ten years."

She rolled up the napkin she had been using to dab at her eyes and tossed it at him. "No matter what the problem is, you always have the right answer," she whimpered. "Sometimes, I don't think I deserve you."

"Don't you think so for a second," he responded quickly.

Tracy just sat there looking at him. He had his moments—not many of them, mind you, but he had them just the same. She let a thin smile creep onto her face. One of the few times she had smiled in the last few days.

"You're right, I should go see her. After all, this is about her—not me," she rationalized. "I'll go over this morning." Tracy was already beginning to feel better. And she hated the fact that she had been so selfish about Jenny's feelings. She just hoped her best friend could forgive her for it.

"What are you saying?" Elise asked her husband in disbelief.

Solomon dropped his head and studied the food on his plate. It was one of his favorite meals. He wasn't quite sure why she had fixed it, but he guessed there were ulterior motives. She usually did.

He poked at the meatloaf, mashed potatoes, and corn on the cob before finally raising his eyes to meet hers. "I mean I think we should go see them. You know, visit them for a while. It's simple enough to understand," he muttered, slipping a forkful of food into his mouth.

"Solomon, I don't know what to say," she breathed out slowly. "When?"

"Why not now? I'm caught up on my work around here and Jeb can keep an eye on the livestock for me. We could leave tomorrow," he suggested.

"I'll start packing right after supper," Elise stated, the excitement spilling from her voice. "How's your supper? Can I get you anything?"

"No, I'm fine." He smiled at her. "Just fine."

"Hello," Tracy called from the kitchen door. "Anybody home?"

Joshua popped his head from around the back of the door. "Yeah, come on in, Tracy. I was just doing some cleaning," he said, motioning for her to enter.

"You're cleaning? Where's Jenny?" she asked hesitantly. Tracy had really expected to see Jenny, at least puttering around in the kitchen, if nothing else. Now she really felt bad for deserting her best friend.

Joshua didn't speak right away. When he did, his voice was strained. "She's upstairs. Has been since the baby di-died. At first, she just stayed in bed. She wouldn't get up for anything except to go to the bathroom and then…right back into bed." Tracy felt sorry for Joshua. She knew he was going through hell. Joshua didn't love anything as much as he loved Jenny. "Now, she just sits in that chair and stares out the window. Never moves. Never gets up. Most of the time she doesn't even rock." His lower lip started to quiver. "She's… she's given up," he stammered.

She put her hand on his arm. He had been so faithful to Jenny, and he didn't deserve this kind of treatment. Tracy was sure that he felt completely alone—deserted. She wished there was something else she could do to console him. But what? There were no words, nothing she could think of that would make any difference.

"She'll come out of it, Joshua. You'll see," Tracy replied. "I know it seems pretty bleak now, but it's just going to take time. Really." Was she trying to convince herself or Joshua?

"I-I know," he managed to say. "I know. Thanks, Tracy, for being such a good friend."

She smiled to let him know she understood. She felt like she was losing her best friend and it was hard on her too. "I'm just going to go up and check on her. Do you need anything?"

"No, nothing. You go ahead."

Tracy started toward the stairs and suddenly had a feeling of déjà vu. At the bottom step, she hesitated before going up. "God, give me strength," she prayed.

As she reached the top step, her pace slowed even more. The deafening silence roared in her head. She thought briefly of leaving before it was too late. Just go back down the stairs, out the front door and all the way home. She looked around her expecting to see the ghosts of Jenny's dead babies dancing around the walls. Tracy reached out and steadied herself as her legs felt weak.

Lord have mercy, she exclaimed to herself, keeping a constant vigil on the hallway.

Finally arriving at Jenny's bedroom door, she stood in the doorway for a minute, looking into the room. Jenny sat in her rocker, just like Joshua had said. The rest of the room was pretty much like it was before the tragedy.

Tracy entered quietly and knelt down beside her friend. "Jenny, it's me. It's Tracy. Jenny, can you hear me?" she asked, tension edging her voice.

There was no indication that Jenny heard or understood. The only sign of life was her barely perceptible breathing. Tracy tried again. "Jenny?" This time she shook the inert woman's shoulder lightly. "Jenny, please," she cried softly. "Please talk to me. Do something." She pleaded hopelessly.

"All right, Jenny," she said in a low voice. "You just sit there and listen. I'll do all the talking."

Tracy stood up and looked around for something to sit on. She spotted an ottoman on the other side of Jenny and moved it around.

Tracy forced Jenny's right hand from her lap, resting it on the arm of the chair where she could hold it in hers.

For the moment, she had no idea how to begin. What should she say? Was there anything that could pierce Jenny's defensive armor? A miracle key, perhaps, that would unlock Jenny's mind? Uncertainty seemed to follow her around lately. Why couldn't she just say the magic words and help her friend?

She was trying too hard. That's what it was. What did Doug say? *Just listen. Just be there for her.*

Suddenly, gripped in a sea of emotions, she tightened her grasp on Jenny's hand, and her tears began to fall. "Jenny, I'm sorry I wasn't here for you. You are my best friend and…and I feel like I let you down," she cried. "I should have been here for you, but I was selfish. I was afraid. I'm not sure of what." She lowered her eyes. "I only thought of myself. I didn't want to…come back in here after… after…oh, God." She looked around the room, sobbing with grief. Not so much for Jenny, although she was part of it, but for the baby that would never grow up. For the baby…

"I'm such a fool. To think you would even care about me after the way I treated you this past week. I-I…" She decided to take Doug's advice and just sit with her friend.

Sit and listen. Sit and listen.

Tracy walked along the road toward the Conners house. She didn't want to feel happy this morning. It didn't seem right to be experiencing pleasantries with Jenny still in a coma.

Joshua was so faithful. He still dressed her every morning and put her in the rocking chair, where she would sit the entire day until he undressed her at night and put her back into bed. He said it was like working with a mummy. She guessed he was probably right.

Still, Tracy would come each day and do the housework and spend the rest of the day sitting with her friend. It had become a ritual. Sometimes she would talk to Jenny. Other times she would just sit and watch her.

The air was unusually fresh this morning. She felt like skipping along the road, instead of walking, but decided that would be an improper display of emotions considering Jenny's condition.

As she approached the house, her mind exploded with strange images and bewildering ruminations. She was still trying to figure out what it meant when she heard someone calling her name. It was Joshua.

"I said, good morning. What's the matter, are you deaf today?" he asked, with a big grin.

"Oh, good morning, Joshua. No, I was just preoccupied," she replied. She continued toward the house and then turned back to face him. "Joshua, has anything peculiar happened since I left yesterday evening?" He gave her a quizzical look. "You know, anything out of the ordinary?"

Joshua looked thoughtful for a minute and then shook his head. "No. Nothing I can think of. Why?" he asked, his curiosity aroused.

"I…don't know. I had an uneasy feeling this morning," she said cautiously. For a fleeting moment, she caught a glimpse of her uneasiness. Then it was gone. "Never mind. It was probably nothing. Any change?"

Joshua shook his head in wonderment. "Same as the last fourteen days."

"I'll be up there," she said.

Joshua returned to his work. As he headed for the barn, he glanced back at Tracy and then let his gaze wander to the upstairs window, where his wife sat in a chair. Their life was so different from when they had come here.

I love you, Jenny Conners. I love you.

The words echoed in his mind as he started again toward the barn.

A few days later, Tracy hurried along the dirt road again that ran in front of their farm. It was a half mile walk to Joshua and Jenny's place from theirs. And today was a perfect day for walking. The morning air was crisp; the sun was shining brightly. It was a day that fairly screamed to be enjoyed. But she couldn't take her time and enjoy it. Not until Jenny came out of her coma.

The only time she was left alone was after Joshua went to work and before Tracy got there each morning. So she tried to arrive as early as possible without disrupting her own household. That was what caused the gap and left Jenny in solitude.

On this particular morning, she hurried even more than usual. She was nagged with the feeling that she should have been there before now. Of course, it was getting to where she felt that way every day, but today the feeling was stronger. She should already be there. She stepped up her pace. By the time she reached the lane to the Conner's house, she had worked up a sweat.

Joshua was emerging from the barn as she drew closer to the house. "Morning, Joshua," she called out. "How's she doing this morning?"

"Morning, Tracy," he called back. "She's the same as usual. No change." He waved as he disappeared around the corner of the barn. *That Tracy is something else*, he thought to himself. *I couldn't get along without her.* He continued toward the hog pen, carrying a board, saw, hammer, and some nails.

"All right, you scoundrels," he scolded the pigs. "I'm going to mend that broken board. See if you can't take it a little easier on it this time, okay?"

Suddenly, a scream that would have woke the dead splintered the air. It came from the house. He dropped the board and tools and broke into a dead run in that direction. He cleared all the front porch steps in one leap and nearly ripped the screen door off as he tore through the house.

"Tracy?" he shouted as he flew up the stairs.

"Joshua, up here. Hurry!" she cried. Tracy disappeared from view as Joshua bolted up the stairs, barely touching them in his ascent.

He skidded to an abrupt halt in the doorway to the bedroom and stared in horror at the terrifying sight. There was blood everywhere. On the bed. On Tracy. And amid this chaotic scene lay the still body of Jenny. A picture of serenity. A smile on her face.

Tracy was desperately trying to stop the bleeding. "Get something to make a tourniquet with," she said quickly. But Joshua stood riveted to the same spot. "Joshua!" she yelled, jerking him back to reality. This time he responded to her instruction.

She kept pressure on the cuts, while Joshua took some leather strings out of a pair of boots in the closet. He tied them midway between Jenny's elbows and wrists. "Jenny!" he shouted. "Jenny, wake up! Oh god, Tracy. What am I going to do?"

"Go get the doctor for one thing—and hurry!"

Joshua raced out of the house leaving Tracy to keep an eye on Jenny. Now it was Tracy's turn to hold her friend's head in her lap. She cradled it carefully and stroked Jenny's hair, rocking back and forth—murmuring over and over.

"Please don't die. Please don't die."

The sun was beginning to set. Soon it would be time for her to go home. Tracy hated to leave. Every day since the suicide attempt, she sat with Jenny hoping—no, praying—that Jenny would come out of her coma. But every evening, she went home disappointed. She glanced at the clock on the dresser. Five o'clock.

She was gathering her things up to leave, when she heard a commotion downstairs. "What in the world is going on down there? Joshua, is that you?" she called out.

Joshua came bounding up the stairs and met her at the door. He stood there in front of her beaming. It was the first time she could remember him smiling since this whole thing began.

There were all sorts of images passing through Tracy's mind. Not the worst of which was what he suddenly had to be so happy about. She couldn't help but feel some trepidation at the sudden change in Joshua's demeanor.

"Joshua? What is it?" she asked, concern etched in her tone.

He took her hand and led her downstairs and into the living room. She pulled up short when suddenly confronted by two people whom she had never seen before. Tracy judged them to be in their late fifties or early sixties. "Oh, I'm sorry. I didn't know you had company," she murmured, starting to back out of the room.

"No, Tracy. It's all right," Joshua said, pulling her back by the elbow. "I want you to meet my father and my mother."

Tracy's head jerked around to face Joshua. He was smiling, but there was something hidden behind the smile. It scared Tracy. She was happy for him, but at the same time, she couldn't shake this feeling of panic that gripped her.

Joshua and Jenny had never talked about their folks. And Tracy didn't want to pry, so she just assumed they were dead or something.

"Tracy, this is my father, Solomon Conners." She turned her attention back to the elderly couple. Solomon had his hand extended toward her.

She took his proffered hand. It was warm but calloused. It felt like picking up a piece of worn leather that was rough but pliable. Here was a man who had spent most of his life working with his hands—outdoors. "Pleased to meet you," she said demurely.

"And this is my mother, Elise Conners."

Tracy shook hands with the elderly grayed woman. "Mrs. Conners." She stared at them. Of course! This must be the curious sensation she had earlier that morning. How bizarre. Was it a premonition, or was she just going crazy?

She suddenly realized she was staring. "I'm sorry," she apologized. "It's just that…this was so unexpected." Tracy knew she sounded clumsy, but she couldn't help it. She turned to leave and was met with an icy stare from Solomon. It was momentary, but it was there. *Why would he be angry with her?* she wondered.

"I've fixed some supper for Joshua," she told them. "There's enough for everyone. I'll set two more places at the table before I leave. You must be hungry after your trip."

"There's plenty of time for that," Solomon replied. "Where is Jenny?" He was met with sad stares from both Tracy and Joshua.

"Something's wrong," Elise gasped as a mother's instinct took over. "What is it, Joshua? What's wrong with my little girl?"

"Mom, Dad, you had better sit down," he said, motioning them toward the sofa. Joshua went to great lengths to explain what had occurred during the past two weeks, going over the nightmare detail by painful detail. By the time he finished, a solemn silence had replaced the joy of Solomon and Elise's arrival.

Solomon cleared his throat. "Take us to see her," he demanded in a low but firm voice.

They filed upstairs led by Joshua. Tracy brought up the rear. It was a glum, dispirited group that gathered in the bedroom that evening. Joshua and Tracy remained in the background while Elise and Solomon stared down at their daughter.

Jenny looked like she was asleep. She was lying on her back, her arms at her sides and her eyes closed. Her breathing was normal, although very shallow. So shallow in fact that, at times, it was difficult to tell whether or not she was actually breathing.

Elise finally spoke. "Jenny, it's me, darling. It's Mother."

Tracy's mouth fell open, and suddenly a lot of things became very clear. She began to think back over the events of the past three years, and she understood a great many things that had eluded her until now.

She tensed.

Tracy could feel Joshua's eyes on her. She was suddenly very uncomfortable and found herself wishing she could drop through the floor and out of sight.

Elise had taken one of Jenny's hands and was rubbing it. She had also leaned forward and was whispering in her daughter's ear. She did that for a long time before straightening up. "It's been so long, my little girl," she said, continuing her ministrations. After what seemed like an interminable length of time, a miracle happened.

Jenny's eyes opened.

It wasn't much, really, but it was more than Tracy, or Joshua for that matter, expected to see.

"Mama? Is that you? Is that really you?"

"Yes, sweetheart. It's me," Elise said lovingly. "I'm here. I'll take care of you now." She looked at Tracy, realizing what she had said. "Oh dear. I didn't mean that the way it sounded. You have done a marvelous job, but there are some things that a mother can do that no one else can. I hope you understand."

At least now Tracy had an excuse for the shocked look on her face. "Yes," she whispered.

Elise's attention returned to her daughter. As Joshua joined his parents at Jenny's bedside, Tracy took the opportunity to ease her way out of the room and eventually out of the house.

She headed for home, puzzling over what had just happened.

Jenny sat in her rocker looking out over the countryside. It had been six months since her harrowing experience, and the only indication of its existence were the scars on her wrists.

Tracy regretted that she had heard what she did, but after carefully considering everything, she decided to ignore it. She decided it wasn't her place to condemn.

For a time, their lives had returned to normal.

Jenny had mended over the following weeks, both physically and mentally. And for a while, she and Joshua had moved on, trying once again to leave the past behind.

They laughed, they loved. The days and nights ran together filled with their happiness—until one day Solomon and Elise had returned for another visit.

The conversation had started off harmlessly enough. Joshua and his father were discussing the best time to sew crops. One thing led to another and there was an argument. It was bound to happen. The signs were all there.

Solomon finally exploded at Joshua over the relationship between him and his sister. He managed to say a lot of things that he had kept bottled up for years. Most of them hurtful. In the end, it completely dismantled the friendship they had been building.

Joshua stormed out of the barn and didn't return home until his parents had left.

Unfortunately, it created a chasm between him and Jenny. She had become accustomed to having her parents around again and, in the heat of the moment, accused Joshua of being the cause for their leaving. They grew further and further apart until all that was left was a recollection of their former love.

The loneliness had crept back into Joshua's life. He moved through the days thinking only of the void left by their father's interference. He had taken to sleeping in a separate room and had written Jenny a letter. But it remained hidden, waiting for the right time.

Then one day, the time was right. He left the letter where Jenny would find it—and headed for Rockhole.

Jenny felt the baby kick as a tear spilled onto the letter that rested on her lap.

She gently laid her hand on her abdomen, making contact with the life that grew inside her. She had meant to tell Joshua about her pregnancy. Maybe if she had, he would still be alive. But by the time she was sure, Joshua had grown very distant. Jenny wasn't sure why, but Tracy had noticed it as well. He seemed to have periods of blackouts, where he wouldn't remember what had occurred. To Joshua, it was like it never happened. She was concerned about those episodes but shrugged them off as part of the ongoing problem. And then from one of them—Joshua didn't return.

She picked the letter up and read it again for the third time.

> My dearest Jenny,
>
> By the time you read this letter, I will already be gone. I'm sorry, my darling, that things had to work out this way. I would rather they had been different. I love you so much, it hurts to think of leaving you.
>
> I thought things had gotten better, especially when Mom and Dad came to see us. Hope began to dawn for the first time in many years. I had some good talks with our father and was convinced that we had worked through the problems that drove us apart to begin with. But evidently, I was wrong. Dad must have simply buried his feelings, but it didn't take long for them to surface again. To this day, I still can't figure out

what set off the argument that got him so angry. Well, what does it matter? We have lost three children, and I've had enough of empty promises from God.

But, my darling, I would rather that my last thoughts were about you. Please do not doubt our love. As far as I'm concerned, it was the most precious thing we had. I adored you more than any man ever adored his wife. I consider myself fortunate, indeed, when I think that I was able to love you twice. First, as my sister and then as my wife.

Have a good life, my love. You deserve it.

Your loving husband,

Joshua

Jenny carefully laid the letter down on her lap again. Tears streamed down her face and cascaded lightly, like raindrops, onto the letter. She moved it so it wouldn't be ruined, like her life was. Besides, this was the last thing Joshua had done out of love.

She flinched as the baby kicked again. Placing her hands on her abdomen, she prayed that it would be a boy—and that it would live. "Please, dear God. Let it live that it might carry its father's name and bear his memory."

Jenny raised her eyes to look out the window at the setting sun. She asked one last time. "Why? Why, Joshua? I loved you…so much."

June 11, 1904

Dear Mama,

Please forgive me for not engaging in any pleasantries, but this letter is not one of chitchat. I don't know how to begin or even how to say it.

So I suppose brevity is the best way. Forgive the bluntness, please.

Joshua is dead!

It came as a great shock to me, as I'm sure it will to you too. I have searched my memory, replayed recent events, and I can't recall even one instance where there was an indication that he would attempt such a thing. I guess you would like to know what happened. They don't really know for sure if it was accidental, or planned, or if someone was responsible.

He was found at Rockhole, floating in the water with several snakebites on his body. The bites were the reason for his death, but what the sheriff doesn't know is how he got there to begin with. I don't think he would just go into the water and wait for the snakes to do their dirty deed. I think there is something that can't be explained. I don't have any premise for it, except that I know, or rather, I knew Joshua well enough to know he wouldn't do such a thing. All I can say now is they are investigating.

I have taken over tending the livestock. I seem to spend a lot of time working around the farm. There always, somehow, seems to be something in need of repair. It can be the smallest thing, that probably wouldn't have any impact on anything, but it takes my mind off Joshua, at least for now. It's not too bad doing this work. He kept everything in tiptop shape. Sounds familiar, doesn't it?

More than he would have admitted, Joshua has—oh god, I don't think I will ever get used to referring to him in the past tense—a lot of Daddy in him. So much so that it was scary at times. Maybe that's why those two didn't get along.

They were just too much alike. Somehow, now, there is a kind of warmth that fills and pervades my being. It reminds me so much of Joshua—and takes away a lot of the hurt.

Well, you should probably know—I'm carrying inside of me the last child Joshua will ever give me. One last try to give you a grandchild and me some remembrance of my husband. Pray that this child will live. I know I can't take any more loss.

I'm going to close this for now. Please keep the baby in your prayers. My love to you and Daddy.

Always,

Jenny

She had no way of knowing it at the time, but this was the last letter Jenny would write to her mother. She was never fully at peace with herself. Tracy and Doug helped a great deal along the way, but her richest reward was her son, Samuel Joshua Conners, named for his father. Included in the letter to her mother was this newspaper clipping.

MAN FOUND DEAD—SNAKES RESPONSIBLE
Story by Storm Wallen

CRATER RIDGE—The body of a man was found floating in Saline Creek early on Friday morning. He was identified as Joshua Conners, a resident of Crater Ridge. Officials say the man had been in the water since late Thursday night. The cause of death was classified as poisoning due to multiple snakebites. There were approximately twenty-two bites all over the body, and they were all, according to an undisclosed source, made by deadly water moccasins. The man's death seems to be shrouded in mystery. No one can account for the reason he was there. They do not seem to know whether it was a suicide or an accidental death. It is common knowledge in these parts that snakes won't normally cohabitate with people, especially in water where there is a lot of motion, like people swimming. It was unclear whether the victim had simply walked off the edge of the rock cliff and into the water accidentally or he had purposely walked into the water and waited for the snakes to administer their fatal poison. Joshua Conners was survived by his wife, Jenny, and their unborn child. They have lived in Crater Ridge for seven years and were respected in the community. In a statement taken by the sheriff's office, it was revealed that the wife had seen what she now classifies as signs of her husband's demise. According to the distressed woman, there were periods of blackouts, when her husband would not remember anything that happened real or imagined. She could offer no reason for the blackouts or what took place during them. Reality takes a back seat, apparently, in this bizarre death. As the sheriff's office tries to unravel this latest mystery, there are those who believe there is a force at work here that goes beyond human understanding. True or not, one thing is certain. Joshua Conners died of deadly, venomous snakebites. Foul play is not ruled out but is suspected. At this time no other information is available.

CHAPTER FIFTEEN

If he was going to do it, it would have to be soon. The best time, Father Pritchard reasoned, was at the dinner hour. That's when the nurses on second shift would be distracted the most. He had been watching them all day, at least since the monsignor had left and he discovered that at break time and mealtime, they gathered in a room behind their work station and visited. About every five minutes, someone came out of the room and checked the monitors and then, if there were no problems, disappeared back inside.

That's when I'll leave.

The priest had successfully resolved the best way to handle his escape.

He had also observed their procedure for operating the monitors and had learned a valuable lesson by watching. One of the patients had, in a frenzy, pulled some of the wires loose from his chest and the electrocardiograph went crazy. It drew erratic lines across the screen and made some rather loud, obnoxious beeping noises—at the patient's bed and at the nurses' station as well. Because of that, he decided the best way to prevent early detection was just to shut the machine off. It would simply go blank at the nurses' station, giving him just enough time to make his getaway without discovery.

Switching the machine off was something else he had learned by watching. A nurse had disconnected one from a patient who had died.

It was almost time for their evening meal. He became wary as he nervously awaited the moment, constantly checking the clock on the wall behind the nurses' station. Seven twenty-seven.

Three minutes until their suppertime.

With each passing second, his mind played tricks on him. He was sure they were aware of what he was planning and were giving him enough rope to hang himself.

Oh, no!

One of the nurses was looking his way. Did she know? Did she suspect he was going to try to make a break for it? Father Pritchard quickly averted his eyes, pretending to be looking at something at the other end of the room, but all the time keeping her in his peripheral vision.

Seven twenty-nine. One minute to go.

His heart raced as he contemplated his escape. *God give me a calmness,* he prayed. If any of his vital signs changed drastically, the monitor would register them and alert the nurses. He had to remain calm. The priest closed his eyes and concentrated on the darkness behind his eyelids. He had used this technique before, when he felt his anger rising. It usually took only a few moments before he felt the effects of his meditation calm him.

It was working now.

And it was a good thing, he noted. He was sure he couldn't have lasted that final minute otherwise.

As soon as the last nurse had vanished through the doorway, he reached over and switched off the machine, then hurriedly pulled all the wires loose from the sticky pods on his body and ducked down so he wouldn't be detected. He inched his way along the room in a crouch, staying close to the counter and out of sight of the ever-watchful medical staff. When he reached the nurses' station, he figured he still had four minutes to make good his escape before they discovered he was missing.

As he quietly sneaked through the double glass doors of ICU, he thanked God that this was not a larger hospital where they would have rotated their lunch break. Safely in the hall outside, he retreated to the nearest stairway and descended to the first floor. He would have to be careful. Wearing only the hospital gown, he stuck out like a Baptist in a Catholic service. He located an exit door at the end of the hall and quickly left the building. Walking in the direction of the church, he was about two blocks from the hospital when he saw car lights dancing on the street. He turned to face the auto approaching from behind him and stuck out his thumb.

The car veered toward the curb, slowing until it came to a stop next to him. The priest leaned over to peer into the car and remarked, somewhat embarrassed, "Oh, it's you."

As they left the hospital, the mood in the car was a somber one for Stoney and Susie. If the truth was known, both were exhausted from the day's activities, which ended happily with the excitement over Mary J.'s recovery.

Stoney turned left out of the parking lot, going north on water street. He crossed Hatcher Street and was halfway through the block when he saw a hitchhiker. "Look at that. What is that? He's wearing a hospital gown?" he asked curiously.

"Yeah," Susie snickered. "That's what it is! Look, he wants a ride. And if anyone ever needed a ride, it's that man." She rolled the window down as they stopped alongside the hitchhiker.

"Oh, it's you," an elderly man said. "Could you give me a ride to the Catholic Church?"

It was all Stoney could do to keep from laughing. He recognized the man as the priest of the Catholic Church, Father Pritchard. Stoney didn't go to his church, but he'd seen him around enough to know who he was. "Sure, get in the back there." Father Pritchard quickly crawled into the back seat holding the split in the back of the gown together.

Stoney pulled away from the curb and continued north on Water Street to the center of town. "What did you mean by 'Oh, it's you'?" he asked, looking at the priest in the rearview mirror.

"Well, it's just funny that it was you who picked me up, when your family is the reason that I left the hospital in the first place."

"What are you talking about?" Susie asked perplexed, turning halfway around to face the priest.

Father Pritchard raised up in the seat a few inches and tugged at the hospital gown, trying modestly to pull it around himself. "Why can't they make these things where they fit a little better? Did they have a shortage of material or something?" He fussed a little longer, still trying to make the material stretch further than it was intended. He finally gave up, deciding it was better to be a little uncomfortable than risk tearing it and exposing himself. "I ended up in the hospital because I was out at Rockhole earlier today. I had an encounter with a rather strange creature and suffered a heart attack as a result."

Susie gasped and covered her mouth with her hand.

"But the attack was the result of the creature's work, not any physical problems of mine. So there's no cause for alarm," he assured Susie, misreading her concern. The young couple in the front seat didn't look convinced. "I'm okay, really." Still no reaction from the front. "Oh, you were wondering why I was out there. Well, I guess I might as well explain myself." He went through a lengthy account of his conversation with the coroner and then the monsignor. He concluded with his confrontation at Rockhole with the demon.

Stoney pulled up in front of the church and stopped. He spoke for the first time since right after they had picked up the priest. "You think this...demon...is what killed Brian?" he asked uncertainly.

"I know it is," the priest answered truthfully. "I knew it was before I went out there." He could tell by their expressions that they had some reservations about his story. But that was all right. Whether they believed him or not made no difference. It didn't affect his plans. It would be better if they stayed out of it. "Well, thanks for the ride," he told them, getting out of the car.

As they drove away, Susie was lost in her own little world as recent events came crashing in around her. "Do you believe that hogwash he just fed us?" Stoney asked amazed. When she didn't answer right away, he glanced over at her. "You do? Don't you?"

"I'll reserve my official opinion until after we read those letters," she said pensively. They drove on in silence.

I wonder if I've been duped, Sheriff Rogers speculated. He sat at his desk staring at the two unsolved one-hundred-year-old cases and couldn't help but feel that there was something in one of these files that was the clue he was looking for. He just wished it was easier to spot.

"Father Pritchard must be pulling my leg," he said out loud. Still, there was the matter of Brian Clark's face. And it wasn't just a figment of his imagination or some made-up story. He had seen it for himself. He would never have believed it otherwise. And if these two cases had been normal, they would have been cleared up a long time ago. "The priest is telling the truth," he said, speaking these words aloud. He needed to hear himself say it.

Something caught his attention.

How in the world had he missed it? It was so clear, at least it was now. Maybe that's why he couldn't see it until this very moment. It was necessary for the creature to be challenged before a human could understand. There had to be a mediator, someone who could approach the creature on its own level and bring it out into the open. Someone to…stir it up. That provocateur was the priest. He had awakened the sleeping beast.

And in its wakefulness, a clue had emerged. It was so plain, now that he knew.

In the first place, a man doesn't die by drowning in water that only comes to his waist at the deepest part. Joshua Conners could have stood up and been well out of danger. The file didn't mention anything about head injuries or any other reason for Joshua being unconscious at the time he drowned. In the second place, the Franklin Baker case was just as ludicrous and not worth going into.

Brian Clark's death was just as implausible as the other two. Jumping from a ten-foot height to the water and your body splitting in half didn't seem right either.

So what did all this mean? He shook his head dejectedly at the files. None of these deaths should have happened, he kept telling himself. They were senseless deaths. And they were not just accidents. So the creature was responsible, just like the priest had said. But what in the hell was he supposed to do now? Confront the beast? Tell it, "You're under arrest for murder"? Hardly. He picked up the Joshua Conners file and started reading again.

Surely, there was another way.

Once again Father Pritchard ducked into the sanctuary for a period of prayer and meditation before facing the demon a second time. He had secluded himself in his office, after getting properly dressed and done some research on exorcism. He had known he was ill prepared for the previous encounter but felt it necessary to kindle a fire within the creature and determine exactly what he was up against. He was sure that if he showed up now, he would have the upper hand. The demon would not be expecting him to return.

After an hour, he was still in the sanctuary, his prayer so intense that he was sweating from the effort. The priest was unaware of anything around him. His mind, his body, and his soul were all in perfect harmony with each other and with God.

As the night wore on, so did Father Pritchard's severity and fierceness of invocation.

Being in the hospital was nothing new to Mary J. She had been in four times already for childbirth. But that was the only reason she had ever been. The rest of the time was to visit friends. She had been healthy her entire life except for occasional colds and flu. She found hospital life extremely boring and hoped she would never have to be a patient herself.

But she had. Regrettably.

Tonight, after everyone had left, she had to face her loneliness. She had to come to grips with the fact that she would never see Brian again. She had, gratefully, worked through her initial grief while her family was around her, but that was just the beginning. Now, she had to be alone with that grief. Now she had to listen to the silent voices reminding her of all the things she and Brian had done together. Her memories. Memories that would stay with her always. And she had to listen to the silent voices telling her of all the things she would never be able to do with her husband again. Telling her of the loneliness that would surround her like a warm winter fire. But instead of comfort for her, there would be only isolation.

Dear God, why did this happen to me? She climbed out of bed and closed the curtains. Then walked over to the door and slowly pulled it open. She was almost afraid that it would be standing on the other side. Suddenly, she jerked the door the rest of the way open, nearly hitting herself as it responded to the violent reaction. She couldn't believe she closed her eyes, but she had. She opened them to thin slivers, peeking out, but there was no one there.

Mary J. walked down the hall, around the corner, and continued along the empty corridor in the direction of the courtyard. Her soft slippers were noiseless on the highly polished tile floor. She was thankful for that. The last thing she needed now was to have to listen to the meaningless dribble of someone she didn't know.

When she reached the courtyard, she pushed the door open just enough to slip through. It was a beautiful setting. She strolled along sluggishly, looking at the mixture of red and yellow roses, blue and purple irises, blue and purple and white wisteria vines, a large assortment of colorful geraniums, bordered with lots of ferns and other ground covers. Normally, Mary J. would have appreciated them, but she hardly noticed them tonight.

She found a park bench and sat down heavily. Her thoughts descended around her until she felt strangled. She wanted to cry but didn't have any more tears to shed or the strength to cry them. She sat there on the bench, only half-aware of her environment. As the minutes dragged by, she fell into a state of lethargy—her mind drugged by the familiar stupor of a dream world.

Mary J. saw herself and Brian in a place she didn't recognize. It looked like a playground, but it was a playground for adults. All the equipment was the same kind that children played on but larger. They were the only people there, and Brian was climbing on the jungle gym. He hung upside down, and Mary J. laughed at his playfulness and his acrobatics. It was like that was his mission in life, to make her laugh.

He could always make her laugh. Now he was turning cartwheels and falling in the middle of them, like it was an accident, but she knew it was on purpose. He only did it to make her laugh—and laugh she did. It came easy for her, especially where Brian was concerned.

Suddenly, the playground disappeared and Brian along with it. A fog had begun to roll in and within minutes, it was the only thing she could see. Her heart stopped, and she held her breath.

"Brian," she called out, into the thick fog. "Brian, where are you. I can't see you." She waited for a bit, but there was no response. A nervous tension set in. "Brian? *Brian!*"

Mary J. tried to get up from the bench but was unable to move. "Brian, where are you!" she yelled. "I need help! Please, Brian!"

Brian is not here. But I know where he is. Would you like for me to take you to him?

She looked around but didn't see anyone. "Where are you?" she asked suspiciously. "How do you know where Brian is?"

I know everything. I see everything. I can take you to him if you follow my instructions. But you must be very careful and not tell anyone where you are going. It is a very special place. How is your baby doing?

"My baby?" she asked suddenly. "What does my baby have to do with anything? What do you want with my baby?" she asked, her tone suggestive of her sudden fear.

The infant is mine. Ask Brian, he will tell you. But if you want to ask him, you will have to follow my instructions. Are you willing?

Mary J. was hesitant to ask, but her need to see Brian was strong. It far outweighed her fear. "Where is this place?"

Rockhole.

"Rockhole? Oh, yes. Now I remember. That's mine and Brian's special place. No wonder he wants to meet me there." She was thoughtful for a minute and then smiled at her inward reflections. "All right, I'll go."

Good. You will not regret it.

Suddenly, the fog began to lift. It just seemed to rise into the air and float away. But the playground never returned. It was replaced by the garden. Somehow, it had lost its original beauty, so she left and returned to her room. But Mary J. didn't go to bed. She wasn't quite sure how she knew it, but somewhere in her mind lingered the notion that there was only one place in the world to find Brian.

She changed into her own clothes and couldn't help but notice that her skirt, which was already extremely short, was even shorter, and was ragged like it had been torn. She frowned at it, then dismissed it and left the hospital.

She had to see Brian. It was the only thing on her mind. She had to get to Rockhole. That's where Brian would be waiting for her. She gave no thought to how she would get there. She struck out on foot, leaving the lighted hospital grounds behind. All she could think about was Brian. She had to get to him.

And to do that she had to get to Rockhole.

Susie sat in their living room, curled up at one end of the sofa, one of the letters, yellowed and brittle with age, in her hands. This handwriting is beautiful, she thought silently. The letters were perfectly formed with flourishes and sweeping strokes. It was definitely an ancestral hand that penned it because people just didn't have that flare anymore. The style of the new millennia was much brasher than in the late nineteenth century.

She glanced at the date on the letter. "February 28, 1895. Stoney, can you imagine what it must have been like to live back then?" she asked, gazing at the old letter. They read the letters one at a time, looking for anything that might explain their weird encounters. "This is like…actually touching a part of history," she said, her emotions aroused.

"Would you like for me to read it?" he asked, impatient with her romanticism.

Susie jerked back involuntarily, cradling the letter to her breast carefully. "No. I'll do it," she said scornfully. She got up from the sofa and started walking aimlessly around the room. Her eyes caressed the paper one more time before she finally started reading out loud. She was saying the words on the brittle, dingy paper, but her mind was not comprehending their meaning. By the time she had finished the second paragraph, tears had formed in her eyes. "My god, they were brother and sister." She said it so softly that Stoney had to strain to hear. She read the next paragraph, and her tears traced erratic patterns down her cheeks.

She stopped reading.

Stoney gently took the letter from her. He finished reading it with a lot less respect than Susie had shown. "This is disgusting," he said with resentment.

"It's beautiful," Susie disagreed with him. "Can't you hear the love in her words, not to mention the fact that she felt badly about what they were doing? Stoney, she knew it was wrong, but she still had to do it. She loved him...and he loved her."

When she was like this—a hopeful romantic, carried away by visceral emotions—he might as well be alone. "Let's read the next one," he suggested doggedly. He took out the next letter in the bundle and removed it from its envelope.

Stoney began reading, moving through the first sections of the letter quickly. They were mostly about the differences between the young couple and their parents concerning improper marriage. But then, about halfway through, the woman identified as Jenny announced that they were going to have a baby. "Who in the hell was Grace?" he asked Susie, frowning.

"I have no idea. Is that the end of that letter?"

He glanced at it and then turned it over. "Yeah, it looks like it. These certainly are short letters," he commented quizzically.

"Considering their circumstances, I don't suppose they had much to say to each other," Susie responded offhandedly. There were times when she was completely exasperated with his lack of romanticism, and then there were times when he truly surprised her with a sudden touch of it.

She took out the next letter and perused it with her smiling eyes. "They had a boy," she said, an almost parental pride in her voice. "They named him after their father. There's some statistics, some dribble about her hospital stay...and that's it," she said, putting the letter back into its envelope.

Stoney already had the next one out. He glanced through it while she was putting the other one up. "Well, this is just telling their parents they are moving. It doesn't say why, but I get the feeling someone, or something is forcing them to move." He read it to her, and they moved on quickly to the next one.

"Oh my god," Susie exclaimed after reading just the first line of the gloomy letter. "Their baby boy died." She read on, tears forming at the corners of her eyes again. Her words became broken and indecipherable, so Stoney took it from her and finished reading. He took Susie in his arms and stroked her hair. "Don't worry, you're not the only one that wept over this letter," he said cryptically.

"What do you mean?"

He released his hold on her and showed her the letter again. "Look here, and here," he said, pointing at some splotches on the page. "Those are dried stains. Most likely from tears." He frowned at the paper like he was trying to figure something out. "But there's no way of knowing if they belonged to the mother or the daughter." He replaced the letter in its holder, leaving Susie to reflect on its contents. He knew that's what she would do. He just hoped all this wouldn't have any lasting effects on her. He didn't think he could stand it if it did.

As he removed the next letter, he scanned it quickly before she figured out what he was doing. He didn't think she could take any more bad news at this time. "Well, this ought to cheer you up," he cried joyfully. "They're going to have another baby. I mean they had another baby," he corrected himself. "Listen to me. I sound like this is happening right now." Stoney refused to admit it, but the letters made him feel like he was right there with them. In some bizarre, rudimentary fashion, he understood the joy and pain of what they went through.

"Her letters almost make you feel that way," Susie said, staring at the letter. Stoney's astonishment reflected his shock at her statement. It was almost like she had read his mind. He shuddered. "It's like in my dreams. The old woman almost made me feel like I was there. Like she was real. I don't know," she said sadly. "It's so confusing."

She picked up the next letter, hoping there was no more bad news. Carefully unfolding it, her eyes lit up immediately. "They had a girl," she squealed. "Her name was Diane Elise and it goes on to tell everything about her. You know," she said, seeing his muddled frown. "Her weight, length, eyes, hair. The things that are important to mothers." She read on in silence. "That's all, really. Except, she still hasn't heard from her mother. For some reason, her mother stopped writing."

"Or wasn't allowed to write," Stoney offered.

Susie hurriedly grabbed the next letter before Stoney's alert reflexes could snatch it away. "Put this one away and I'll read it to you," she demanded. She began reading aloud, but it wasn't long before it turned gloomy—again. She dropped it, letting the two horrifying pages flutter to the carpet, stung by its lurid contents. Stoney bent down and picked the letter up. He read slowly, softly while his words told them about Diane's disappearance.

There didn't seem to be much hope.

The next letter not only verified the disparity but explained what happened. Diane's body had been found. Another battle for the beguiled parents to wage, as they fought desperately to hold on to their sanity. How much could a mother and father take? Exactly the question Jenny put to her own mother. However, instead of a mother's comforting words, which was the least a daughter should expect, she was met with a lonely silence. Susie contemplated how alike she and Jenny were. Her tears started anew as she read on. But were the tears for Jenny or for herself?

The only bright spot was the fact that Jenny was pregnant again. But could she bear to have another child, considering what had happened to the first two? Could she carry another life inside her, knowing the doubts she harbored against the unfairness of the last five years?

Susie hastily picked up the next letter. Although she hated to read about another crisis in the Connerses' lives, she had to know what came next. Could this be the reason for the Curse that the old woman told her about? If so, why did it affect Brian and Mary J.? Puzzled but curious, she dove into the next letter. At first, she thought it was a letter to Jenny from her mother, but soon realized it was from Joshua to his wife. She read it silently, then handed it to Stoney. A longer letter was in the same envelope. Susie took it out and read it while Stoney read Joshua's note. This was a much longer letter than the others had been. It described what Jenny intended to do with her life, now that she was alone. The one good thing that came out of all this surrealistic imagery was the fact that Jenny was pregnant one last time with Joshua's child. Had she not been, their family would have ended a hundred years ago.

Included with the note to Jenny and the letter to her mother was a newspaper article. There was no date, but it was from the *Crater Ridge Gazette*, which had been renamed the *Crater Ridge Times* in 1940.

The article was an account of Joshua's death. Susie gasped as she read it. "What an awful way to die," she said aloud. "I never knew anyone had died so horribly at Rockhole."

Stoney quickly read the article she handed to him. "Wow!" he blurted out.

A shriek broke his concentration. "Stoney! Look at these pictures." He had never seen her so excited. "These were in the bottom of the chest. Look! Oh, she's beautiful. Oh my god!" Her eyes were as big as saucers. He looked to see what had caused her mortified stare. It was a picture of an attractive young woman, but he didn't see anything to get upset about.

Susie couldn't remove her eyes from the image displayed in a simple photograph taken over a hundred years ago. "It's her," she breathed the words out slowly.

"Her? Her who?" he asked suspiciously.

"The old woman in my dreams. It's her. I swear to you on my mother's gr—I swear to you," she said, unwilling to complete the oath that she had originally intended to utter. Yesterday she might very well have said it but not now. They had reconciled their differences. That was enough.

Stoney started putting all the letters back into the chest. "What are you doing?" she asked dubiously.

"I think we should take these and go see Mom and Dad," he answered plaintively. They gathered up the letters and pictures, put them back in the chest, and left quickly.

Mary J. wandered along the highway in the dark. She was scared, alone and seriously considering turning back when a car approached her from behind. She stepped off the side of the road, wondering if she should hide, as the headlights bounced in the air throwing shadows where there should have been none. She quickly reasoned that no one would be looking for her out here. So she boldly stepped back up on the edge of the pavement and waited for the car to draw near. Somewhere, behind her in the darkness, an owl hooted. She suddenly felt alone again and scared. She hoped the vehicle would stop and give her a ride. She stuck her thumb out, hesitantly at first. It was the first time she had ever hitchhiked, and she didn't like doing it. Then she thought about Brian and was more determined.

The vehicle slowed as it came alongside her.

Mary J. was suddenly apprehensive about the whole incident. For a moment—a very brief moment—she thought about running off and taking her chances with the creatures of the night. But where would she go and how could she possibly elude an attacker if he really wanted her. Besides, she probably wouldn't get very far in the dark. So she waited and when the window of the car rolled down, she bent over and looked in.

A sudden gush of relief flooded over her. "Can I offer you a ride, young lady? I'm about as safe as you'll find in the middle of the night out here. And I'm pretty sure we're going to the same place," the priest informed her.

"How do you know that?" Mary J. asked suspiciously, momentarily thwarted by the priest's overwhelming confidence. "Do I know you?"

"No! But I know you and your family," he continued, unwavering in his certainty. "And the very problem you're thinking of attacking personally tonight, I'm willing to take on myself. I am certain I can do more about it than you can. Why don't you get in and let's discuss it while we drive to Rockhole."

Mary J. was tentative about opening the car door but finally decided that if he knew that much about it, it was worth listening to his proposition. She slid onto the seat, staying as close to the door as she could.

Father Pritchard sensed her trepidation and tried to put her at ease. "I'm sorry about your husband. I know that was a great loss to you."

"You know about Brian?" she asked, shocked by the priest's statement.

"Oh, yes. And the creature that is responsible for ending his life," he added. "That is the curse that hounds your family—and has for many generations. It should have ended when Joshua Conners died at Rockhole almost a hundred years ago, but the demon held on and has been attacking your family ever since." She looked at him like he had completely lost it. "It's the truth, my dear. There's no doubt about it. And I intend to put an end to it this very night. I cannot allow Satan to hold this kind of council in my parish. There would never be any ministry but his."

"What are you going to do? How do you intend to stop it?"

The priest looked over at her. "My dear, I am just a man. I could never presume to try and win a battle against Satan—not without God's help. This is His war, His battle. I'm just doing His bidding." He smiled at her. It was obvious that she didn't know much about the Bible, let alone the book of Revelation. "I'm sorry. I don't have time to explain the entire concept of spiritual warfare right now. But if we both come out of this night alive, I'd like the opportunity to try."

Mary J. nodded and then leaned against the door, staring out at the night. It was a gorgeous night, with a full moon and so many stars that they alone could have lit up the earth. Unconsciously, she realized, she was searching for some familiar constellations. She didn't really know that many, their small high school didn't offer much in the field of astronomy. She probably learned more, she noted with some alacrity, by watching *Star Trek* on TV. But still, she had picked up a few basic formations in science class.

There are so many, she decided as she mournfully thought of Brian. *Are you up there my love? I miss you so much. And it hurts so bad,* she cried silently. Then she thought of the baby. The baby! Oh my god! She had forgotten about the baby.

"It wants my baby," she told the priest quietly.

He glanced over at her and nodded.

Sheriff Rogers had reluctantly left his office and gone home. He hated leaving things undone. And when he finally decided to leave, he had a distinct impression that he had neglected to do something. Whatever it was flirted with the edges of his awareness but stayed just out of reach. It was irritating to Rogers. He hated the unknown.

He took a bottle of beer out of the refrigerator, sat down in his recliner, and picked up the TV remote. He turned the TV on to watch his favorite late-night news. But as he sipped at the cold beer, he was oblivious to the program. As the newscaster droned on covering story after story, the images floated in and out of his consciousness, never making an impression.

He might be at home, but his mind was still back at the office—going over those three files that still lay on his desk. He had refused to bring them home with him, although the temptation was enormous, but they were what was on his mind.

He tried again to concentrate on the TV. What was the newscaster saying? Something about animal control getting out of hand? And the city council needed to take appropriate action. *This is real news*, he thought to himself. Unable to fully concentrate, again his thoughts roamed, casting about randomly. It was useless. His mind was one track tonight.

Rogers sipped thoughtfully on his bottle of beer. Already it was getting warm. Had he been sitting there that long? He looked at the miniature grandfather clock that sat atop the console TV. The pendulum, busy swinging back and forth while marking time, could put him into a hypnotic state if he stared at it long enough.

He shook his head. *Ten thirty-five*, the hands on the clock silently shouted.

Damn!

He focused on the TV screen. Sure enough, the news was over. Rogers picked up the remote and clicked the power button. The screen went black. He went into the kitchen and poured the remainder of his warm beer in the sink.

The telephone chirped out its insistent tone. It annoyed him. He wished now he had bought one that had an actual ring to it. This one sounded more like a cricket in love than a telephone.

He picked up the receiver. "Hello," he answered gruffly, still angry at the tone.

The caller hesitated before saying anything. "Uh, hello, Sheriff. This is Mike."

"I know who it is," he responded shortly. After working with him for two years, you'd think the young deputy would come to understand the sheriff's moods and pretenses. He forced himself to calm down, as he reminded himself that not everyone was as proficient at these things as he was. "What do you want, Mike?" he asked ambiguously.

The deputy apologized quickly before relaying his message. "Sorry to disturb you so late, Sheriff. But I thought you ought to know. The priest left the hospital—"

"What time?" Rogers demanded, interrupting the deputy.

Mike hesitated but only briefly. "Close as they can figure, 'round seven-thirty," he said, knowing what was coming next. He had, in fact, worked with the sheriff long enough to know ahead of time what kind of response to expect in this situation.

"What!" Rogers exploded. "And you're just now calling me?"

"Wait a minute, Sheriff. The hospital just notified me a little while ago," he said quickly, defending his position. "I can't help it if they're slow."

"Shit!" he exploded again.

The deputy almost wished he didn't have to say any more. He wished he could hang up the phone and get back to reading the detective novel he kept around for boring nights like this one. It was a lot more interesting than the palling stuff that usually went on around here. "Sheriff, that's not all." He could hear the thunder now.

Rogers didn't disappoint him. But not right away. Instead, the question that came over the wire to the deputy had an enormous icy chill to it. "What else?"

Mike blurted it out, wanting to get through as fast as possible. "The Conners girl is missing too."

"Son of a bitch," the sheriff cursed silently. A wealth of suspicions began to flood through his mind. He had suspected something was afoot, but without any proof, he had no choice but to sit back and wait—for something like this to happen, he supposed. "What time?" The cool tone had returned.

"As close as we can determine, it must have been around the same time as the priest," the deputy informed his superior.

"How in the world can a person walk out of ICU and not be seen? Never mind," he said swiftly. "I forgot. We're working with Miller County Community Hospital. That's how. Those people really need to install some security over there." He mulled over what the deputy had told him. "Anything else?"

"That's all, Sheriff. What do you want me to do?"

Rogers thought about it for a minute before answering. He decided his deputy could serve him better if he stayed where he was. "Just hang around there until you hear from me." He hung up.

Something was about to happen, and when it did, Rogers wanted to be there. He was pretty sure he knew where those two were going. Had they been planning this together? He didn't think so, but it seemed too coincidental to him. "But that must be all it is," he said aloud. "Coincidence." He grabbed his pistol belt, which also contained his nightstick, a handheld radio, extra bullets, and mace and left.

Rockhole.

That's where they're going. And that's where he was going.

The bright headlights alerted the Clark's that they had company. Daniel walked out onto the porch and greeted his son and stepdaughter. He thought he should try to enjoy what few minutes of peace remained, for he knew it would end soon. When these two kids found out what horrible secrets, he and Sadie had been hiding all these years—well, he wished there was some other way.

"Stoney, Susie. We've been expecting you," he said with a note of apprehension. Daniel was getting mixed signals from the two young people. Stoney glared, his expression full of contempt. Susie, on the other hand, was much more placid, if not downright sad—regrettable almost. He gave them both a hug and then led them into the house.

"Sadie, the kids are here!" he yelled in the direction of the kitchen. They could hear her rummaging around. It was a familiar sound. One they had grown up with. After a minute or so, the noises ceased and she came into the living room, carrying a tray of drinks.

She sat the tray down on the coffee table. "Something to drink?" she asked softly. Sadie had believed all along that their children should have been told about their family secrets. But now that the moment was here, she was a bundle of nervous tension. She poured Daniel a cup of coffee trying not to spill it in the process.

"I'll have a cup of that coffee," Stoney said, as she finished with Daniel's. She poured him a cup, finding it easier to handle than the first one. When she handed it to him, she raised her eyebrows at Susie. But her daughter was too involved in her thoughts and didn't see her mother's silent question.

Stoney looked at her. "Susie? Do you want something to drink?"

She gazed at him, her expression clouded. He repeated his question and she seemed to snap out of the spell she was under. "Uh…I'll have a Coke," she replied dully when she realized what the question was. Sadie poured one over a glass of ice and handed it to her, but not letting go until she was sure Susie had a good grip on it.

"So what did you two find in that chest?" Daniel asked, breaking an uncomfortable silence. "Anything of interest?"

The question was innocent enough, and heaven knows he never intended, or wanted, Susie to be hurt by it. But her tears said otherwise. Stoney did his best to relate the contents of the letters from Jenny to her mother, ending with the horrible death of Joshua, thereby explaining Susie's reaction.

Daniel was happy to know that he didn't do anything to cause Susie to be upset, but now the deafening silence returned to the Clark living room. It seemed like it went on far too long but was only about three or four minutes.

He did.

With a sadness that only Sadie could understand, he told them—everything. "You'll find the same thing happened on our side of the family. Sadie and I found some letters, pictures and other things left from Franklin and Carlotta Baker, your great-grandparents, Stoney, on my side. I don't think we were intended to see them. We found them out at the old family home, under a pile of bricks and wood that hadn't quite burned completely." Stoney and Susie exchanged knowing glances. They had been right. "They are a lot like those you found, with some differences, but the circumstances are the same." He coughed and poured himself another cup of coffee. He wished he could pour a shot of sour mash in his cup with the coffee. He could sure use it right now. "What I'm about to tell you two, you may find difficult to accept."

Daniel coughed again, cleared his throat, and then began. Slowly. "Believe me, kids, this is not the way we wanted to do this." Another cough. "To be honest with you, I didn't want to do it all. But Sadie thinks we should have said something a long time ago. There's no telling which way it should have been. But what's done is done."

"Daddy, you're scaring me," Susie winced. "What's the matter?"

He fidgeted around, wringing his hands nervously. Suddenly, Daniel had no idea how to begin. To be truthful, he didn't want to. Nor did he have to.

"Brian is my son," Sadie said, staring through hollow, vacant eyes.

Susie tensed. What was her mother saying? Brian couldn't be her son. Mary J. was the first baby she ever had—wasn't she? Brian was Elizabeth Clark's son. He was Stoney's brother.

She stared at her mother, whose face was drained of color. Sadie's eyes betrayed the guilt she had harbored too long. And now her daughter and stepson knew. Thank God, someone besides her and Daniel finally knew.

"What do you mean he's your son?" Susie asked, her voice barely above a squeak. It was kind of strange. To her, it sounded—and felt—like someone else asked that question, and she stood by and listened. "You mean, like your stepson, right?" Susie looked around. She wished she didn't feel so detached.

Sadie shook her head. "No, baby girl! I mean he's my son," she declared. Then she went on to explain. "Before any of you were born, Daniel and I had a very brief affair. It lasted one night and wasn't meant to have any repercussions. But it did," she said vacuously. "And Brian was the result."

"But I don't understand," Stoney interrupted. "Everybody always said Mom—I mean Elizabeth, our mother—was Brian's mother." His gesture alone indicated his utter confusion.

Sadie knew she should answer him, but what could she say? Now that the moment had come, the words wouldn't. She began to shake. Maybe if she got up and walked around, she would feel better. Sadie stood up and knew right away that she had made a mistake. She lost all feeling in her legs, her stomach turned flip-flops, her head reeled, and finally—as her eyes rolled back into her head—she crumpled into a heap on the floor.

Susie had watched the entire scene with a detached sentiment, wondering all the time who this woman was. Stoney stood still, paralyzed by what happened and didn't do anything until Daniel rousted him from his frozen stance.

"Help me get her to the couch," he said to his son while lifting Sadie by the shoulders. The boy hadn't moved. "Stoney!" he shouted. That did it. He took his stepmother's legs, and together they laid her on the sofa. Mechanically, Susie placed a pillow under her mother's head. Daniel was patting his wife's hand and talking to her. "Susie, get me a glass of water," he said gruffly. Moving on sheer will alone, she went into the kitchen and drew a tumbler full of water from the faucet and returned to the living room. But instead of handing it to Daniel, she stood behind the couch and poured it in her mother's face.

"Susie, what the hell?" Daniel shouted, trying to block the rushing torrent. All he managed to do was get his arm wet, while most of the water found its way to Sadie's face after all. Sadie gurgled and sputtered but regained consciousness—thanks to her daughter.

Daniel attempted to dry her face, but Sadie fought at him, struggling to get up. "How could you do that, Mother?" Susie cried. "Don't you know what that means?" She went on as though she was the only one who understood. "It means that Brian and Mary J. were brother and sister. Unless we're not your daughters," she said scornfully. "Well, which is it?"

She stood with her arms crossed, a defiant look on her face. But it was Daniel who answered. "Susie, honey, we can't change what's already done. No one was ever supposed to know about Brian. Believe us, we didn't like the fact that those two kids fell in love and then got married. But it was either tell the truth then and ruin their lives or be silent and let everyone go on being happy. I suppose we should have just told the truth seven years ago and went ahead and ruined their lives then. At least we wouldn't be having this discussion now," he said, hanging his head, his dejection all too apparent. "But now that Brian's dead, I guess it no longer matters, does it?" His shoulders sagged like a man laboring under tremendous weight.

The telephone rang.

Stoney went to answer it, while Susie came around from behind the couch and hugged Daniel. "I suppose, like you said, the damage is done. There's no sense in crying over spilled milk. The only real problem is, do we tell Mary J.?"

"That was the hospital," Stoney said, turning everyone's attention to him. "Mary J. left the hospital. As close as they can figure, it was about an hour ago. They didn't miss her until the night nurse went in to give her a sleeping pill," he said by way of explanation. "Her clothes were gone, and she was gone."

"Where in the hell could she be going?" Daniel asked of no one in particular.

Stoney glanced at Susie. She covered her mouth. "Rockhole," she gasped.

"I think we should go out there," Stoney replied. He took Susie's arm and steered her toward the door.

"I'm coming with you," Daniel told him. He looked down at his wife. "Will you be all right by yourself for a while?"

"Forget that. I'm coming too," she stated firmly. She got up from the couch, a renewed determination in her manner and her color returned. "She's my daughter too. Let's go." When they hesitated, she added, "Come on, time is wasting."

They all four piled into Stoney's car.

CHAPTER SIXTEEN

It was just like before, only this time there was a light penetrating the darkness. It started out nothing more than a single speck. But it soon developed into a lusterless glow that had a defined focus which was difficult to isolate. Somehow, as dull as the light was, it managed to completely encircle him so that he was actually a part of the light.

Your time is growing close.

"Close? Already? But it's too soon. I'm not ready," Franklin said helplessly. He couldn't leave now. He just wasn't ready. It was too soon.

When it is your time, you must go. It cannot be altered.

Franklin shuddered at the intonation of the voice. It was completely emotionless. It lacked any depth. He couldn't remember the last time he heard such an obdurate, hardened being. "How can you be so…so…cold and heartless? Don't you feel anything?"

There is no place for feelings here. When it is time, it is time. You have no say in it.

"What do you want from me?" Franklin shouted, shaking his fist in the air.

To tell you that your time is coming soon. I thought you should know.

Franklin glared at the light. This was impossible. It didn't make any sense. "But how do I know if I'm ready? What preparations do I make?" he asked confused.

You'll know…you'll know.

Franklin made his way back home, practically retracing his original steps. He walked parallel to the creek on a trail that led to the road. But halfway between Rockhole and the road, he cut across the field to the south and followed it to the hillside. Then he climbed the hill and followed the ridge to his property. There, he angled across his own pasture and came up behind the barn.

"I'm gonna get you," Kelly rasped in a low voice. She was creeping toward, Jeff, one of Carlotta's twin boys, flexing her fingers like they were spider legs and making faces at him. The baby started giggling, already expecting the fingers to dig into his sides and tickle him. It was a game that they had played over and over again.

Carlotta looked over at them from where she was changing Seth. "You always find a way to make these boys laugh," she said, chuckling at them.

The twins had been born early, so they were a little underweight at birth. But they had come along nicely and gained the weight they needed as long as she nursed them. But then their weight had dropped some when she stopped nursing. And they were still extremely thin in Carlotta's estimation. Kelly had remarked about it one day but didn't think it was cause for worry.

"Lord knows they get enough exercise," Carlotta fussed. "They follow Imogene around like two little shadows." She winked at Kelly. "But she likes it you know. I think Imogene sees them as her own kids. She'll go traipsing all over that back pasture, and those boys will stay right with her. If she starts out and they aren't around, she'll go looking for them. I don't know. It worries me sometimes how they all stick so close together."

Kelly tipped her head, as though that would help her think a little better. "I should think that would make better. You know, knowing that she looks after them so well."

"Oh, it does. Don't get me wrong," she added quickly. I like the way she takes care of them. But she's a lot older you understand. Imogene can go places and do things that the boys can't yet." She paused, letting her thoughts wander, as worry lines wrinkled her face. "I'm just afraid that they might try to copy her when she does something difficult and get hurt, that's all."

"Do you really think Imogene would let those boys get hurt?

Carlotta shook her head and smiled. "You're right. I'm probably worrying for nothing." She finished buttoning up Seth's shirt and held him up in the air. "There, how does that feel? You know, you boys are two years old now. I think it's time you learned to dress yourselves, don't you?" She tossed him around in the air for a minute. "We'll start tomorrow." She lowered him when he started dribbling. "All right, Aunt Kelly, let's switch. You take this roustabout and let me have that little stinker."

Imogene and Kimberly trooped into the room, their lower lips jutted out in an obvious pout. "Can the boys come out and play now?" Imogene asked, screwing her face up at Seth, making him laugh.

Carlotta looked at her daughter's funny face and then gasped. "You two go wash your faces and hands. Then we'll talk about it. How in the world did you get so dirty?" She clucked her tongue at them as they dashed off to the kitchen.

Within seconds, the two girls were back. "Okay, now can they come outside and play?"

Carlotta took one look at them and dropped her head. "Imogene, you call that washing? That was no more than a lick and a promise."

"Mooom," she drawled.

Carlotta let them whine until she was through dressing Jeff. "Oh, all right. Go on and get out of here." She gave Seth a pat on the bottom as he trotted off. "Stay close by," she yelled at them on their way out the door.

Exhausted from the simple effort of chasing after the boys and changing their clothes, she flopped back on the sofa and closed her eyes. "Those kids will be the death of me," she declared.

Tracy smiled at her, understanding in her smile. Carlotta would have it no other way. And she knew it.

Franklin didn't go straight to the house when he returned from Rockhole. Instead, he slipped into the barn. He felt like he needed some time alone. Instinctively, he tried to recall what had occurred only moments before, but something didn't quite fit.

It was like a dream.

If you couldn't remember what the dream was about as soon as you wake up, it would begin to fade from memory with celeritous haste. Franklin had tried to recollect almost immediately but found that even though he was thinking of it, he had still waited too long. With each passing minute, he forgot more and more.

Now, he simply wanted to clear his head of the hazy fog drifting around inside it.

Like a thief, he skulked around outside the barn until he was sure no one would see him. And then he opened the door a crack and slithered through. Once inside, he walked with a resolute swiftness to the toolshed at the back and closed the door behind him.

There were no windows in the little room, and he didn't bother to light a lantern. Had he wanted to, it wouldn't have done him any good. He never had found his missing lantern. The lantern he normally kept in the barn was now in Imogene's secret hiding place.

In nearly total darkness, a small shaft of light streamed in under the crack of the door, he wandered over to where he kept a stool at the end of the room in front of the wall to wall workbench. "What is wrong with me?" he wondered aloud. He shook his head again, but it didn't seem to help.

Rising from the stool to leave, he strode halfway across the room and then stopped in midstep. He stood motionless, not making a sound, and turned one ear toward the noise. Voices. He heard children's voices.

Lurking in the wings, spying on others was abnormal behavior. He felt guilty, even though he hadn't planned to do so. But for some reason, he couldn't bring himself to exit the room. He remained rooted to the same spot, quietly listening like a traitorous spy.

He listened intently for a minute as the voices got closer and closer. Just at the moment, he was sure they would walk in and discover him, the voices were silenced. He strained even harder to hear, but the voices were gone.

Franklin slowly opened the door of the dark little room and immediately shielded his eyes from the bright light that exploded over him. He peeked out from under the edge of his hand and scoured the barn but didn't see anyone. Slowly, as his eyes adjusted to the light, he removed his hand and gave the huge barn a more thorough investigation.

Still no sign that anyone had been in here.

"That's impossible," he groaned out loud. Franklin wasn't sure but what he didn't imagine the whole thing.

Falteringly, he walked out of the barn, a heavy feeling of foreboding pressing in on him.

Carlotta stared intently at her husband, as she tried to make up her mind what was really bothering him. He had been moody for a few days, and she had started several times to ask him about it but each time dismissed it as just being tired from working too hard. She made a mental note to suggest swimming or some other activity to give him a break. Franklin was an unusual person; he didn't like to take any time for himself as long as there was work to do.

Tonight, as they sat on the front porch gazing at the crystal-clear sky, watching the stars twinkle as though the radiant beams flexed their romantic shafts of light just for them, she would ask him. Carlotta loved the feeling of the crisp evening wind blowing gently through her hair. She smiled at the dark, looming silhouettes of the trees that dotted the landscape across their front yard. Tonight, they were her friends. There was nothing threatening or menacing about them. On the contrary, they offered a comforting presence to her pleasant evening.

Oblivious to the romantic air that his wife enjoyed, Franklin sat in the porch swing oscillating back and forth in perfect rhythm, privy to some distant sound only he could hear. He began to hum a tune that Carlotta was unfamiliar with.

She had been leaning against the porch rail and came over to the swing to sit beside him. "What is that tune you're humming?" she asked curiously.

He turned his head and looked at her, but it was a blank stare.

It was time. "Franklin, what has gotten into you lately?" He continued to stare, as though he hadn't heard. She started to repeat her question. "Frank—"

"I'm sorry, darling. Did you say something?" Now his eyes were clear. She was alarmed at the rapid change, and it filled her with panic. She quickly averted her eyes and hoped he didn't see the fear that crept into them. As quickly as it had come, the stupor had disappeared. Now he was like before, like nothing had ever happened.

"It's just that you've been sort of distant lately," she muttered, brushing a lock of hair from her face. "I've been worried about you, that's all."

"I'm fine," he retorted. "There's no need to worry. Besides, you usually make more out of something than it is," he teased her. Franklin could feel another crappy nag session coming on. He hated these things and never understood why they were necessary to begin with.

"No need to be spiteful," she said, discomfited by his sharp reply.

This conversation was already headed toward disaster. They loved each other, so why all the bickering? What had gotten into their relationship recently? Franklin decided to be bold for once. He half turned in the swing and took one of Carlotta's hands in his. She was amazed that this rough and tumble farmer with his calloused, rugged features could be so gentle as he held her hand in his. Tears sprang to her eyes, and she used her free hand to wipe them away. Carlotta was embarrassed at her sudden display of feminine weakness.

In a surprising gesture of romantic foreplay, Franklin reached up and wiped the remaining tears from her cheeks and tenderly cupped her face in his hand. And then he kissed her. It was warm and responsive, and the first time he had shown her such affection or given her more than a peck on the cheek in several weeks. One thing led to another, and before long, he had gathered her in his arms and carried her upstairs to their waiting bed.

That night, Franklin and Carlotta made mad, passionate love with an intensity that belied their normally tranquil relationship. It was that night, amid their feverish, unbridled almost sexual exposé, that his seed found the object of its desire. Carlotta would look back later and remember it as the moment of their final creation.

The pungent aroma of coffee brewing, mixed with the piquant odor of bacon frying in the skillet, wafted its way up the stairs, curling around the hallway and into the second-floor rooms.

They weren't strange smells or even unusual. He had coffee and bacon for breakfast every morning, as well as, eggs, toast, and jam. The only deviant was when they had biscuits and gravy to go along with all that on Sunday mornings.

But somehow, it seemed different this morning.

The combination of the aforementioned aromas seemed to poise themselves above Franklin, and at the appropriate moment, woke him with a gentle tickling of his nose. He stirred and sat up on the side of the bed. At first, it didn't register, but as his mind cleared, he understood. He jumped up and stared at the window.

The morning sun was streaming through as the curtains fluttered in the gentle breeze of the open window.

Carlotta was just putting the finishing touches on the breakfast, when Franklin barreled down the stairs and clomped into the kitchen. "Why did you let me sleep so late? I've got cows to milk and feed, not to mention the hogs and chickens to tend. There's a fence to mend and fields to plow." He stopped his verbal libations when he realized his wife was staring at him but not listening to a word he said. "Carlotta, are you listening to me?"

"No, I'm not," she pointed out. Franklin recoiled at her abrupt answer. She quickly explained before he got the wrong idea. "All that will get done…and probably on time. Franklin, you're a wonderful farmer. A couple of hours off right now will not make one iota's difference in the overall scheme of things. You forget, I've seen you work. You've been at this for several years and neither your crops nor your other work has ever come in late." She sat down at the table next to him, which was not her customary place. "Now, eat your breakfast."

Chewing a mouthful of eggs and toast, he raised his eyes, glanced at his wife and told her, "Last night? I really enjoyed that." And then he lowered his eyes before she could see the smile that danced in them.

She laid her hand on his arm. "I know. It was special for me too."

Franklin went about his work with renewed ambition. For a while, he labored with the drive of a madman, accomplishing more in a short time than he had in the several weeks since his encounter with the mysterious phenomenon.

Carlotta was concerned at first about the funk he wandered around in. He seemed to move mechanically through his chores and other work and never wanted to do anything socially. Doug and Kelly had also noticed and were puzzled by Franklin's disassociation but didn't give it more than a passing thought.

But now, Carlotta was concerned for the opposite reason. She felt he was working too hard and was afraid he might collapse from overexertion. Her worst fears surfaced when Franklin came in complaining of pain and excessive tiredness one evening.

They were at the supper table when it began. "Franklin, are you okay? Do you feel all right? You look kind of pale," Carlotta said, worriedly.

"I'm just tired," he replied, picking at his food. "I moved some hay today and you know how heavy those bales can get after a while." He sat there a little while longer, stabbing at his food with his fork and occasionally slipping a small bite into his mouth.

"Daddy, why don't you sit in your easy chair if you're tired?" Imogene asked innocently. "You always feel better after you sit in your chair for a while."

"Thank you, sweetheart," he replied, smiling at her. "I think I will. Excuse me please," he said, looking at his wife. Franklin shuffled off to the living room and plopped down into his overstuffed chair. Carlotta had followed as far as the door and watched him for a few minutes. To her apparent uneasiness, she saw him rubbing his chest with his fist. His face was even more ashen than before.

Returning to the kitchen table, she sat down heavily in her chair. Something was wrong. What should she do? Get Doug? No! Get the doctor. No! Get both of them. Her mind made up, she took Imogene aside and sent her to get Doug. Then she hurried the twins through the rest of their supper before marching them upstairs and to bed early.

"Come on, boys," she urged them. "Your daddy doesn't feel well, and I need for you to do as I ask tonight."

"Is Daddy gonna be all right?" the twins asked in unison.

"He's going to be fine," she assured them. "Your daddy is a strong man. He's just tired that's all." She was slipping Seth's pajamas on while Jeff washed his face and hands. When he stomped into the bedroom, she asked, "Did you wash behind your ears?"

"Yes, ma'am," he answered politely. "See." He pulled his ear out as far as it would go, as though that would prove to her that he did.

"Okay," she laughed. "Let's get your pajamas on." She sent Seth toward his bed and helped Jeff into his pajamas.

While she was slipping the top over his head and searching for his evasive arms, Jeff began plying her with questions. "Is something terrible wrong with Daddy? What happened to him? Is he gonna die?"

"Whoa, there, mister." She finally located one of his active arms and pushed it through the sleeve. "Where is all this coming from?"

"I don't know. He just looks…weird."

"Honey, he's going to be fine. You heard him. He's just tired, that's all. You'll see. Tomorrow he'll be his jolly old self," she said, unconvinced of her own words. Having succeeded with the pajamas, she sent Jeff to his bed and kissed them both good night.

By the time she got back downstairs, Imogene had returned with Michael, Kelly, and Kimberly. They were in the living room checking on Franklin, with the two girls looking on, fear in their eyes.

Michael was shaking him awake. "Come on, Franklin, wake up." He stirred and opened his eyes. Everyone could see the dazed look, as though Franklin had no idea where he was. After a minute, his eyes began to clear.

"Oh, hello." He sat up in the chair and shook his head. "I must have dozed off. What are you all doing here?" Suddenly his head snapped up. "Were we doing something tonight?" he asked.

"I sent Imogene after them." Carlotta stepped in. "I was worried about you."

"What on earth for?" he asked, looking at his wife in a strange way. "What made you think there was something wrong with me?" Franklin sat up in the chair. He had slouched down, as was his custom when he was tired, and fell asleep sitting crossways in the comfortable chair.

"You feel all right, now?" Carlotta asked, annoyed at him for not being sick. "I could have sworn you were on the verge of collapsing."

"I'm fine," he said with a note of finality.

"If you're sure you're okay, I think we'll be going on home," Michael said, standing up and frowning at Franklin. He and Kelly crossed the room to the door. "Kimberly, let's go." They waited for her to catch up. "Just in case, we'll drop by tomorrow and check on you." He glanced one more time at Franklin, who had stood up. "You might want to consider taking a break every now and then."

"I told you, Michael, there's nothing wrong with me. I just slung too many bales of hay today. Now, don't be worrying about me. You've got enough to take care of without shouldering any of my problems. Thanks for coming," he said gruffly, glancing at his wife. "Good night."

The Bakers turned in early that night, and no more was said about Franklin's incident.

The next morning dawned bright as the sun came up over the horizon. Franklin had already been out for a couple of hours, tending to his livestock and planning his day. He stood on the north side of the barn, just outside the corral, watching the sunrise. This was one of the reasons why he enjoyed being a farmer. He was up before the sun each morning and worked hard until it was time for the immense globe of warmth and light to make its appearance. No matter where he was or what he was doing, he always found the time to stop and watch this great miracle of nature.

"It's going to be a beautiful day," he said, gazing at the horizon and smelling the air. As soon as the first rays of the sun peeked over the neighboring hillside, he returned to the barn where he had been about to clean out the horses' stalls. Unknown to him, there was one thing different this morning from every other morning.

Someone was watching.

Carefully, so she wouldn't be seen or heard, Carlotta had tiptoed to the kitchen window and stood so that she could see out but not be seen by her husband. She slid the curtain aside, just a fraction of an inch, and watched his early morning ritual.

Something is wrong, echoed through her mind.

When he returned to the barn, she went about her morning chore of fixing breakfast. But for some reason, she couldn't get the notion out of her head that something terrible was going to happen. It was as though a threatening message hovered, just out of grasp in a remote, uncluttered, seldom used corner of her conscience.

Carlotta went about her task mechanically, her mind occupied with trying to sort through her strange feelings. It was something she was not used to and was severely distracted by it. She tried to shrug it off, but it was strong and hung around, lingering in the wings waiting for another chance to divert her attention once again.

Somehow, she managed to finish breakfast without burning the food. She called the children down to the table, stuck her head out the back door and hollered for Franklin, then ducked back inside to retrieve the biscuits from the oven before they turned into a collection of solid black rocks.

The children drifted down the stairs, one at a time. By the time the last one, Imogene—it was usually her that was last—plodded into the kitchen, Franklin was drying his hands and took his chair.

As he pulled his chair out from under the table, scraping its legs on the hardwood floor, he posed a question to the smaller members of his family. "I'm missing a lantern in the barn. Anyone seen it lately?"

He was looking at his plate while he shoveled some eggs into it, but he had one eye raised slightly, casting it about the table at his three children. They were all extremely busy filling their plates—in silence, which in itself was unusual—and trying desperately not to look in their father's direction. He was sure they knew where the missing lantern was, but he wouldn't press it any further, not at the table. Rather, he would let the guilty party have the chance to return it, no questions asked.

The rest of the meal was spent talking about everything but the missing lantern.

True to their word, the Warrens showed up the next morning. Michael claimed they were on their way to town and just stopped by to see if the Bakers needed anything since they were going anyway.

"Figured we might save you a trip, just in case you did need something," Michael said doggedly. He wasn't quite sure how to broach the subject without making his friend angry, but he would feel better if he heard it from Franklin himself that he was all right after last night's episode.

"No. We're doing all right," Franklin responded suspiciously. "Something else on your mind, Michael? Just come right out and say it."

Michael shrugged and pretended to be tightening the reins on his horses. "You feeling okay this morning? You look better," he commented while adjusting the bit in one of the horse's mouths.

"I'm fine."

"Just thought I'd ask," Michael said dourly. An uneasy silence formed and was finally broken when Kimberly ran up and skidded to a halt next to her dad. She yanked on her dad's jeans.

"Daddy, can I stay here while you and Mama go into town?" she asked hopefully, her eyebrows raised, as though that might help her cause in his decision. She thought for a minute he was going to say yes, but then he gave her a very resounding "*No!*"

"But, Daddy. It's going to be boring," she complained shrilly.

"Honey, you know Mama's going to have you fitted for a new pair of shoes, and unfortunately you have to be there so we get the right size. I'm sorry, pumpkin, but you have to go." She stared at the ground as her foot drew designs in the dirt. Suddenly, she looked up, her eyes shining again. "Can Seth go with us? Please? At least it won't be so boring."

Franklin had been quiet through the dialogue between father and daughter. He finally decided to speak up. "Kimberly, if it's all right with your father, it's all right with me. But you better go ask his mother too."

"Daddy? Is it all right?"

"Yes, honey. It's fine with me." She didn't wait for any more talk but darted immediately for the house. Several minutes later, as the Warrens' wagon was disappearing down the lane, two sets of eyes watched the dust settling with disappointment etched in their faces.

"Well, it's just you and me, Jeff," Imogene said, unhappy that all four of them wouldn't be able to play together. "Come on, let's go to our secret hiding place." They trooped off together toward the barn.

Carlotta thought that Imogene and Jeff were the picture of solemnity as they walked toward the barn. She continued staring out the kitchen window long after they had closed the barn door. Well, they would get used to disappointment. They had better anyway. It wouldn't be the last time that wily devil would visit their door.

She returned to her work without giving their little problem another thought.

"I don't want to play anymore," Jeff whined. "I want to go swing." The two despondent children had tried to carry on without their brother and best friend but weren't having much fun. Imogene was resolute in trying to keep their attention focused on the two of them having fun all by themselves.

"No! Let's stay and play a while longer," she said, sardonically. Not intentionally, a note of cynicism had crept into her voice. Immediately, she was sorry for the way she snapped at her little brother.

Jeff had jerked backward at her indignant attitude, afraid she might strike out at him. His fear mounting, Jeff started crawling toward the exit tunnel as fast as he could. Imogene felt bad about the way she had yelled at him and grabbed at Jeff to apologize. But in his present state of mind, Jeff was sure she was going to hit him for being such a spoilsport. He jumped sideways to evade her grasping fingers, but Imogene's arms were longer than he realized, plus she was extremely agile.

Just as she latched onto Jeff's arm, he kicked out with his foot to try to loosen her grip. His bad aim and short legs only resulted in his kick careening off Imogene's leg and into the lantern. The impact was enough to catapult the flaming light into the hay at the mouth of the tunnel, where it seemed to explode on impact.

Both children stared in shock as the flames engulfed the opening, which was their only escape. Imogene realized their peril almost immediately and still holding Jeff's arm, backed away from the rapidly spreading fire, while frantically searching for another way out.

But the fire blocked the only exit.

The sudden movement awoke Jeff from his frozen panic, and he started screaming. Imogene's heart sank into her stomach, but her only reaction was the tears streaming down her face.

The flames were getting closer and closer, while the heat was almost unbearable. Within seconds, the fire had consumed most of the oxygen in the small play area, and both children started choking from the lack of breathable air and the overwhelming smoke.

Imogene shrank into a corner as far away from the quickly approaching flames as she could with Jeff at her side. Somehow, she knew.

They were going to die.

Carlotta kicked the back door open with her foot and crossed the porch, balancing a pan of dirty dishwater. Still a couple of feet from the porch railing, she rotated the pan slinging it out and down with the practiced hand of one who has done it many times before. She pulled the pan back and was just turning to retreat to the kitchen when she smelled it before seeing it.

Her curiosity getting the best of her, Carlotta sniffed the air as she ascended the steps to the ground and made her way across the yard to the barn. The door felt warm to her touch when she unlatched it and pulled it open. *Dear God, please don't let this be what I think it is*, she prayed silently. She swung the door open and gasped as flames licked their way up the wooden supports to the roof.

It covered nearly half the barn. How in the world could it be that big and she just now found out about it? Suddenly, Carlotta recovered from her initial shock and screamed. "*Imogene! Jeff!*" She didn't see them or hear a response. But she was sure they were in there somewhere. She hadn't seen them come out.

Even though the heat was incredible, Carlotta went into the barn to look for her children. She shielded her face with her arm and skirted the side of the barn that was not in flames yet. About halfway through the barn, she dropped to her knees and erupted into a coughing fit. She was beginning to feel dizzy. But she had to find her children.

"*Imogene! Jeff!*" Still nothing.

The smoke was so thick she could hardly see—or breath. But she continued searching anyway. Carlotta got up by leaning against a stall railing. She staggered a few steps and fell face forward.

Franklin had seen the smoke from the field a quarter of a mile away, where he was plowing. He quickly unhooked the plow from the horse, leaped onto the horse's back, and whipped it into a dead run toward the barn.

As soon as he got there, he jumped down from the still moving horse and ran into the barn. The smoke was already so thick he could barely see through it, but he bolted into the barn and looked around quickly. He spotted Carlotta lying on the floor, apparently unconscious, and worked his way over to her. "Carlotta, honey, get up!" No response. He picked her up and carried her out of the barn, away from the fire.

In the fresh air, the oxygen revived Carlotta and sent her into another violent coughing fit. It took a few minutes to clear the smoke from her lungs before she could say anything. "The—" More coughing. "The children."

Franklin's throat constricted, so his question came out a squeak. "What about them?"

Michael and Kelly's wagon came flying around the corner of the house. Even before it stopped, they were climbing down. "Kelly, watch her," he shouted. "Michael, the children are in the barn."

They raced toward the already huge incinerator and started in, but the shooting flames drove them back. Franklin started again to enter the blazing inferno, but Michael caught hold of his arm and yanked him back. "Franklin, you can't go in there!"

"I've got to. My kids—"

"Franklin, it's too late," Michael shouted, to be heard above the noise of the flaming furnace. Franklin tried to pull away from his friend's grip on his arm. But Michael held on tight. "*It's too late!*" he bellowed.

Franklin turned to look at Michael, an absolute look of horror on his face. He fell to his knees and yelled in anguish as the awful truth slowly sank in.

"*Nooo!*" Franklin clasped his hands on his head and rocked back and forth.

The shock of losing two of their children in the fire was more than Franklin could handle. He went about his chores mechanically, not really caring if they got done correctly. Michael and Kelly felt certain he never really came out of the shock, that his vacant, dead stare was his constant companion now. His and Carlotta's relationship had slowly, at first, deteriorated. Franklin had even taken to sleeping on the sofa, claiming he didn't want to ruin what sleep Carlotta might get.

Neighbors from all around offered to help rebuild the barn, but Franklin declined. All he would say was, it was his constant reminder. He believed it was his fault. Seth and Kimberly had finally told them about the secret hiding place, and it was then that Franklin realized with a sense of dread that he had intended to remove that old hay. It wasn't any good for feed and didn't seem to bother anyone where it was, so he just left it. But he shouldn't have. It was his fault his two children were dead.

Carlotta did everything she could to try to bring him around, but it was pretty evident that he wouldn't respond. She hated the way they had drifted apart. From the very beginning, they had been so close that nothing could separate them. But something finally did. Franklin was in his own little bubble, and nothing could penetrate it.

Then one day he began to act even stranger. His movements seemed even more mechanical than before. He paid less and less attention to his family. And of late, he seemed to drift in and out of reality. He stopped eating, and Carlotta was becoming more frightened with each passing moment.

She finally decided to confront him. "Franklin, what is wrong with you lately?" Carlotta asked, a nervous tic playing at the corner of her eye. At first, she wasn't sure he had heard her. But then he peered at her, puzzled himself at the queer things that were going on in his head.

"I don't know. I just feel strange. I can't explain it." It had been going on for a lot longer than he had let on to Carlotta. At first, he thought he was sick or something. But the symptoms were different from a cold or flu. It really was hard to explain.

"Maybe you should see the doctor," she suggested.

The last thing Franklin wanted to do right now was to see a doctor. He'd never been on to go running off to a sawbones when the least little thing cropped up. "I'll be all right," he told her. "Don't say anything to the children. They don't need to be worrying about me, especially after what happened to their brother and sister."

Carlotta was nearly two months pregnant. But with the deaths of their two children, she thought it best to not say anything for a while. She would just play it day by day until she felt the time was right. That time would be determined by Franklin himself.

Her greatest fear was that he would completely ignore his only living child. Franklin never really had any favorites among his children, however, Imogene being his firstborn and, according to his own words, the prettiest little girl he had ever laid eyes on, did hold a special place in his heart.

Seth was very patient for such a young person, to the point that Carlotta was concerned for his welfare as well. The toddler had cried at the loss of his siblings. He seemed to understand that they were lost forever. He had even come to grips with the loss, but there was something that didn't feel right to his mother. She supposed it was because he and Jeff were twins, and that somehow that would have a profound effect on the one remaining alive. She was uncertain but based her conclusion on the fact that the two had been inseparable.

They were never apart, even for a minute. And they thought so much alike, sometimes she couldn't tell which one to credit for an idea.

Carlotta did her best to take up the slack of a practically non-existent father. But just like Franklin was missing something in his life, so was she and Seth. They each needed him for different reasons.

That was what their lives had been reduced to, mechanical, programmed movements by day and loneliness by night.

Until one day…

Franklin was outside chopping firewood. Seth was in the house helping his mother with her chores. He had taken to doing that a lot lately. Especially since his father didn't seem to want his company. He didn't mind helping his mother. It helped to pass the time.

Suddenly, a scream pierced the dreadful silence that held their home in its chilling grip. Carlotta grabbed a towel and was drying her hands as she rushed to the back door. A hurried glance around the backyard revealed nothing. Franklin was not in sight. She had completely forgotten about Seth, who was standing next to her with a terrified look on his face. He was moaning in a low voice. Not knowing what to expect, she quickly knelt down and turned the boy to face her.

"No matter what happens, I want you to stay in the house." He didn't seem to hear her. "Do you understand?" she shouted at the youngster.

Carlotta slammed the screen door back against the side of the house as she bolted through. Her eyes quickly scanned the yard in search of Franklin. She finally detected him lying on the ground near the woodpile where he had been working. He was twisting and writhing in pain, lying on his side with his arms wrapped around his head. Carlotta was still twenty feet from him when he suddenly stopped moving. His arms relaxed and fell to the ground and he went completely limp. Her heart leaped into her throat, and her chest pounded until she was sure it would burst.

"*Franklin!*" she shouted, stepping up her pace even more. A few feet away, she dropped suddenly and slid with her legs folded under her, coming to a stop at his side. "Franklin!" she shouted at him again, grabbing his arm and turning him over until he lay on his back.

Carlotta drew back involuntarily when she saw his face.

There was immense pain scrolled over it, or was it fear? She wasn't sure, but it was the most atrocious thing she had ever seen. His eyes were open and had a death stare in them. In fact, he looked like he was dead. But he was still breathing.

After a few minutes, he began to stir.

"Franklin?"

He moaned and said something indistinct. At first, she thought it was some kind of strange language but decided that was stupid. He was just in pain.

"Franklin, honey, are you all right?" she asked softly, holding his shoulders. She gently lifted his head and scooted around so that she could lay it in her lap. She stroked his hair letting her fingers trail down the ridge of his cheek. "Darling, talk to me. Say something," she almost cried, beginning to lose control.

Again, he mumbled something unintelligible.

"Franklin, I don't understand what you're saying," she cried desperately. She was losing it. She had to get hold of herself.

"I'm all…right," he finally responded, in words she could understand.

"Honey, what happened?" she asked tersely.

"I don't know," he whispered, trembling slightly. "I don't have any idea. The last thing I remember was laying that ax into a chunk of wood."

Carlotta couldn't help but laugh at his statement. She was just so glad he was all right. So many terrible things went through her mind when she saw him lying there. She sat caressing his head for the longest time. Finally, she suggested, "Why don't we take Seth and go swimming over at Rockhole this afternoon? You've been working hard. You could use a little rest and relaxation," she chided him.

"Sounds like a good idea to me," he replied, grinning at her. "Here, help me up."

Carlotta walked him to the house and made him sit down while she packed them a lunch. When she was finished and they had changed clothes, they headed for Saline Creek. Franklin and Carlotta never swam with the children. They usually just sat on a blanket spread out on the bluff, but since Seth was alone now, they preferred to keep a closer eye on him. So this time, they got wet.

Saline Creek was narrow for the most part, but at this juncture, it widened enough to create a perfect swimming area. The rock cliff on which they sat plummeted straight down for about ten feet to the water's surface and then continued for four or five feet more under water. The gravel bottom began to slant upward from the point where it met the rock face until it came to a zero point approximately fifteen feet on the other side. The gravel continued its upward climb to form a rugged shelf for visitors to sit on, although it could be pretty rough with some of the sharper rocks.

To the left of the rock cliff was a natural stairstep descending into the creek. It had been carved out of the rock by father time. Those who were not adept at diving or jumping from a ten-foot height into a shallow pool like Rockhole could use the steps to gain access at water level.

After they had splashed, dunked, and spent enough time in the water to shrivel up, they climbed the stone stairs to the top and spread out their picnic lunch. After a nice quiet meal and a short time to relax, they packed up their picnic basket and began to ascend the short incline to the dirt road above.

At the top, they climbed into the wagon and headed east toward the road. They were a few hundred feet away when Seth suddenly started screaming bloody murder. He quickly hopped off the back of the wagon and started running back toward the swimming hole.

Franklin reined the horses in when he realized Seth had jumped off. He vaulted from the wagon and ran after his young son. His longer, stronger legs allowed him to catch up to Seth in no time.

"Whoa, young man," he said, scooping the toddler up in his arms, before Seth could take one more step. "What are you carrying on about?"

"I left Miss Peebles," he cried, struggling against his dad's strong arms. "I left Miss Peebles." After the fire, Seth had taken to playing with and carrying his sister's favorite rag doll around. It was his way of, somehow, keeping Imogene with him.

Franklin held the boy out away from him far enough to see his face. "Well, I tell you what. I'll go get her for you, okay? You stay with Mommy," he said, setting Seth down on the seat of the buckboard. "I'll be back in a minute," he told his wife, grinning at them both.

He trotted back down the road toward Rockhole. Carlotta turned and watched as Franklin disappeared into the trees. In her mind, she could trace his steps as he descended to the bluff they had just vacated. She pulled Seth over close to her and hugged him. They sat like that while they waited for Franklin to reemerge from the trees.

Several minutes passed and Franklin had not returned. Carlotta began to get worried. Her mind conjured up all sorts of terrible images. His earlier incident that day didn't help. Now, she was really getting worried. She climbed down from the wagon and instructed Seth to stay where he was. "Daddy's probably having a hard time finding Miss Peebles. I'll go help him, so we can get home sooner," she told her son.

She started off at a fast walk which soon turned into a full run. From the top of the incline, she scoured the area below but didn't see Franklin. He was nowhere on the bluff. Seth must have left the doll down below, she reasoned to herself. She navigated the short incline to the level solid surface below and walked over to the edge, scanning the area for her husband.

Suddenly, she saw him.

He was floating facedown in the water, still clutching Miss Peebles in his hand. He wasn't moving. Carlotta jumped in without thinking. She landed within inches of his body and grabbed at him, turning him over. She shook him. "Franklin! *Franklin!*" she cried several times. This time there was no movement. There was no breathing. She gathered his inert body in her arms and held him close as she cried into his already wet face.

This time, he was dead.

ROCK HOLE CLAIMS ITS SECOND VICTIM
Story by Storm Wallen

CRATER RIDGE—Although it is still early in the investigation, Rockhole, the popular swimming haunt for most folks around Crater Ridge, has claimed its second victim in two years. For the moment, Sheriff Eason is calling it an accidental death. Franklin Baker, who lived on the ridge itself, died from drowning late yesterday afternoon when he fell from the top of the bluff overlooking the creek to his death below. While there seems to be no doubt as to the cause of death, Sheriff Eason is concerned there seems to be no apparent connection between the two deaths. Sheriff Eason alluded to the fact that his office would certainly not disregard this as a brutal murder by an unknown assailant. The coroner's report should provide additional information concerning the unusual events of Baker's mysterious death. But the sheriff says he will not sit idly by and wait for the report, which will come out of St. Louis and could take several weeks to arrive. The investigation will proceed. Even though Conners' death two years ago was never resolved to the satisfaction of the sheriff. Eason remains hopeful that this case will produce enough viable clues to unravel the cabalistic death of Franklin Baker. It is interesting to note that the Joshua Conners case was never closed, and the official cause of death was listed as murder at the hands of person or persons unknown. Reliable sources say that the victim's wife and child were nearby but did not see or hear what happened. Franklin Baker is survived by his wife, Carlotta, and his son, Seth. The face of so little to go on, Eason says he will not rule out suicide or even murder. Foul play, says Eason, could easily have been covered up. The absence of any signs of a struggle is what the sheriff bases his assumption on. You will remember that on June 5, 1904, Joshua Conners died of several deadly, venomous snakebites. That incident was also ruled an accidental death, but just as in this case, everyone was mystified as to some of the strange events surrounding that young man's death.

Chapter Seventeen

The last part of their ride was in silence. Mary J. was content to lean cozily against the car door and stare up at the stars. The same stars, which she and Brian had lain under that night not so long ago, twinkled at her as though they were saying to her, *Everything will be fine. There's no need to worry.* She smiled appreciatively and silently thanked them for their reticent approval.

Now she knew!

Everything would be fine. She was going to meet Brian, and they would be together forever. She smiled again as the affection of the soft moonlight penetrated her body and nurtured her unborn child. She felt it stir as the gentle fingers of its love nudged the baby into activity.

Father Pritchard slowed the car as County Road 135 came into the farthest reach of the car's lights. He turned onto the gravel road and eased across the low water bridge that gave them passage to the south side of Saline Creek.

Still gazing out the window of the car, Mary J. tried to see beyond the black curtain of night to the place she knew was Rockhole. The place she knew Brian waited for her. The place she knew it waited for her baby.

But it was too dark to see.

As Father Pritchard stopped alongside the fence that ran perpendicular to the dirt lane leading to Rockhole, a huge black cloud passed in front of the moon. It and the stars disappeared, and they suddenly found themselves gathered in the arms of night.

That was appropriate, the priest thought silently. Demons preferred complete darkness to any kind of light. It's an unwritten rule, he reminded himself.

The prince of darkness.

The master of wickedness.

The lord of the night.

Whatever you wanted to call it, darkness was its friend.

As he shut the motor off and the last bit of light faded into the shadow of night, Mary J. shuddered.

Before the light completely disappeared, she had seen the fence that guarded the dirt lane. Suddenly she felt uneasy. It had awakened a forgotten memory. But only briefly. Then it was gone.

Something had happened to her here. Something terrible. She wished she could remember what it was, but her memory failed her. It had flickered on for one brief second before winking out of existence again.

She did remember the basic things like getting there, carrying the blanket, and Brian carrying the picnic basket as they walked down the dirt lane, arm in arm, not a care in the world. She smiled at the memory. Then they were at Rockhole, and she was spreading out the blanket for them to sit on. Little fragments of that night flickered in and out of her memory. The way she had teased Brian, showing off her legs every chance she got. That was why she had worn the short skirt, the one she still had on that was so badly torn. She felt the ragged edges and was puzzled by it.

What came next? Oh, yes! She had forgotten. She had taken the lantern out of the basket and given it to Brian to light. He had such a time getting it lighted. She laughed softly at his clumsiness. He had lit the lantern many times. It wasn't that he suddenly didn't know how something was wrong with him. He had even said so. But she hadn't listened. Why hadn't she listened to him?

Then they had eaten.

Afterward, they drank champagne, while they lay on the blanket under the stars. That was when it all started. She seduced him—starting with a flashy show of her legs—and they had just started to make love and...and...

Damn it! She couldn't remember. Everything was a blank after that. Why couldn't she remember what came next? Why? Why? Why?

"What is it, young lady?"

She started at the sound of his voice. "What?" she asked, trembling.

"You were a long way from here." He frowned at her. "I was talking to you and noticed that you weren't listening. I thought maybe something was wrong." She glanced into the night at the fence. Then again, she tried to look past the darkness to where she knew Rockhole was. Suddenly it dawned on him. "You don't remember, do you? You don't remember what happened to you that night."

She shook her head slowly in agreement. He was right. She didn't remember, at least the things she needed to remember. "No," she replied quietly. "I don't. But you must know something, or else you wouldn't be out here." She looked back around at the priest, who was facing her, his left arm draped over the steering wheel. "Why are you here?" she asked.

"For the same reason you are," he told her. "To confront the demon." When she appeared confused, he went on. "What happened to your husband was no accident, Mrs. Clark. Do you know about your family's curse?"

She nodded at him. "Only because of an old woman who appeared to me in a dream." Now it was his turn to express confusion. Mary J. didn't know this man very well and wasn't sure she should say anymore. He might think she was certifiable, and well, she already had enough people thinking that. Of course, he was a priest, so maybe he would be sympathetic and not judge her so readily. "While I was in the coma, a woman came to me one night and told me about a curse. She said a lot of other things that didn't make much sense, but I gathered that it had something to do with me and Brian. I really don't know any more than that." She secretly hoped he would accept her abbreviated explanation.

He gave her a fatherly smile meant to ease her discomfort, but she wasn't in the mood for it right now. "There's a lot you don't know," he commented dryly. "I think I should fill you in before we go any further."

She was beginning to like this priest. He was gentle and kind and did seem to want to help her. She decided to trust him and prayed she wasn't wrong about him.

"Why were you in the hospital?" she asked suddenly.

There was that mysterious yet comforting smile. She wondered if that was common among priests or if it was special just to him. *I think just to him*, she decided. He was special, and the smile was genuine.

"I had a heart attack," he informed her.

She frowned. "Your health is failing? Maybe you shouldn't be here," she declared innocently. "I wouldn't want my problems to become your problems or a detriment to your health."

"It's not that simple," he said cautiously. "Besides, the demon was responsible for the heart condition, not poor health." Again, she frowned, her confusion mounting. He went on to explain his previous trip out here and what happened as a result of it.

Panic spread across her face.

Father Pritchard had watched her and figured she had a completely different concept of the demon than what he was telling her. "Is there something you'd like to tell me?"

The panic was gone. It had been replaced by anger. "You're just trying to keep me and Brian apart," she said accusingly.

That wasn't the response he expected. "What do you mean? Your dead husband?"

"It said that if I would come to Rockhole, Brian and I would be together again."

"Mary J., that's impossible. You know that he's dead. No matter how much you want it, Brian cannot come back—"

"No! I won't listen to your lies," she yelled, interrupting him. "It said you would lie to me and try to deceive me. You just don't want me and Brian to be together again."

She was losing control. He needed to do something to regain her confidence, or it was over for her. "Tell me about the baby."

There was that gentle, condescending smile again. How could she stay mad at that? Her anger subsided, and she calmly told him about *it* wanting her baby. In her mind, the whole thing seemed rational. Mary J. didn't see the need to question *its* motives. In her present state of chaotic confusion, the tradeoff was worth it.

"So you see, I have to," she said bleakly. "It's the only way I can get Brian back."

"What about the baby?"

Mary J. was amused at the priest's misplaced concern. "All you can think about is the baby," she replied, sarcastically. "What about me? What about Brian? Don't we matter? The baby isn't even a real person. Why can't you care as much for us as you do for it?"

"But it is a real person, Mary J.," he replied. "It became a real living being at the moment of conception." Father Pritchard now knew the demon had control of her mind, and if he was to have any chance at saving her, it would only be by persuading her to see the fallibility of the beast's demands. By showing her that God loved her and the child and cared for them more than the demon did. He continued. "God gave that life to you and Brian to love and care for." She looked thoughtful. He prayed he was beginning to break through the barrier the demon had created around her. "It has no claim on your child, Mary J. That child is a gift from God. The beast has taken your husband, just as *it* has taken other of your family members in the past. There is nothing you can do to help Brian now. You should be thinking about yourself and your baby. Brian's baby."

Mary J. wiped the few tears from her eyes that had appeared as the priest talked about Brian and Brian's baby. She felt her stomach. It wasn't flat, but she was just now developing a bulge. Not unusual for her. She usually didn't start to show with her previous children until she was about five months along. It was something in her genetic makeup she supposed. "I can't even feel it," she cried. She peered through her tears at the priest. "I can't feel it!" Fear crept into her voice.

"It's there—"

"*No!* It's not. You're trying to fool me with your fancy talk about Brian and the baby and God." Once again, her fear turned to anger.

"If God cared so much, why did He let Brian die? Why did He separate us? Answer me that!" she continued shouting at the priest.

Father Pritchard shook his head. "That wasn't God's doing, Mary J. That was Satan's work. But through God's love and our acceptance of His Son, we can be reunited with our loved ones again. No demon can do that. Believe me."

Her anger was still prevalent but was more controlled than before. She looked menacingly at the priest. He was losing ground with her. The priest had to concede that the beast already had too firm a grip on Mary J. He decided to try a new line of attack.

"Your great-grandparents had the same problem. Each of your great-grandmothers lost their husbands—at Rockhole. It was the same demon who took their lives, as well as their children, leaving at least one in each family to continue the line." He stared at her in the darkness and wondered how much she understood or if it was the demon listening, and she understood nothing.

"They were cursed," she said defiantly.

"So are you, Mary J. This demon has you under the same curse as your ancestors."

She glared at him through the dark night, the dash lights providing just enough light to cast an eerie shadow on her pretty face. "They were brothers and sisters who married. That's why they were cursed. Brian and I were normal. There was nothing wrong with our marriage."

"Are you sure?"

Her hand went unconsciously to the door handle. "You have no right to say that!" she yelled. Suddenly the interior of the car lighted up as another car approached from the south and bathed them in bright light.

They watched the approaching car for a moment and then Mary J. looked at the priest before opening the door. "I'm going after my husband." She got out of the car and slammed the door shut. Then she looked back in at the priest. "Don't try to stop me!" she hissed and disappeared over the fence.

No one spoke on the trip to Rockhole. Stoney drove as fast as he safely could. As they rounded the curve in front of the Matthews farm, their headlights confirmed what everyone had suspected. There sat a car next to the fence. Susie, who was sitting next to Stoney in the front seat, was sure she heard a sigh of relief from the back seat.

They watched as someone got out of the car and climbed over the fence. "I think that was Mary J.," Susie said, breaking the silence. Stoney brought his car to a halt in front of the other car. He quickly got out and looked down the dirt lane but saw no sign of Mary J.

He walked over to the other car, followed by Susie and eventually his folks. "Father Pritchard," he gasped, surprised at the priest's presence. "Why are you out here? Did Mary J. call you for a ride?"

"No. I picked her up on my way out here," he explained. "She was hitchhiking."

"I don't understand. What the hell is going on?" Stoney demanded. "Was that Mary J. that went over the fence?"

"Yes, I'm afraid it was," he replied. Father Pritchard went through a hasty explanation of the evening's events and his conversation with Mary J. And then he suggested they should go after her.

"I don't know, Father," Daniel drawled. "I mean, demons and curses. This whole thing sounds pretty bizarre."

"Yes, it does," Pritchard confirmed. "And it doesn't usually happen like this anymore. But I can assure you that what's happening to your daughter is real, especially to her. And right now, the demon has more influence over her than God does."

Susie had heard enough. "It's true, Dad. Just like he says. My dreams were like Mary J.'s." She looked toward the trees. "We have to go stop her."

Under cover of darkness, a night so black that a hand in front of the face was invisible, Mary J. climbed the fence with relative ease. As soon as her feet hit the ground on the other side, she broke into a run, looking back only to check the lights on the car that drove up.

She was halfway to Rockhole and, as far as she could tell, no one was following her. She maintained her pace until she reached the trail that descended to the bluff. She cast one more wary glance in the direction of the road. Still no one followed.

As she started down the slope, she remembered there was a low hanging tree branch and put her left arm up. She felt her hand contact it and grabbed it, using it to balance her as she skated down the trail.

On the flat rock that formed the bluff, overlooking Rockhole, she stood in silent anticipation. *It* was here. She could feel *its* presence.

In the calmness that surrounded her—a light appeared.

It was Brian.

Everyone had crossed the fence except for Stoney who was holding the wire. He ducked down to climb through just as a car turned the corner off Highway 38 onto the gravel road. It pulled up behind the priest's car and stopped.

Stoney went out to the road to see who it was. When he was within a few feet, he recognized the sheriff's car by the lights on top. "Sheriff Rogers. What brings you out here?" he asked.

"I got a phone call that your sister-in-law left the hospital, as did the priest," Rogers stated cautiously.

"Do you really think you need to be here, Sheriff?"

"Until I find out what the hell is going on, yes. I need to be here. Besides, I think I know why they're here," he said lugubriously. Rogers took out his flashlight. "Let's go."

Mary J.'s eyes lit up. "Brian," she gasped. "The priest said you wouldn't be here, but I knew you would. That's why I came."

The baby. I want the unborn child.

"Brian, why are you talking so weird?" she asked, her words strangled by her emotions. It was his voice and his face, but he didn't talk like that. "Of course, honey. It's your baby too. Oh, Brian. I'm so glad to see you."

He came closer and placed his hand on her stomach. The baby moved. A pleasing smile spread over Mary J.'s face.

Take off your clothes and lie down. Right here.

Still smiling and happy to finally be with her husband, Mary J. complied, no questions asked. She slipped out of her skirt, removed her blouse, and lay down on the smooth, cool surface of the rock bluff.

She sucked in her breath as her bare skin touched the coolness of the rock.

While Mary J. lay naked, her body glistening from the light that surrounded them, Brian put his hand out and let it hover over her stomach.

Her eyes closed, her lips half-parted, Mary J. felt the baby stirring again. Boy, it sure was active for five and a half months, she thought.

Suddenly the movement was increased, and she began to feel pain. Mary J. tried to lift her arms to grab her stomach, but they wouldn't move.

The pain—it was getting worse.

She opened her eyes and saw Brian's hand—that couldn't be Brian's hand. He didn't have fingernails six inches long. She raised her eyes to meet his. That wasn't Brian. She was terrified. The priest had been right. It was the demon, and it wanted her baby. She tried to scream, but no sound came out.

Mary J. watched in horror, unable to move, as the knifelike fingernails slashed across her stomach and abdomen. Blood gushed out of her body, and as though it were happening in slow motion, the intense pain registered in her brain.

She screamed with every ounce of strength she had left. Tears sprang to her eyes as she looked and saw the demon holding a baby.

Her baby!

The demon released her, and Mary J. screamed again and again.

The group walking hurriedly along the dirt lane froze when the first scream pierced the darkness. They looked around at each other and then broke into a run toward the terrifying sounds.

Rogers did his best to keep the flashlight shining on the path but found it difficult to keep up with Stoney and Susie who had youth and fear for Mary J. on their side.

The sheriff arrived at the slope on the heels of the young couple but came to a sudden halt when he realized they weren't moving. He looked past them to see what had stopped them so suddenly.

There, below them on the bluff, lying on the ground, her guts ripped open and spilling out, was Mary J. Something inside Susie awoke and she went screaming, stumbling, and sliding down the slope. She came to a sudden stop next to Mary J. and fell to her knees beside her sister.

"*Nooo!*"

Susie gently tried to put Mary J.'s insides back where they belonged. By then, the rest of the entourage had arrived. When Sadie came alongside her two daughters, the bloody melee was too much for her, and she passed out.

Daniel attended to her while keeping one eye on the horror next to him.

They were all so busy watching Susie that no one noticed the sinister presence a few feet to their left.

Suddenly the baby cried, and several things happened at the same time.

"Oh, shit!" Rogers exclaimed, pulling his pistol and aiming it at the smirking demon.

"No!" Father Pritchard shouted, grabbing the sheriff's arm. "You might hit the child. You can't harm the creature with that. Besides, this is where I come in," he reassured the terrified lawman. Rogers released the hammer on the pistol but kept it aimed at the gruesome sight.

The priest took a hesitant step toward the beast. He ignored everything going on behind him. The dead girl lying on the ground, the sister covered with the blood of her sibling, the mother who fainted and was being treated by her husband and the sheriff who had an itchy trigger finger.

He hurriedly crossed himself and said a silent prayer before speaking to the creature. Reassured by God's power, he started. "Give the child to me."

It was a simple, straightforward demand. And one that brought a deep, hearty laugh from the demon. It seemed like the laughing went on for a good while, and then finally the beast put the crying baby on the ground beside him.

I didn't convince you the last time, priest?

"Not only did you not convince me, but I do not acknowledge your power. Your rampaging destruction of this family is at an end."

Again, the peculiar laugh came from the demon. Father Pritchard knew that his only chance was to remain calm, contain his anger, and keep a clear head. Suddenly the beast reached out, his hand slashed the air as the razor-sharp claws sliced across the priest's face, opening four identical cuts on his left cheek.

This time it was his turn to laugh. He threw his head back and laughed with a fervor that started deep inside his gut and worked its way up and outward. Then he turned the other cheek. The beast laid identical marks on that cheek.

Before Father Pritchard had time to recover from those wounds, a well-aimed punch caught him full in the stomach taking his breath away and sending him flying to the ground.

With the priest out of his line of fire and the baby safely on the ground, Rogers decided to take his shot. He fired his nine mil into the beast until he emptied the clip. He then stared in disbelief. Every round in his weapon and the creature was not fazed. It should be dead. But instead, it roared and shot twin lightning bolts at the sheriff.

Rogers, who was on the side of Mary J. nearest the water, flew over the edge of the cliff and into the creek below. Stoney jumped in after him to keep him from drowning. He found the unconscious sheriff and pulled him onto the gravel bar on the opposite side.

Distracted by his pursuit of the sheriff, the demon didn't see the priest approach him from the opposite side.

Father Pritchard reached out and wrapped his hands around what he presumed was the demon's throat. It didn't make any difference what body part it was, the contact between human flesh and evil spirit created the subsequent conduit of supernatural consequences.

With the power of God flowing through him, the priest held on while the screaming, flailing demon used up its last bit of strength. With its final roar, it uttered these words of warning to the priest.

I'll be back!

Father Pritchard handed the newborn baby to Susie once she had finally calmed down. She sat in Stoney's car, covered with Mary J.'s blood, holding the infant which she had wrapped in a sweater that was on the back seat until they could get the premature baby to the hospital.

Then the four men had gone back to the bluff and placed Mary J.'s body in a body bag that Rogers kept in his trunk for situations like this.

Two weeks later, Susie was sitting in the window seat thinking about Mary J. and Brian. Her eyes glistened with tears, as they did every time she thought of her sister and—she now knew—her brother. It was funny to think of Brian as a brother after all these years of referring to him as a brother-in-law.

She and Stoney had made doubly sure that they were not related, other than by the marriage of Daniel and Sadie. In so doing, she saw no reason for them to sever their relationship or for Stoney to move out.

But move he did.

Brian and Mary J. had willed their house and their share of the business to Stoney and Susie. So he had already moved into their house to go through their things and store what was personal to them. Susie was just waiting, unable to face that task, until he was through. Then she would move in with him along with—

"Aunt Susie." Michele stood a few feet away, rubbing her eyes. "I had a bad dream," she whimpered.

She was so wrapped up in her thoughts, Susie hadn't even heard her niece get up. "Come here, baby girl. It's going to be all right. You just sit right here with Aunt Susie," she said, lifting the little girl—who was a mirror image of her mother—to her lap. "Tell Aunt Susie all about it."

Susie and Stoney were getting married the following week and had already filed for custody of Michele and baby Brian. They had named the baby after its father.

Brian weighed two pounds, four ounces at birth. By the time they got him to the hospital, he had some fluid in his lungs, which was cleaned out. Other than that, they declared him a healthy baby. He was coming home from the hospital tomorrow.

Susie and Michele sat quietly, looking out the bay window.

Epilogue

Michele drove into Crater Ridge and sighed heavily as she started down Main Street. Was she holding her breath? She hadn't realized it. She let her breath out slowly while weaving her way through the morning traffic. She had anticipated this moment for several years, and now that it was here, she could feel her pulse racing. For a moment, just a fleeting moment, she thought about turning around and leaving before anyone knew she was here.

But she didn't.

She continued her slow push through her hometown.

The town itself hadn't changed as much as she thought it would. There were a couple of new businesses. One was a convenience store on Highway 54 coming in from the west, and the other was a new restaurant at the stoplight where a bank used to be.

When she left Crater Ridge to go to college, the one thing she swore to her Aunt Susie was that she had no plans to return to this town that held so many terrible memories for her. But as a last-minute decision, after her graduation, she had decided to pay her Uncle Stoney and Aunt Susie a visit before getting on with her life.

She figured they were at the hardware store but wanted to drop by the house first and freshen up after the long trip. She pulled into the driveway and turned the motor off. Michele just sat there for a minute and looked at the house.

More than anything in the world, she wished her mother and father were coming out of the house she grew up in to welcome her home. Unwanted tears wet her eyes. When she saw Dala come out of the house next door, she hurriedly dried her eyes and got out of the car. She walked back to the trunk, unlocked it, and took her bags out. Then she stood there and waited until her mother's best friend crossed the yard.

"Hi, Aunt Dala."

"Well, Michele Clark, as I live and breathe. If you aren't a sight for sore eyes." She gave the trim, well-tanned girl a hug. "My god, if you aren't the spitting image of your mother."

Michele smiled. It did her heart good to hear that. Nothing would please her more than to know that she looked like her mother—and that people could see it. "Really?" she asked politely.

"Believe me, honey. It's the truth. Nobody knew your mother better than I did. She, Susie, and I were the triplets in high school. Are you home for good?"

A shadow crossed Michele's face. "No, I'm just here for a visit. I plan on leaving in a few days. I'm going to New York City to work and live."

Dala picked up one of Michele's bags and carried it to the back porch for her. "What I want to know is, why didn't you come home to visit while you were away at college?"

Setting the suitcase down on the porch, Michele looked at her surrogate aunt. "Because it was just too hard," she replied. "I needed a change, and I needed it for longer than a few months. Can you understand that?"

"Yes, honey. I can."

"Do you think Aunt Susie will?"

Dala was reflective for a minute. "I think she'll understand, but I also think she'll be hurt. You have to remember, honey, that you and little Brian are all she has to remind her of her sister."

That brought a smile from Michele, how Dala still referred to Michele's brother as little when he was twenty years old now. The last she heard, he was away at college too. "Heard from Brian lately?" she asked.

"He's supposed to be home either today or tomorrow."

Michele nodded. "Well, I've got to get in here and get a quick shower before Aunt Susie gets home. It's good to see you again, Aunt

Dala." She gave the woman a quick kiss on the cheek and then disappeared inside.

Dala crossed the yard to her house very pensive about her conversation with Michele. Something was wrong with that girl, she decided. And it has nothing to do with her memories of this place. She looked up at the sky as a cloud passed in front of the sun. "It's an omen," she said softly to herself.

On impulse, she glanced back next door and was startled when she realized that Michele had been watching her. She went quickly inside.

Michele had just finished showering and dressing when she heard her name being called. "Aunt Susie, I'm in here!" she shouted back. Susie rushed through the door and gathered Michele in her arms. It wasn't an entirely easy thing to do now that they were about the same size. But somehow, she managed to do just that.

"I can't believe you're actually here," she remarked, misty-eyed.

"Believe me, I thought seriously about not coming," Michele replied, still holding her aunt's hands in hers. "Where's Uncle Stoney?"

"Oh, he'll be home this afternoon late. He's got business at the store. I'll call him later and tell him to pick up Rachel and Renee on his way home." She smiled at her niece. "It's just the two of us."

"Aunt Susie."

For a brief moment, Michele had several worry lines scrolled across her forehead. "What is it, baby girl?"

Michele had thought about it hundreds of times in the last several years. She didn't think she would ever be asking this question, but she had to see it for herself. She had finally reconciled everything about her parents' deaths, except the place where they died. "Could we go…out there?"

Susie was astonished that Michele would even consider it. "To Rockhole?"

Michele's nod was almost imperceptible.

Against her better judgment, Susie had consented to go with Michele to the place where, first, her father and then her mother had died. It was a gruesome thought, but she was almost positive that her niece had not yet come to terms with the events that took place there twenty years earlier.

Susie figured she just needed closure.

The fence had long been torn down, and there was barely a path at all leading to what used to be the most popular swimming hole around. "It's not used anymore," Susie explained at Michele's curious look. "After your mother's and father's deaths, it kind of lost its popularity."

They found the trail, after careful searching, that descended the slope to the bluff. Except for the fact that it was solid rock, it probably would have grown over as well.

Standing on the edge of the cliff, Susie couldn't help but think that the water below still looked as clear, cool, and inviting as it had twenty years ago.

She concentrated on the water and the gravel bar on the other side while Michele stared at the spot where her mother had lain as she died. Here was where her lifeblood had flowed from her torn body. The only sound that could be heard was her tears splattering on the ground.

Michele thought it was strange, as she knelt down and touched a dark spot. She didn't think blood would stain solid rock or that it would still show after twenty years. But Michele was positive the longer she stared at it that this odd discoloration was some of her mother's blood that had stained the flat, smooth rock. It was a deeper brown than the rest.

Susie took her eyes from the opposite side of the creek long enough to see how Michele was doing. She wanted to go to her and hold her and tell her it was all right. But it wasn't all right. Here her mother and father had met up with the past. Here they had met the monster that had haunted their family for a hundred years. They had battled—and they had lost. She wondered if Michele would ever understand the significance of what happened here. Susie turned away to face the other side again.

You have finally come.

Michele looked around quickly, but no one was there. There shouldn't be anyway, she thought. It was in my mind. The voice was in my mind.

Your mother and father will be happy to know you have come.

"Tell me about them," she asked the voice.

Susie glanced again at her niece. She gasped, and her hand went to her mouth.

Oh my god, she cried silently. *It's starting again!*

THE END

About the Author

Jesse was born and raised in the Missouri Ozarks for the first seven years of his life. His family then moved to Kansas, where he graduated from high school before entering the US Army that summer. He eventually returned to his roots in Missouri, graduating from the University of Southwest Missouri. Searching for greener pastures, Jesse relocated to South Texas, where he lived and raised his family. Having suffered a disability while serving in Vietnam, Jesse was forced to retire from physical labor. With so much extra time on his hands, he turned to writing. Rockhole is a real place from his childhood days in Missouri. While the events and characters in the story are fictional, some personal privileges have crept into the work. Jesse and his family still live in Texas, where he continues his writing. First and foremost, he considers himself a Texan.